Praise for Dean Koontz and his masterworks of suspense

"Koontz barely lets the reader come up for air between terrors."
—*The Washington Post*

"Koontz's skill at edge-of-the-seat writing has improved with each book. He can scare our socks off." —*Boston Herald*

"Koontz's imagination is not only as big as the Ritz, it is also as wild as an unbroken stallion." —*Los Angeles Times*

"Koontz puts his readers through the emotional wringer."
—*The Associated Press*

"His prose mesmerizes . . . Koontz consistently hits the bull's-eye."
—*Arkansas Democrat-Gazette*

"First-class entertainment." —*The Cleveland Plain Dealer*

"An exceptional novelist . . . top notch." —*Lincoln Journal Star*

"Koontz is an expert at creating believable characters."
—*Detroit News and Free Press*

"One of our finest and most versatile suspense writers."
—*The Macon Telegraph & News*

"Koontz does it so well!" —*The Baton Rouge Advocate*

"Koontz's prose is as smooth as a knife through butter and his storytelling ability never wavers." —*The Calgary Sun*

"Koontz's gift is that he makes his monsters seem 'realer,' and he makes the characters who fight [them] as normal as anyone you'd meet on a street."
—*Orlando Sentinel*

DEAN KOONTZ

whispers

BERKLEY BOOKS, NEW YORK

THE BERKLEY PUBLISHING GROUP
Published by the Penguin Group
Penguin Group (USA) Inc.
375 Hudson Street, New York, New York 10014, USA
Penguin Group (Canada), 90 Eglinton Avenue East, Suite 700, Toronto, Ontario M4P 2Y3, Canada
(a division of Pearson Penguin Canada Inc.)
Penguin Books Ltd., 80 Strand, London WC2R 0RL, England
Penguin Group Ireland, 25 St. Stephen's Green, Dublin 2, Ireland (a division of Penguin Books Ltd.)
Penguin Group (Australia), 250 Camberwell Road, Camberwell, Victoria 3124, Australia
(a division of Pearson Australia Group Pty. Ltd.)
Penguin Books India Pvt. Ltd., 11 Community Centre, Panchsheel Park, New Delhi—110 017, India
Penguin Group (NZ), Cnr. Airborne and Rosedale Roads, Albany, Auckland 1310, New Zealand
(a division of Pearson New Zealand Ltd.)
Penguin Books (South Africa) (Pty.) Ltd., 24 Sturdee Avenue, Rosebank, Johannesburg 2196,
South Africa

Penguin Books Ltd., Registered Offices: 80 Strand, London WC2R 0RL, England

This is a work of fiction. Names, characters, places, and incidents either are the product of the author's imagination or are used fictitiously, and any resemblance to actual persons, living or dead, business establishments, events, or locales is entirely coincidental.

PRINTING HISTORY
G. P. Putnam's Sons hardcover edition / June 1980
Berkley mass-market edition / April 1981
Berkley trade paperback edition / July 2006

Berkley trade paperback ISBN: 0-425-20992-X

The Library of Congress has catalogued the G. P. Putnam's Sons hardcover edition as follows:

Koontz, Dean, 1945–
  Whispers / by Dean Koontz.
    p. cm.
  ISBN 0-399-12351-2
    1. Women—Crimes against—Fiction.   2. Stalkers—Fiction.   I. Title.
PZ4.K8335 Wh 1980 PS3561.O55
813'.5'4—dc19   79022858

PRINTED IN THE UNITED STATES OF AMERICA

10   9   8   7   6   5   4   3   2

This book is dedicated to
Rio and Battista Locatelli,
two very nice people who
deserve the very best.

part one

THE LIVING
AND THE DEAD

The forces that affect our lives, the influences that mold and shape us, are often like whispers in a distant room, teasingly indistinct, apprehended only with difficulty.

—Charles Dickens

chapter one

Tuesday at dawn, Los Angeles trembled. Windows rattled in their frames. Patio wind chimes tinkled merrily even though there was no wind. In some houses, dishes fell off shelves.

At the start of the morning rush hour, KFWB, all-news radio, used the earthquake as its lead story. The tremor had registered 4.8 on the Richter Scale. By the end of the rush hour, KFWB demoted the story to third place behind a report of terrorist bombings in Rome and an account of a five-car accident on the Santa Monica Freeway. After all, no buildings had fallen. By noon, only a handful of Angelenos (mostly those who had moved west within the past year) found the event worthy of even a minute's conversation over lunch.

•

The man in the smoke-gray Dodge van didn't even feel the earth move. He was at the northwest edge of the city, driving south on the San Diego Freeway, when the quake struck. Because it is difficult to feel any but the strongest tremors while in a moving vehicle, he wasn't aware of the shaking until he stopped for breakfast at a diner and heard one of the other customers talking about it.

He knew at once that the earthquake was a sign meant just for him. It had been sent either to assure him that his mission in Los Angeles would be a success—or to warn him that he would fail. But which message was he supposed to perceive in this sign?

He brooded over that question while he ate. He was a big strong man—six-foot-four, two hundred and thirty pounds, all muscle—and he took more than an hour and a half to finish his meal. He started with two eggs, bacon, cottage fries, toast and a glass of milk. He chewed slowly, methodically, his eyes focused on his food as if he were entranced by it. When he finished his first plateful, he asked for a tall stack of pancakes and more milk. After the pancakes, he ate a cheese omelet with three pieces of Canadian bacon on the side, another serving of toast, and orange juice.

By the time he ordered the third breakfast, he was the chief topic of conversation in the kitchen. His waitress was a giggly redhead named Helen, but each of the other waitresses found an excuse to pass by his table and get a better look at him. He was aware of their interest, but he didn't care.

When he finally asked Helen for the check, she said, "You must be a lumberjack or something."

He looked up at her and smiled woodenly. Although this was the first time he had been in the diner, although he had met Helen only ninety minutes ago, he knew exactly what she was going to say. He had heard it all a hundred times before.

She giggled self-consciously, but her blue eyes fixed unwaveringly on his. "I mean, you eat enough for three men."

"I guess I do."

She stood beside the booth, one hip against the edge of the table, leaning slightly forward, not-so-subtly letting him know that she might be available. "But with all that food . . . you don't have an ounce of fat on you."

Still smiling, he wondered what she'd be like in bed. He pictured himself taking hold of her, thrusting into her—and then he pictured his hands around her throat, squeezing, squeezing, until her face slowly turned purple and her eyes bulged out of their sockets.

She stared at him speculatively, as if wondering whether he satisfied *all* of his appetites with such single-minded devotion as he had shown toward the food. "Must get a lot of exercise."

"I lift weights," he said.

"Like Arnold Schwarzenegger."

"Yeah."

She had a graceful, delicate neck. He knew he could break it as if it were a dry twig, and the thought of doing that made him feel warm and happy.

"You sure do have a set of big arms," she said, softly, appreciatively. He was wearing a short-sleeved shirt, and she touched his bare forearm with one finger. "I guess, with all that pumping iron, no matter how much you eat, it just turns into more muscle."

"Well, that's the idea," he said. "But I also have one of those metabolisms."

"Huh?"

"I burn up a lot of calories in nervous energy."

"You? Nervous?"

"Jumpy as a Siamese cat."

"I don't believe it. I bet there's nothing in the world could make you nervous," she said.

She was a good-looking woman, about thirty years old, ten years younger than he was, and he figured he could have her if he wanted her. She would need a little wooing, but not much, just enough so she could convince herself that he had swept her off her feet, playing Rhett to her Scarlett, and had tumbled her into bed against her will. Of course, if he made love to her, he would have to kill her afterward. He'd have to put a knife through her pretty breasts or cut her throat, and he really didn't want to do that. She wasn't worth the bother or the risk. She simply wasn't his type, he didn't kill redheads.

He left her a good tip, paid his check at the cash register by the door, and got out of there. After the air conditioned restaurant, the September heat was like a pillow jammed against his face. As he walked toward the Dodge van, he knew that Helen was watching him, but he didn't look back.

From the diner he drove to a shopping center and parked in a corner of the large lot, in the shade of a date palm, as far from the stores as he could get. He climbed between the bucket seats, into the back of the van, pulled down a bamboo shade that separated the driver's compartment from the cargo area, and stretched out on a thick but tattered mattress that was too short for him. He had been driving all night without rest, all the way from St. Helena in the wine country. Now, with a big breakfast in his belly, he was drowsy.

Four hours later, he woke from a bad dream. He was sweating, shuddering, burning up and freezing at the same time, clutching the mattress with one hand and punching the empty air with the other. He was trying to scream, but his voice was stuck far down in his throat; he made a dry, gasping sound.

At first, he didn't know where he was. The rear of the van was saved from utter darkness only by three thin strips of pale light that came through narrow slits in the bamboo blind. The air was warm and stale. He sat up, felt the metal wall with one hand, squinted at what little there was to see, and gradually oriented himself. When at last he realized he was in the van, he relaxed and sank back onto the mattress again.

He tried to remember what the nightmare had been about, but he could not. That wasn't unusual. Nearly every night of his life, he suffered through horrible dreams from which he woke in terror, mouth dry, heart pounding; but he never could recall what had frightened him.

Although he knew where he was now, the darkness made him uneasy. He kept hearing stealthy movement in the shadows, soft scurrying sounds that put the hair up on the back of his neck even though he knew he was imagining them. He raised the bamboo shade and sat blinking for a minute until his eyes adjusted to the light.

He picked up a bundle of chamois-textured cloths that lay on the floor beside the mattress. The bundle was tied up with dark brown cord. He loosened the knot and unrolled the soft cloths, four of them, each rolled around the other. Wrapped in the center were two big knives. They were very sharp. He had spent a lot of time carefully honing the gracefully tapered blades. When he took one of them in his hand, it felt strange and wonderful, as if it were a sorcerer's knife, infused with magic energy that it was now transmitting to him.

The afternoon sun had slipped past the shadow of the palm tree in which he had parked the Dodge. Now the light streamed through the windshield, over his shoulder, and struck the ice-like steel; the razor-edge glinted coldly.

As he stared at the blade, his thin lips slowly formed a smile. In spite of the nightmare, the sleep had done him a lot of good. He felt refreshed and confident. He was absolutely certain that the morning's earthquake had been a sign that everything would go well for him in Los Angeles. He would find the woman. He would get his hands on her. Today. Or Wednesday at the latest. As he thought about her smooth, warm body and the flawless texture of her skin, his smile swelled into a grin.

•

Tuesday afternoon, Hilary Thomas went shopping in Beverly Hills. When she came home early that evening, she parked her coffee-brown Mercedes in the circular driveway, near the front door. Now that fashion designers had decided women finally would be allowed to look feminine again, Hilary had bought all the clothes she hadn't been able to find during the dress-like-an-army-sergeant fever that had seized everyone in the fashion industry for at least the past five years. She needed to make three trips to unload the trunk of the car.

As she was picking up the last of the parcels, she suddenly had the feeling that she was being watched. She turned from the car and looked toward the street. The low westering sun slanted between the big houses and through the feathery palm fronds, streaking everything with gold. Two children were playing on a lawn, half a block away, and a floppy-eared cocker spaniel was padding happily along the sidewalk. Other than that, the neighborhood was silent and almost preternaturally still. Two cars and a gray Dodge van were parked on the other side of the street, but as far as she could see, there wasn't anyone in them.

Sometimes you act like a silly fool, she told herself. Who would be watching?

But after she carried the last of the packages inside, she came out to park the car in the garage, and again she had the unshakable feeling that she was being observed.

•

Later, near midnight, as Hilary was sitting in bed reading, she thought she heard noises downstairs. She put the book aside and listened.

Rattling sounds. In the kitchen. Near the back door. Directly under her bedroom.

She got out of bed and put on a robe. It was a deep blue silk wrapper she had bought just that afternoon.

A loaded .32 automatic lay in the top drawer of the nightstand. She hesitated, listened to the rattling sounds for a moment, then decided to take the gun with her.

She felt slightly foolish. What she heard was probably just settling noises, the natural sounds a house makes from time to time. On the other hand, she had lived here for six months and had not heard anything like it until now.

She stopped at the head of the stairs and peered down into the darkness and said, "Who's there?"

No answer.

Holding the gun in her right hand and in front of her, she went downstairs and across the living room, breathing fast and shallow, unable to stop her gun hand from shaking just a bit. She switched on every lamp that she passed. As she approached the back of the house, she still could hear the strange noises, but when she stepped into the kitchen and hit the lights, there was only silence.

The kitchen looked as it should. Dark pegged pine floor. Dark pine cabinets with glossy white ceramic fixtures. White tile counters, clean and uncluttered. Shining copper pots and utensils hanging from the high white ceiling. There was no intruder and no sign that there had been one before she arrived.

She stood just inside the doorway and waited for the noise to begin again.

Nothing. Just the soft hum of the refrigerator.

Finally she walked around the gleaming central utility island and tried the back door. It was locked.

She turned on the yard lights and rolled up the shade that covered the window above the sink. Outside, off to the right, the forty-foot-long swimming pool shimmered prettily. The huge shadowy rose garden lay to the left, a dozen bright blossoms glowing like bursts of phosphorescent gas in the dark green foliage. Everything out there was silent and motionless.

What I heard was the house settling, she thought. Jeez. I'm getting to be a regular spooky old maid.

She made a sandwich and took it upstairs with a cold bottle of beer. She left all the lights burning on the first floor, which she felt would discourage any prowler—if there actually was someone lurking about the property.

Later, she felt foolish for leaving the house so brightly lit.

She knew exactly what was wrong with her. Her jumpiness was a symptom of the I-don't-deserve-all-this-happiness disease, a mental disorder with which she was intimately acquainted. She had come from nowhere, from nothing, and now she had everything. Subconsciously, she was afraid that God would take notice of her and decide that she didn't deserve what she'd been given. Then the hammer would fall. Everything she had accumulated would be smashed and swept away: the house, the car, the bank accounts. . . . Her new life seemed like a fantasy, a marvelous fairytale, too good to be true, certainly too good to last.

No. Dammit, no! She had to stop belittling herself and pretending that her accomplishments were only the result of good fortune. Luck had nothing to do with it. Born into a house of despair, nurtured not with milk and kindness but with uncertainty and fear, unloved by her father and merely tolerated by her mother, raised in a home where self-pity and bitterness had driven out all hope, she had of course grown up without a sense of real worth. For years she had struggled with an inferiority complex. But that was behind her now. She had been through therapy. She understood herself. She didn't dare let those old doubts rise again within her. The house and car and money would *not* be taken away; she *did* deserve them. She worked hard, and she had talent. Nobody had given her a job simply because she was a relative or friend; when she'd come to Los Angeles, she hadn't known anyone. No one had heaped money in her lap just because she was pretty. Drawn by the wealth of the entertainment industry and by the promise of fame, herds of beautiful women arrived every day in L.A. and were usually treated worse than cattle. She had made it to the top for one reason: she was a good writer, a superb craftsman, an imaginative and energetic artist who knew how to create the motion pictures that a lot of people would pay money to see. She earned every dime she was paid, and the gods had no reason to be vindictive.

"So relax," she said aloud.

No one had tried to get in the kitchen door. That was just her imagination.

She finished the sandwich and beer, then went downstairs and turned out the lights.

She slept soundly.

•

The next day was one of the best days of her life. It was also one of the worst.

Wednesday began well. The sky was cloudless. The air was sweet and clear. The morning light had that peculiar quality found only in Southern California and only on certain days. It was crystalline light, hard yet warm, like the sunbeams in a cubist painting, and it gave you the feeling that at any moment the air would part like a stage curtain to reveal a world beyond the one in which we live.

Hilary Thomas spent the morning in her garden. The walled half-acre behind the two-story neo-Spanish house was adorned with two dozen species of roses—beds and trellises and hedges of roses. There were the Frau Karl Druschki Rose, the Madame Pierre Oger Rose, the rosa muscosa, the Souvenir de la Malmaison Rose, and a wide variety of modern hybrids. The garden blazed with white roses and red roses, orange and yellow and pink and purple and even green roses. Some blooms were the size of saucers, and others were small enough to pass through a wedding ring. The velvety green lawn was speckled with windblown petals of every hue.

Most mornings, Hilary worked with the plants for two or three hours. No matter how agitated she was upon entering the garden, she was always completely relaxed and at peace when she left.

She easily could have afforded a gardener. She still received quarterly payments from her first hit film, *Arizona Shifty Pete*, which had been released more than two years ago and which had been an enormous success. The new movie, *Cold Heart*, in the theaters less than two months, was doing even better than *Pete*. Her twelve-room house in Westwood, on the fringes of Bel Air and Beverly Hills, had cost a great deal, yet six months ago she had paid cash for the place. In show business circles, she was called a "hot property." That was exactly how she felt, too. Hot. Burning. Ablaze with plans and possibilities. It was a glorious feeling. She was a damned successful screenwriter, a hot property indeed, and she could hire a platoon of gardeners if she wanted them.

She tended to the flowers and the trees herself because the garden was a special place for her, almost sacred. It was the symbol of her escape.

She had been raised in a decaying apartment building in one of Chicago's worst neighborhoods. Even now, even here, even in the middle of her fragrant rose garden, she could close her eyes and see every detail of that long-ago place. In the foyer, the mailboxes had been smashed open by thieves looking for welfare checks. The hallways were narrow and poorly lit. The rooms were tiny, dreary, the furniture tattered and worn. In the small kitchen, the ancient gas range had seemed about to spring a leak and explode; Hilary had lived for years in fear of the stove's irregular, spurting blue flames. The refrigerator was yellow with age; it wheezed and rattled, and its warm motor attracted what her father called "the local wildlife." As she stood now in her lovely garden, Hilary clearly remembered the wildlife with which she'd spent her childhood, and she shuddered. Although she and her mother had kept the four rooms spotlessly clean, and although they had used great quantities of insecticide, they had never been able to get rid of the cockroaches because the damned things came through the thin walls from the other apartments where people were *not* so clean.

Her most vivid childhood memory was of the view from the single window in her cramped bedroom. She had spent many lonely hours there, hiding while her father and mother argued. The bedroom had been a haven from those terrible bouts of cursing and screaming, and from the sullen silences when her parents weren't speaking to each other. The view from the window wasn't inspiring: nothing more than the soot-streaked brick wall on the far side of the four-foot-wide serviceway that led between the tenements. The window would not open; it was painted shut.

She'd been able to see a thin sliver of sky, but only when she'd pressed her face against the glass and peered straight up the narrow shaft.

Desperate to escape from the shabby world in which she lived, young Hilary learned to use her imagination to see *through* the brick wall. She would set her mind adrift, and suddenly she would be looking out upon rolling hills, or sometimes the vast Pacific Ocean, or great mountain ranges. Most of the time, it was a garden that she conjured up, an enchanted place, serene, with neatly trimmed shrubs and high trellises twined about with thorny rose vines. In this fantasy there was a great deal of pretty wrought-iron lawn furniture that had been painted white. Gaily striped umbrellas cast pools of cool shadow in the coppery sunlight. Women in lovely long dresses and men in summer suits sipped iced drinks and chatted amiably.

And now I'm living in that dream, she thought. That make-believe place is real, and I own it.

Maintaining the roses and the other plants—palms and ferns and jade shrubs and a dozen other things—was not a chore. It was a joy. Every minute she worked among the flowers, she was aware of how far she had come.

At noon, she put away her gardening tools and showered. She stood for a long while in the steaming water, as if it were sluicing away more than dirt and sweat, as if it were washing off ugly memories as well. In that depressing Chicago apartment, in the minuscule bathroom, where all the faucets had dripped and where all the drains had backed up at least once a month, there never had been enough hot water.

She ate a light lunch on the glassed-in patio that overlooked the roses. While she nibbled at cheese and slices of an apple, she read the trade papers of the entertainment industry—*Hollywood Reporter* and *Daily Variety*—which had come in the morning mail. Her name appeared in Hank Grant's column in the *Reporter*, in a list of movie and television people whose birthday it was. For a woman just turned twenty-nine, she had come a long, long way indeed.

Today, the chief executives at Warner Brothers were discussing *The Hour of the Wolf*, her latest screenplay. They would decide either to buy or reject by the close of the business day. She was tense, anxious for the telephone to ring, yet dreading it because it might bring disappointing news. This project was more important to her than anything else she'd ever done.

She had written the script without the security of a signed contract, strictly on speculation, and she had made up her mind to sell it only if she was signed to direct and was guaranteed final cut. Already, Warners had hinted at a record offer for the screenplay if she would reconsider her conditions of sale. She knew she was demanding a lot; however, because of her success as a screenwriter, her demands were not entirely unreasonable. Warners reluctantly would agree to let her direct the picture; she would bet anything on that. But the sticking point would be the final cut. That honor, the power to decide exactly what would appear on the screen, the ultimate authority over every shot and every frame and every nuance of the film, usually was bestowed upon directors who had proven themselves on a number of money-making movies; it was seldom granted to a fledgling director, especially not to a fledgling *female* director. Her insistence on total creative control might queer the deal.

Hoping to take her mind off the pending decision from Warner Brothers, Hilary spent Wednesday afternoon working in her studio, which overlooked the pool. Her desk was large, heavy, custom-made oak, with a dozen drawers and two dozen cubbyholes. Several pieces of Lallique crystal stood on the desk, refracting the soft glow from the two brass piano lamps. She struggled through the second draft of an article she was writing for *Film Comment*, but her thoughts constantly wandered to *The Hour of the Wolf*.

The telephone rang at four o'clock, and she jerked in surprise even though she'd been waiting all afternoon for that sound. It was Wally Topelis.

"It's your agent, kid. We have to talk."

"Isn't that what we're doing now?"

"I mean face to face."

"Oh," she said glumly. "Then it's bad news."

"Did I say it was?"

"If it was good," Hilary said, "you'd just give it to me on the phone. Face to face means you want to let me down easy."

"You're a classic pessimist, kid."

"Face to face means you want to hold my hand and talk me out of suicide."

"It's a damned good thing this melodramatic streak of yours never shows up in your writing."

"If Warners said no, just tell me."

"They haven't decided yet, my lamb."

"I can take it."

"Will you listen to me? The deal hasn't fallen through. I'm still scheming, and I want to discuss my next move with you. That's all. Nothing more sinister than that. Can you meet me in half an hour?"

"Where?"

"I'm at the Beverly Hills Hotel."

"The Polo Lounge?"

"Naturally."

•

As Hilary turned off Sunset Boulevard, she thought the Beverly Hills Hotel looked unreal, like a mirage shimmering in the heat. The rambling building that thrust out of stately palms and lush greenery, a fairytale vision. As always, the pink stucco did not look as garish as she remembered it. The walls seemed translucent, appeared almost to shine with a soft inner light. In its own way, the hotel was rather elegant—more than a bit decadent, but unquestionably elegant nonetheless. At the main entrance, uniformed valets were parking and delivering cars: two Rolls-Royces, three Mercedes, one Stuts, and a red Maserati.

A long way from the poor side of Chicago, she thought happily.

When she stepped into the Polo Lounge, she saw half a dozen movie actors and actresses, famous faces, as well as two powerful studio executives, but none of them was sitting at table number three. That was generally considered to be the most desirable spot in the room, for it faced the entrance and was the best place to see and be seen. Wally Topelis was at table three because he was one of the most powerful agents in Hollywood and because he charmed the maître d' just as he charmed everyone who met him. He was a small lean man in his fifties, very well dressed. His white hair was thick and lustrous. He also had a neat white mustache. He looked quite distinguished, exactly the kind of man you expected to see at table number three. He was talking on a telephone that had been plugged in just for him. When he saw Hilary approaching, he hastily concluded his conversation, put the receiver down, and stood.

"Hilary, you're lovely—as usual."

"And you're the center of attention—as usual."

He grinned. His voice was soft, conspiratorial. "I imagine everyone's staring at us."

"I imagine."

"Surreptitiously."

"Oh, of course," she said.

"Because they wouldn't want us to know they're looking," he said happily.

As they sat down, she said, "And we dare not look to see if they're looking."

"Oh, heavens no!" His blue eyes were bright were merriment.

"We wouldn't want them to think we care."

"God forbid."

"That would be gauche."

"Trés gauche." He laughed.

Hilary sighed. "I've never understood why one table should be so much more important than another."

"Well, I can sit and make fun of it, but I understand," Wally said. "In spite of everything Marx and Lenin believed, the human animal thrives on the class system—so long as that system is based primarily on money and achievement, not on pedigree. We establish and nurture class systems everywhere, even in restaurants."

"I think I've just stumbled into one of those famous Topelis tirades."

A waiter arrived with a shiny silver ice bucket on a tripod. He put it down beside their table, smiled and left. Apparently, Wally had taken the liberty of ordering for both of them before she arrived. But he didn't take this opportunity to tell her what they were having.

"Not a tirade," he said. "Just an observation. People *need* class systems."

"I'll bite. Why?"

"For one thing, people must have aspirations, desires beyond the basic needs of food and shelter, obsessive wants that will drive them to accomplish things. If there's a best neighborhood, a man will hold down two jobs to raise money for a house there. If one car is better than another, a man—or a woman, for that matter; this certainly isn't a sexist issue—will work harder to be able to afford it. And if there's a best table in the Polo Lounge, everyone who comes here will want to be rich enough or famous enough—or even infamous enough—to be seated there. This almost manic desire for status generates wealth, contributes to the gross national product, and creates jobs. After all, if Henry Ford hadn't wanted to move up in life, he'd never have built the company that now employs tens of thousands. The class system is one of the engines that drive the wheels of commerce; it keeps our standard of living high. The class system gives people goals—and it provides the maître d' with a satisfying sense of power and importance that makes an otherwise intolerable job seem desirable."

Hilary shook her head. "Nevertheless, being seated at the best table doesn't mean I'm automatically a better person than the guy who gets second-best. It's no accomplishment in itself."

"It's a *symbol* of accomplishment, of position," Wally said.

"I still can't see the sense of it."

"It's just an elaborate game."

"Which you certainly know how to play."

He was delighted. "Don't I though?"

"I'll never learn the rules."

"You should, my lamb. It's more than a bit silly, but it helps business. No one likes to work with a loser. But everyone playing the game wants to deal with the kind of person who can get the best table at the Polo Lounge."

Wally Topelis was the only man she knew who could call a woman "my lamb" and sound neither patronizing nor smarmy. Although he was a small man, about the right size to be a professional jockey, he somehow made her think of Cary Grant in movies like *To Catch a Thief*. He had Grant's style: excellent manners observed without flourish; balletic grace in every movement, even in casual gestures; quiet charm; a subtle look of amusement, as if he found life to be a gentle joke.

Their captain arrived, and Wally called him Eugene and inquired about his children. Eugene seemed to regard Wally with affection, and Hilary realized that getting the best table in the Polo Lounge might also have something to do with treating the staff as friends rather than servants.

Eugene was carrying champagne, and after a couple of minutes of small talk, he held the bottle for Wally's inspection.

Hilary glimpsed the label. "Dom Perignon?"

"You deserve the best, my lamb."

Eugene removed the foil from the neck of the bottle and began to untwist the wire that caged the cork.

Hilary frowned at Wally. "You must *really* have bad news for me."

"What makes you say that?"

"A hundred-dollar bottle of champagne. . . ." Hilary looked at him thoughtfully. "It's supposed to soothe my hurt feelings, cauterize my wounds."

The cork popped. Eugene did his job well; very little of the precious liquid foamed out of the bottle.

"You're such a pessimist," Wally said.

"A realist," she said.

"Most people would have said, 'Ah, champagne. What are we celebrating?' But not Hilary Thomas."

Eugene poured a sample of Dom Perignon. Wally tasted it and nodded approval.

"*Are* we celebrating?" Hilary asked. The possibility really had not occurred to her, and she suddenly felt weak as she considered it.

"In fact, we are," Wally said.

Eugene slowly filled both glasses and slowly screwed the bottle into the shaved ice in the silver bucket. Clearly, he wanted to stick around long enough to hear what they were celebrating.

It was also obvious that Wally wanted the captain to hear the news and spread it. Grinning like Cary Grant, he leaned toward Hilary and said, "We've got the deal with Warner Brothers."

She stared, blinked, opened her mouth to speak, didn't know what to say. Finally: "We don't."

"We do."

"We can't."

"We can."

"Nothing's that easy."

"I tell you, we've got it."

"They won't let me direct."

"Oh, yes."

"They won't give me final cut."

"Yes, they will."

"My God."

She was stunned. Felt numb.

Eugene offered his congratulations and slipped away.

Wally laughed, shook his head. "You know, you could have played that a lot better for Eugene's benefit. Pretty soon, people are going to see us celebrating, and they'll ask Eugene what it's about, and he'll tell them. Let the world think you always knew you'd get exactly what you wanted. Never show doubt or fear when you're swimming with sharks."

"You're not kidding about this? We've actually got what we wanted?"

Raising his glass, Wally said, "A toast. To my sweetest client, with the hope she'll eventually learn there *are* some clouds with silver linings and that a lot of apples *don't* have worms in them."

They clinked glasses.

She said, "The studio must have added a lot of tough conditions to the deal. A bottom of the barrel budget. Salary at scale. No participation in the gross rentals. Stuff like that."

"Stop looking for rusty nails in your soup," he said exasperatedly.

"I'm not eating soup."

"Don't get cute."

"I'm drinking champagne."

"You know what I mean."

She stared at the bubbles bursting in her glass of Dom Perignon.

She felt as if hundreds of bubbles were rising within her, too, chains of tiny, bright bubbles of joy; but a part of her acted like a cork to contain the effervescent emotion, to keep it securely under pressure, bottled up, safely contained. She was afraid of being too happy. She didn't want to tempt fate.

"I just don't get it," Wally said. "You look as if the deal fell through. You did hear me all right, didn't you?"

She smiled. "I'm sorry. It's just that . . . when I was a little girl, I learned to expect the worst every day. That way, I was never disappointed. It's the best outlook you can have when you live with a couple of bitter, violent alcoholics."

His eyes were kind.

"Your parents are gone," he said, quietly, tenderly. "Dead. Both of them. They can't touch you, Hilary. They can't hurt you ever again."

"I've spent most of the past twelve years trying to convince myself of that."

"Ever consider analysis?"

"I went through two years of it."

"Didn't help?"

"Not much."

"Maybe a different doctor—"

"Wouldn't matter," Hilary said. "There's a flaw in Freudian theory. Psychiatrists believe that as soon as you fully remember and understand the childhood traumas that made you into a neurotic adult, you can change. They think finding the key is the hard part, and that once you have it you can open the door in a minute. But it's not that easy."

"You have to want to change," he said.

"It's not that easy, either."

He turned his champagne glass around and around in his small well-manicured hands. "Well, if you need someone to talk to now and then, I'm always available."

"I've already burdened you with too much of it over the years."

"Nonsense. You've told me very little. Just the bare bones."

"Boring stuff," she said.

"Far from it, I assure you. The story of a family coming apart at the seams, alcoholism, madness, murder, and suicide, an innocent child caught in the middle. . . . As a screenwriter, you should know that's the kind of material that never bores."

She smiled thinly. "I just feel I've got to work it out on my own."

"Usually it helps to talk about—"

"Except that I've already talked about it to an analyst, and I've talked about it to you, and that's only done me a little bit of good."

"But talking has helped."

"I've got as much out of it as I can. What I've got to do now is talk to *myself* about it. I've got to confront the past alone, without relying on your support or a doctor's, which is something I've never been able to do." Her long dark hair had fallen over one eye; she pushed it out of her face and tucked it behind her ears. "Sooner or later, I'll get my head on straight. It's only a matter of time."

Do I really believe that? she wondered.

Wally stared at her for a moment, then said, "Well, I suppose you know best. At least, in the meantime, drink up." He raised his champagne glass. "Be cheerful and full of laughter so all these important people watching us will envy you and want to work with you."

She wanted to lean back and drink lots of icy Dom Perignon and let happiness consume her, but she could not totally relax. She was always sharply aware of that spectral darkness at the edges of things, that crouching nightmare waiting to spring and devour her. Earl and Emma, her parents, had jammed her into a tiny box of fear, had slammed the heavy lid and locked it; and since then she had looked out at the world from the dark confines of that box. Earl and Emma had instilled in her a quiet but ever-present and unshakable paranoia that stained everything good, everything that should be right and bright and joyful.

In that instant, her hatred of her mother and father was as hard, cold, and immense as it had ever been. The busy years and the many miles that separated her from those hellish days in Chicago suddenly ceased to act as insulation from the pain.

"What's wrong?" Wally asked.

"Nothing. I'm okay."

"You're so pale."

With an effort, she pushed down the memories, forced the past back where it belonged. She put one hand on Wally's cheek, kissed him. "I'm sorry. Sometimes I can be a real pain in the ass. I haven't even thanked you. I'm happy with the deal, Wally. I really am. It's wonderful! You're the best damned agent in the business."

"You're right," he said. "I am. But this time I didn't have to do a lot of selling. They liked the script so much they were willing to give us almost anything just to be sure they'd get the project. It wasn't luck. And it wasn't just having a smart agent. I want you to understand that. Face it, kid, you deserve success. Your work is about the best thing being written for the screen these days. You can go on living in the shadow of your parents, go on expecting the worst, as you always do, but from here on out it's going to be nothing but the best for you. My advice is, get used to it."

She desperately wanted to believe him and surrender to optimism, but black weeds of doubt still sprouted from the seeds of Chicago. She saw those familiar lurking monsters at the fuzzy edges of the paradise he described. She was a true believer in Murphy's Law: *If anything can go wrong, it will.*

Nevertheless, she found Wally's earnestness so appealing, his tone so nearly convincing, that she reached down into her bubbling cauldron of confused emotions and found a genuine radiant smile for him.

"That's it," he said, pleased. "That's better. You have a beautiful smile."

"I'll try to use it more often."

"I'll keep making the kind of deals that'll force you to use it more often."

They drank champagne and discussed *The Hour of the Wolf* and made plans and laughed more than she could remember having laughed in years. Gradually her mood lightened. A macho movie star—icy eyes, tight thin lips, muscles, a swagger in his walk when he was on screen; warm, quick to laugh, somewhat shy in real life—whose last picture had made fifty million dollars, was the first to stop by to say hello and inquire about the celebration. The sartorially impeccable studio executive with the lizard eyes tried subtly, then blatantly, to learn the plot of *Wolf*, hoping it would lend itself to a quick, cheap television movie-of-the-week rip-off. Pretty soon, half the room was table-hopping, stopping by to congratulate Hilary and Wally, flitting away to confer with one another about her success, each of them wondering if there was any percentage in it for him. After all, *Wolf* would need a producer, stars, someone to write the musical score. . . . Therefore, at the best table in the room, there was a great deal of back-patting and cheek-kissing and hand-holding.

Hilary knew that most of the glittery denizens of the Polo Lounge weren't actually as mercenary as they sometimes appeared to be. Many of them had begun at the bottom, hungry, poor, as she had been herself. Although their fortunes were now made and safely invested, they couldn't stop hustling; they'd been at it so long that they didn't know how to live any other way.

The public image of Hollywood life had very little to do with the facts. Secretaries, shopkeepers, clerks, taxi drivers, mechanics, housewives, waitresses, people all over the country, in everyday jobs of all kinds came home weary from work and sat in front of the television and dreamed about life among the stars. In the vast collective mind that brooded and murmured from Hawaii to Maine and from Florida to Alaska, Hollywood was a sparkling blend of wild parties, fast women, easy money, too much whiskey, too much cocaine, lazy sunny days, drinks by the pool, vacation in Acapulco and Palm Springs, sex in the back seat of a fur-lined Rolls-Royce. A fantasy. An illusion. She supposed that a society long abused by corrupt and incompetent leaders, a society standing upon pilings that had been rotted by inflation and excess taxation, a society existing in the cold shadow of sudden nuclear annihilation, needed its illusions if it were to survive. In truth, people in the movie and television industries worked harder than almost anyone else, even though the product of their labor was not always, perhaps not even often, worth the effort. The star of a successful television series worked from dawn till nightfall, often fourteen or sixteen hours a day. Of course, the rewards were enormous. But in reality, the parties were not so wild, the women no faster than women in Philadelphia or Hackensack or Tampa, the days sunny but seldom lazy, and the sex exactly the same as it was for secretaries in Boston and shopkeepers in Pittsburgh.

Wally had to leave at a quarter past six in order to keep a seven o'clock engagement, and a couple of the table-hoppers in the Polo Lounge asked Hilary to have dinner with them. She declined, pleading a prior commitment.

Outside the hotel, the autumn evening was still bright. A few high clouds tracked across the technicolor sky. The sunlight was the color of platinum-blonde hair, and the air was surprisingly fresh for mid-week Los Angeles. Two young couples laughed and chattered noisily as they climbed out of a blue Cadillac, and farther away, on Sunset Boulevard, tires hummed and engines roared and horns blared as the last of the rush hour crowd tried to get home alive.

As Hilary and Wally waited for their cars to be brought around by the smiling valets, he said, "Are you really having dinner with someone?"

"Yeah. Me, myself, and I."

"Look, you can come along with me."

"The uninvited guest."

"I just invited you."

"I don't want to spoil your plans."

"Nonsense. You'd be a delightful addition."

"Anyway, I'm not dressed for dinner."

"You look fine."

"I want to be alone," she said.

"You do a terrible Garbo. Come to dinner with me. Please. It's just an informal evening at The Palm with a client and his wife. An up and coming young television writer. Nice people."

"I'll be okay, Wally. Really."

"A beautiful woman like you, on a night like this, with so much to celebrate—there ought to be candlelight, soft music, good wine, a special someone to share it with."

She grinned. "Wally, you're a closet romantic."

"I'm serious," he said.

She put one hand on his arm. "It's sweet of you to be concerned about me, Wally. But I'm perfectly all right. I'm happy when I'm alone. I'm very good company for myself. There'll be plenty of time for a meaningful relationship with a man and skiing weekends in Aspen and chatty evenings at The Palm after *The Hour of the Wolf* is finished and in the theaters."

Wally Topelis frowned. "If you don't learn how to relax, you won't survive for very long in a high-pressure business like this. In a couple of years, you'll be as limp as a rag doll, tattered, frayed, worn out. Believe me, kid, when the physical energy is all burnt up, you'll suddenly discover that the mental energy, the creative juice, has also evaporated with it."

"This project is a watershed for me," she said. "After it, my life won't be the same."

"Agreed. But—"

"I've worked hard, damned hard, single-mindedly, toward this chance. I'll admit it: I've been obsessed with my work. But once I've made a reputation as a good writer *and* a good director, I'll feel secure. I'll finally be able to cast out the demons—my parents, Chicago, all those bad memories. I'll be able to relax and lead a more normal life. But I can't rest yet. If I slack off now, I'll fail. Or at least I think I will, and that's the same thing."

He sighed. "Okay. But we would have had a lot of fun at The Palm."

A valet arrived with her car.

She hugged Wally. "I'll probably call you tomorrow, just to be sure that this Warner Brothers thing wasn't all a dream."

"Contracts will take a few weeks," he told her. "But I don't anticipate any serious problems. We'll have the deal memo sometime next week, and then you can set up a meeting at the studio."

She blew him a kiss, hurried to the car, tipped the valet, and drove away.

She headed into the hills, past the million-dollar houses, past lawns greener than money, turning left, then right, at random, going nowhere in particular, just driving for relaxation, one of the few escapes she allowed herself. Most of the streets were shrouded in purple shadows cast by canopies of green branches; night was stealing across the pavement even though daylight still existed above the interlaced palms, oaks, maples, cedars, cypresses, jacarandas, and pines. She switched on the headlights and explored some of the winding canyon roads until, gradually, her frustration began to seep away.

Later, when night had fallen above the trees as well as below them, she stopped at a Mexican restaurant on La Cienega Boulevard. Rough beige plaster walls. Photographs of Mexican bandits. The rich odors of hot sauce, taco seasoning, and corn meal tortillas. Waitresses in scoop-necked peasant blouses and many-pleated red skirts. South-of-the-border Muzak. Hilary ate cheese enchiladas, rice, refried beans. The food tasted every bit as good as it would have tasted if it had been served by candle-light, with string music in the background, and with someone special seated beside her.

I'll have to remember to tell Wally that, she thought as she washed down the last of the enchiladas with a swallow of Dos Equis, a dark Mexican beer.

But when she considered it for a moment, she could almost hear his reply: My lamb, that is nothing but blatant psychological rationalization. It's true that loneliness doesn't change the taste of food, the quality of candlelight, the sound of music—but that doesn't mean that loneliness is desirable or good or healthy." He simply wouldn't be able to resist launching into one of his fatherly lectures about life; and listening to that would not be made any easier by the fact that whatever he had to say would make sense.

You better not mention it, she told herself. You are never going to get one up on Wally Topelis.

In her car again, she buckled her seatbelt, brought the big engine to life, snapped on the radio, and sat for a while, staring at the flow of traffic on La Cienega. Today was her birthday. Twenty-ninth birthday. And in spite of the fact that it had been noted in Hank Grant's *Hollywood Reporter* column, she seemed to be the only one in the world who cared. Well, that was okay. She was a loner. Always had been a loner. Hadn't she told Wally that she was perfectly happy with only her own company?

The cars flashed past in an endless stream, filled with people who were going places, doing things—usually in pairs.

She didn't want to start for home yet, but there was nowhere else to go.

•

The house was dark.

The lawn looked more blue than green in the glow of the mercury-vapor streetlamp.

Hilary parked the car in the garage and walked to the front door. Her heels made an unnaturally loud *tock-tock-tock* sound on the stone footpath.

The night was mild. The heat of the vanished sun still rose from the earth, and the cooling sea wind that washed the basin city in all seasons had not yet brought the usual autumn chill to the air; later, toward midnight, it would be coat weather.

Crickets chirruped in the hedges.

She let herself into the house, found the entranceway light, closed and locked the door. She switched on the living room lights as well and was a few steps from the foyer when she heard movement behind her and turned.

A man came out of the foyer closet, knocking a coat off a hanger as he shouldered out of that confining space, throwing the door back against the wall with a loud *bang!* He was about forty years old, a tall man wearing dark slacks and a tight yellow pullover sweater—and leather gloves. He had the kind of big, hard muscles that could be gotten only from years of weightlifting; even his wrists, between the cuffs of the sweater and the gloves, were thick and sinewy. He stopped ten feet from her and grinned broadly, nodded, licked his thin lips.

She wasn't quite sure how to respond to his sudden appearance. He wasn't an ordinary intruder, not a total stranger, not some punk kid or some shabby degenerate with a drug-blur in his eyes. Although he didn't belong here, she knew him, and he was just about the last man she would expect to encounter in a situation of this sort. Seeing gentle little Wally Topelis come out of that closet was the only thing that could have shocked her more than this. She was less frightened than confused. She had met him three weeks ago, while doing research for a screenplay set in the wine country of Northern California, a project meant to take her mind off Wally's marketing of *The Hour of the Wolf*, which she had finished about that time. He was an important and successful man up there in the Napa Valley. But that didn't explain what the hell he was doing in her house, hiding in her closet.

"Mr. Frye," she said uneasily.

"Hello, Hilary." He had a deep, somewhat gravelly voice which seemed reassuring and fatherly when she had taken an extensive private tour of his winery near St. Helena, but which now sounded coarse, mean, threatening.

She cleared her throat nervously. "What are you doing here?"

"Come to see you."

"Why?"

"Just had to see you again."

"About what?"

He was still grinning. He had a tense, predatory look. His was the smile of the wolf just before it closed hungry jaws on the cornered rabbit.

"How did you get in?" she demanded.

"Pretty."

"What?"

"So pretty."

"Stop it."

"Been looking for one like you."

"You're scaring me."

"You're a real pretty one."

He took a step toward her.

She knew then, beyond doubt, what he wanted. But it was crazy, unthinkable. Why would a wealthy man of his high social position travel hundreds of miles to risk his fortune, reputation, and freedom for one brief violent moment of forced sex?

He took another step.

She backed away from him.

Rape. It made no sense. Unless. . . . If he intended to kill her afterwards, he would not be taking much of a risk at all. He was wearing gloves. He would leave no prints, no clues. And no one would believe that a prominent and highly-respected vintner from St. Helena would drive all the way to Los Angeles to rape and murder. Even if some would believe it, they'd have no reason to think of him in the first place. The homicide investigation would never move in his direction.

He kept coming. Slowly. Relentlessly. Heavy steps. Enjoying the suspense. Grinning more than ever as he saw comprehension enter her eyes.

She backed past the huge stone fireplace, briefly considered grabbing one of the heavy brass implements on the hearth, but realized that she would not be quick enough to defend herself with it. He was a powerful, athletic man in excellent physical condition; he would be all over her before she could seize the poker and swing it at his damned thick skull.

He flexed his big hands. The knuckles strained at the snug-fitting leather.

She backed past a grouping of furniture—two chairs, a coffee table, a long sofa. She started moving toward her right, trying to put the sofa between her and Frye.

"Such pretty hair," he said.

A part of her wondered if she were losing her mind. This could not be the Bruno Frye she had met in St. Helena. There had been not even the slightest hint of the madness that now contorted his broad, sweat-greased face. His eyes were blue-gray chips of ice, and the frigid passion that shone in them was surely too monstrous to have been concealed when she last saw him.

Then she saw the knife, and the sight of it was like a blast of furnace heat that turned her doubts to steam and blew them away. He meant to kill her. The knife was fixed to his belt, over his right hip. It was in an open sheath, and he could free it simply by popping the metal snap on a single narrow leather strap. In one second, the blade could be slipped from the holder and wrapped tightly in his fist; in two seconds, it could be jammed deep into her soft belly, slicing through warm meat and jelly organs, letting loose the precious store of blood.

"I've wanted you since I first saw you," Frye said. "Just wanted to get at you."

Time seemed to stop for her.

"You're going to be a good little piece," he said. "Real good."

Abruptly, the world was a slow-motion movie. Each second seemed like a minute. She watched him approach as if he were a creature in a nightmare, as if the atmosphere had suddenly become as thick as syrup.

The instant that she spotted the knife, Hilary froze. She stopped backing away from him, even though he continued to approach. A knife will do that. It chokes you up, freezes your heart, brings an uncontrollable tremor to your guts. Surprisingly few people have the stomach to use a knife against another living thing. More than any other weapon, it makes you aware of the delicacy of flesh, the terrible fragility of human life; in the damage that he wreaks, the attacker can see all too clearly the nature of his own mortality. A gun, a draught of poison, a firebomb, a blunt instrument, a strangler's piece of rope—all can be used relatively cleanly, most of them at a distance. But the man with a knife must be prepared to get dirty, and he must get in close, so close that he can feel the heat escaping from the wounds as he makes them. It takes a special courage, or insanity, to slash at another person and not be repelled by the warm blood spurting over your hand.

Frye was upon her. He placed one large hand on her breasts, rubbed and squeezed them roughly through the silky fabric of her dress.

That rude contact snapped her out of the trance into which she'd fallen. She knocked his hand away, twisted out of his grasp, and ran behind the couch.

His laugh was hearty, disconcertingly pleasant, but his hard eyes glinted with a macabre amusement. It was a demon joke, the mad humor of hell. He wanted her to fight back, for he enjoyed the chase.

"Get out!" she said. "Get out!"

"Don't want to get out," Frye said, smiling, shaking his head. "I want to get *in*. Oh yeah. That's it. I want to get in you, little lady. I want to rip that dress off your back, get you naked, and get right up in there. All the way up, all the way inside where it's warm and wet and dark and soft."

For a moment, the fear that made her legs rubbery and turned her insides to water was supplanted by more powerful emotions: hate, anger, fury. Hers was not the reasoned anger of a woman toward an arrogant man's usurpation of her dignity and rights; not an intellectual anger based on the social and biological injustices of the situation; it was more fundamental than that. He had entered her private space uninvited, had pushed his way into her modern cave, and she was possessed by a primitive rage that blurred her vision and made her heart race. She bared her teeth at him, growled in the back of her throat; she was reduced to an almost unconscious animal response as she faced him and looked for a way out of the trap.

A low, narrow, glass-topped display table stood flush against the back of the sofa. Two eighteen-inch-high pieces of fine porcelain statuary rested upon it. She grabbed one of the statues and hurled it at Frye.

He ducked with a primitive, instinctual quickness of his own. The porcelain struck the stone fireplace and exploded like a bomb. Dozens of chunks and hundreds of chips of it rained down on the hearth and on the surrounding carpet.

"Try again," he said, mocking her.

She picked up the other porcelain, hesitated. She watched him through narrowed eyes, weighed the statue in her hand, then faked a pitch.

He was deceived by the feint. He dipped down and to one side to avoid the missile.

With a small cry of triumph, she threw the statue for real.

He was too surprised to duck again, and the porcelain caught him on the side of the head. It was a glancing blow, less devastating than she'd hoped, but he staggered back a step or two. He didn't go down. He wasn't seriously injured. He wasn't even bleeding. But he was hurt, and the pain transformed him. He was no longer in a perversely playful mood. The crooked smile disappeared. His mouth was set in a straight, grim line, lips tightly compressed. His face was red. Fury wound him up as if he were a watch spring; under the strain, the muscles in his massive neck popped up, taut, impressive. He crouched slightly, ready to charge.

Hilary expected him to come around the couch, and she intended to circle it, staying away from him, keeping the couch between them until she could reach something else worth throwing. But when he moved at last, he didn't stalk her as she'd anticipated. Instead, he rushed straight at her without finesse, as if he were a bull in a blind rage. He bent in front of the couch, gripped it with both hands, tilted it up, and in one smooth movement pushed it over backwards as if it weighed only a few pounds. She jumped out of the way as the big piece of furniture crashed down where she'd been standing. Even as the sofa fell, Frye vaulted over it. He reached for her, and he would have had her if he hadn't stumbled and gone down on one knee.

Her anger gave way to fear again, and she ran. She headed toward the foyer and the front door, but she knew she would not have time to throw off both bolt locks and get out of the house before he got hold of her. He was too damned close, no more than two or three steps away. She darted to the right and dashed up the winding stairs, two at a time.

She was breathing hard, but over her own gasping she heard him coming. His footfalls were thunderous. He was cursing her.

The gun. In the nightstand. If she could get to her bedroom far enough ahead of him to slam and lock the door, that ought to hold him for a few seconds, at least, certainly long enough for her to get the pistol.

At the top of the stairs, as she came into the second-floor hallway, when she was certain she had put another few feet between them, he caught her right shoulder and yanked her back against him. She screamed, but she didn't try to pull away, as he evidently expected her to do. Instead, the instant he grabbed her, she turned on him. She pushed into him before he could get a restraining arm around her, pressed so tight against him that she could feel his erection, and she drove one knee hard into his crotch. He reacted as if he'd been hit by lightning. The red flush of anger went out of his face, and his skin flashed bone-white, all in a fraction of a second. He lost his grip on her and staggered back and slipped on the edge of the first step and windmilled his arms and toppled over, cried out, threw himself to one side, clutched the bannister and was lucky enough to arrest his fall.

Apparently, he hadn't had much experience with women who fought back effectively. She had tricked him twice. He thought he was on the trail of a nice, fluffy, harmless bunny, timid prey that could be subdued easily and used and then broken with a flick of the wrist. But she turned and showed long fangs and claws to him, and she was exhilarated by his shocked expression.

She had hoped he would tumble all the way to the bottom of the staircase, breaking his neck as he went. Even now, she thought the blow to his privates would take him out of action at least a minute or two, long enough for her to get the upper hand. She was shocked when, after only the briefest pause, before she could even turn and run, he shoved away from the bannister and, wincing with pain, struggled up toward her.

"Bitch," he said between clenched teeth, barely able to get his breath.

"No," she said. "No. Stay back."

She felt like a character in one of those old horror movies that Hammer Films used to do so well. She was in a battle with a vampire or a zombie, repeatedly astonished and disheartened by the beast's supernatural reserves of strength and endurance.

"Bitch."

She ran down the shadow-draped hallway, into the master bedroom. She slammed the door, fumbled for the lock button in the dark, finally hit the light switch, engaged the lock.

There was a strange and frightening noise in the room. It was a loud hoarse sound filled with terror. She looked around wildly for the source of it before she realized that she was listening to her own ragged and uncontrollable sobbing.

She was dangerously close to panic, but she knew she must control herself if she wanted to live.

Suddenly, Frye tried the locked door behind her, then threw his weight against it. The barrier held. But it would not hold much longer, certainly not long enough for her to call the police and wait for help.

Her heart was beating furiously, and she was shaking as if she were standing naked on a vast field of ice; but she was determined not to be incapacitated by fear. She hurried across the big room, around the bed, toward the far nightstand. On the way, she passed a full-length wall mirror that seemed to throw back to her the image of a total stranger, an owl-eyed and harried woman with a face as pale as the painted visage of a mime.

Frye kicked the door. It shook violently in the frame but didn't let go.

The .32 automatic was on top of three pairs of folded pajamas in the nightstand drawer. The loaded magazine lay beside it. She picked up the gun and, with jittery hands that nearly failed her, rammed the magazine into the butt. She faced the doorway.

Frye kicked the lock again. The hardware was flimsy. It was the kind of interior lock primarily meant to keep children and nosey house guests out of a room. It was useless against an intruder like Bruno Frye. On the third kick, the workings burst from the mounting, and the door clattered open.

Panting, sweating, he looked more than ever like a mad bull as he lumbered out of the dark hall and crossed the threshold. His broad shoulders were hunched, and his hands were fisted at his sides. He wanted to lower his head and charge, smash and destroy everything that stood in his way. Blood lust shone in his eyes as clearly as his reflection glowered back at him from the wall mirror beside Hilary. He wanted to smash his way through the china shop and stomp on the proprietor.

Hilary pointed the pistol at him, holding it firmly with both hands.

He kept coming.

"I'll shoot! I will! I swear to God I will!" she said frantically.

Frye stopped, blinked at her, saw the gun for the first time.

"Out," she said.

He didn't move.

"Get the hell out of here!"

Incredibly, he took one more step toward her. It was no longer the smug, calculating, game-playing rapist she had faced downstairs. Something had happened to him; deep inside, relay switches had clicked into place, setting up new patterns in his mind, new wants and needs and hungers that were more disgusting and perverted than any he had revealed thus far. He was no longer even half rational. His demeanor was that of a lunatic. His eyes flashed, not icy as they had been, but watery and hot, fevered. Sweat streamed down his face. His lips worked ceaselessly, even though he was not speaking; they writhed and twisted, pulled back over his teeth, then pushed out in a childish pout, formed a sneer, then a weird little smile, then a fierce scowl, then an expression for which there was no name. He was no longer driven by lust or the desire to utterly dominate her. The secret motor that drove him now was darker in design than the one that had powered him just a few minutes ago, and she had the terrible crazy feeling that it would somehow provide him with enough energy to shield him from harm, to let him advance untouched through a hail of bullets.

He took the large knife from the sheath on his right hip and thrust it in front of him.

"Back off," she said desperately.

"Bitch."

"I mean it."

He started toward her again.

"For God's sake," she said, "be serious. That knife's no good against a gun."

He was twelve or fifteen feet from the other side of the bed.

"I'll blow your goddamned head off."

Frye waved the knife at her, drew small rapid circles in the air with the point of the blade, as if it were a talisman and he were chasing off evil spirits that stood between him and Hilary.

And he took another step.

She lined up the forward sight with the center of his abdomen, so that no matter how high the recoil kicked her hands and no matter whether the gun pulled to the left or the right, she would hit something vital. She squeezed the trigger.

Nothing happened.

Please, God!

He took two steps.

She stared at the pistol, stunned. She had forgotten to throw off the safety catches.

He was maybe eight feet from the other side of the bed. Maybe only six.

Swearing at herself, she thumbed the two tiny levers on the side of the pistol, and a pair of red dots appeared on the black metal. She aimed and pulled the trigger a second time.

Nothing.

Jesus! What? It can't be jammed!

Frye was so completely disassociated from reality, so thoroughly possessed by his madness, that he did not realize immediately that she was having problems with the weapon. When he finally saw what was happening, he moved in fast, while the advantage was his. He reached the bed, scrambled onto it, stood up, started straight across the mattress like a man walking a bridge of barrels, swaying on the springy surface.

She had forgotten to jack a bullet into the chamber. She did that and retreated two steps until she backed into the wall. She squeezed off a shot without taking aim, fired up at him as he loomed directly over her like a demon leaping out of a crack in hell.

The sound of the shot filled the room. It slapped off the walls and reverberated in the windows.

She saw the knife shatter, saw the fragments arc out of Frye's right hand. The sharp steel flew up and back, sparkling for a moment in the shaft of light that escaped through the open top of the bedside lamp.

Frye howled as the knife spun away from him. He fell backwards and rolled off the far side of the bed. But he was up as soon as he went down, cradling his right hand in his left.

Hilary didn't think she had hit him. There wasn't any blood. The bullet must have struck the knife, breaking it and tearing it out of his grasp. The shock would have stung his fingers worse than the crack of a whip.

Frye wailed in pain, screamed in rage. It was a wild sound, a jackal's bark, but it was definitely not the cry of an animal with its tail between its legs. He still intended to come after her.

She fired again, and he went down again. This time he stayed down.

With a little whimper of relief, Hilary sagged wearily against the wall, but she did not take her eyes off the place where he had gone down and where he now lay out of sight beyond the bed.

No sound.

No movement.

She was uneasy about not being able to see him. Head cocked, listening intently, she moved cautiously to the foot of the bed, out into the room, then around to the left until she spotted him.

He was belly-down on the chocolate-brown Edward Fields carpet. His right arm was tucked under him. His left arm was flung straight out in front, the hand curled slightly, the still fingers pointing back toward the top of his head. His face was turned away from her. Because the carpet was so dark and plush and eye-dazzlingly textured, she had some difficulty telling from a distance if there was any blood soaked into it. Quite clearly, there was not an enormous sticky pool like the one she had expected to find. If the shot had hit him in the chest, the blood might be trapped under him. The bullet might even have taken him squarely in the forehead, bringing instant death and abrupt cessation of heartbeat; in which case, there would be only a few drops of blood.

She watched him for a minute, two minutes. She could not detect any movement, not even the subtle rise and fall of his breathing.

Dead?

Slowly, timidly, she approached him.

"Mr. Frye?"

She didn't intend to get too close. She wasn't going to endanger herself, but she wanted a better look at him. She kept the gun trained on him, ready to put another round into him if he moved.

"Mr. Frye?"

No response.

Funny that she should keep calling him "Mr. Frye." After what had happened tonight, after what he had tried to do to her, she was still being formal and polite. Maybe because he was dead. In death, the very worst man in town is accorded hushed respect even by those who know that he was a liar and a scoundrel all his life. Because every one of us must die, belittling a dead man is in a way like belittling ourselves. Besides, if you speak badly about the dead, you somehow feel that you are mocking that great and final mystery—and perhaps inviting the gods to punish you for your effrontery.

Hilary waited and watched as another minute dragged past.

"You know what, Mr. Frye? I think I won't take any chances with you. I think I'll just put another bullet in you right now. Yeah. Fire a round right in the back of your head."

Of course, she wasn't able to do that. She wasn't violent by nature. She had fired the gun on a shooting range once, shortly after she bought it, but she had never killed a living thing larger than the cockroaches in that Chicago apartment. She had found the will to shoot at Bruno Frye only because he had been an immediate threat and she had been pumped full of adrenaline. Hysteria and a primitive survival instinct had made her briefly capable of violence. But now that Frye was on the floor, quiet and motionless, no more menacing than a pile of dirty rags, she could not easily bring herself to pull the trigger. She couldn't just stand there and watch as she blew the brains out of a corpse. Even the thought of it turned her stomach. But the threat of doing it was a good test of his condition. If he was faking, the possibility of her shooting pointblank at his skull ought to make him give up his act.

"Right in the head, you bastard," she said, and she fired a round into the ceiling.

He didn't flinch.

She sighed and lowered the pistol.

Dead. He was dead.

She had killed a man.

Dreading the coming ordeal with police and reporters, she edged around the outstretched arm and headed for the hall door.

Suddenly, he was not dead any more.

Suddenly, he was very much alive and moving.

He anticipated her. He'd known exactly how she was trying to trick him. He'd seen through the ruse, and he'd had nerves of steel. He hadn't even flinched!

Now he used the arm under him to push up and forward, striking at Hilary as if he were a snake, and with his left hand he seized her ankle and brought her down, screaming and flailing, and they rolled over, a tangle of arms and legs, then over again, and his teeth were at her throat, and he was snarling like a dog, and she had the crazy fear that he was going to bite her and tear open her jugular vein and suck out all of her blood, but then she got a hand between them, got her palm under his chin and levered his head away from her neck as they rolled one last time, and then they came up against the wall with jarring impact and stopped, dizzy, gasping, and he was like a great beast on her, so rough, so heavy, crushing her, leering down at her, his hideous cold eyes so frighteningly close and deep and empty, his breath foul with onions and stale beer, and he had one hand under her dress, shredding her pantyhose, trying to get his big blunt fingers under her panties and gain a grip on her sex, not a lover's grip but a fighter's grip, and the thought of the damage he might do to her softest tissues made her gag with horror, and she knew it was even possible to kill a woman that way, to reach up inside and claw and rip and pull, so she tried frantically to scratch his cobalt eyes and blind him, but he swiftly drew his head back, out of range, and then they both abruptly froze, for they realized simultaneously that she had not dropped the pistol when he had pulled her down onto the floor. It was wedged between them, the muzzle pressed firmly into his crotch—and although her finger was on the trigger guard instead of the trigger itself, she was able to slip it back a notch and put it in the proper place even as she became aware of the situation.

His heavy hand was still on her pubis. An obscene thing. A leathery, demonic, disgusting hand. She could feel the heat of it even through the glove he was wearing. He was no longer clawing at her panties. Trembling. His big hand was trembling.

The bastard's scared.

His eyes seemed to be fastened to hers by an invisible thread, a strong thread that would not break easily. Neither of them could look away.

"If you make one wrong move," she said weakly, "I'll blow your balls off."

He blinked.

"Understand?" she asked, unable to put any force in her voice. She was wheezing and breathless with exertion and, mostly, with fear.

He licked his lips.

Blinked slowly.

Like a goddamned lizard.

"Do you understand?" she demanded, putting bite into it this time.

"Yeah."

"You can't fool me again."

"Whatever you say."

His voice was deep and gruff, as before, and it did not waver. There wasn't anything in his voice or eyes or face to betray his hard-muscled tough guy image. But his gloved hand continued to spasm nervously on the sensitive juncture of her thighs.

"Okay," she said. "What I want you to do is move very slowly. Very, very slowly. When I give the word, we're going to roll over very slowly, until you're on the bottom and I'm on the top."

Without being the least amused, she was aware that what she had said bore a grotesque resemblance to an eager lover's suggestion in the middle of the sex act.

"When I tell you to, and not a second before I tell you to, you'll roll to your right," she said.

"Okay."

"And I'll move with you."

"Sure."

"Nice and easy."

"Sure."

"And I'll keep the gun where it is."

His eyes were still hard and cold, but the insanity and the rage had gone out of them. The thought of having his sex organs shot off had snapped him back into the real world—at least temporarily.

She poked the barrel of the gun hard against his privates, and he grimaced with pain.

"Now roll over *easy*," she said.

He did exactly what she had instructed him to do, moved onto his side with exaggerated care, then onto his back, never taking his eyes from hers. He slipped his hand out from under her dress as they reversed positions, but he didn't attempt to take the pistol from her.

She clung to him with her left hand, the gun clenched in her right, and she went over with him, keeping the muzzle firmly in his crotch. Finally she was atop him, one arm trapped between them, the .32 automatic still strategically placed.

Her right hand was beginning to go numb because of the awkward position, but also because she was squeezing the pistol with all of her might and was afraid to hold it any less surely. Her grip was so fierce that her fingers and the muscles up the length of her arm ached with the effort. She was worried that somehow he would sense the growing weakness in her hand—or that she would actually let go of the gun against her will as her fingers lost all feeling.

"Okay," she said. "I'm going to slide off you. I'm going to keep the gun where it is, and I'm going to slip off beside you. Don't move. Don't even blink."

He stared at her.

"You got that?" she asked.

"Yeah."

Keeping the .32 on his scrotum, she disengaged herself from him as if she were rising from a bed of nitroglycerin. Her abdominal muscles were painfully tight with tension. Her mouth was dry and sour. Their noisy breathing seemed to fill the bedroom like rushing wind, yet her hearing was so acute that she could detect the soft ticking of her Cartier watch. She slid to one side, got up on her knees, hesitated, finally pushed all the way to her feet and shuffled quickly out of his reach before he could trip her again.

He sat up.

"No!" she said.

"What?"

"Lie down."

"I'm not coming after you."

"Lie down."

"Just relax."

"Dammit, lie down!"

He would not obey her. He just sat there. "So what happens next?"

Waving the pistol at him, she said, "I told you to lie down. Flat on your back. Do it. Now."

He twisted his lips into one of those ugly smiles that he did so well. "And I asked *you* what happens next."

He was trying to regain control of the situation, and she did not like that. On the other hand, did it really matter whether he was sitting or lying down? Even sitting up, he could not get to his feet and cross the space between them faster than she could put a couple of bullets into him.

"Okay," she said reluctantly. "Sit up if you insist. But you make one move toward me, and I'll empty the gun on you. I'll spread your guts all over the room. I swear to Christ I will."

He grinned and nodded.

Shivering, she said, "Now, I'm going to the bed. I'll sit down there and phone the police."

She moved sideways and backwards, crablike, one small step at a time, until she got to the bed. The telephone was on the nightstand. The moment she sat down and lifted the receiver, Frye disobeyed her. He stood up.

"Hey."

She dropped the receiver and clutched the pistol with both hands, trying to keep it steady.

He held his hands out placatingly, palms toward her. "Wait. Just wait a second. I'm not going to touch you."

"Sit down."

"I'm not coming anywhere near you."

"Sit down right now."

"I'm going to walk out of here," Frye said.

"Like hell you are."

"Out of this room and out of this house."

"No."

"You won't try to shoot me if I just leave."

"Try me and you'll be sorry."

"You won't," he said confidently. "You aren't the type to pull the trig-ger unless you don't have any other choice. You couldn't kill me in cold blood. You couldn't shoot me in the back. Not in a million years. Not you. You don't have that kind of strength. You're weak. Just too damned weak." He gave her that ghastly grin again, that wide death's head smile, and he took one step toward the door. "You can call the cops when I'm gone." Another step. "It would be different if I was a stranger. Then I might have a chance to get away scot-free. But after all, you can tell them who I am." Another step. "See, you've already won, and I've lost. All I'm doing is buying a little time. A very little bit of time."

She knew he was right about her. She could kill him if he attacked, but she was not capable of shooting him while he retreated.

Sensing her unspoken acknowledgment of the truth in what he had said, Frye turned his back on her. His smug self-confidence infuriated her, but she could not pull the trigger. He had been sidling carefully toward the exit. Now, he strode boldly out of the room, not bothering to glance back. He disappeared through the broken door, and his footsteps echoed along the hallway.

When Hilary heard him thumping down the stairs, she realized that he might not leave the house. Unobserved, he could slip into one of the downstairs rooms and hide in a closet, wait patiently until the police had come and gone, then slither out of his hole and strike her by surprise. She hurried to the head of the stairs and got there just in time to see him turn right, into the foyer. A moment later, she heard him rattling the locks; then he went out and threw the door shut behind him with a loud *wham!*

She was three-quarters of the way down the stairs when she realized he might have faked his departure. He might have slammed the door without leaving. He might be waiting for her in the foyer.

Hilary was carrying the pistol at her side, the muzzle directed safely at the floor, but she raised it in dread anticipation. She descended the stairs, and on the bottom step she paused for a long while, listening. At last, she eased forward until she could see into the foyer. It was empty. The closet door stood open. Frye wasn't in there either. He was really gone.

She closed the closet door.

She went to the front door and double-locked it.

Weaving slightly, she walked across the living room, in the study. The room smelled of lemon-scented furniture polish; the two women from the cleaning agency had been in yesterday. Hilary switched on the light and drifted to the big desk. She put the gun in the center of the blotter.

Red and white roses filled the vase on the window table. They added a sweet contrasting fragrance to the lemon air.

She sat down at the desk and pulled the telephone in front of her. She looked up the number for the police.

Suddenly, unexpectedly, her vision blurred with hot tears. She tried to hold them back. She was Hilary Thomas, and Hilary Thomas did not cry. Not ever. Hilary Thomas was tough. Hilary Thomas could take all the crap the world wanted to throw at her and keep on taking it and never break down. Hilary Thomas could handle herself perfectly well, thank you. Even though she squeezed her eyes shut, the flood would not be contained. Fat tears tracked down her cheeks and settled saltily in the corners of her mouth, then dribbled over her chin. At first she wept in eerie silence, emitting not even the shallowest whimper. But after a minute or so, she began to twitch and shiver, and her voice was shaken loose. In the back of her throat, she made a wet choking sound which swiftly grew into a sharp little cry of despair. She broke. She let out a terrible quaverous wail and hugged herself. She sobbed and sputtered and gasped for breath. She pulled Kleenex from a decorator dispenser on one corner of the desk, blew her nose, got hold of herself—then shuddered and began to sob again.

She was not crying because he had hurt her. He hadn't caused her any lasting or unbearable pain—at least not physically. She was weeping because, in some way she found difficult to define, he had violated her. She boiled with outrage and shame. Although he had not raped her, although he had not even managed to tear off her clothes, he had demolished her crystal bubble of privacy, a barrier that she had constructed with great care and upon which she had placed a great value. He had smashed into her snug world and had pawed everything in it with his dirty hands.

Tonight, at the best table in the Polo Lounge, Wally Topelis had begun to convince her that she could let down her guard at least a fraction of an inch. For the first time in her twenty-nine years, she seriously had considered the possibility of living much less defensively than she had been accustomed to living. With all the good news and Wally's urging, she had been willing to look at the idea of a life with less fear, and she had been attracted to it. A life with more friends. More relaxation. More fun. It was a shining dream, this new life, not easily attained but worth the struggle to achieve it. But Bruno Frye had taken that fragile dream by the throat and had throttled it. He had reminded her that the world was a dangerous place, a shadowy cellar with nightmare creatures crouching in the dark corners. Just as she was struggling out of her pit, before she had a chance to enjoy the world above ground, he kicked her in the face and sent her tumbling back where she came from, down into doubt and fear and suspicion, down into the awful safety of loneliness.

She wept because she felt violated. And because she was humiliated. And because he had taken her hope and stomped on it the way a school-yard bully crushes the favorite toy of a weaker child.

chapter two

Patterns.

They fascinated Anthony Clemenza.

At sundown, before Hilary Thomas had even gone home, while she was still driving through the hills and canyons for relaxation, Anthony Clemenza and his partner, Lieutenant Frank Howard, were questioning a bartender in Santa Monica. Beyond the enormous windows in the room's west wall, the sinking sun created constantly changing purple and orange and silver-fleck patterns on the darkening sea.

The place was a singles' bar called Paradise, meeting ground for the chronically lonely and terminally horny of both sexes in an age when all the traditional meeting grounds—church suppers, neighborhood dances, community picnics, social clubs—had been leveled with real (and socio-logical) bulldozers, the ground where they once stood now covered with high-rise offices, towering cement and glass condominiums, pizza parlors, and five-story parking garages. The singles' bar was where space-age boy met space-age girl, where the macho stud connected with the nymphoma-niac, where the shy little secretary from Chatsworth met the socially inept computer programmer from Burbank, and, where, sometimes, the rapist met the rapee.

To Anthony Clemenza's eye, the people in Paradise made patterns that identified the place. The most beautiful women and the handsomest men sat very erect on barstools and at minuscule cocktail tables, legs crossed in geometric perfection, elbows bent just so, posing to display the clean lines of their faces and their strong limbs; they made elegantly angular patterns as they watched and courted one another. Those who were less physically attractive than the *crème de la crème*, but who were nonetheless undeniably appealing and desirable, tended to sit and stand with less than ideal posture, choosing to make up in attitude and image what they lacked in form. Their posture made a statement: I am at ease here, relaxed, unimpressed with those gorgeous straight-backed girls and guys, confident, my own person. This group slouched and slumped gracefully, using the eye-pleasing rounded lines of a body at rest to conceal slight imperfections of bone and muscle. The third and largest group of people in the bar was composed of the plain ones, neither pretty nor ugly, who made jagged anxious patterns as they huddled in corners and darted from table to table to exchange gaping smiles and nervous gossip, worried that no one would love them.

The overall pattern of Paradise is sadness, Tony Clemenza thought. Dark strips of unfulfilled need. A checkered field of loneliness. Quiet desperation in a colorful herringbone.

But he and Frank Howard were not there to study the patterns in the sunset and the customers. What they were there to do was get a lead on Bobby "Angel" Valdez.

Last April, Bobby Valdez had been released from prison after serving seven years and a few months of a fifteen-year sentence for rape and manslaughter. It looked like letting him go had been a big mistake.

Eight years ago, Bobby had raped as few as three and as many as sixteen Los Angeles women. The police could prove three; they suspected the others. One night, Bobby accosted a woman in a parking lot, forced her into his car at gunpoint, drove her to a little-traveled dirt connecting road high in the Hollywood Hills, tore off her clothes, raped her repeatedly, then pushed her out of the car and drove off. He had been parked on the verge of the lane, and the narrow shoulder had opened on a long nasty drop. The woman, thrust naked from the car, lost her balance and went over the edge. She landed on a broken-down fence. Splintery wooden fence posts. With rusted wire. Barbed wire. The wire lacerated her badly, and a jagged four-inch-wide section of weathered pine railing slammed through her belly and out her back, impaling her. Incredibly, while submitting to Bobby in the car, she had put her hand upon a flimsy copy of a Union 76 credit card purchase slip, had realized what it was, and had held on to it all the way down to the fence, all the way down into death. Furthermore, police learned that the deceased wore only one kind of panties, a gift from her boyfriend. Every pair she owned bore this embroidered legend on the silky crotch: HARRY'S PROPERTY. A pair of those panties, torn and soiled, were found in a collection of underthings in Bobby's apartment. Those and the scrap of paper in the victim's hand led to the suspect's arrest.

Unfortunately for the people of California, circumstances conspired to get Bobby off lightly. The arresting officers made a minor procedural error when they took him into custody, just the sort of thing to stir some judges to passionate rhetoric about constitutional guarantees. The district attorney at that time, a man named Kooperhausen, had been busy responding to charges of political corruption in his own office. Aware that the improper handling of the accused at the time of arrest might have jeopardized the state's case, preoccupied with saving his own ass from the muckrakers, the D.A. had been receptive to the defense attorney's offer to plead Bobby guilty to three counts of rape and one of manslaughter in return for the dropping of all other and more serious charges. Most homicide detectives, like Tony Clemenza, felt that Kooperhausen should have tried to get convictions for second-degree murder, kidnapping, assault, rape, and sodomy. The evidence was overwhelmingly in favor of the state's position. The deck was stacked against Bobby—and then fate dealt him an unexpected ace.

Today, Bobby was a free man.

But maybe not for long, Tony thought.

In May, one month after his release from prison, Bobby "Angel" Valdez failed to keep an appointment with his parole officer. He moved out of his apartment without filing the required change of address form with the proper authorities. He vanished.

In June, he started raping again. Just as easy as that. As casually as some men start smoking again after shaking the habit for a few years. Like renewed interest in an old hobby. He molested two women in June. Two in July. Three in August. Two more in the first ten days of September. After eighty-eight months behind bars, Bobby had a craving for woman-flesh, an insatiable need.

The police were convinced that those nine crimes—and perhaps a few others that had gone unreported—were the work of one man, and they were equally certain the man was Bobby Valdez. For one thing each of the victims had been approached in the same way. A man walked up to her as she got out of her car alone, at night, in a parking lot. He put a gun in her ribs or back or belly, and he said, "I'm a fun guy. Come to the party with me, and you won't get hurt. Turn me down, and I'll blow you away right now. Play along, and you've got no worries. I'm really a fun guy." He said pretty much the same thing every time, and the victims remembered it because the "fun guy" part sounded so weird, especially when spoken in

Bobby's soft, high-pitched, almost girlish voice. It was identical to the approach Bobby had used more than eight years ago, during his first career as a rapist.

In addition to that, the nine victims gave strikingly similar descriptions of the man who had abused them. Slender. Five-foot-ten. A hundred and forty pounds. Dusky complexion. Dimpled chin. Brown hair and eyes. The girlish voice. Some of Bobby's friends called him "Angel" because of his sweet voice and because he had a cute baby face. Bobby was thirty years old, but he looked sixteen. Each of the nine victims had seen her assailant's face, and each had said he looked like a kid, but handled himself like a tough, cruel, clever, and sick man.

The chief bartender in Paradise left the business to his two subordinates and examined the three glossy mug shots of Bobby Valdez that Frank Howard had put on the bar. His name was Otto. He was a good-looking man, darkly tanned and bearded. He wore white slacks and a blue body shirt with the top three buttons undone. His brown chest was matted with crisp golden hairs. He wore a shark's tooth on a gold chain around his neck. He looked up at Frank, frowned. "I didn't know L.A. police had jurisdiction in Santa Monica."

"We're here by sufferance of the Santa Monica P.D.," Tony said.

"Huh?"

"Santa Monica police are cooperating with us in this investigation," Frank said impatiently. "Now, did you ever see the guy?"

"Yeah, sure. He's been in a couple of times," Otto said.

"When?" Frank asked.

"Oh . . . a month ago. Maybe longer."

"Not recently?"

The band, just returned from a twenty-minute break, struck up a Billy Joel song.

Otto raised his voice above the music. "Haven't seen him for at least a month. The reason I remember is because he didn't look old enough to be served. I asked to see some ID, and he got mad as hell about that. Caused a scene."

"What kind of scene?" Frank asked.

"Demanded to see the manager."

"That's all?" Tony asked.

"Called me names." Otto looked grim. "Nobody calls me names like that."

Tony cupped one hand around his ear to funnel in the bartender's voice and block some of the music. He liked most Billy Joel tunes, but not when they were played by a band that thought enthusiasm and amplification could compensate for poor musicianship.

"So he called you names," Frank said. "Then what?"

"Then he apologized."

"Just like that? He demands to see the manager, calls you names, then right away apologizes?"

"Yeah."

"Why?"

"I asked him to," Otto said.

Frank leaned farther over the bar as the music swelled into a deafening chorus. "He apologized just because you asked him to?"

"Well . . . first, he wanted to fight."

"Did you fight him?" Tony shouted.

"Nah. If even the biggest and meanest son of a bitch in the place gets rowdy, I don't ever have to touch him to quiet him down."

"You must have a hell of a lot of charm," Frank yelled.

The band finished the chorus, and the roar descended from a decibel level high enough to make your eyeballs bleed. The vocalist did a bad imitation of Billy Joel on a verse played no louder than a thunderstorm.

A stunning green-eyed blonde was sitting at the bar next to Tony. She had been listening to the conversation. She said, "Go on, Otto. Show them your trick."

"You're a magician?" Tony asked Otto. "What do you do—make unruly customers disappear?"

"He scares them," the blonde said. "It's neat. Go on, Otto. Show them your stuff."

Otto shrugged and reached under the bar and took a tall beer glass from a rack. He held it up so they could look at it, as if they had never seen a beer glass before. Then he bit off a piece of it. He clamped his teeth on the rim and snapped a chunk out of it, turned, spat the sharp fragment into a garbage can behind him.

The band exploded through the last chorus of the song and gifted the audience with merciful silence.

In the sudden quiet between the last note and the burst of scattered applause, Tony heard the beer glass crack as Otto took another bite out of it.

"Jesus," Frank said.

The blonde giggled.

Otto chomped on the glass and spat out a mouthful and chomped

some more until he had reduced it to an inch-thick base too heavy to suc-
cumb to human teeth and jaws. He threw the remaining hunk in the can
and smiled. "I chew up the glass right in front of the guy who's making
trouble. Then I look mean as a snake, and I tell him to settle down. I tell
him that if he doesn't settle down I'll bite his goddamned nose off."

Frank Howard gaped at him, amazed. "Have you ever done it?"

"What? Bitten off someone's nose? Nah. Just the threat's enough to
make them behave."

"You get many hard cases here?" Frank asked.

"Nah. This is a class place. We have trouble maybe once a week. No
more than that."

"How do you do that trick?" Tony asked.

"Biting the glass? There's a little secret to it. But it's not really hard to
learn."

The band broke into Bob Seger's *Still the Same* as if they were a
bunch of juvenile delinquents breaking into a nice house with the intention of trashing it.

"Ever cut yourself?" Tony shouted to Otto.

"Every once in a while. Not often. And I've never cut my tongue. The
sign of someone who can do the stunt well is the condition of his tongue,"
Otto said. "My tongue has never been cut."

"But you have injured yourself."

"Sure. My lips a few times. Not often."

"But that only makes the trick more effective," the blonde said. "You
should see him when he cuts himself. Otto stands there in front of the jerk
who's been causing all the trouble, and he just pretends like he doesn't
know he's hurt himself. He lets the blood run." Her green eyes shone with
delight and with a hard little spark of animal passion that made Tony
squirm uneasily on his barstool. "He stands there with bloody teeth and
with the blood oozing down into his beard, and he warns the guy to stop
making a ruckus. You wouldn't believe how fast they settle down."

"I believe," Tony said. He felt queasy.

Frank Howard shook his head and said, "Well. . . ."

"Yeah," Tony said, unable to find words of his own.

Frank said, "Okay . . . let's get back to Bobby Valdez." He tapped the
mug shots that were lying on the bar.

"Oh. Well, like I told you, he hasn't been in for at least a month."

"That night, after he got angry with you, after you settled him down
with the glass trick, did he stick around for a drink?"

"I served him a couple."

"So you saw his ID."

"Yeah."

"What was it—driver's license?"

"Yeah. He was thirty, for God's sake. He looked like he was in maybe eleventh grade, a high school junior, maybe at most a senior, but he was thirty."

Frank said, "Do you remember what the name was on the driver's license?"

Otto fingered his shark's tooth necklace. "Name? You already know his name."

"What I'm wondering," Frank said, "is whether or not he showed you a phony driver's license."

"His picture was on it," Otto said.

"That doesn't mean it was genuine."

"But you can't change pictures on a California license. Doesn't the card self-destruct or something if you mess around with it?"

"I'm saying the whole card might be a fake."

"Forged credentials," Otto said, intrigued. "Forged credentials. . . ." Clearly, he had watched a couple of hundred old espionage movies on television. "What is this, some sort of spy thing?"

"I think we've gotten turned around here," Frank said impatiently.

"Huh?"

"*We're* supposed to be the ones asking questions," Frank said. "You just answer them. Understand?"

The bartender was one of those people who reacted quickly, strongly, and negatively to a pushy cop. His dark face closed up. His eyes went blank.

Aware that they were about to lose Otto while he still might have something important to tell them, Tony put a hand on Frank's shoulder, squeezed gently. "You don't want him to start munching on a glass, do you?"

"I'd like to see it again," the blonde said, grinning.

"You'd rather do it your way?" Frank asked Tony.

"Sure."

"Go ahead."

Tony smiled at Otto. "Look, you're curious, and so are we. Doesn't hurt a thing if we satisfy your curiosity, so long as you satisfy ours."

Otto opened up again. "That's the way I see it, too."

"Okay," Tony said.

"Okay. So what's this Bobby Valdez done that makes you want him so bad?"

"Parole violations," Tony said.

"And assault," Frank said grudgingly.

"And rape," Tony said.

"Hey," Otto said, "didn't you guys say you were with the homicide squad?"

The band finished *Still the Same* with a clatter-bang-boom of sound not unlike the derailment of a speeding freight train. Then there were a few minutes of peace while the lead singer made unamusing small talk with the ringside customers who sat in clouds of smoke that, Tony felt sure, had come partly from cigarettes and partly from burning eardrums. The musicians pretended to tune their instruments.

"When Bobby Valdez comes across an uncooperative woman," Tony explained to Otto, "he pistol-whips her a little to make her more eager to please. Five days ago, he went after victim number ten, and she resisted, and he hit her on the head so hard and so often that she died in the hospital twelve hours later. Which brought the homicide squad into it."

"What I don't understand," the blonde said, "is why any guy would take it by force when there's girls willing to give it away." She winked at Tony, but he didn't wink back.

"Before the woman died," Frank said, "she gave us a description that fit Bobby like a custom-made glove. So if you know anything about the slimy little bastard, we've got to hear it."

Otto hadn't spent all his time watching spy movies. He had seen his share of police shows, too. He said, "So now you want him for murder-one."

"Murder-one," Tony said. "Precisely."

"How'd you know to ask me about him?"

"He accosted seven of those ten women in singles' bar parking lots—"

"None of them in our lot," Otto interrupted defensively. "Our lot is very well lighted."

"That's true," Tony said. "But we've been going to singles' bars all over the city, talking to bartenders and regular customers, showing them those mug shots, trying to get a line on Bobby Valdez. A couple of people at a place in Century City told us they thought they'd seen him here, but they couldn't be sure."

"He was here all right," Otto said.

Now that Otto's feathers had been smoothed, Frank took over the questioning again. "So he caused a commotion, and you did your beer glass trick, and he showed you his ID."

"Yeah."

"So what was the name on the ID?"

Otto frowned. "I'm not sure."

"Was it Robert Valdez?"

"I don't think so."

"Try to remember."

"It was a Chicano name."

"Valdez is a Chicano name."

"This was more Chicano than that."

"What do you mean?"

"Well . . . longer . . . with a couple Zs in it."

"Zs?"

"And Qs. You know the kind of name I mean. Something like Velazquez."

"Was it Velazquez?"

"Nah. But like that."

"Began with a V?"

"I couldn't say for sure. I'm just talking about the sound of it."

"What about the first name?"

"I think I remember that."

"And?"

"Juan."

"J-U-A-N?"

"Yeah. Very Chicano."

"You notice an address on his ID?"

"I wasn't looking for that."

"He mention where he lived?"

"We weren't exactly chummy."

"He say anything at all about himself?"

"He just drank quietly and left."

"And never came back?"

"That's right."

"You're positive?"

"He's never been back on my shift, anyway."

"You got a good memory."

"Only for the troublemakers and the pretty ones."

"We'd like to show those mug shots to some of your customers," Frank said.

"Sure. Go ahead."

The blonde sitting next to Tony Clemenza said, "Can I get a closer look at them? Maybe I was in here when he was. Maybe I even talked to him."

Tony picked up the photographs and swiveled on his barstool.

She swung toward him as he swung toward her, and she pressed her pretty knees against his. When she took the pictures from him, her fingers lingered for a moment on his. She was a great believer in eye contact. She seemed to be trying to stare right through his brain and out the back of his skull.

"I'm Judy. What's your name?"

"Tony Clemenza."

"I *knew* you were Italian. I could tell by your dark soulful eyes."

"They give me away every time."

"And that thick black hair. So curly."

"And the spaghetti sauce stains on my shirt?"

She looked at his shirt.

"There aren't really any stains," he said.

She frowned.

"Just kidding. A little joke," he said.

"Oh."

"Do you recognize Bobby Valdez?"

She finally looked at the mug shot. "Nope. I must not have been here the night he came in. But he's not all that bad, is he? Kind of cute."

"Baby face."

"It would be like going to bed with my kid brother," she said. "Kinky." She grinned.

He took the pictures from her.

"That's a very nice suit you're wearing," she said.

"Thank you."

"It's cut really nice."

"Thank you."

This was not just a liberated woman exercising her right to be the sexual aggressor. He liked liberated women. This one was something else. Something weird. The whips and chains type. Or worse. She made him feel like a tasty little morsel, a very edible canapé, the last tiny piece of toast and caviar on a silver tray.

"You sure don't see many suits in a place like this," she said.

"I guess not."

"Body shirts, jeans, leather jackets, the Hollywood look—that's what you see in a place like this."

He cleared his throat. "Well," he said uneasily, "I want to thank you for helping us as much as you could."

She said, "I like men who dress well."

Their eyes locked again, and he saw that flicker of ravenous hunger and animal greed. He had the feeling that if he let her lead him into her apartment, the door would close behind him like a set of jaws. She'd be all over him in an instant, pushing and pulling and whirling him around as if she were a wave of digestive juices, breaking him down and sucking the nutrients out of him, using him until he fragmented and dissolved and simply ceased to exist except as a part of her.

"Got to go to work," he said, sliding off the barstool. "See you around."

"I hope so."

For fifteen minutes, Tony and Frank showed the mug shots of Bobby Valdez to the customers in Paradise. As they moved from table to table, the band played Rolling Stones and Elton John and Bee Gees material at a volume that set up sympathetic vibrations in Tony's teeth. It was a waste of time. No one in Paradise remembered the killer with the baby face.

On the way out, Tony stopped at the long oak bar where Otto was mixing strawberry Margaritas. "Tell me something," he shouted above the music.

"Anything," Otto yelled.

"Don't people come to these places to meet each other?"

"Making connections. That's what it's all about."

"Then why the hell do so many singles' bars have bands like that one?"

"What's wrong with the band?"

"A lot of things. But mostly it's too damned loud."

"So?"

"So how can anyone possibly strike up an interesting conversation?"

"Interesting conversation?" Otto said. "Hey man, they don't come here for interesting conversation. They come to meet each other, check each other out, see who they want to go to bed with."

"But no conversation?"

"Look at them. Just look around at them. What would they talk about? If we didn't play music loud and fairly steady, they'd get nervous."

"All those maddeningly quiet spaces to fill."

"How right you are. They'd go somewhere else."

"Where the music was louder and they only needed body language."

Otto shrugged. "It's a sign of the times."

"Maybe I should have lived in another time," Tony said.

Outside, the night was mild, but he knew it would get colder. A thin mist was coming off the sea, not genuine fog yet, but a sort of damp greasy breath that hung in the air and made halos around all the lights.

Frank was waiting behind the wheel of the unmarked police sedan. Tony climbed in on the passenger's side and buckled his seatbelt.

They had one more lead to check out before they quit for the day. Earlier, a couple of people at that Century City singles' bar had said they'd also seen Bobby Valdez at a joint called The Big Quake on Sunset Boulevard, over in Hollywood.

Traffic was moderate to heavy heading toward the heart of the city. Sometimes Frank got impatient and darted from lane to lane, weaving in and out with toots of the horn and little squeals of the brakes, trying to get ahead a few car lengths, but not tonight. Tonight, he was going with the flow.

Tony wondered if Frank Howard had been discussing philosophy with Otto.

After a while, Frank said, "You could have had her."

"Who?"

"That blonde. That Judy."

"I was on duty, Frank."

"You could have set something up for later. She was panting for you."

"Not my type."

"She was gorgeous."

"She was a killer."

"She was what?"

"She'd have eaten me up alive."

Frank considered that for about two seconds, then said, "Bullshit. I'd take a crack at her if I had the chance."

"You know where she's at."

"Maybe I'll mosey back there later, when we're done."

"You do that," Tony said. "Then I'll come visit you in the rest home when she's finished with you."

"Hell, what's the matter with you? She wasn't *that* special. That kind of stuff can be handled easy."

"Maybe that's why I didn't want it."

"Send that one by me again."

Tony Clemenza was tired. He wiped his face with his hands as if weariness was a mask that he could pull off and discard. "She was too well-handled, too well-used."

"Since when did you become a Puritan?"

"I'm not," Tony said, "Or . . . yeah . . . okay, maybe I am. Just a little. Just a thin streak of Puritanism in there somewhere. God knows, I've had more than a few of what they now call 'meaningful relationships.' I'm far from pure. But I just can't see myself on the make in a place like Paradise, cruising, calling all the women 'foxes,' looking for fresh meat. For one thing, I couldn't keep a straight face making the kind of chatter that fills in between the band's numbers. Can you hear me making that scene? 'Hi, I'm Tony. What's your name? What's your sign? Are you into numerology? Have you taken est training? Do you believe in the incredible totality of cosmic energy? Do you believe in destiny as an arm of some all-encompassing cosmic consciousness? Do you think we were destined to meet? Do you think we could get rid of all the bad karma we've generated individually by creating a good energy gestalt together? Want to fuck?' "

"Except for the part about fucking," Frank said, "I didn't understand a thing you said."

"Neither did I. That's what I mean. In a place like Paradise, it's all plastic chatter, glossy surface jive talk formulated to slide everyone into bed with as little friction as possible. In Paradise, you don't ask a woman anything really important. You don't ask about her feelings, her emotions, her talents, her fears, hopes, wants, needs, dreams. So what happens is you end up going to bed with a stranger. Worse than that, you find yourself making love to a fox, to a paper cut-out from a men's magazine, an image instead of a woman, a piece of meat instead of a person, which means you aren't making love at all. The act becomes just the satisfying of a bodily urge, no different than scratching an itch or having a good bowel movement. If a man reduces sex to that, then he might as well stay home alone and use his hand."

Frank braked for a red light and said, "Your hand can't give you a blow job."

"Jesus, Frank, sometimes you can be crude as hell."

"Just being practical."

"What I'm trying to say is that, for me at least, the dance isn't worth the effort if you don't know your partner. I'm not one of those people who'd go to a disco just to revel in my own fancy choreography. I've got to know what the lady's steps are, how she wants to move and why, what she feels and thinks. Sex is just so damned much better if she means something to you, if she's an individual, a quirky person all her own, not just a smooth sleek body that's rounded in all the right places, but a unique personality, a character with chips and dents and marks of experience."

"I can't believe what I'm hearing," Frank said as he drove away from the traffic signal. "It's that old bromide about sex being cheap and unfulfilling if love isn't mixed up with it somehow."

"I'm not talking about undying love," Tony said. "I'm not talking about unbreakable vows of fidelity until the end of time. You can love someone for a little while, in little ways. You can go on loving her even after the physical part of the relationship is over. I'm friends with old lovers because we didn't look at each other as new notches on the gun; we had something in common even after we stopped sharing a bed. Look, before I'm going to go for a tumble in the sack, before I'm going to get bare-assed and vulnerable with a woman, I want to know I can trust her. I want to feel she's special in some way, dear to me, a person worth knowing, worth revealing myself to, worth being a part of for a while."

"Garbage," Frank said scornfully.

"It's the way I feel."

"Let me give you a warning."

"Go ahead."

"The best advice you'll ever get."

"I'm listening."

"If you think there's really something called love, if you honest-to-God believe there's actually a thing called love that's as strong and real as hate or fear, then all you're doing is setting yourself up for a lot of pain. It's a lie. A big lie. Love is something writers invented to sell books."

"You don't really mean that."

"The hell I don't." Frank glanced away from the road for a moment, looked at Tony with pity. "You're how old—thirty-three?"

"Almost thirty-five," Tony said as Frank looked back at the street and pulled around a slow-moving truck that was loaded down with scrap metal.

"Well, I'm ten years older than you," Frank said. "So listen to the wisdom of age. Sooner or later, you're going to think you're in true love with some fluff, and while you're bending over to kiss her pretty feet she's going to kick the shit out of you. Sure as hell, she'll break your heart if you let her know you have one. Affection? Sure. That's okay. And lust. Lust is the word, my friend. Lust is what it's really all about. But not love. What you've got to do is forget all this love crap. Enjoy yourself. Get all the ass you can while you're young. Fuck 'em and run. You can't get hurt that way. If you keep daydreaming about love, you'll only go on making a complete goddamned fool out of yourself, over and over and over again, until they finally stick you in the ground."

"That's too cynical for me."

Frank shrugged.

Six months ago, he had gone through a bitter divorce. He was still sour from the experience.

"And you're not really that cynical, either," Tony said. "I don't think you really believe what you said."

Frank didn't say anything.

"You're a sensitive man," Tony said.

Frank shrugged again.

For a minute or two, Tony tried to revive the dead conversation, but Frank had said everything he intended to say about the subject. He settled into his usual sphinxlike silence. It was surprising that he had said all he said, for Frank was not much of a talker. In fact, when Tony thought about it, the brief discussion just concluded seemed to have been the longest they'd ever had.

Tony had been partners with Frank Howard for more than three months. He still was not sure if the pairing was going to work out.

They were so different from each other in so many ways. Tony *was* a talker. Frank usually did little more than grunt in response. Tony had a wide variety of interests other than his job: films, books, food, the theater, music, art, skiing, running. So far as he could tell, Frank didn't care a great deal about anything except his work. Tony believed that a detective had many tools with which to extract information from a witness, including kindness, gentleness, wit, sympathy, empathy, attentiveness, charm, persistence, cleverness—and of course, intimidation and the rare use of mild force. Frank felt he could get along fine with just persistence, cleverness, intimidation, and a bit more force than the department thought acceptable; he had no use whatsoever for the other approaches on Tony's list. As a result, at least twice a week, Tony had to restrain him subtly but firmly. Frank was subject to eye-bulging, blood-boiling rages when too many things went wrong in one day. Tony, on the other hand, was nearly always calm. Frank was five-nine, stocky, solid as a blockhouse. Tony was six-one, lean, rangy, rugged looking. Frank was blond and blue-eyed.

Tony was dark. Frank was a brooding pessimist. Tony was an optimist. Sometimes it seemed they were such totally opposite types that the partnership never could be successful.

Yet they were alike in some respects. For one thing, neither of them was an eight-hour-a-day cop. More often than not, they worked an extra two hours, sometimes three, without pay, and neither of them complained about it. Toward the end of a case, when evidence and leads developed faster and faster, they would work on their days off if they thought it necessary. No one asked them to do overtime. No one ordered it. The choice was entirely theirs.

Tony was willing to give more than a fair share of himself to the department because he was ambitious. He did not intend to remain a detective-lieutenant for the rest of his life. He wanted to work his way up at least to captain, perhaps higher than that, perhaps all the way to the top, right into the chief's office, where the pay and retirement benefits were a hell of a lot better than what he would get if he stayed where he was. He had been raised in a large Italian family in which parsimony had been a religion as important as Roman Catholicism. His father, Carlo, was an immigrant who worked as a tailor. The old man had labored hard and long to keep his children housed, clothed, and fed, but quite often he had come perilously close to destitution and bankruptcy. There had been much sickness in the Clemenza family, and the unexpected hospital and pharmacy bills had eaten up a frighteningly high percentage of what the old man earned. While Tony was still a child, even before he was old enough to understand about money and household budgets, before he knew anything about the debilitating fear of poverty with which his father lived, he sat through hundreds, maybe thousands, of short but strongly worded lectures on fiscal responsibility. Carlo instructed him almost daily in the importance of hard work, financial shrewdness, ambition, and job security. His father should have worked for the CIA in the brainwashing department. Tony had been so totally indoctrinated, so completely infused with his father's fears and principles, that even at the age of thirty-five, with an excellent bank account and a steady job, he felt uneasy if he was away from work more than two or three days. As often as not, when he took a long vacation, it turned into an ordeal instead of a pleasure. He put in a lot of overtime every week because he was Carlo Clemenza's son, and Carlo Clemenza's son could not possibly have done otherwise.

Frank Howard had other reasons for giving a big piece of himself to the department. He did not appear to be any more ambitious than the next guy, and he did not seem unduly worried about money. As far as Tony could tell, Frank put in the extra hours because he really lived only when he was on the job. Being a homicide detective was the only role he knew how to play, the one thing that gave him a sense of purpose and worth.

Tony looked away from the red taillights of the cars in front of them and studied his partner's face. Frank wasn't aware of Tony's scrutiny. His attention was focused on his driving; he peered intently at the quicksilver flow of traffic on Wilshire Boulevard. The green glow from the dashboard dials and gauges highlighted his bold features. He was not handsome in the classic sense, but he was good-looking in his own way. Broad brow. Deeply-set blue eyes. The nose a bit large and sharp. The mouth well-formed but most often set in a grim scowl that flexed the strong jawline. The face unquestionably contained power and appeal—and more than a hint of unyielding single-mindedness. It was not difficult to picture Frank going home and sitting down and, every night without fail, dropping into a trance that lasted from quitting time until eight the next morning.

In addition to their willingness to work extended hours, Tony and Frank had a few other things in common. Although many plainclothes detectives had tossed out the old dress code and now reported for duty in everything from jeans to leisure suits, Tony and Frank still believed in wearing traditional suits and ties. They thought of themselves as professionals, doing a job that required special skills and education, a job as vital and demanding as that of any trial attorney or teacher or social worker—more demanding, in fact—and jeans simply did not contribute to a professional image. Neither of them smoked. Neither of them drank on the job. And neither of them attempted to foist his paperwork on the other.

So maybe it'll work out between us, Tony thought. Maybe in time I can quietly convince him to use more charm and less force with witnesses. Maybe I can get him interested in films and food, if not in books and art and theater. The reason I'm having so much trouble adjusting to him is that my expectations are far too high. But Jesus, if only he'd talk a little more instead of sitting there like a lump!

For the rest of his career as a homicide detective, Tony would expect a great deal of anyone who rode with him because, for five years, until last May 7, he had worked with a nearly perfect partner, Michael Savatino. He and Michael were both from Italian families; they shared certain ethnic memories, pains, and pleasures. More important than that, they employed similar methods in their police work, and they enjoyed many of the same extracurricular activities. Michael was an avid reader, a film buff, and an excellent cook. Their days had been punctuated by fascinating conversations.

Last February, Michael and his wife, Paula, had gone to Las Vegas for a weekend. They saw two shows. They ate dinner twice at Battista's Hole in the Wall, the best restaurant in town. They filled out a dozen Keno cards and won nothing. They played two-dollar blackjack and lost sixty bucks. And one hour before their scheduled departure, Paula put a silver dollar in a slot machine that promised a progressive jackpot, pulled the handle, and won slightly more than two hundred and twenty thousand dollars.

Police work never had been Michael's first choice for a career. But like Tony, he was a seeker of security. He attended the police academy and climbed relatively quickly from uniformed patrolman to detective because public service offered at least moderate financial security. In March, however, Michael gave the department a sixty-day notice, and in May he quit. All of his adult life, he had wanted to own a restaurant. Five weeks ago, he opened Savatino's, a small but authentic Italian *ristorante* on Santa Monica Boulevard, not far from the Century City complex.

A dream come true.

How likely is it that I could make *my* dream come true the same way? Tony wondered as he studied the night city through which they moved. How likely is it that I could go to Vegas, win two hundred thousand bucks, quit the police force, and take a shot at making it as an artist?

He did not have to ask the question aloud. He didn't need Frank Howard's opinion. He knew the answer. How likely was it? Not very damned likely. About as likely as suddenly learning he was the long-lost son of a rich Arabian prince.

As Michael Savatino had always dreamed of being a restaurateur, so Tony Clemenza dreamed of earning his living as an artist. He had talent. He produced fine pieces in a variety of media: pen and ink, watercolor, oil. He was not merely technically skilled; he had a sharp and unique creative imagination as well. Perhaps if he had been born into a middle-class family with at least modest financial resources, he would have gone to a good school, would have received the proper training from the best professors, would have honed his God-given abilities, and would have become tremendously successful. Instead, he had educated himself with hundreds of art books and through thousands of hours of painstaking drawing practice and experimentation with materials. And he suffered from that pernicious lack of self-confidence so common to those who are self-taught in any field. Although he had entered four art shows and had twice won top prize in his division, he never seriously considered quitting his job and plunging into the creative life. That was nothing more than a pleasant fantasy, a bright daydream. No son of Carlo Clemenza would ever forsake a weekly paycheck for the dread uncertainties of self-employment, unless he had first banked a windfall from Las Vegas.

He was jealous of Michael Savatino's good fortune. Of course, they were still close friends, and he was genuinely happy for Michael. Delighted. Really. But also jealous. He was human, after all, and in the back of his mind, the same petty question kept blinking off and on, off and on, like a neon sign: *Why couldn't it have been me?*

Slamming on the brakes, jolting Tony out of his reverie, Frank blew the horn at a Corvette that cut him off in traffic. "Asshole!"

"Easy, Frank."

"Sometimes I wish I was back in uniform again, handing out citations."

"That's the last thing you wish."

"I'd nail his ass."

"Except maybe he'd turn out to be out of his skull on drugs or maybe just plain crazy. When you work the traffic detail too long, you tend to forget the world's full of nuts. You fall into a habit, a routine, and you get careless. So maybe you'd stop him and walk up to his door with your ticket book in hand, and he'd greet you with a gun. Maybe he'd blow your head off. No. I'm thankful traffic detail's behind me forever. At least when you're on a homicide assignment, you know the kind of people you're going to have to deal with. You never forget there's going to be someone with a gun or a knife or a piece of lead pipe up ahead somewhere. You're a lot less likely to walk into a nasty little surprise when you're working homicide."

Frank refused to be drawn into another discussion. He kept his eyes on the road, grumbled sullenly, wordlessly, and settled back into silence.

Tony sighed. He stared at the passing scenery with an artist's eye for unexpected detail and previously unnoticed beauty.

Patterns.

Every scene—every seascape, every landscape, every street, every building, every room in every building, every person, every thing—had its own special patterns. If you could perceive the patterns in a scene, you could then look beyond the patterns to the underlying structure that supported them. If you could see and grasp the method by which a surface harmony had been achieved, you eventually could understand the deepest meaning and mechanisms of any subject and then make a good painting of it. If you picked up your brushes and approached the canvas without first performing that analysis, you might wind up with a pretty picture, but you would not produce a work of art.

Patterns.

As Frank Howard drove east on Wilshire, on the way to the Hollywood singles' bar called The Big Quake, Tony searched for patterns in the city and the night. At first, coming in from Santa Monica, there were the sharp low lines of the sea-facing houses and the shadowy outlines of tall feathery palms—patterns of serenity and civility and more than a little money. As they entered Westwood, the dominant pattern was rectilinear: clusters of office highrises, oblong patches of light radiating from scattered windows in the mostly dark faces of the buildings. These neatly ordered rectangular shapes formed the patterns of modern thought and corporate power, patterns of even greater wealth than had been evident in Santa Monica's seaside homes. From Westwood they went to Beverly Hills, an insulated pocket within the greater fabric of the metropolis, a place through which the Los Angeles police could pass but in which they had no authority. In Beverly Hills, the patterns were soft and lush and flowing in a graceful continuum of big houses, parks, greenery, exclusive shops, and more ultra-expensive automobiles than you could find anywhere else on earth. From Wilshire Boulevard to Santa Monica Boulevard to Doheny, the pattern was one of ever-increasing wealth.

They turned north on Doheny, crawled up the steep hills, and swung right onto Sunset Boulevard, heading for the heart of Hollywood. For a couple of blocks, the famous street delivered a little bit on the promise of its name and legend. On the right stood Scandia, one of the best and most elegant restaurants in town, and one of the half dozen best in the entire country. Glittering discos. A nightclub specializing in magic. Another spot owned and operated by a stage hypnotist. Comedy clubs. Rock and roll clubs. Huge flashy billboards advertising current films and currently popular recording stars. Lights, lights, and more lights. Initially, the boulevard supported the university studies and government reports that claimed Los Angeles and its suburbs formed the richest metropolitan area in the nation, perhaps the richest in the world. But after a while, as Frank continued to drive eastward, the blush of glamor faded. Even L.A. suffered from senescence. The pattern became marginally but unmistakably cancerous. In the healthy flesh of the city, a few malignant growths swelled here and there: cheap bars, a striptease club, a shuttered service station, brassy massage parlors, an adult book store, a few buildings desperately in need of renovation, more of them block by block. The disease was not terminal in this neighborhood, as it was in others nearby, but every day it gobbled up a few more bites of healthy tissue. Frank and Tony did not have to descend into the scabrous heart of the tumor, for The Big Quake was still on the edge of the blight. The bar appeared suddenly in a blaze of red and blue lights on the righthand side of the street.

Inside, the place resembled Paradise, except that the decor relied more heavily on colored lights and chrome and mirrors than it did in the Santa Monica bar. The customers were somewhat more consciously stylish, more aggressively *au courant*, and generally a shade better looking than the crowd in Paradise. But to Tony the patterns appeared to be the same as they were in Santa Monica. Patterns of need, longing, and loneliness. Desperate, carnivorous patterns.

The bartender wasn't able to help them, and the only customer who had anything for them was a tall brunette with violet eyes. She was sure they would find Bobby at Janus, a discotheque in Westwood. She had seen him there the previous two nights.

Outside, in the parking lot, bathed in alternating flashes of red and blue light, Frank said, "One thing just leads to another."

"As usual."

"It's getting late."

"Yeah."

"You want to try Janus now or leave it for tomorrow?"

"Now," Tony said.

"Good."

They turned around and traveled west on Sunset, out of the area that showed signs of urban cancer, into the glitter of the Strip, then into greenery and wealth again, past the Beverly Hills Hotel, past mansions and endless marching rows of gigantic palm trees.

As he often did when he suspected Tony might attempt to strike up another conversation, Frank switched on the police band radio and listened to Communications calling black-and-whites in the division that provided protection for Westwood, toward which they were heading. Nothing much was happening on that frequency. A family dispute. A fender-bender at the corner of Westwood Boulevard and Wilshire. A suspicious man in a parked car on a quiet residential street off Hilgarde had attracted attention and needed checking out.

In most of the city's other sixteen police divisions, the night was far less safe and peaceful than it was in privileged Westwood. In the Seventy-seventh, Newton, and Southwest divisions, which served the black community south of the Santa Monica Freeway, none of the mid-watch patrol officers would be bored; in their bailiwicks the night was jumping. On the east side of town, in the Mexican-American neighborhoods, the gangs would continue to give a bad name to the vast majority of law-abiding Chicano citizens. By the time the mid-watch went off duty at three o'clock—three hours after the morning watch came on line—there would be several ugly incidents of gang violence on the east side, a few punks stabbing other punks, maybe a shooting and a death or two as the macho maniacs tried to prove their manhood in the wearisome, stupid, but timeless blood ceremonies they had been performing with Latin passion for generations. To the northwest, on the far side of the hills, the affluent valley kids were drinking too damned much whiskey, smoking too much pot, snorting too much cocaine—and subsequently ramming their cars and vans and motorcycles into one another at ghastly speeds and with tiresome regularity.

As Frank drove past the entrance to Bel Air Estates and started up a hill toward the UCLA campus, the Westwood scene suddenly got lively. Communications put out a woman-in-trouble call. Information was sketchy. Apparently, it was an attempted rape and assault with a deadly weapon. It was not clear if the assailant was still on the premises. Shots had been fired, but Communications had been unable to ascertain from the complainant whether the gun belonged to her or the assailant. Likewise, they didn't know if anyone was hurt.

"Have to go in blind," Tony said.

"That address is just a couple of blocks from here," Frank said.

"We could be there in a minute."

"Probably a lot faster than the patrol car."

"Want to assist?"

"Sure."

"I'll call in and tell them."

Tony picked up the microphone as Frank hung a hard left at the first intersection. A block later they turned left again, and Frank accelerated as much as he dared along the narrow, tree-flanked street.

Tony's heart accelerated with the car. He felt an old excitement, a cold hard knot of fear in his guts.

He remembered Parker Hitchison, a particularly quirky, morose, and humorless partner he had endured for a short while during his second year as a patrol officer, long before he won his detective's badge. Every

time they answered a call, every damned time, whether it was a Code
Three emergency or just a frightened cat stuck in a tree, Parker Hitchison
sighed mournfully and said, "Now, we die." It was weird and decidedly
unsettling. Over and over again on every shift, night after night, with sincere and unflagging pessimism, he said it—"Now, we die"—until Tony
was almost crazy.

Hitchison's funereal voice and those three somber words still haunted
him in moments like this.

Now we die?

Frank wheeled around another corner, nearly clipping a black BMW
that was parked too close to the intersection. The tires squealed, and the
sedan shimmied, and Frank said, "That address ought to be right around
here somewhere."

Tony squinted at the shadowy houses that were only partly illuminated by the streetlamps. "There it is, I think," he said, pointing.

It was a large neo-Spanish house set well back from the street on a
spacious lot. Red tile roof. Cream-colored stucco. Leaded windows. Two
big wrought-iron carriage lamps, one on each side of the front door.

Frank parked in the circular driveway.

They got out of the unmarked sedan.

Tony reached under his jacket and slipped the service revolver out of
his shoulder holster.

•

After Hilary had finished crying at her desk in the study, she had decided,
in a daze, to go upstairs and make herself presentable before she reported
the assault to the police. Her hair had been in complete disarray, her dress
torn, her pantyhose shredded and hanging from her legs in ludicrous
loops and tangles. She didn't know how quickly the reporters would arrive once the word had gotten out on the police radio, but she had no
doubt that they would show up sooner or later. She was something of a
public figure, having written two hit films and having received an Academy Award nomination two years ago for her *Arizona Shifty Pete* screenplay. She treasured her privacy and preferred to avoid the press if at all
possible, but she knew that she would have little choice but to make a
statement and answer a few questions about what had happened to her
this night. It was the wrong kind of publicity. It was embarrassing. Being
the victim in a case like this was always humiliating. Although it should
make her an object of sympathy and concern, it actually would make her

look like a fool, a patsy just waiting to be pushed around. She had successfully defended herself against Frye, but that would not matter to the sensation seekers. In the unfriendly glare of the television lights and in the flat gray newspaper photos, she would look weak. The merciless American public would wonder why she had let Frye into her house. They would speculate that she had been raped and that her story of fending him off was just a coverup. Some of them would be certain that she had invited him in and had asked to be raped. Most of the sympathy she received would be shot through with morbid curiosity. The only thing she could control was her appearance when the newsmen arrived. She simply could not allow herself to be photographed in the pitiable, disheveled state in which Bruno Frye had left her.

As she washed her face and combed her hair and changed into a silk robe that belted at the waist, she was not aware that these actions would damage her credibility with the police, later. She didn't realize that, in making herself presentable, she was actually setting herself up as a target for at least one policeman's suspicion and scorn, as well as for charges of being a liar.

Although she thought she was in command of herself, Hilary got the shakes again as she finished changing clothes. Her legs turned to jelly, and she was forced to lean against the closet door for a minute.

Nightmarish images crowded her mind, vivid flashes of unsummoned memories. At first, she saw Frye coming at her with a knife, grinning like a death's head, but then he changed, melted into another shape, another identity, and he became her father, Earl Thomas, and then it was Earl who was coming at her, drunk and angry, cursing, taking swipes at her with his big hard hands. She shook her head and drew deep breaths and, with an effort, banished the vision.

But she could not stop shaking.

She imagined that she heard strange noises in another room of the house. A part of her knew that she was merely imagining it, but another part was sure that she could hear Frye returning for her.

By the time she ran to the phone and dialed the police, she was in no condition to give the calm and reasoned report she had planned. The events of the past hour had affected her far more profoundly than she had thought at first, and recovering from the shock might take days, even weeks.

After she hung up the receiver, she felt better, just knowing help was on the way. As she went downstairs, she said aloud, "Stay calm. Just stay calm. You're Hilary Thomas. You're tough. Tough as nails. You aren't scared. Not ever. Everything will be okay." It was the same litany that she had repeated as a child so many nights in that Chicago apartment. By the time she reached the first door, she had begun to get a grip on herself.

She was standing in the foyer, staring out the narrow leaded window beside the door, when a car stopped in the driveway. Two men got out of it. Although they had not come with sirens blaring and red lights flashing, she knew they were the police, and she unlocked the door, opened it.

The first man onto the front stoop was powerfully built, blond, blue-eyed, and had the hard no-nonsense voice of a cop. He had a gun in his right hand. "Police. Who're you?"

"Thomas," she said. "Hilary Thomas. I'm the one who called."

"This your house?"

"Yes. There was a man—"

A second detective, taller and darker than the first, appeared out of the night and interrupted her before she could finish the sentence. "Is he on the premises?"

"What?"

"Is the man who assaulted you still here?"

"Oh, no. Gone. He's gone."

"Which way did he go?" the blond man asked.

"Out this door."

"Did he have a car?"

"I don't know."

"Was he armed?"

"No. I mean, yes."

"Which is it?"

"He had a knife. But not now."

"Which way did he run when he left the house?"

"I don't know. I was upstairs. I—"

"How long ago did he leave?" the tall dark one asked.

"Maybe fifteen, maybe twenty minutes ago."

They exchanged a look that she did not understand but which she knew, immediately, was not good for her.

"What took you so long to call it in?" the blond asked.

He was slightly hostile.

She felt she was losing some important advantage that she could not identify.

"At first I was . . . confused," she said. "Hysterical. I needed a few minutes to get myself together."

"Twenty minutes?"

"Maybe it was only fifteen."

Both detectives put away their revolvers.

"We'll need a description," the dark one said.

"I can give you better than that," she said as she stepped aside to let them enter. "I can give you a name."

"A name?"

"His name. I know him," she said. "The man who attacked me. I know who he is."

The two detectives gave each other that look again.

She thought: *What have I done wrong?*

•

Hilary Thomas was one of the most beautiful women Tony had ever seen. She appeared to have a few drops of Indian blood. Her hair was long and thick, darker than his own, a glossy raven-black. Her eyes were dark, too, the whites as clear as pasteurized cream. Her flawless complexion was a light milky bronze shade, probably largely the result of carefully measured time in the California sun. If her face was a bit long, that was balanced by the size of her eyes (enormous) and by the perfect shape of her patrician nose, and by the almost obscene fullness of her lips. Hers was an erotic face, but an intelligent and kind face as well, the face of a woman capable of great tenderness and compassion. There was also pain in that countenance, especially in those fascinating eyes, the kind of pain that came from experience, knowledge; and Tony expected that it was not merely the pain she'd suffered that night; some of it went back a long, long time.

She sat on one end of the brushed corduroy sofa in the book-lined study, and Tony sat on the other end. They were alone.

Frank was in the kitchen, talking on the phone to a desk man at headquarters.

Upstairs, two uniformed patrolmen, Whitlock and Farmer, were digging bullets out of the walls.

There was not a fingerprint man in the house because, according to the complainant, the intruder had worn gloves.

"What's he doing now?" Hilary Thomas asked.

"Who?"

"Lieutenant Howard."

"He's calling headquarters and asking someone to get in touch with the sheriff's office up there in Napa County, where Frye lives."

"Why?"

"Well, for one thing, maybe the sheriff can find out how Frye got to L.A."

"What's it matter how he got here?" she asked. "The important thing is that he's here and he's got to be found and stopped."

"If he flew down," Tony said, "it doesn't matter much at all. But if Frye drove to L.A., the sheriff up in Napa County might be able to find out what car he used. With a description of the vehicle and a license number, we've got a better chance of nailing him before he gets too far."

She considered that for a moment, then said, "Why did Lieutenant Howard go to the kitchen? Why didn't he just use the phone in here?"

"I guess he wanted you to have a few minutes of peace and quiet," Tony said uneasily.

"I think he just didn't want me to hear what he was saying."

"Oh, no. He was only—"

"You know, I have the strangest feeling," she said, interrupting him. "I feel like I'm the suspect instead of the victim."

"You're just tense," he said. "Understandably tense."

"It isn't that. It's something about the way you're acting toward me. Well . . . not so much you as him."

"Frank can seem cool at times," Tony said. "But he's a good detective."

"He thinks I'm lying."

Tony was surprised by her perspicacity. He shifted uncomfortably on the sofa. "I'm sure he doesn't think any such thing."

"He does," she insisted. "And I don't understand why." Her eyes fixed on his. "Level with me. Come on. What is it? What did I say wrong?"

He sighed. "You're a perceptive lady."

"I'm a writer. It's part of my job to observe things a little more closely than most people do. And I'm also persistent. So you might as well answer my question and get me off your back."

"One of the things that bothers Lieutenant Howard is the fact that you know the man who attacked you."

"So?"

"This is awkward," he said unhappily.

"Let me hear it anyway."

"Well . . ." He cleared his throat. "Conventional police wisdom says that if the complainant in a rape or an attempted rape knows the victim, there's a pretty good chance that she contributed to the crime by enticing the accused to one degree or another."

"Bullshit!"

She got up, went to the desk, and stood with her back to him for a minute. He could see that she was struggling to maintain her composure. What he had said had made her extremely angry.

When she turned to him at last, her face was flushed. She said, "This is horrible. It's outrageous. Every time a woman is raped by someone she knows, you actually believe she asked for it."

"No. Not every time."

"But *most* of the time, that's what you think," she said angrily.

"No."

She glared at him. "Let's stop playing semantical games. You believe it about *me*. You believe I enticed him."

"No," Tony said. "I merely explained what conventional police wisdom is in a case like this. I didn't say that I put much faith in conventional police wisdom. I don't. But Lieutenant Howard does. You asked me about him. You wanted to know what he was thinking, and I told you."

She frowned. "Then . . . you believe me?"

"Is there any reason I shouldn't?"

"It happened exactly the way I said."

"All right."

She stared at him. "Why?"

"Why what?"

"Why do you believe me when he doesn't?"

"I can think of only two reasons for a woman to bring false rape charges against a man. And neither of them makes any sense in your case."

She leaned against the desk, folded her arms in front of her, cocked her head, and regarded him with interest. "What reasons?"

"Number one, he has money, and she doesn't. She wants to put him on the spot, hoping she can pry some sort of big settlement out of him in return for dropping the charges."

"But I've got money."

"Apparently, you've got quite a lot of it," he said, looking around admiringly at the beautifully furnished room.

"What's the other reason?"

"A man and a woman are having an affair, but he leaves her for another lady. She feels hurt, rejected, scorned. She wants to get even with him. She wants to punish him, so she accuses him of rape."

"How can you be sure that doesn't fit me?" she asked.

"I've seen both your movies, so I figure I know a little bit about the way your mind works. You're a very intelligent woman, Miss Thomas. I don't think you could be foolish or petty or spiteful enough to send a man to prison just because he hurt your feelings."

She studied him intently.

He felt himself being weighed and judged.

Obviously convinced that he was not the enemy, she returned to the couch and sat down in a swish of dark-blue silk. The robe molded to her, and he tried not to show how aware he was of her strikingly female lines.

She said, "I'm sorry I was snappish."

"You weren't," he assured her. "Conventional police wisdom makes me angry, too."

"I suppose if this gets into court, Frye's attorney will try to make the jury believe that I enticed the son of a bitch."

"You can count on it."

"Will they believe him?"

"They often do."

"But he wasn't just going to rape me. He was going to *kill* me."

"You'll need proof of that."

"The broken knife upstairs—"

"Can't be connected to him," Tony said. "It won't be covered with his prints. And it's just a common kitchen knife. There's no way we can trace it to the point of purchase and tie it to Bruno Frye."

"But he looked so crazy. He's . . . unbalanced. The jury would see that. Hell, you'll see it when you arrest him. There probably won't even be a trial. He'll probably just be put away."

"If he'a lunatic, he knows how to pass for normal," Tony said. "After all, until tonight, he's been regarded as an especially responsible and up-standing citizen. When you visited his winery near St. Helena, you didn't realize you were in the company of a madman, did you?"

"No."

"Neither will the jury."

She closed her eyes, pinched the bridge of her nose. "So he's probably going to get away clean."

"I'm sorry to say there's a good chance that he will."

"And then he'll come back for me."

"Maybe."

"Jesus."

"You wanted the unvarnished truth."

She opened her lovely eyes. "I did, yes. And thank you for giving it to me." She even managed a smile.

He smiled back at her. He wanted to take her in his arms, hold her close, comfort her, kiss her, make love to her. But all he could do was sit on his end of the couch like a good officer of the law and smile his witless smile and say, "Sometimes it's a lousy system."

"What are the other reasons?"

"Excuse me?"

"You said *one* reason Lieutenant Howard didn't believe me was because I knew the assailant. What are the other reasons? What else makes him think I'm lying?"

Tony was about to answer her when Frank Howard walked into the room.

"Okay," Frank said brusquely. "We've got the sheriff looking into it up there in Napa County, trying to get a line on when and how this Frye character left town. We also have an APB out, based on your description, Miss Thomas. Now, I went to the car and got my clipboard and this crime report form." He held up the rectangular piece of masonite and the single sheet of paper affixed to it, took a pen from his inside coat pocket. "I want you to walk Lieutenant Clemenza and me through your entire experience just once more, so I can write it all down precisely in your own words. Then we can get out of your way."

She led them to the foyer and began her story with a detailed recounting of Bruno Frye's surprise appearance from the coat closet. Tony and Frank followed her to the overturned sofa, then upstairs to the bedroom, asking questions as they went. During the thirty minutes they needed to complete the form, as she reenacted the events of the evening, her voice now and then became tremulous, and again Tony had the urge to hold and soothe her.

Just as the crime report was completed, a few newsmen arrived. She went downstairs to meet them.

At the same time, Frank got a call from headquarters and took it on the bedroom phone.

Tony went downstairs to wait for Frank and to see how Hilary Thomas would deal with the reporters.

She handled them expertly. Pleading weariness and a need for privacy, she did not allow them into her house. She stepped outside, onto the stone walk, and they gathered in front of her. A television news crew had arrived, complete with a minicam and the standard actor-reporter, one of those men who had gotten his job largely because of his chiseled features and penetrating eyes and deep fatherly voice. Intelligence and journalistic ability had little to do with being a performer in television news; indeed, too much of either quality could be seriously disadvantageous; for optimum success, the career-minded television reporter had to think much the same way that his program was structured—in three- and four- and five-minute segments, never dwelling longer than that on any one subject, and never exploring anything at great depth. A newspaperman and his photographer, not so pretty as the television man and a bit rumpled, were also present. Hilary Thomas fielded their questions with ease, answering only those that she wanted to answer, smoothly turning away all of those that were too personal or impertinent.

The thing that Tony found most interesting about her performance was the way she kept the news people out of the house and out of her most private thoughts without offending them. That was no easy trick. There were many excellent reporters who could dig for the truth and write fine stories without violating the subject's rights and dignity; but there were just as many of the other kind, the boars and the con men. With the rise of what the *Washington Post* glowingly referred to as "advocacy journalism"—the despicable slanting of a story to support the reporter's and the editor's personal political and social beliefs—some members of the press, the con men and the boars, had gone on a power trip of unprecedented irresponsibility. If you bristled at a reporter's manner and methods or at his obvious bias, if you dared to offend him, he might decide to use his pen to make you look like a fool, a liar, or a criminal; and he would see himself as the champion of enlightenment in a battle against evil. Clearly, Hilary was aware of the danger, for she dealt masterfully with them. She answered more questions than not, stroked the news people, accorded them respect, charmed them, and even smiled for the cameras. She didn't say that she knew her assailant. She didn't mention the name Bruno Frye. She didn't want the media speculating about her previous relationship with the man who had attacked her.

Her awareness forced Tony to reevaluate her. He already knew that she was talented and intelligent; now he saw she was also shrewd. She was the most intriguing woman he had encountered in a long time.

She was nearly finished with the reporters, carefully extricating herself from them, when Frank Howard came down the stairs and stepped to the doorway, where Tony stood in the cool night breeze. Frank watched Hilary Thomas as she answered a reporter's question, and he scowled fiercely. "I've got to talk to her."

"What did headquarters want?" Tony asked.

"That's what I've got to talk to her about," Frank said grimly. He had decided to be tight-lipped. He wasn't going to reveal his information until he was damned good and ready. That was another of his irritating habits.

"She's almost through with them," Tony said.

"Strutting and preening herself."

"Not at all."

"Sure. She's loving every minute of it."

"She handles them well," Tony said, "but she really doesn't seem to enjoy it."

"Movie people," Frank said scornfully. "They need that attention and publicity like you and I need food."

The reporters were only eight feet away, and although they were noisily questioning Hilary Thomas, Tony was afraid they might hear Frank. "Not so loud," he said.

"I don't care if they know what I think," Frank said. "I'll even give them a statement about publicity hounds who make up stories to get newspaper coverage."

"Are you saying she made this all up? That's ridiculous."

"You'll see," Frank said.

Tony was suddenly uneasy. Hilary Thomas brought out the chivalrous knight in him; he wanted to protect her. He didn't want to see her hurt, but Frank apparently had something decidedly unpleasant to discuss with her.

"I've got to talk to her now," Frank said. "I'll be damned if I'll stand around cooling my heels while she sucks up to the press."

Tony put a hand on his partner's shoulder. "Wait here. I'll get her."

Frank was angry about whatever headquarters had told him, and Tony knew the reporters would recognize that anger and be irritated by it. If they thought there was progress in the investigation—especially if it looked to be a juicy bit, a scandalous twist—they would hang around all night, pestering everybody. And if Frank actually had uncovered unflattering information about Hilary Thomas, the press would make headlines out of it, trumpet it with that unholy glee they reserved for choice dirt. Later, if Frank's information proved inaccurate, the television people most likely wouldn't make any correction at all, and the newspaper retraction, if there ever was one, would be four lines on page twenty of the second section. Tony wanted her to have an opportunity to refute whatever Frank might say, a chance to clear herself before the whole thing became a tawdry media carnival.

He went to the reporters and said, "Excuse me, ladies and gentlemen, but I believe Miss Thomas has already told you more than she's told us. You've squeezed her dry. Now, my partner and I were scheduled to go off duty a few hours ago, and we're awfully tired. We've put in a hard day, beating up innocent suspects and collecting bribes, so if you would let us finish with Miss Thomas, we would be most grateful."

They laughed appreciatively and began to ask questions of him. He answered a few of them, giving out nothing more than Hilary Thomas had done. Then he hustled the woman into her house and closed the door.

Frank was in the foyer. His anger had not subsided. He looked as if steam should be coming from his ears. "Miss Thomas, I have some more questions to ask you."

"Okay."

"Quite a few questions. It'll take a while."

"Well . . . shall we go into the study?"

Frank Howard led the way.

To Tony, Hilary said, "What's happening?"

He shrugged. "I don't know. I wish I did."

Frank had reached the center of the living room. He stopped and looked back at her. "Miss Thomas?"

She and Tony followed him into the study.

•

Hilary sat on the brushed corduroy couch, crossed her legs, straightened her silk robe. She was nervous, wondering why Lieutenant Howard disliked her so intensely. His manner was cold. He was filled with an icy anger that made his eyes look like cross sections of two steel rods. She thought of Bruno Frye's strange eyes, and she could not suppress a shiver. Lieutenant Howard glowered at her. She felt like the accused at a trial during the Spanish Inquisition. She would not have been terribly surprised if Howard had pointed a finger and charged her with witchcraft.

The nice one, Lieutenant Clemenza, sat in the brown armchair. The warm amber light from the yellow-shaded floor lamp fell over him and cast soft shadows around his mouth and nose and deeply set eyes, giving him an even gentler and kinder aspect than he ordinarily possessed. She wished he was the one asking questions, but at least for the moment, his role was evidently that of an observer.

Lieutenant Howard stood over her, looked down at her with unconcealed contempt. She realized that he was trying to make her look away in shame or defeat, playing some police version of a childish staring contest. She looked back at him unwaveringly until he turned from her and began to pace.

"Miss Thomas," Howard said, "there are several things about your story that trouble me."

"I know," she said. "It bothers you that I know the assailant. You figure I might have enticed him. Isn't that conventional police wisdom?"

He blinked in surprise but quickly recovered. "Yes. That's one thing. And there's also the fact that we can't find out how he got into this house. Officer Whitlock and Officer Farmer have been from one end of the place to the other, twice, three times, and they can't find any sign of forced entry. No broken windows. No smashed or jimmied locks."

"So you think I let him in," she said.

"I certainly must consider it."

"Well, consider this. When I was up there in Napa County a few weeks ago, doing research for a screenplay, I lost my keys at his winery. House keys, car keys—"

"You drove all the way up there?"

"No. I flew. But all my keys were on the same ring. Even the keys for the rental car I picked up in Santa Rosa; they were on a flimsy chain, and I was afraid I'd lose them, so I slipped them on my own key ring. I never found them. The rental car people had to send out another set. And when I got back to L.A., I had to have a locksmith let me into my house and make new keys for me."

"You didn't have the locks changed?"

"It seemed like a needless expense," she said. "The keys I lost didn't have any identification on them. Whoever found them wouldn't know where to use them."

"And it didn't occur to you they might have been stolen?" Lieutenant Howard asked.

"No."

"But now you think Bruno Frye took the keys with the intention of coming here to rape and kill you."

"Yes."

"What does he have against you?"

"I don't know."

"Is there any reason he should be angry with you?"

"No."

"Any reason he should hate you?"

"I hardly know him."

"It's an awfully long way for him to come."

"I know."

"Hundreds of miles."

"Look, he's crazy. And crazy people do crazy things."

Lieutenant Howard stopped pacing, stood in front of her, glared down like one of the faces on a totempole of angry gods. "Doesn't it seem odd to you that a crazy man would be able to conceal his madness so well at home, that he would have the iron control needed to keep it all bottled up until he was off in a strange city?"

"Of course it seems odd to me," she said. "It's weird. But it's true."

"Did Bruno Frye have an opportunity to steal those keys?"

"Yes. One of the winery foremen took me on a special tour. We had to clamber up scaffolding, between fermentation vats, between storage barrels, through a lot of tight places. I couldn't have easily taken my purse with me. It would have been in my way. So I left it in the main house."

"Frye's house."

"Yes."

He was crackling with energy, supercharged. He began to pace again, from the couch to the windows, from the windows to the bookshelves, then back to the couch again, his broad shoulders drawn up, head thrust forward.

Lieutenant Clemenza smiled at her, but she was not reassured.

"Will anyone at the winery remember you losing your keys?" Lieutenant Howard asked.

"I guess so. Sure. I spent at least half an hour looking for them. I asked around, hoping someone might have seen them."

"But no one had."

"That's right."

"Where did you think you might have left them?"

"I thought they were in my purse."

"That was the last place you remembered putting them?"

"Yes. I drove the rental car to the winery, and I was sure I'd put the keys in my purse when I'd parked."

"Yet when you couldn't find them, you never thought they might have been stolen?"

"No. Why would someone steal my keys and not my money? I had a couple hundred dollars in my wallet."

"Another thing that bothers me. After you drove Frye out of the house at gunpoint, why did you take so long to call us?"

"I didn't take long."

"Twenty minutes."

"At most."

"When you've just been attacked and nearly killed by a maniac with a knife, twenty minutes is a hell of a long time to wait. Most people want to get hold of the police right away. They want us on the scene in ten seconds, and they get furious if it takes us a few minutes to get there."

She glanced at Clemenza, then at Howard, then at her fingers, which were tightly laced, white-knuckled. She sat up straight, squared her shoulders. "I . . . I guess I . . . broke down." It was a difficult and shameful admission for her. She had always prided herself on her strength. "I went to that desk and sat down and began to dial the police number and . . . then . . . I just . . . I cried. I started to cry . . . and I couldn't stop for a while."

"You cried for twenty minutes?"

"No. Of course not. I'm really not the crying type. I mean, I don't fall apart easily."

"How long did it take you to get control of yourself?"

"I don't know for sure."

"Fifteen minutes?"

"Not that long."

"Ten minutes?"

"Maybe five."

"When you regained control of yourself, why didn't you call us then? You were sitting right there by the phone."

"I went upstairs to wash my face and change my clothes," she said. "I've already told you about that."

"I know," he said. "I remember. Primping yourself for the press."

"No," she said, beginning to get angry with him. "I wasn't 'primping' myself. I just thought I should—"

"That's the fourth thing that makes me wonder about your story," Howard said, interrupting her. "It absolutely amazes me. I mean, after you were almost raped and murdered, after you broke down and wept, while you were still afraid that Frye might come back here and try to finish the job he started, you nevertheless took time out to make yourself look presentable. Amazing."

"Excuse me," Lieutenant Clemenza said, leaning forward in the brown armchair. "Frank, I know you've got something, and I know you're leading up to it. I don't want to spoil your rhythm or anything. But I don't think we can make assumptions about Miss Thomas's honesty and integrity based on how long she took to call in the complaint. We both know that people sometimes go into a kind of shock after an experience like this. They don't always do the rational thing. Miss Thomas's behavior isn't all that peculiar."

She almost thanked Lieutenant Clemenza for what he had said, but she sensed a low-grade antagonism between the two detectives, and she did not want to fan that smoldering fire.

"Are you telling me to get on with it?" Howard asked Clemenza.

"All I'm saying is, it's getting late, and we're all very tired," Clemenza told him.

"You admit her story's riddled with holes?"

"I don't know that I'd put it quite like that," said Clemenza.

"How would you put it?" Howard asked.

"Let's just say there are some parts of it that don't make sense yet."

Howard scowled at him for a moment, then nodded. "Okay. Good enough. I was only trying to establish that there are at least four big problems with her story. If you agree, then I'll get on with the rest of it." He turned to Hilary. "Miss Thomas, I'd like to hear your description of the assailant just once more."

"Why? You've got his name."

"Indulge me."

She couldn't understand where he was going with his questioning. She knew he was trying to set a trap for her, but she hadn't the faintest idea what sort of trap or what it would do to her if she got caught in it. "All right. Just once more. Bruno Frye is tall, about six-four—"

"No names, please."

"What?"

"Describe the assailant without using any names."

"But I know his name," she said slowly, patiently.

"Humor me," he said humorlessly.

She sighed and settled back against the sofa, feigning boredom. She didn't want him to know that he was rattling her. What the hell was he after? "The man who attacked me," she said, "was about six-feet-four, and he weighed maybe two hundred and forty pounds. Very muscular."

"Race?" Howard asked.

"He was white."

"Complexion?"

"Fair."

"Any scars or moles?"

"No."

"Tattoos?"

"Are you kidding?"

"Tattoos?"

"No."

"Any other identifying marks?"

"No."

"Was he crippled or deformed in any way?"

"He's a big healthy son of a bitch," she said crossly.

"Color of hair?"

"Dirty blond."

"Long or short?"

"Medium length."

"Eyes?"

"Yes."

"What?"

"Yes, he had eyes."

"Miss Thomas—"

"Okay, okay."

"This is serious."

"He had blue eyes. An unusual shade of blue-gray."

"Age?"

"Around forty."

"Any distinguishing characteristics?"

"Like what?"

"You mentioned something about his voice."

"That's right. He had a deep voice. It rumbled. A gravelly voice. Deep and gruff and scratchy."

"All right," Lieutenant Howard said, rocking slightly on his heels, evidently pleased with himself. "We have a good description of the assailant. Now, describe Bruno Frye for me."

"I just did."

"No, no. We're pretending that you didn't know the man who attacked you. We're playing this little game to humor me. Remember? You just described your assailant, a man without a name. Now, I want you to describe Bruno Frye for me."

She turned to Lieutenant Clemenza. "Is this really necessary?" she asked exasperatedly.

Clemenza said, "Frank, can you hurry this along?"

"Look, I've got a point I'm trying to make," Lieutenant Howard said. "I'm building up to it the best way I know how. Besides, *she's* the one slowing it down."

He turned to her, and again she had the creepy feeling she was on trial in another century and that Howard was some religious inquisitionist. If Clemenza would permit it, Howard would simply take hold of her and shake until she gave the answers he wanted, whether or not they were the truth.

"Miss Thomas," he said, "if you'll just answer all of my questions, I'll be finished in a few minutes. Now, will you describe Bruno Frye?"

Disgustedly, she said, "Six-four, two hundred and forty pounds, muscular, blond, blue-gray eyes, about forty years old, no scars, no deformities, no tattoos, a deep gravelly voice."

Frank Howard was smiling. It was not a friendly smile. "Your description of the assailant and Bruno Frye are exactly the same. Not a single discrepancy. Not one. And of course, you've told us that they were, in fact, one and the same man."

His line of questioning seemed ridiculous, but there was surely a purpose to it. He wasn't stupid. She sensed that already she had stepped into the trap, even though she could not see it.

"Do you want to change your mind?" Howard asked. "Do you want to say that perhaps there's a small chance it was someone else, someone who only resembled Frye?"

"I'm not an idiot," Hilary said. "It was him."

"There wasn't even maybe some slight difference between your assailant and Frye? Some little thing?" he persisted.

"No."

"Not even the shape of his nose or the line of his jaw?" Howard asked.

"Not even that."

"You're certain that Frye and your assailant shared precisely the same hairline, exactly the same cheekbones, the same chin?"

"Yes."

"Are you positive beyond a shadow of a doubt that it was Bruno Frye who was here tonight?"

"Yes."

"Would you swear to that in court?"

"*Yes, yes, yes!*" she said, tired of his badgering.

"Well, then. Well, well. I'm afraid if you testified to that effect, you'd wind up in jail yourself. Perjury's a crime."

"What? What do you mean?"

He grinned at her. His grin was even more unfriendly than his smile. "Miss Thomas, what I mean is—you're a liar."

Hilary was so stunned by the bluntness of the accusation, by the boldness of it, so disconcerted by the ugly snarl in his voice, that she could not immediately think of a response. She didn't even know what he meant.

"A liar, Miss Thomas. Plain and simple."

Lieutenant Clemenza got out of the brown armchair and said, "Frank, are we handling this right?"

"Oh, yeah," Howard said. "We're handling it exactly right. While she was out there talking to the reporters and posing so prettily for the photographers, I got a call from headquarters. They heard back from the Napa County Sheriff."

"Already?"

"Oh, yeah. His name's Peter Laurenski. Sheriff Laurenski looked into things for us up there at Frye's vineyard, just like we asked him to, and you know what he found? He found that Mr. Bruno Frye didn't come to Los Angeles. Bruno Frye never left home. Bruno Frye is up there in Napa County right now, right this minute, in his own house, harmless as a fly."

"Impossible!" Hilary said, pushing up from the sofa.

Howard shook his head. "Give up, Miss Thomas. Frye told Sheriff Laurenski that he *intended* to come to L.A. today for a week-long stay. Just a short vacation. But he didn't manage to clear off his desk in time, so he cancelled out and stayed home to get caught up on his work."

"The sheriff's wrong!" she said. "He couldn't have talked to Bruno Frye."

"Are you calling the sheriff a liar?" Lieutenant Howard asked.

"He . . . he must have talked to someone who was covering for Frye," Hilary said, knowing how hopelessly implausible that sounded.

"No," Howard said. "Sheriff Laurenski talked to Frye himself."

"Did he see him? Did he actually *see* Frye?" she demanded. "Or did he only talk to someone on the phone, someone claiming to be Frye?"

"I don't know if it was a face to face chat or a phone conversation," Howard said. "But remember, Miss Thomas, you told us about Frye's unique voice. Extremely deep. Scratchy. A guttural, gravelly voice. Are you saying someone could have easily imitated it on the phone?"

"If Sheriff Laurenski doesn't know Frye well enough, he might be fooled by a bad imitation. He—"

"It's a small county up there. A man like Bruno Frye, an important man like that, is known to just about everyone. And the sheriff has known him *very* well for more than twenty years," Howard said triumphantly.

Lieutenant Clemenza looked pained. Although she did not care much what Howard thought of her, it was important to Hilary that Clemenza believed the story she had told. The flicker of doubt in his eyes upset her as much as Howard's bullying.

She turned her back on them, went to the mullioned window that looked out on the rose garden, tried to control her anger, couldn't suppress it, and faced them again. She spoke to Howard, furious, emphasizing every word by pounding her fist against the window table: "Bruno—Frye—was—here!" The vase full of roses rocked, toppled off the table, bounced on the thick carpet, scattering flowers and water. She ignored it. "What about the sofa he overturned? What about the broken porcelain I threw at him and the bullets I fired at him? What about the broken knife he left behind? What about the torn dress, the pantyhose?"

"It could be just clever stage dressing," Howard said. "You could have done it all yourself, faked it up to support your story."

"That's absurd!"

Clemenza said, "Miss Thomas, maybe it really was someone else. Someone who looked a lot like Frye."

Even if she had wanted to retreat in that fashion, she could not have done it. By forcing her to repeatedly describe the man who attacked her, by drawing several assurances from her that the assailant had been none other than Bruno Frye, Lieutenant Howard had made it difficult if not impossible for her to take the way out that Clemenza was offering. Anyway, she didn't want to back up and reconsider. She knew she was right. "It was Frye," she said adamantly. "Frye and nobody else but Frye. I didn't make the whole thing up. I didn't fire bullets into the walls. I didn't overturn the sofa and tear up my own clothes. For God's sake, why would I do a crazy thing like that? What reason could I possibly have for a charade of that sort?"

"I've got some ideas," Howard said. "I figure you've known Bruno Frye for a long time, and you—"

"I told you. I only met him three weeks ago."

"You've told us other things that turned out not to be true," Howard said. "So I think you knew Frye for years, or at least for quite a while, and the two of you were having an affair—"

"No!"

"—and for some reason, he threw you over. Maybe he just got tired of you. Maybe it was another woman. Something. So I figure you didn't go up to his winery to research one of your screenplays, like you said. I think you went up there just to get together with him again. You wanted to smooth things over, kiss and make up—"

"No."

"—but he wasn't having any of it. He turned you away again. But while you were there, you found out that he was coming to L.A. for a little vacation. So you made up your mind to get even with him. You figured he probably wouldn't have anything planned his first night in town, probably just a quiet dinner alone and early to bed. You were pretty sure he wouldn't have anyone to vouch for him later on, if the cops wanted to know his every move that night. So you decided to set him up for a rape charge."

"Damn you, this is disgusting!"

"It backfired on you," Howard said. "Frye changed his plans. He didn't even come to L.A. So now you're caught in the lie."

"He was here!" She wanted to take the detective by the throat and choke him until he understood. "Look, I have one or two friends who know me well enough to know if I'd been having an affair. I'll give you their names. Go see them. They'll tell you I didn't have anything going with Bruno Frye. Hell, they might even tell you I haven't had anything going with anyone for a while. I've been too busy to have much of a private life. I work long hours. I haven't had a lot of time for romance. And I sure as hell haven't had time to carry on with a lover who lives at the other end of the state. Talk to my friends. They'll tell you."

"Friends are notoriously unreliable witnesses," Howard said. "Besides, it might have been that one affair you kept all to yourself, the secret little fling. Face it, Miss Thomas, you painted yourself into a corner. The facts are these. You say Frye was in this house tonight. But the sheriff says he was up there, in his own house, as of thirty minutes ago. Now, St. Helena is over four hundred miles by air, over five hundred by car. He simply could not have gotten home that fast. And he could not have been in two places at once because, in case you haven't heard, that's a serious violation of the laws of physics."

Lieutenant Clemenza said, "Frank, maybe you should let me finish up with Miss Thomas."

"What's to finish? It's over, done, kaput." Howard pointed an accusing finger at her. "You're damned lucky, Miss Thomas. If Frye had come to L.A. and this had gotten into court, you'd have committed perjury. You might have wound up in jail. You're also lucky that there's no sure way for us to punish someone like you for wasting our time like this."

"I don't know that we've wasted our time," Clemenza said softly.

"Like hell we haven't." Howard glared at her. "I'll tell you one thing: If Bruno Frye wants to pursue a libel suit, I sure to God will testify for him." Then he turned and walked away from her, toward the study door.

Lieutenant Clemenza didn't make any move to leave and obviously had something more to say to her, but she didn't like having the other one walk out before some important questions were answered. "Wait a minute," she said.

Howard stopped and looked back at her. "Yeah?"

"What now? What are you going to do about my complaint?" she said.

"Are you serious?"

"Yes."

"I'm going to the car, cancel that APB on Bruno Frye, then call it a day. I'm going home and drink a couple cold bottles of Coors."

"You aren't going to leave me here alone? What if he comes back?"

"Oh, Christ." Howard said. "Will you please drop the act?"

She took a few steps toward him. "No matter what you think, no matter what the Napa County Sheriff says, I'm not putting on an act. Will you at least leave one of those uniformed men for an hour or so, until I can get a locksmith to replace the locks on my doors?"

Howard shook his head. "No. I'll be damned if I'll waste more police time and taxpayers' money to provide you with protection you don't need. Give up. It's all over. You lost. Face it, Miss Thomas." He walked out of the room.

Hilary went to the brown armchair and sat down. She was exhausted, confused, and scared.

Clemenza said, "I'll make sure Officers Whitlock and Farmer stay with you until the locks have been changed."

She looked up at him. "Thank you."

He shrugged. He was noticeably uncomfortable. "I'm sorry there's not much more I can do."

"I didn't make up the whole thing," she said.

"I believe you."

"Frye really was here tonight," she said.

"I don't doubt that someone was here, but—"

"Not just someone. Frye."

"If you'd reconsider your identification, we could keep working on the case and—"

"It was Frye," she said, not angrily now, just wearily. "It was him and no one else but him."

For a long moment, Clemenza regarded her with interest, and his clear brown eyes were sympathetic. He was a handsome man, but it was not his good looks that most pleased the eye; there was an indescribably warm and gentle quality in his Italian features, a special concern and understanding so visible in his face that she felt he truly cared what happened to her.

He said, "You've had a very rough experience. It's shaken you. That's perfectly understandable. And sometimes, when you go through a shock like this, it distorts your perceptions. Maybe when you've had a chance to calm down, you'll remember things a little . . . differently. I'll stop by sometime tomorrow. Maybe by then you'll have something new to tell me."

"I won't," Hilary said without hesitation. "But thanks for . . . being kind."

She thought he seemed reluctant to leave. But then he was gone, and she was alone in the study.

For a minute or two, she could not find the energy to get out of the armchair. She felt as if she had stepped into a vast pool of quicksand and had expended every bit of her strength in a frantic and futile attempt to escape.

At last she got up, went to the desk, picked up the telephone. She thought of ringing the winery in Napa County, but she realized that would accomplish nothing. She knew only the business office number. She didn't have Frye's home phone listing. Even if his private number was available through Information—and that was highly unlikely—she would not gain any satisfaction by dialing it. If she tried calling him at home, only one of two things could happen. One, he wouldn't answer, which would neither prove her story nor disprove what Sheriff Laurenski had said. Two, Frye would answer, surprising her. And then what? She would have to reevaluate the events of the night, face the fact that the man with whom she had fought was someone who only resembled Bruno Frye. Or perhaps he didn't look like Frye at all. Maybe her perceptions were so askew that she had perceived a resemblance where there was none. How could you tell when you were losing your grip on reality? How did madness begin? Did it creep up on you, or did it seize you in an instant, without warning? She had to consider the possibility that she was losing her mind because, after all, there was a history of insanity in her family. For more than a decade, one of her fears had been that she would die as her father had died; wild-eyed, raving, incoherent, waving a gun and trying to hold off monsters that were not really there. Like father, like daughter?

"I saw him," she said aloud. "Bruno Frye. In my house. Here. Tonight. I didn't imagine or hallucinate it. I saw him, dammit."

She opened the telephone book to the yellow pages and called a twenty-four-hour-a-day locksmith service.

•

After he fled Hilary Thomas's house, Bruno Frye drove his smoke-gray Dodge van out of Westwood. He went west and south to Marina Del Rey, a small-craft harbor on the edge of the city, a place of expensive garden apartments, even more expensive condominiums, shops, and unexceptional but lushly decorated restaurants, most with unobstructed views of the sea and the thousands of pleasure boats docked along the manmade channels.

Fog was rolling in along the coast, as if a great cold fire burned upon the ocean. It was thick in some places and thin in others, getting denser all the time.

He tucked the van into an empty corner of a parking lot near one of the docks, and for a minute he just sat there, contemplating his failure. The police would be looking for him, but only for a short while, only until they found out that he had been at his place in Napa County all evening. And even while they were looking for him in the L.A. area, he would not be in much danger, for they wouldn't know what sort of vehicle he was driving. He was sure Hilary Thomas had not seen the van when he left because it was parked three blocks from her house.

Hilary Thomas.

Not her real name, of course.

Katherine. That's who she really was. Katherine.

"Stinking bitch," he said aloud.

She scared him. In the past five years, he had killed her more than twenty times, but she had refused to stay dead. She kept coming back to life, in a new body, with a new name, a new identity, a cleverly constructed new background, but he never failed to recognize Katherine hiding in each new persona. He had encountered her and killed her again and again, but she would not stay dead. She knew how to come back from the grave, and her knowledge terrified him more than he dared let her know.

He was frightened of her, but he couldn't let her see that fear, for if she became aware of it, she'd overwhelm and destroy him.

But she can be killed, Frye told himself. I've done it. I've killed her many times and buried many of her bodies in secret graves. I'll kill her again, too. And maybe this time she won't be able to come back.

As soon as it was safe for him to return to her house in Westwood, he would try to kill her again. And this time he planned to perform a number of rituals that he hoped would cancel out her supernatural power of regeneration. He had been reading books about the living dead—vampires and other creatures. Although she was not really any of those things, although she was horrifyingly unique, he believed that some of the methods of extermination that were effective against vampires might work on her as well. Cut out her heart while it was still beating. Drive a wooden stake through it. Cut off her head. Stuff her mouth full of garlic. It would work. Oh, God, it *had* to work.

He left the van and went to a public phone close by. The damp air smelled vaguely of salt, seaweed, and machine oil. Water slapped against the pilings and the hulls of the small yachts, a curiously forlorn sound. Beyond the plexiglas walls of the booth, rank upon rank of masts rose from the tethered boats, like a defoliated forest looming out of the night mist. About the same time that Hilary was calling the police, Frye phoned his own house in Napa County and gave an account of his failed attack on the woman.

The man on the other end of the line listened without interruption, then said, "I'll handle the police."

They spoke for a few minutes, then Frye hung up. Stepping out of the booth, he looked around suspiciously at the darkness and swirling fog. Katherine could not possibly have followed him, but nevertheless, he was afraid she was out there in the gloom, watching, waiting. He was a big man. He should not have been afraid of a woman. But he was. He was afraid of the one who would not die, the one who now called herself Hilary Thomas.

He returned to the van and sat behind the wheel for a few minutes, until he realized that he was hungry. Starving. His stomach rumbled. He hadn't eaten since lunch. He was familiar enough with Marina Del Rey to know there was not a suitable restaurant in the neighborhood. He drove south on the Pacific Coast Highway to Culver Boulevard, then west, then south again on Vista Del Mar. He had to proceed slowly, for the fog was heavy along that route; it threw the van's headlight beams back at him and reduced visibility to thirty feet, so that he felt as if he was driving underwater in a murky phosphorescent sea. Almost twenty minutes after he completed the telephone call to Napa County (and about the same time that Sheriff Laurenski was looking into the case up there in behalf of the L.A. police), Frye found an interesting restaurant on the northern edge of El Segundo. The red and yellow neon sign cut through the fog: GARRIDO'S. It was a Mexican place, but not one of those *norteamericano* chrome and glass outlets serving imitation *comida;* it appeared to be authentically Mexican. He pulled off the road and parked between two hotrods that were equipped with the hydraulic lifts so popular with young Chicano drivers. As he walked around to the entrance, he passed a car bearing a bumper sticker that proclaimed CHICANO POWER. Another one advised everyone to SUPPORT THE FARM WORKERS' Union. Frye could already taste the enchiladas.

Inside, Garrido's looked more like a bar than a restaurant, but the close warm air was redolent with the odors of a good Mexican kitchen. On the left, a stained and scarred wooden bar ran the length of the big rectangular room. Approximately a dozen dark men and two lovely young señoritas sat on stools or leaned against the bar, most of them chattering in rapid Spanish. The center of the room was taken up by a single row of twelve tables running parallel to the bar, each covered with a red tablecloth. All of the tables were occupied by men and women who laughed and drank a lot as they ate. On the right, against the wall, there were booths with red leatherette upholstery and high backs; Frye sat down in one of them.

The waitress who hustled up to his table was a short woman, almost as wide as she was tall, with a very round and surprisingly pretty face. Raising her voice above Freddie Fender's sweet and plaintive singing, which came from the jukebox, she asked Frye what he wanted and took his order: a double platter of chili verde and two cold bottles of Dos Equis.

He was still wearing leather gloves. He took them off and flexed his hands.

Except for a blonde in a low-cut sweater, who was with a mustachioed Chicano stud, Frye was the only one in Garrido's who didn't have Mexican blood in his veins. He knew some of them were staring at him, but he didn't care.

The waitress brought the beer right away. Frye didn't bother with the glass. He put the bottle to his lips, closed his eyes, tilted his head back, and chugged it down. In less than a minute, he had drained it. He drank the second beer with less haste than he had consumed the first, but it was also gone by the time she brought his dinner. He ordered two more bottles of Dos Equis.

Bruno Frye ate with voracity and total concentration, unwilling or unable to look away from his plate, oblivious of everyone around him, head lowered to receive the food in the fevered manner of a graceless glutton. Making soft animal murmurs of delight, he forked the chili verde into his mouth, gobbled up huge dripping bites of the stuff, one after the other, chewed hard and fast, his cheeks bulging. A plate of warm tortillas was served on the side, and he used those to mop up the delicious sauce. He washed everything down with big gulps of icy beer.

He was already two-thirds finished when the waitress stopped by to ask if the meal was all right, and she quickly realized the question was unnecessary. He looked up at her with eyes that were slightly out of focus. In a thick voice that seemed to come from a distance, he asked for two beef tacos, a couple of cheese enchiladas, rice, refried beans, and two more bottles of beer. Her eyes went wide, but she was too polite to comment on his appetite.

He ate the last of the chili verde before she brought his second order, but he did not rise out of his trance when the plate was clean. Every table had a bowl of taco chips, and he pulled his in front of him. He dipped the chips into the cup of hot sauce that came with them, popped them into his mouth whole, crunched them up with enormous pleasure and a lot of noise. When the waitress arrived with more food and beer, he mumbled a thank you and immediately began shoveling cheese enchiladas into his mouth. He worked his way through the tacos and the side dishes. A pulse thumped visibly in his bull neck. Veins stood out boldly across his forehead. A film of sweat sheathed his face, and beads of sweat began to trickle down from his hairline. At last he swallowed the final mouthful of refried beans and chased it with beer and pushed the empty plates away. He sat for a while with one hand on his thigh, one hand wrapped around a bottle, staring across the booth at nothing in particular. Gradually, the sweat dried on his face, and he became aware of the jukebox music again; another Freddie Fender tune was playing.

He sipped his beer and looked around at the other customers, taking an interest in them for the first time. His attention was drawn to a group at the table nearest the door. Two couples. Good-looking girls. Darkly handsome men. All in their early twenties. The guys were putting on an act for the women, talking just a fraction too loud and laughing too much, doing the rooster act, trying too hard, determined to impress the little hens.

Frye decided to have some fun with them. He thought about it, figured out how he would set it up, and grinned happily at the prospect of the excitement he would cause.

He asked the waitress for his check, gave her more than enough money to cover it, and said, "Keep the change."

"You're very generous," she said, smiling and nodding as she went off to the cash register.

He pulled on the leather gloves.

His sixth bottle of beer was still half-full, and he took it with him when he slid out of the booth. He headed toward the exit and contrived to hook a foot on a chair leg as he passed the two couples who had interested him. He stumbled slightly, easily regained his balance, and leaned toward the four surprised people at the table, letting them see the beer bottle, trying to look like a drunk.

He kept his voice low, for he didn't want others in the restaurant to be aware of the confrontation he was fomenting. He knew he could handle two of them, but he wasn't prepared to fight an army. He peered blearily at the toughest looking of the two men, gave him a big grin, and spoke in a low mean snarl that belied his smile. "Keep your goddamned chair out of the aisle, you stupid spic."

The stranger had been smiling at him, expecting some sort of drunken apology. When he heard the insult, his wide brown face went blank, and his eyes narrowed.

Before that man could get up, Frye swung to the other one and said, "Why don't you get a foxy lady like that blonde back there? What do you want with these two greasy wetback cunts?"

Then he made swiftly for the door, so the fight wouldn't start inside the restaurant. Chuckling to himself, he pushed through the door, staggered into the foggy night, and hurried around the building to the parking lot on the north side to wait.

He was only a few steps from his van when one of the men he had left behind called to him in Spanish-accented English. "Hey! Wait a second, man!"

Frye turned, still pretending drunkenness, weaving and swaying as if he found it difficult to keep the ground under his feet. "What's up?" he asked stupidly.

They stopped, side by side, apparitions in the mist. The stocky one said, "Hey, what the hell you think you're doin', man?"

"You spics looking for trouble?" Frye asked, slurring his words.

"*Cerdo!* the stocky one said.

"*Mugriento cerdo!*" said the slim man.

Frye said, "For Christ's sake, stop jabbering that damn monkey talk at me. If you have something to say, speak English."

"Miguel called you a pig," said the slim one. "And I called you a filthy pig."

Frye grinned and made an obscene gesture.

Miguel, the stocky man, charged, and Frye waited motionless, as if he didn't see him coming. Miguel rushed in with his head down, his fists up, his arms tucked close to his sides. He threw two quick and powerful punches at Frye's iron-muscled midsection. The brown man's granite hands made sharp, hard slapping sounds as they landed, but Frye took both blows without flinching. By design, he was still holding the beer bottle, and he smashed it against the side of Miguel's head. Glass exploded and rained down on the parking lot in dissonant musical notes. Beer and beer foam splashed over both men. Miguel dropped to his knees with a horrible groan, as if he had been poleaxed. "Pablo," he called pleadingly to his friend. Grabbing the injured man's head with both hands, Frye held him steady long enough to ram a knee into the underside of his chin. Miguel's teeth clacked together with an ugly noise. As Frye let go of him, the man fell sideways, unconscious, his breath bubbling noisily through bloody nostrils.

Even as Miguel crumpled onto the fog-damp pavement, Pablo came after Frye. He had a knife. It was a long thin weapon, probably a switchblade, probably sharpened into cutting edges on both sides, certain to be as wickedly dangerous as a razor. The slim man was not a charger as Miguel had been. He moved swiftly but gracefully, almost like a dancer, gliding around to Frye's right side, searching for an opening, making an opening by virtue of his speed and agility, striking with the lightning moves of a snake. The knife flashed in, from left to right, and if Frye had not jumped back, it would have torn open his stomach, spilling his guts. Crooning eerily to himself, Pablo pressed steadily forward, slashing at Frye again and again, from left to right, from right to left. As Frye retreated, he studied the way Pablo used the knife, and by the time he backed up against the rear end of the Dodge van, he saw how to handle him. Pablo made long sweeping passes with the knife instead of the short vicious arcs employed by skilled knife fighters; therefore, on the outward half of each swing, after the blade had passed Frye but before it started coming back again, there was a second or two when the weapon was moving away from him, posing no threat whatsoever, a moment when Pablo was vulnerable. As the slim man edged in for the kill, confident that his prey had nowhere to run, Frye timed one of the arcs and sprang forward at precisely the right instant. As the blade swung away from him, Frye seized Pablo's wrist, squeezing and twisting it, bending it back against the joint. The slim man cried out in agony. The knife flew out of his slender fingers. Frye stepped behind him, got a hammerlock on him, and ran him face-first into the rear end of the van. He twisted Pablo's arm even farther, got the hand all the way up between the shoulder blades, until it seemed something would have to snap. With his free hand, Frye gripped the seat of the man's trousers, literally lifted him off his feet, all hundred and forty pounds of him, and slammed him into the van a second time, a third, a fourth, a fifth, a sixth, until the screaming stopped. When he let go of Pablo, the slim man went down like a sack of rags.

Miguel was on his hands and knees. He spit blood and shiny white bits of teeth onto the black macadam.

Frye went to him.

"Trying to get up, friend?"

Laughing softly, Frye stepped on his fingers. He ground his heel on the man's hand, then stepped back.

Miguel squealed, fell on his side.

Frye kicked him in the thigh.

Miguel did not lose consciousness, but he closed his eyes, hoping Frye would just go away.

Frye felt as if electricity was coursing through him, a million-billion volts, bursting from synapse to synapse, hot and crackling and sparking within him, not a painful feeling, but a wild and exciting experience, as if he had just been touched by the Lord God Almighty and filled up with the most beautiful and bright and holy light.

Miguel opened his swollen dark eyes.

"All the fight gone out of you?" Frye asked.

"Please," Miguel said around broken teeth and split lips.

Exhilarated, Frye put a foot against Miguel's throat and forced him to roll onto his back.

"Please."

Frye took his foot off the man's throat.

"Please."

High with a sense of his own power, floating, flying, soaring, Frye kicked Miguel in the ribs.

Miguel choked on his own scream.

Laughing exuberantly, Frye kicked him repeatedly, until a couple of ribs gave way with an audible crunch.

Miguel began to do something he had struggled manfully not to do for the past few minutes. He began to cry.

Frye returned to the van.

Pablo was on the ground by the rear wheels, flat on his back, unconscious.

Saying, "Yeah, yeah, yeah, yeah, yeah, yeah," over and over again, Frye circled Pablo, kicking him in the calves and knees and thighs and hips and ribs.

A car started to pull into the lot from the street, but the driver saw what was happening and wanted no part of it. He put the car in reverse, backed out of there, and sped off with a screech of tires.

Frye dragged Pablo over to Miguel, lined them up side by side, out of the way of the van. He didn't want to run over anyone. He didn't want to kill either of them, for too many people in the bar had gotten a good look at him. The authorities wouldn't have much desire to pursue the winner of an ordinary street fight, especially when the losers had intended to gang up on a lone man. But the police would look for a killer, so Frye made sure that both Miguel and Pablo were safe.

Whistling happily, he drove back toward Marina Del Rey and stopped at the first open service station on the right-hand side of the street. While the attendant filled the tank, checked the oil, and washed the windshield, Frye went to the men's room. He took a shaving kit with him and spent ten minutes freshening up.

When he traveled, he slept in the van, and it was not as convenient as a camper; it did not have running water. On the other hand, it was more maneuverable, less visible, and far more anonymous than a camper. To take full advantage of the many luxuries of a completely equipped motor home, he would have to stop over at a campground every night, hooking up to sewer and water and electric lines, leaving his name and address wherever he went. That was too risky. In a motor home, he would leave a trail that even a noseless bloodhound could follow, and the same would be true if he stayed at motels where, if the police asked about him later, desk clerks would surely remember the tall and extravagantly muscled man with the penetrating blue eyes.

In the men's room at the service station, he stripped out of his gloves and yellow sweater, washed his torso and underarms with wet paper towels and liquid soap, sprayed himself with deodorant, and dressed again. He was always concerned about cleanliness; he liked to be clean and neat at all times.

When he felt dirty, he was not only uncomfortable but deeply depressed as well—and somewhat fearful. It was as if being dirty stirred up vague recollections of some intolerable experience long forgotten, brought back hideous memories to the edge of his awareness, where he could sense but not see them, perceive but not understand them. Those few nights when he had fallen into bed without bothering to wash up, his repeating nightmare had been far worse than usual, expelling him from sleep in a screaming flailing terror. And although he had awakened on those occasions, as always, with no clear memory of what the dreams had been about, he had felt as if he'd just clawed his way out of a sickeningly filthy place, a dark and close and foul hole in the ground.

Rather than risk intensifying the nightmare that was sure to come, he washed himself there in the men's room, shaved quickly with an electric razor, patted his face with aftershave lotion, brushed his teeth, and used the toilet. In the morning, he would go to another service station and repeat the routine, and he would also change into fresh clothes at that time.

He paid the attendant for the gasoline and drove back to Marina Del Rey through ever-thickening fog. He parked the van in the same dockside lot from which he had made the call to his house in Napa County. He got out of the Dodge and walked to the public phone booth and called the same number again.

"Hello?"

"It's me," Frye said.

"The heat's off."

"The police called?"

"Yeah."

They talked for a minute or two, and then Frye returned to the Dodge.

He stretched out on the mattress in the back of the van and switched on a flashlight he kept there. He could not tolerate totally dark places. He could not sleep unless there was at least a thread of illumination under a door or a night light burning dimly in a corner. In perfect darkness, he began to imagine that strange things were crawling on him, skittering over his face, squirming under his clothes. Without light, he was assaulted by the threatening but wordless whispers that he sometimes heard for a minute or two after he awakened from his nightmare, the blood-freezing whispers that loosened his bowels and made his heart skip.

If he could ever identify the source of those whispers or finally hear what they were trying to tell him, he would know what the nightmare was about. He would know what caused the recurring dream, the icy fear, and he might finally be able to free himself from it.

The problem was that whenever he woke and heard the whispers, that tail end of the dream, he was in no state of mind to listen closely and to analyze them; he was always in a panic, wanting nothing more than to have the whispers fade away and leave him in peace.

He tried to sleep in the indirect glow of the flashlight, but he could not. He tossed and turned. His mind raced. He was wide awake.

He realized that it was the unfinished business with the woman that was keeping him from sleep. He had been primed for the kill, and it had been denied him. He was edgy. He felt hollow, incomplete.

He had tried to satisfy his hunger for the woman by feeding his stomach. When that had not worked, he had tried to take his mind off her by provoking a fight with those two Chicanos. Food and enormous physical exertion were the two things he had always used to stifle his sexual urges, and to divert his thoughts from the secret blood lust that sometimes burned fiercely within him. He wanted sex, a brutal and bruising kind of sex that no woman would willingly provide, so he gorged himself instead. He wanted to kill, so he spent four or five hard hours lifting progressive weights until his muscles cooked into pudding and the violence steamed out of him. The psychiatrists called it *sublimation*. Lately, it had been less and less effective in dissipating his unholy cravings.

The woman was still on his mind.

The sleekness of her.

The swell of hips and breasts.

Hilary Thomas.

No. That was just a disguise.

Katherine.

That was who she really was.

Katherine. Katherine the bitch. In a new body.

He could close his eyes and picture her naked upon a bed, pinned under him, thighs spread, squirming, writhing, quivering like a rabbit that sees the muzzle of a gun. He could envision his hand moving over her heavy breasts and taut belly, over her thighs and the mound of her sex . . . and then his other hand raising the knife, plunging it down, jamming the silvered blade into her, all the way into her softness, her flesh yielding to him, the blood springing up in bright wet promise. He could see the stark terror and excruciating pain in her eyes as he smashed through her chest and dug for her living heart, trying to rip it out while it was still beating. He could almost feel her slick warm blood and smell the slightly bitter coppery odor of it. As the vision filled his mind and took command of all his senses, he felt his testicles draw tight, felt his penis twitch and grow stiff—another knife—and he wanted to plunge it into her, all the way into her marvelous body, first his thick pulsing penis and then the blade, spurting his fear and weakness into her with one weapon, drawing out her strength and vitality with the other.

He opened his eyes.

He was sweating.

Katherine. The bitch.

For thirty-five years, he had lived in her shadow, had existed miserably in constant fear of her. Five years ago, she had died of heart disease, and he had tasted freedom for the first time in his life. But she kept coming back from the dead, pretending to be other women, looking for a way to take control of him again.

He wanted to use her and kill her to show her that she did not scare him. She had no power over him any more. He was now stronger than she was.

He reached for the bundle of chamois cloths that lay beside the mattress, untied them, unwrapped his spare knife.

He wouldn't be able to sleep until he killed her.

Tonight.

She wouldn't be expecting him back so soon.

He looked at his watch. Midnight.

People would still be returning home from the theater, late dinner, parties. Later, the streets would be deserted, the houses lightless and quiet, and there would be less chance of being spotted and reported to the police.

He decided that he would leave for Westwood at two o'clock.

chapter three

The locksmith came and changed the locks on the front and back doors, then went on to another job in Hancock Park.

Officers Farmer and Whitlock left.

Hilary was alone.

She didn't think she could sleep, but she knew for sure she couldn't spend the night in her own bed. When she stood in that room, her mind's eye filled with vivid images of terror: Frye smashing through the door, stalking her, grinning demoniacally, moving inexorably toward the bed and suddenly leaping onto it, rushing across the mattress with the knife raised high. . . . As before, in a curious dreamlike flux, the memory of Frye became a memory of her father, so that for an instant she had the crazy notion that it had been Earl Thomas, raised from the dead, who had tried to kill her tonight. But it was not merely the residual vibrations of evil in the room that put it off limits. She was also unwilling to sleep there until the ruined door had been removed and a new one hung, a job that couldn't be taken care of until she could get hold of a carpenter tomorrow. The flimsy door that had been there had not held long against Frye's assault, and she had decided to have it replaced with a solid-core hardwood door and a brass deadbolt. But if Frye came back and somehow got into the house tonight, he would be able to walk right into her room while she slept—if she slept.

And sooner or later he would come back. She was as certain of that as she ever had been about anything.

She could go to a hotel, but that didn't appeal to her. It would be like hiding from him. Running away. She was quietly proud of her courage. She never ran away from anyone or anything; she fought back with all of her ingenuity and strength. She hadn't run away from her violent and unloving parents. She had not even sought psychological escape from the searing memory of the final monstrous and bloody events in that small Chicago apartment, had not accepted the kind of peace that could be found in madness or convenient amnesia, which were two ways out that most people would have taken if they'd been through the same ordeal. She had never backed away from the endless series of challenges she had encountered while struggling to build a career in Hollywood, first as an actress, then as a screenwriter. She had gotten knocked down plenty of times, but she had picked herself up again. And again. She persevered, fought back, and won. She would also win this bizarre battle with Bruno Frye, even though she would have to fight it alone.

Damn the police!

She decided to sleep in one of the guest rooms, where there was a door she could lock and barricade. She put sheets and a blanket on the queen-size bed, hung towels in the adjoining guest bathroom.

Downstairs, she rummaged through the kitchen drawers, taking out a variety of knives and testing each for balance and sharpness. The large butcher's knife looked deadlier than any of the others, but in her small hand it was unwieldy. It would be of little use in close quarters fighting, for she needed room to swing it. It might be an excellent weapon for attack, but it was not so good for self-defense. Instead, she chose an ordinary utility knife with a four-inch blade, small enough to fit in a pocket of her robe, large enough to do considerable damage if she had to use it.

The thought of plunging a knife into another human being filled her with revulsion, but she knew that she could do it if her life was threatened. At various times during her childhood, she had hidden a knife in her bedroom, under the mattress. It had been insurance against her father's unpredictable fits of mindless violence. She had used it only once, that last day, when Earl had begun to hallucinate from a combination of delirium tremens and just plain lunacy. He had seen giant worms coming out of the walls and huge crabs trying to get in through the windows. In a paranoid schizophrenic fury, he had transformed that small apartment into a reeking charnel house, and she had saved herself only because she'd had a knife.

Of course, a knife was inferior to a gun. She wouldn't be able to use it against Frye until he was on top of her, and then it might be too late. But the knife was all she had. The uniformed patrolmen had taken her .32 pistol with them when they left right behind the locksmith.

Damn them to hell!

After Detectives Clemenza and Howard had gone, Hilary and Officer Farmer had had a maddening conversation about the gun laws. She became furious every time she thought of it.

"Miss Thomas, about this pistol. . . ."

"What about it?"

"You need a permit to keep a handgun in your house."

"I know that. I've got one."

"Could I see the registration?"

"It's in the nightstand drawer. I keep it with the gun."

"May Officer Whitlock go upstairs and get it?"

"Go ahead."

And a minute or two later:

"Miss Thomas, I gather you once lived in San Francisco."

"For about eight months. I did some theater work up there when I was trying to break in as an actress."

"This registration bears a San Francisco address."

"I was renting a North Beach apartment because it was cheap, and I didn't have much money in those days. A woman alone in that neighborhood sure needs a gun."

"Miss Thomas, aren't you aware that you're required to fill out a new registration form when you move from one county to another?"

"No."

"You really aren't aware of that?"

"Look, I just write movies. Guns aren't my business."

"If you keep a handgun in your house, you're obliged to know the laws governing its registration and use."

"Okay, okay. I'll register it as soon as I can."

"Well, you see, you'll have to come in and register it if you want it back."

"Get it back?"

"I'll have to take it with me."

"Are you kidding?"

"It's the law, Miss Thomas."

"You're going to leave me alone, unarmed?"

"I don't think you need to worry about—"

"Who put you up to this?"

"I'm only doing my job."

"Howard put you up to it, didn't he?"

"*Detective Howard did suggest I check the registration. But he didn't—*"

"*Jesus!*"

"*All you have to do is come in, pay the proper fee, fill out a new registration—and we'll return your pistol.*"

"*What if Frye comes back here tonight?*"

"*It isn't very likely, Miss Thomas.*"

"*But what if he does?*"

"*Call us. We've got some patrol cars in the area. We'll get here—*"

"*—just in time to phone for a priest and a morgue wagon.*"

"*You've got nothing to fear but—*"

"*—fear itself? Tell me, Officer Farmer, do you have to take a college course in the use of the cliché before you can become a cop?*"

"*I'm only doing my duty, Miss Thomas.*"

"*Ahhh . . . what's the use.*"

Farmer had taken the pistol, and Hilary had learned a valuable lesson. The police department was an arm of the government, and you could not rely on the government for anything. If the government couldn't balance its own budget and refrain from inflating its own currency, if it couldn't find a way to deal with the rampant corruption within its own offices, if it was even beginning to lose the will and the means to maintain an army and to provide national security, then why should she expect it to stop a single maniac from cutting her down?

She had learned long ago that it was not easy to find someone in whom she could place her faith and trust. Not her parents. Not relatives, every one of whom preferred not to get involved. Not the paper-shuffling social workers to whom she had turned for help when she was a child. Not the police. In fact, she saw now that the only person anyone could trust and rely on was himself.

All right, she thought angrily. Okay. I'll deal with Bruno Frye myself.

How?

Somehow.

She left the kitchen with the knife in her hand, went to the mirrored wet bar that was tucked into a niche between the living room and the study, and poured a generous measure of Remy Martin into a large crystal snifter. She carried the knife and the brandy upstairs to the guest room, defiantly switching off the lights as she went.

She closed the bedroom door, locked it, and looked for some way to fortify it. A highboy stood against the wall to the left of the door, a heavy dark pine piece taller than she was. It weighed too much to be moved as it was, but she made it manageable by taking out all the drawers and setting them aside. She dragged the big wooden chest across the carpet, pushed it squarely against the door, and replaced the drawers. Unlike many high-boys, this one had no legs at all; it rested flat on the floor and had a relatively low center of gravity that made it a formidable obstacle for anyone trying to bull his way into the room.

In the bathroom, she put the knife and the brandy on the floor. She filled the tub with water as hot as she could stand it, stripped, and settled slowly into it, wincing and gasping as she gradually submerged. Ever since she had been pinned beneath Frye on the bedroom floor, ever since she'd felt his hand pawing at her crotch and shredding her panty-hose, she had felt dirty, contaminated. Now, she soaked herself with great pleasure, worked up a thick lilac-scented lather, scrubbed vigor-ously with a washcloth, pausing occasionally to sip Remy Martin. At last, when she felt thoroughly clean again, she put the bar of soap aside and settled down even farther in the fragrant water. Steam rose over her, and the brandy made steam within her, and the pleasant combina-tion of inner and outer heat forced fine drops of perspiration out of her brow. She closed her eyes and concentrated on the contents of the crys-tal snifter.

The human body will not run for long without the proper mainte-nance. The body, after all, is a machine, a marvelous machine made of many kinds of tissues and fluids, chemicals and minerals, a sophisticated assemblage with one heart-engine and a lot of little motors, a lubricating system and an air-cooling system, ruled by the computer brain, with drive trains made out of muscles, all constructed upon a clever calcium frame. To function, it needs many things, not the least of which are food, relax-ation, and sleep. Hilary had thought she would be unable to sleep after what had happened, that she would spend the night like a cat with its ears up, listening for danger. But she had exerted herself tonight in more ways than one, and although her conscious mind was reluctant to shut down for repairs, her subconscious knew it was necessary and inevitable. By the time she finished the brandy, she was so drowsy that she could hardly keep her eyes open.

She climbed out of the tub, opened the drain, and dried herself on a big fluffy towel as the water gurgled away. She picked up the knife and walked out of the bathroom, leaving the light on, pulling the door halfway shut. She switched off the lights in the main room. Moving languorously in the soft glow and velvet shadows, she put the knife on the nightstand and slid naked into bed.

She felt loose, as if the heat had unscrewed her joints.

She was a bit dizzy, too. The brandy.

She lay with her face toward the door. The barricade was reassuring. It looked very solid. Impenetrable. Bruno Frye wouldn't get through it, she told herself. Not even with a battering ram. A small army would find it difficult to get through that door. Not even a tank would make it. What about a big old dinosaur? she wondered sleepily. One of those tyrannosaurus rex fellas like in the funny monster pictures. Godzilla. Could Godzilla bash through that door . . . ?

By two o'clock Thursday morning, Hilary was asleep.

•

At 2:25 Thursday morning, Bruno Frye drove slowly past the Thomas place. The fog was into Westwood now, but it was not as turbid as it was nearer the ocean. He could see the house well enough to observe that there was not even the faintest light beyond any of the front windows.

He drove two blocks, swung the van around, and went by the house again, even slower this time, carefully studying the cars parked along the street. He didn't think the cops would post a guard for her, but he wasn't taking any chances. The cars were empty; there was no stakeout.

He put the Dodge between the pair of Volvos two blocks away and walked back to the house through pools of foggy darkness, through pale circles of hazy light from the mist-cloaked streetlamps. As he crossed the lawn, his shoes squished in the dew-damp grass, a sound that made him aware of how ethereally quiet the night was otherwise.

At the side of the house, he crouched next to a bushy oleander plant and looked back the way he had come. No alarm had been set off. No one was coming after him.

He continued to the rear of the house and climbed over a locked gate. In the back yard, he looked up at the wall of the house and saw a small square of light on the second floor. From the size of it, he supposed it was a bathroom window; the larger panes of glass to the right of it showed vague traces of light at the edges of the drapes.

She was up there.

He was sure of it.

He could sense her. Smell her.

The bitch.

Waiting to be taken and used.

Waiting to be killed.

Waiting to kill me? he wondered.

He shuddered. He wanted her, had a fierce hard-on for her, but he was also afraid of her.

Always before, she had died easily. She had always come back from the dead in a new body, masquerading as a new woman, but she had always died without much of a struggle. Tonight, however, Katherine had been a regular tigress, shockingly strong and clever and fearless. This was a new development, and he did not like it.

Nevertheless, he had to go after her. If he didn't pursue her from one reincarnation to the next, if he didn't keep killing her until she finally stayed dead, he would never have any peace.

He did not bother to try opening the kitchen door with the keys he had stolen out of her purse the day she'd been to the winery. She had probably had new locks installed. Even if she hadn't taken that precaution, he would be unable to get in through the door. Tuesday night, the first time he had attempted to get into the house, she had been at home, and he had discovered that one of the locks would not open with a key if it had been engaged from inside. The upper lock opened without resistance, but the lower one would only release if it had been locked from outside, with a key. He had not gotten into the house on that occasion, had had to come back the next night, Wednesday night, eight hours ago, when she was out to dinner and both of his keys were useable. But now she was in there, and although she might not have had the locks replaced, she had turned those special deadbolts from the inside, effectively barring entrance regardless of the number of keys he possessed.

He moved along to the corner of the house, where a big mullioned window looked into the rose garden. It was divided into a lot of six-inch-square panes of glass by thin strips of dark, well-lacquered wood. The book-lined study lay on the other side. He took a penlight from one pocket, flicked it on, and directed the narrow beam through the window. Squinting, he searched the length of the sill and the less visible horizontal center bar until he located the latch, then turned off the penlight. He had a roll of masking tape, and he began to tear strips from it, covering the small pane that was nearest the window lock. When the six-inch square was completely masked over, he used his gloved fist to smash through it: one hard blow. The glass shattered almost soundlessly and did not clatter to the floor, for it stuck onto the tape. He reached inside and unlatched the window, raised it, heaved himself up and across the sill. He barely avoided making a hell of a racket when he encountered a small table and nearly fell over it.

Standing in the center of the study, heart pounding, Frye listened for movement in the house, for a sign that she had heard him.

There was only silence.

She was able to rise up from the dead and come back to life in a new identity, but that was evidently the limit of her supernatural power. Obviously, she was not all-seeing and all-knowing. He was in her house, but she did not know it yet.

He grinned.

He took the knife from the sheath that was fixed to his belt, held it in his right hand.

With the penlight in his left hand, he quietly prowled through every room on the ground floor. They were all dark and deserted.

Going up the stairs to the second floor, he stayed close to the wall, in case any of the steps creaked. He reached the top without making a sound.

He explored the bedrooms, but he encountered nothing of interest until he approached the last room on the left. He thought he saw light coming under the door, and he switched off his flash. In the pitch-black corridor only a nebulous silvery line marked the threshold of the last room, but it was more marked than any of the others. He went to the door and cautiously tried the knob. Locked.

He had found her.

Katherine.

Pretending to be someone named Hilary Thomas.

The bitch. The rotten bitch.

Katherine, Katherine, Katherine. . . .

As the name echoed through his mind, he clenched his fist around the knife and made short jabbing motions at the darkness, as if he were stabbing her.

Stretching out face-down on the floor of the hallway, Frye looked through the inch-high gap at the bottom of the door. A large piece of furniture, perhaps a dresser, was pushed up against the other side of the entrance. A vague indirect light spread across the bedroom from an unseen source on the right, some of it finding its way around the edges of the dresser and under the door.

He was delighted by what little he could see, and a flood of optimism filled him. She had barricaded herself in the room, which meant the hateful bitch was afraid of him. *She* was afraid of *him*. Even though she knew how to come back from the grave, she was frightened of dying. Or maybe she knew or sensed that this time she would not be able to return to the living. He was going to be damned thorough when he disposed of the corpse, far more thorough than he had been when he'd disposed of the many other women whose bodies she had inhabited. Cut out her heart. Pound a wooden stake through it. Cut off her head. Fill her mouth with garlic. He also intended to take the head and the heart with him when he left the house; he would bury the pair of grisly trophies in separate and secret graves, in the hallowed ground of two different churchyards, and far away from wherever the body itself might be interred. Apparently, she was aware that he planned to take extraordinary precautions this time, for she was resisting him with a fury and a purpose the likes of which she had never shown before.

She was very quiet in there.

Asleep?

No, he decided. She was too scared to sleep. She was probably sitting up in bed with the pistol in her hands.

He pictured her hiding in there like a mouse seeking refuge from a prowling cat, and he felt strong, powerful, like an elemental force. Hatred boiled blackly within him. He wanted her to squirm and shake with fear as she had made him do for so many years. An almost overpowering urge to scream at her took hold of him; he wanted to shout her name—Katherine, Katherine—and fling curses at her. He kept control of himself only with an effort that brought sweat to his face and tears to his eyes.

He got to his feet and stood silently in the darkness, considering his options. He could throw himself against the door, break through it, and push the obstacle out of the way, but that would surely be suicidal. He wouldn't get through the fortifications fast enough to surprise her. She would have plenty of time to line up the sights of the gun and put half a dozen bullets into him. The only other thing he could do was wait for her to come out. If he stayed in the hallway and didn't make a sound all night, the uneventful hours might wear the edges off her watchfulness. By morning, she might get the idea that she was safe and that he wasn't ever coming back. When she walked out of there, he could seize her and force her back to the bed before she knew what was happening.

Frye crossed the corridor in two steps and sat on the floor with his back against the wall.

In a few minutes, he began to hear rustling sounds in the dark, soft scurrying noises.

Imagination, he told himself. That familiar fear.

But then he felt something creeping up his leg, under his trousers.

It's not really there, he told himself.

Something slithered under one sleeve and started up his arm, something awful but unidentifiable. And something ran across his shoulder and up his neck, onto his face, something small and deadly. It went for his mouth. He pressed his lips together. It went for his eyes. He squeezed his eyes shut. It went for his nostrils, and he brushed frantically at his face, but he couldn't find it, couldn't knock it off. *No!*

He switched on the penlight. He was the only living creature in the hallway. There was nothing moving under his trousers. Nothing under his sleeves. Nothing on his face.

He shuddered.

He left the penlight on.

•

At nine o'clock Thursday morning, Hilary was awakened by the telephone. There was an extension in the guest room. The bell switch accidentally had been turned all the way up to maximum volume, probably by someone from the house-cleaning service that she employed. The strident ringing broke into Hilary's sleep and made her sit up with a start.

The caller was Wally Topelis. While having breakfast, he had seen the morning paper's account of the assault and attempted rape. He was shocked and concerned.

Before she would tell him any more than the newspaper had done, she made him read the article to her. She was relieved to hear that it was short, just a small picture and a few column inches on the sixth page. It was based entirely on the meager information that she and Lieutenant Clemenza had given the reporters last night. There was no mention of Bruno Frye—or of Detective Frank Howard's conviction that she was a liar. The press had come and gone with perfect timing, just missing the kind of juicy angle that would have put the story at least a few pages closer to page one.

She told Wally all of it, and he was outraged. "That stupid goddamned cop! If he'd made any effort at all to find out about you, what kind of person you are, he'd have known you couldn't possibly make up a story like that. Look, kid, I'll take care of this. Don't worry. I'll get some action for you."

"How?"

"I'll call some people."

"Who?"

"How about the chief of police for starters?"

"Oh, sure."

"Hey, he owes me," Wally said. "For the past five years in a row, who was it that organized the annual police benefit show? Who was it that got some of the biggest Hollywood stars to appear for nothing? Who was it got singers and comedians and actors and magicians all free for the police fund?"

"You?"

"Damn right it was me."

"But what can he do?"

"He can reopen the case."

"When one of his detectives swears it was a hoax?"

"His detective is brain-damaged."

"I have a hunch this Frank Howard might have a very good record," she said.

"Then the way they rate their people is a disgrace. Their standards are either very low or all screwed up."

"You might have a pretty hard time convincing the chief of that."

"I can be very persuasive, my lamb."

"But even if he owes you a favor, how can he reopen the case without new evidence? He may be the chief, but he has to follow the rules, too."

"Look, he can at least talk to the sheriff up there in Napa County."

"And Sheriff Laurenski will give the chief the same story he was putting out last night. He'll say Frye was at home baking cookies or something."

"Then the sheriff's an incompetent fool who took the word of some-one on Frye's household staff. Or he's a liar. Or maybe he's even in on this with Frye somehow."

"You go to the chief with that theory," she said, "and he'll have both of us tested for paranoid schizophrenia."

"If I can't squeeze some action out of the cops," Wally said, "then I'll hire a good PI team."

"Private investigators?"

"I know just the agency. They're good. Considerably better than most cops. They'll pry open Frye's life and find all the little secrets in it. They'll come up with the kind of evidence that'll get the case reopened."

"Isn't that expensive?"

"I'll split the cost with you," he said.

"Oh, no."

"Oh, yes."

"That's generous of you, but—"

"It's not generous of me at all. You're an extremely valuable property, my lamb. I own a percentage of you, so anything I pay to a PI team is just insurance. I only want to protect my interests."

"That's baloney, and you know it," she said. "You *are* generous, Wally. But don't hire anyone just yet. The other detective that I told you about, Lieutenant Clemenza, said he'd stop around later this afternoon to see if I remembered anything more. He still sort of believes me, but he's confused because Laurenski shot a big hole in my story. I think Clemenza would use just about any excuse he could find to get the case reopened. Let's wait until I've seen him. Then if the situation still looks bleak, we'll hire your PI."

"Well . . . all right," Wally said reluctantly. "But in the meantime, I'm going to tell them to send a man over to your place for protection."

"Wally, I don't need a bodyguard."

"Like hell you don't."

"I was perfectly safe all night, and I—"

"Listen, kid, I'm sending someone over. That's final. There won't be any arguing with Uncle Wally. If you won't let them inside, he'll just stand by your front door like a palace guard."

"Really, I—"

"Sooner or later," Wally said gently, "you're going to have to face the fact that you can't get through life alone, entirely on your own steam. No one does. No one, kid. Now and then everyone has to accept a little help. You should have called me last night."

"I didn't want to disturb you."

"For God's sake, you wouldn't have disturbed me! I'm your friend. In fact, you disturbed me a whole lot more by not disturbing me last night. Kid, it's all right to be strong and independent and self-reliant. But when you carry it too far, when you isolate yourself like this, it's a slap in the face to everybody who cares about you. Now, will you let the guard in when he arrives?"

She sighed. "Okay."

"Good. He'll be there within an hour. And you'll call me as soon as you've talked to Clemenza?"

"I will."

"Promise."

"I promise."

"Did you sleep last night?"

"Surprisingly, yes."

"If you didn't get enough sleep," he said, "take a nap this afternoon."
Hilary laughed. "You'd make a wonderful Jewish mother."

"Maybe I'll bring over a big pot of chicken soup this evening. Good-bye, dear."

"Good-bye, Wally. Thanks for calling."

When she hung up the receiver, she glanced at the highboy that stood in front of the door. After the uneventful night, the barricade looked foolish. Wally was right: the best way to handle this was to hire around-the-clock bodyguards and then put a first-rate team of private investigators on Frye's trail. Her original plan for dealing with the problem was ludicrous. She simply could not board up the windows and play Battle of the Alamo with Frye.

She got out of bed, put on her silk robe, and went to the highboy. She took the drawers out and put them aside. When the tall chest was light enough to be moved, she dragged it away from the door, back to the indentation in the carpet that marked where it had rested until last night. She replaced the drawers.

She went to the nightstand, picked up the knife, and smiled ruefully as she realized how naive she had been. Hand-to-hand combat with Bruno Frye? Knife-fighting with a maniac? How could she have thought that she would have any chance whatsoever in such an uneven contest? Frye was many times stronger than she was. She had been fortunate last night when she had managed to get away from him. Luckily, she'd had the pistol. But if she tried fencing with him, he would cut her to ribbons.

Intending to return the knife to the kitchen, wanting to be dressed for the day by the time the bodyguard arrived, she went to the bedroom door, unlocked it, opened it, stepped into the hallway, and screamed as Bruno Frye grabbed her and slammed her up against the wall. The back of her head hit the plaster with a sharp crack, and she struggled to remain above a wave of darkness that washed in behind her eyes. He clutched her throat with his right hand, pinned her in place. With his left hand, he tore open the front of her robe and squeezed her bare breasts, leering at her, calling her a bitch and a slut.

He must have been listening when she talked to Wally, must have heard that the police had taken away her pistol, for he had absolutely no fear of her. She hadn't mentioned the knife to Wally, and Frye was not prepared for it. She rammed the four-inch blade into his flat, hard-muscled belly. For a few seconds, he seemed unaware of it; he slid his hand down from her breasts, tried to thrust a couple of fingers into her vagina. As she jerked the knife out of him, he was stricken by pain. His eyes went wide, and he let out a high-pitched yelp. Hilary stuck the blade into him again, piercing him high and toward the side this time, just under the ribs. His face was suddenly as white and greasy looking as lard. He howled, let go of her, stumbled backwards until he collided with the other wall and knocked an oil painting to the floor.

A violent spasmodic shiver of revulsion snapped through Hilary as she realized what she had done. But she did not drop the knife, and she was fully prepared to stab him again if he attacked her.

Bruno Frye looked down at himself in astonishment. The blade had sunk deep. A thin stream of blood oozed from him, rapidly staining his sweater and pants.

Hilary did not wait for his expression of amazement to metamorphose into agony and anger. She turned and hurried into the guest room, threw the door shut and locked it. For half a minute she listened to Frye's soft groans and curses and clumsy movements, wondering if he had sufficient strength left to smash through the door. She thought she heard him lumbering down the hall toward the stairs, but she couldn't be sure. She ran to the telephone. With bloodless and palsied hands, she picked up the receiver and dialed the operator. She asked for the police.

•

The bitch! The rotten bitch!

Frye slipped one hand under the yellow sweater and gripped the lower of the two wounds, the gut puncture, for that was the one doing the most bleeding. He squeezed the lips of the cut together as best he could, trying to stop the life from flowing out of him. He felt the warm blood soaking through the stitching of the gloves, onto his fingers.

He was suffering very little pain. A dull burning in his stomach. An electric tingle along his left side. A mild rhythmic twinge timed to his heartbeat. That was the extent of it.

Nevertheless, he knew that he had been badly hurt and was getting worse by the second. He was pathetically weak. His great strength had gushed out of him suddenly and completely.

Holding his belly with one hand, clutching the bannister with the other, he descended to the first floor on steps as treacherous as those in a carnival funhouse; they seemed to tip and pitch and roll. By the time he reached the bottom, he was streaming sweat.

Outside, the sun stung his eyes. It was brighter than he had ever seen it, a monstrous sun that filled the sky and beat mercilessly upon him. He felt as if it were shining through his eyes and starting tiny fires on the surface of his brain.

Bending over his wounds, cursing, he shuffled south along the sidewalk until he came to the smoke-gray van. He pulled himself up into the driver's seat, drew the door shut as if it weighed ten thousand pounds.

He drove with one hand to Wilshire Boulevard, turned right, went to Sepulveda, made a left, looking for a public telephone that offered a lot of privacy. Every bump in the road was like a blow to his solar plexus. At times, the automobiles around him appeared to stretch and flex and balloon, as if they were constructed of a magical elastic metal, and he had to concentrate to force them back into more familiar shapes.

Blood continued to trickle out of him no matter how tightly he pressed on the wound. The burning in his stomach grew worse. The rhythmic twinge became a sharp pinch. But the catastrophic pain that he knew was coming had not yet arrived.

He drove an interminable distance on Sepulveda before he finally located a pay phone that suited his needs. It was in a back corner of a supermarket parking lot, eighty or a hundred yards from the store.

He parked the van at an angle, screening the phone from everyone at the market and from motorists passing on Sepulveda. It was not a booth, just one of those plastic windscreens that were supposed to provide excellent sound-proofing but which had no effect at all on background noise; but at least it appeared to be in service, and it was private enough. A high cement block fence rose behind it, separating the supermarket property from the fringes of a housing tract. On the right, a cluster of shrubs and two small palms shielded the phone from the side street leading off Sepulveda. No one was likely to see him well enough to realize he was hurt; he didn't want anyone nosing around.

He slid across the seat to the passenger's side and got out that door. When he looked down at the thick red muck oozing between the fingers that were clamped over the worse wound, he felt dizzy, and he looked quickly away. He only had to take three steps to reach the phone, but each of them seemed like a mile.

He could not remember his telephone credit card number, which had been as familiar to him as his birthdate, so he called collect to Napa Valley.

The operator rang it six times.

"Hello?"

"I have a collect call for anyone from Bruno Frye. Will you accept the charges?"

"Go ahead, operator."

There was a soft click as she went off the line.

"I'm hurt real bad. I think . . . I'm dying," Frye told the man in Napa County.

"Oh, Jesus, no. No!"

"I'll have to . . . call an ambulance," Frye said. "And they . . . everyone will know the truth."

They spoke for a minute, both of them frightened and confused.

Suddenly, Frye felt something loosen inside him. Like a spring popping. And a bag of water bursting. He screamed in pain.

The man in Napa County cried out in sympathy, as if he felt the same pain.

"Got to . . . get an ambulance," Frye said.

He hung up.

Blood had run all the way down his pants to his shoes, and now it was dribbling onto the pavement.

He lifted the receiver off the hook and put it down on the metal shelf beside the phone box. He picked up a dime from the same shelf, on which he had put his pocket change, but his fingers weren't working properly; he dropped it and looked down stupidly as it rolled across the macadam. Found another dime. Held this one as tightly as he could. He lifted the dime as if it were a lead disc as big as an automobile tire, finally put it in the proper slot. He tried to dial 0. He didn't even have enough energy to perform that small chore. His muscle-packed arms, his big shoulders, his gigantic chest, his powerful back, his hard rippled belly, and his massive thighs all failed him.

He couldn't make the call, and he couldn't even stand up any longer. He fell, rolled over once, and lay face-down on the macadam.

He couldn't move.

He couldn't see. He was blind.

It was a very black darkness.

He was scared.

He tried to tell himself that he would come back from the dead as Katherine had done. *I'll come back and get her,* he thought. *I'll come back.* But he really didn't believe it.

As he lay there getting increasingly light-headed, he had a surprisingly lucid moment when he wondered if he had been all wrong about Katherine coming back from the dead. Had it been his imagination? Had he just been killing women who resembled her? Innocent women? Was he mad?

A new explosion of pain blew those thoughts away and forced him to consider the smothering darkness in which he lay.

He felt things moving on him.

Things crawling on him.

Things crawling on his arms and legs.

Things crawling on his face.

He tried to scream. Couldn't.

He heard the whispers.

No!

His bowels loosened.

The whispers swelled into a raging sibilant chorus and, like a great dark river, swept him away.

•

Thursday morning, Tony Clemenza and Frank Howard located Jilly Jenkins, an old friend of Bobby "Angel" Valdez. Jilly had seen the baby-faced rapist and killer in July, but not since. At that time, Bobby had just quit a job at Vee Vee Gee Laundry on Olympic Boulevard. That was all Jilly knew.

Vee Vee Gee was a large one-story stucco building dating from the early fifties, when an entire Los Angeles school of benighted architects first thought of crossing ersatz Spanish texture and form with utilitarian factory design. Tony had never been able to understand how even the most insensitive architect could see beauty in such a grotesque crossbreed. The orange-red tile roof was studded with dozens of firebrick chimneys and corrugated metal vents; steam rose from about half of those outlets. The windows were framed with heavy timbers, dark and rustic, as if this were the *casa* of some great and rich *terrateniente;* but the ugly factory-window glass was webbed with wire. There were loading docks where the verandas should have been. The walls were straight, the corners sharp, the overall shape boxlike—quite the opposite of the graceful arches and rounded edges of genuine Spanish construction. The place was like an aging whore wearing more refined clothes than was her custom, trying desperately to pass for a lady.

"Why did they do it?" Tony asked as he got out of the unmarked police sedan and closed the door.

"Do what?" Frank asked.

"Why did they put up so many of these offensive places? What was the point of it?"

Frank blinked. "What's so offensive?"

"It doesn't bother you?"

"It's a laundry. Don't we need laundries?"

"Is anybody in your family an architect?"

"Architect? No," Frank said. "Why'd you ask?"

"I just wondered."

"You know, sometimes you don't make a whole hell of a lot of sense."

"So I've been told," Tony said.

In the business office at the front of the building, when they asked to see the owner, Vincent Garamalkis, they were given worse than a cool reception. The secretary was downright hostile. The Vee Vee Gee Laundry had paid four fines in four years for employing undocumented aliens. The secretary was certain that Tony and Frank were agents with the Immigration and Naturalization Service. She thawed a bit when she saw their LAPD identification, but she was still not cooperative until Tony convinced her that they hadn't even a smidgen of interest in the nationalities of the people working at Vee Vee Gee. At last, reluctantly, she admitted that Mr. Garamalkis was on the premises. She was about to take them to him when the phone rang, so she gave them hasty directions and asked them to find him on their own.

The enormous main room of the laundry smelled of soap and bleach and steam. It was a damp place, hot and noisy. Industrial washing machines thumped, buzzed, sloshed. Huge driers whirred and rumbled monotonously. The clacking and hissing of automatic folders put Tony's teeth on edge. Most of the workers unloading the laundry carts, and the husky men feeding the machines, and the women tagging linens at a double row of long tables were speaking to one another in loud and rapid Spanish. As Tony and Frank walked from one end of the room to the other, some of the noise abated, for the workers stopped talking and eyed them suspiciously.

Vincent Garamalkis was at a battered desk at the end of the big room. The desk was on a three-foot-high platform that made it possible for the boss to watch over his employees. Garamalkis got up and walked to the edge of the platform when he saw them coming. He was a short, stocky man, balding, with hard features and a pair of gentle hazel eyes that didn't match the rest of his face. He stood with his hands on his hips, as if he were defying them to step onto his level.

"Police," Frank said, flashing ID.

"Yeah," Garamalkis said.

"Not Immigration," Tony assured him.

"Why should I be worried about Immigration?" Garamalkis asked defensively.

"Your secretary was," Frank said.

Garamalkis scowled down at them. "I'm clean. I hire nobody but U.S. citizens or documented aliens."

"Oh, sure," Frank said sarcastically. "And bears don't shit in the woods any more."

"Look," Tony said, "we really don't care about where your workers come from."

"So what do you want?"

"We'd like to ask a few questions."

"About what?"

"This man," Frank said, passing up the three mug shots of Bobby Valdez.

Garamalkis glanced at them. "What about him?"

"You know him?" Frank asked.

"Why?"

"We'd like to find him."

"What for?"

"He's a fugitive."

"What'd he do?"

"Listen," Frank said, fed up with the stocky man's sullen responses, "I can make this hard or easy for you. We can do it here or downtown. And if you want to play Mr. Hardass, we can bring the Immigration and Naturalization Service into it. We don't really give a good goddamned whether or not you hire a bunch of Mexes, but if we can't get cooperation from you, we'll see that you get busted every which way but loose. You got me? You hear it?"

Tony said, "Mr. Garamalkis, my father was an emigrant from Italy. He came to this country with his papers in order, and eventually he became a citizen. But one time he had some trouble with agents from the Immigration Service. It was just a mistake in their records, a paperwork foul-up. But they hounded him for more than five weeks. They called him at work and paid surprise visits to our apartment at odd hours. They demanded records and documentation, but when Papa provided those things, they called them forgeries. There were threats. Lots of threats. They even served deportation papers on him before it was all straightened out. He had to hire a lawyer he couldn't afford, and my mother was hysterical most of the time until it was settled. So you see, I don't have any love for the Immigration Service. I wouldn't go one step out of my way to help them pin a rap on you. Not one damn step, Mr. Garamalkis."

The stocky man looked down at Tony for a moment, then shook his head and sighed. "Don't they burn you up? I mean, a year or two ago, when all those Iranian students were making trouble right here in L.A., overturning cars and trying to set houses on fire, did the damn Immigration Service even consider booting their asses out of the country? Hell, no! The agents were too busy harassing my workers. These people I employ don't burn down other people's houses. They don't overturn cars and throw rocks at policemen. They're good hardworking people. They only want to make a living. The kind of living they can't make south of the border. You know why Immigration spends all its time chasing them? I'll tell you. I've got it figured out. It's because these Mexicans don't fight back. They're not political or religious fanatics like a lot of these Iranians. They aren't crazy or dangerous. It's a whole hell of a lot safer and easier for Immigration to come after these people 'cause they generally just go along quietly. Ahh, the whole damned system's a disgrace."

"I can understand your point of view," Tony said. "So if you'd just take a look at these mug shots—"

But Garamalkis was not ready to answer their questions. He still had a few things to get off his chest. Interrupting Tony, he said, "Four years ago, I got fined the first time. The usual things. Some of my Mexican employees didn't have green cards. Some others were working on expired cards. After I settled up in court, I decided to play it straight from then on. I made up my mind to hire only Mexicans with valid work cards. And if I couldn't find enough of those, I was going to hire U.S. citizens. You know what? I was stupid. I was really stupid to think I could stay in business that way. See, I can only afford to pay minimum wage to most of these workers. Even then, I'm stretching myself thin. The problem is Americans won't work for minimum wage. If you're a citizen, you can get more from welfare for not working than you can make at a job that pays minimum wage. And the welfare's tax-free. So I just about went crazy for about two months, trying to find workers, trying to keep the laundry going out on schedule. I nearly had a heart attack. See, my customers are places like hotels, motels, restaurants, barber shops . . . and they all need to get their stuff back fast and on a dependable schedule. If I hadn't started hiring Mexicans again, I'd have gone out of business."

Frank didn't want to hear any more. He was about to say something sharp, but Tony put a hand on his shoulder and squeezed gently, urging him to be patient.

"Look," Garamalkis said, "I can understand not giving illegal aliens welfare and free medical care and like that. But I can't see the sense in deporting them when they're only doing jobs that no one else wants to do. It's ridiculous. It's a disgrace." He sighed again, looked at the mug shots of Bobby Valdez that he was holding, and said, "Yeah, I know this guy."

"We heard he used to work here."

"That's right."

"When?"

"Beginning of the summer, I think. May. Part of June."

"After he skipped out on his parole officer," Frank said to Tony.

"I don't know anything about that," Garamalkis said.

"What name did he give you?" Tony asked.

"Juan."

"Last name?"

"I don't remember. He was only here six weeks or so. But it'll still be in the files."

Garamalkis stepped down from the platform and led them back across the big room, through the steam and the smell of detergent and the suspicious glances of the employees. In the front office he asked the secretary to check the files, and she found the right pay record in a minute. Bobby had used the name Juan Mazquezza. He had given an address on La Brea Avenue.

"Did he really live at this apartment?" Frank asked.

Garamalkis shrugged. "It wasn't the sort of important job that required a background credit check."

"Did he say why he was quitting?"

"No."

"Did he tell you where he was going?"

"I'm not his mother."

"I mean, did he mention another job?"

"No. He just cut out."

"If we don't find Mazquezza at this address," Tony said, "we'd like to come back and talk to your employees. Maybe one of them got to know him. Maybe somebody here's still friends with him."

"You can come back if you want," Garamalkis said. "But you'll have some trouble talking to my people."

"Why's that?"

Grinning, he said, "A lot of them don't speak English."

Tony grinned back at him and said, "*Yo leo, escribo y hablo español.*"

"Ah," Garamalkis said, impressed.

The secretary made a copy of the pay record for them, and Tony thanked Garamalkis for his cooperation.

In the car, as Frank pulled into traffic and headed toward La Brea Avenue, he said, "I've got to hand it to you."

Tony said, "What's that?"

"You got more out of him quicker than I could have."

Tony was surprised by the compliment. For the first time in their three-month association, Frank had admitted that his partner's techniques were effective.

"I wish I had a little bit of your style," Frank said. "Not all of it, you understand. I still think my way's best most of the time. But now and then we run across someone who'd never open up to me in a million years, but he'd pour out his guts to you in about a minute flat. Yeah, I wish I had a little of your smoothness."

"You can do it."

"Not me. No way."

"Of course, you can."

"You've got a way with people," Frank said. "I don't."

"You can learn it."

"Nah. It works out well enough the way it is. We've got the classic mean-cop-nice-cop routine, except we aren't playing at it. With us, it just sort of naturally works out that way."

"You're not a mean cop."

Frank didn't respond to that. As they stopped at a red light, he said, "There's something else I've got to say, and you probably won't like it."

"Try me," Tony said.

"It's about that woman last night."

"Hilary Thomas?"

"Yeah. You liked her, didn't you?"

"Well . . . sure. She seemed nice enough."

"That's not what I mean. I mean, you *liked* her. You had the hots for her."

"Oh, no. She was good looking, but I didn't—"

"Don't play innocent with me. I saw the way you looked at her."

The traffic light changed.

They rode in silence for a block.

Finally, Tony said; "You're right. I don't get all hot and bothered by every pretty girl I see. You know that."

"Sometimes I think you're a eunuch."

"Hilary Thomas is . . . different. And it's not just the way she looks. She's gorgeous, of course, but that's not all of it. I like the way she moves, the way she handles herself. I like to listen to her talk. Not just the sound of her voice. More than that. I like the way she expresses herself. I like the way she thinks."

"I like the way she looks," Frank said, "but the way she thinks leaves me cold."

"She wasn't lying," Tony said.

"You heard what the sheriff—"

"She might have been mixed up about exactly what happened to her, but she didn't create the whole story out of thin air. She probably saw someone who looked like Frye, and she—"

Frank interrupted. "Here's where I've got to say what you won't want to hear."

"I'm listening."

"No matter how hot she made you, that's no excuse for what you did to me last night."

Tony looked at him, confused. "What'd I do?"

"You're supposed to support your partner in a situation like that."

"I don't understand."

Frank's face was red. He didn't look at Tony. He kept his eyes on the street and said, "Several times last night, when I was questioning her, you took her side against mine."

"Frank, I didn't intend—"

"You tried to keep me from pursuing a line of questioning that I *knew* was important."

"I felt you were too harsh with her."

"Then you should have indicated your opinion a whole hell of a lot more subtly than you did. With your eyes. With a gesture, a touch. You handle it that way all the time. But with her, you came charging in like a white knight."

"She had been through a very trying ordeal and—"

"Bullshit," Frank said. "She hadn't been through any ordeal. She made it all up!"

"I still won't accept that."

"Because you're thinking with your balls instead of your head."

"Frank, that's not true. And it's not fair."

"If you thought I was being so damned rough, why didn't you take me aside and ask what I was after?"

"I *did* ask, for Christ's sake!" Tony said, getting angry in spite of himself. "I asked you about it just after you took the call from HQ, while she was still out on the lawn talking to the reporters. I wanted to know what you had, but you wouldn't tell me."

"I didn't think you'd listen," Frank said. "By that time, you were mooning over her like a lovesick boy."

"That's crap, and you know it. I'm as good a cop as you are. I don't let personal feelings screw up my work. But you know what? I think you *do*."

"Do what?"

"I think you do let personal feelings screw up your work sometimes," Tony said.

"What the hell are you talking about?"

"You have this habit of hiding information from me when you come up with something really good," Tony said. "And now that I think about it . . . you only do it when there's a woman in the case, when it's some bit of information you can use to hurt her, something that'll break her down and make her cry. You hide it from me, and then you spring it on her by surprise, in the nastiest way possible."

"I always get what I'm after."

"But there's usually a nicer and easier way it could be gotten."

"Your way, I suppose."

"Just two minutes ago you admitted my way works."

Frank didn't say anything. He glowered at the cars ahead of them.

"You know, Frank, whatever your wife did to you through the divorce, no matter how much she hurt you, that's no reason to hate every woman you meet."

"I don't."

"Maybe not consciously. But subconsciously—"

"Don't give me any of that Freud shit."

"Okay. All right," Tony said. "But I'll swap accusation for accusation. You say I was unprofessional last night. And I say you were unprofessional. Stalemate."

Frank turned right on La Brea Avenue.

They stopped at another traffic signal.

The light changed, and they inched forward through the thickening traffic.

Neither of them spoke for a couple of minutes.

Then Tony said, "Whatever weakness and faults you might have, you're a pretty damned good cop."

Frank glanced at him, startled.

"I mean it," Tony said. "There's been friction between us. A lot of the time, we rub each other the wrong way. Maybe we won't be able to work together. Maybe we'll have to put in requests for new partners. But that'll just be a personality difference. In spite of the fact that you're about three times as rough with people as you ever need to be, you're good at what you do."

Frank cleared his throat. "Well . . . you, too."

"Thank you."

"Except sometimes you're just too . . . sweet."

"And you can be a sour son of a bitch sometimes."

"Want to ask for a new partner?"

"I don't know yet."

"Me either."

"But if we don't start getting along better, it's too dangerous to go on together much longer. Partners who make each other tense can get each other killed."

"I know," Frank said. "I know that. The world's full of assholes and junkies and fanatics with guns. You have to work with your partner as if he was just another part of you, like a third arm. If you don't, you're a lot more likely to get blown away."

"So I guess we should think seriously about whether we're right for each other."

"Yeah," Frank said.

Tony started looking for street numbers on the buildings they passed. "We should be just about there."

"That looks like the place," Frank said, pointing.

The address on Juan Mazquezza's Vee Vee Gee pay record was a sixteen-unit garden apartment complex in a block largely taken over by commercial interests: service stations, a small motel, a tire store, an all-night grocery. From a distance the apartments looked new and somewhat expensive, but on closer inspection Tony saw signs of decay and neglect. The exterior walls needed a new coat of stucco; they were badly chipped and cracked. The wooden stairs and railings and doors all needed new paint. A signpost near the entrance said the place was *Las Palmeras Apartments*. The sign had been hit by a car and badly damaged, but it hadn't been replaced. Las Palmeras looked good from a distance because it was cloaked in greenery that masked some of its defects and softened the splintery edges. But even the landscaping, when scrutinized closely, betrayed the seediness of Las Palmeras; the shrubs had not been trimmed in a long time, and the trees were raggedy, and the jade shrubs were in need of care.

The pattern at Las Palmeras could be summed up in one word: transition. The few cars in the parking area reinforced that evaluation. There were two middle-priced new cars that were lovingly cared for, gleaming with fresh wax. No doubt they belonged to young men and women of optimism and were signs of accomplishment to them. A battered and corroded old Ford leaned on one flat tire, unused and unuseable. An eight-year-old Mercedes stood beyond the Ford, washed and waxed, but a bit worse for wear; there was a rusty dent in one rear fender. In better days, the owner was able to purchase a twenty-five-thousand-dollar automobile, but now he apparently couldn't come up with the two-hundred-dollar deductible part of the repair bill. Las Palmeras was a place for people in transition. For some of them, it was a way station on the upward climb to bright and beckoning careers. For others, it was a precarious spot on the cliff, the last respectable toehold on a sad and inevitable fall into total ruin.

As Frank parked by the manager's apartment, Tony realized that Las Palmeras was a metaphor for Los Angeles. This City of Angels was perhaps the greatest land of opportunity the world had ever known. Incredible quantities of money moved through here, and there were a thousand ways to earn a sizable bankroll. L.A. produced enough success stories to fill a daily newspaper. But the truly astounding affluence also created a variety of tools for self-destruction and made them widely available. Any drug you wanted could be found and bought easier and quicker in Los Angeles than in Boston or New York or Chicago or Detroit. Grass, hashish, heroin, cocaine, uppers, downers, LSD, PCP. . . . The city was a junkie's supermarket. Sex was freer, too. Victorian principles and sensibilities had collapsed in Los Angeles faster than they had in the rest of the country, partly because the rock music business was centered there, and sex was an integral part of that world. But there were other vastly more important factors that had contributed to the unchaining of the average

Californian's libido. The climate had something to do with it; the warm dry days and the subtropical light and the competing winds—desert and sea winds—had a powerful erotic influence. The Latin temperament of the Mexican immigrants made its mark on the population at large. But perhaps most of all, in California you felt that you were on the edge of the Western world, on the brink of the unknown, facing an abyss of mystery. It was seldom a conscious awareness of being on the cultural edge, but the subconscious mind was bathed in that knowledge at all times, an exhilarating and sometimes scary feeling. Somehow, all of those things combined to break down inhibitions and stir the gonads. A guilt-free view of sex was healthy, of course. But in the special atmosphere of L.A., where even the most bizarre carnal tastes could be indulged with little difficulty, some men (and women) could become as addicted to sex as to heroin. Tony had seen it happen. There were some people, certain personality types, who chose to throw everything away—money, self-respect, reputation—in an endless party of fleshy embraces and brief wet thrills. If you couldn't find your personal humiliation and ruin in sex and drugs, L.A. provided a smorgasbord of crackpot religions and violence-prone radical political movements for your consideration. And of course, Las Vegas was only one hour away by cheap regularly scheduled airlines, free if you could qualify as a high-rolling junketeer. All of those tools for self-destruction were made possible by the truly incomprehensible affluence. With its wealth and its joyous celebration of freedom, Los Angeles offered both the golden apple and the poisoned pear: positive transition and negative transition. Some people stopped at places like Las Palmeras Apartments on their way up, grabbed the apple, moved to Bel Air or Beverly Hills or Malibu or somewhere else on the Westside, and lived happily ever after. Some people tasted the contaminated fruit, and on the way down they made a stop at Las Palmeras, not always certain how or why they'd wound up there.

In fact, the manager of the apartment complex did not appear to understand how the patterns of transition had brought her to her current circumstances. Her name was Lana Haverby. She was in her forties, a well-tanned blonde in shorts and halter. She had a good opinion of her sexual attractiveness. She walked and stood and sat as if she were posing. Her legs were okay, but the rest of her was far from prime. She was thicker in the middle than she seemed to realize, too big in hips and butt for her skimpy costume. Her breasts were so huge that they were not attractive but freakish. The thin halter top exposed canyonesque cleavage and accentuated the large turgid nipples, but it could not give her breasts the shape and uplift they so desperately needed. When she wasn't changing her pose or adjusting it, when she wasn't trying to gauge what effect her body had on Frank and Tony, she seemed confused, distracted. Her eyes didn't always appear to be focused. She tended to leave sentences unfinished. And several times she looked around in wonder at her small dark living room and at the threadbare furniture, as if she had absolutely no idea how she had come to this place or how long she'd been here. She cocked her head as if she heard whispering voices, just out of range, that were trying to explain it all to her.

Lana Haverby sat in a chair, and they sat on the sofa, and she looked at the mug shots of Bobby Valdez.

"Yeah," she said. "He was a sweetie."

"Does he live here?" Frank asked.

"He lived . . . yeah. Apartment nine . . . was it? But not any more."

"He moved out?"

"Yeah."

"When was that?"

"This summer sometime. I think it was. . . ."

"Was what?" Tony asked.

"First of August," she said.

She recrossed her bare legs, put her shoulders back a bit farther to elevate her breasts as much as possible.

"How long did he live here?" Frank asked.

"I guess it was three months," she said.

"He live alone?"

"You mean was there a chick?"

"A girl, a guy, anybody," Frank said.

"Just him," Lana said. "He was a sweetie, you know."

"Did he leave a forwarding address?"

"No. But I wish he would have."

"Why? Did he skip out on the rent?"

"No. Nothing like that. I'd just like to know where I could . . ."

She cocked her head, listening to the whispers again.

"Where you could what?" Tony asked.

She blinked. "Oh . . . I'd sure like to know where I could visit him. I was kind of working on him. He turned me on, you know. Got my juices running. I was trying to get him into bed, but he was, you know, sort of shy."

She had not asked why they wanted Bobby Valdez, alias Juan

Mazquezza. Tony wondered what she would say if she knew her shy little sweetie was an aggressive, violent rapist.

"Did he have any regular visitors?"

"Juan? Not that I noticed."

She uncrossed her legs, sat with her thighs spread, and watched Tony for his reaction.

"Did he say where he worked?" Frank asked.

"When he first moved in, he worked at some laundry. Later, he got something else."

"Did he say what it was?"

"No. But he was, you know, making good money."

"He have a car?" Frank asked.

"Not at first," she said. "But later. A Jaguar two-plus-two. That was beautiful, man."

"And expensive," Frank said.

"Yeah," she said. "He paid a bundle for it and all in cold hard cash."

"Where would he get that kind of money?"

"I told you. He was making good bread at his new job."

"Are you sure you don't know where he was working?"

"Positive. He wouldn't talk about it. But, you know, as soon as I saw that Jaguar, I knew . . . he wasn't long for this place," she said wistfully. "He was moving up fast."

They spent another five minutes asking questions, but Lana Haverby had nothing more of consequence to tell them. She was not a very observant person, and her recollection of Juan Mazquezza seemed to have tiny holes in it, as if moths had been nibbling at her store of memories.

When Tony and Frank got up to leave, she hurried to the door ahead of them. Her gelatinous breasts jiggled and swayed alarmingly, in what she evidently thought was a wildly provocative display. She affected that ass-swinging, tippy-toewalk that didn't look good on any coquette over twenty-one; she was forty, a grown woman, unable to discover and explore the dignity and special beauty of her own age, trying to pass for a teenager, and she was pathetic. She stood in the doorway, leaning back slightly against the open door, one long leg bent at the knee, copying a pose she'd seen in a men's magazine or on a cheesecake calendar, virtually begging for a compliment.

Frank turned sideways as he went through the door, barely able to avoid brushing against her breasts. He strode quickly down the walk toward the car, not looking back.

Tony smiled and said, "Thanks for your cooperation, Miss Haverby."

She looked up at him, and her eyes focused on his eyes more clearly than they had focused on anything during the past fifteen minutes. She held his gaze, and a spark of something vital glimmered in her eyes—intelligence, genuine pride, maybe a shred of self-respect—something better and cleaner than had been there before. "I'm going to move up and out of here, too, you know, like Juan did. I wasn't always just a manager at Las Palmeras. I moved in some, you know, pretty rich circles."

Tony didn't want to hear what she had to tell him, but he felt trapped and then mesmerized, like the man who was stopped in the street by the Ancient Mariner.

"Like when I was twenty-three," she said. "I was working as a waitress, but I got up and out of that. That was when the Beatles, you know, were just getting started, like seventeen years ago, and the whole rock thing was really exploding then. You know? A good-looking girl back then, she could connect with the stars, make those important connections, you know, and go just about everywhere with the big groups, travel all over the country with them. Oh, wow, man, those were some fantastic times! Like there wasn't anything you couldn't have or do. They had it all, those groups, and they spread it around, you know. And I was with them. I sure was. I slept with some very famous people, you know. Household names. I was very popular, too. They liked me."

She began to list bestselling rock groups from the sixties. Tony didn't know how many of them she'd actually been with and how many she only imagined she'd been with, but he noticed that she never mentioned individuals; she had been to bed with *groups*, not people.

He had never wondered what became of groupies, those bouncy child-women who wasted some of their best years as hangers-on in the rock music world. But now he knew at least one way they could end up. They trailed after the current idols, offering inarticulate praise, sharing drugs, providing convenient receptacles for the sperm of the rich and famous, giving no thought to time and the changes it would bring. Then one day, after a girl like that had been burnt out by too much booze and too much pot and too much cocaine and maybe a little heroin, when the first hard wrinkles came at the corners of the eyes, when the laugh lines grew a shade too deep, when the pneumatic breasts began to show the first signs of sagging, she was eased out of one group's bed—and discovered that, this time, there was no other group willing to take her in. If she wasn't averse to turning tricks, she could still make a living that way, for a few years. But to some of them that was a turnoff; they didn't think of themselves as hookers but as "girlfriends." For a lot of them, marriage was out, for they'd seen too much and done too much to willingly settle for a tame domestic life. One of them, Lana Haverby, had taken a job at Las Palmeras, a position she thought of as temporary, just a way to swing free rent until she could reconnect with the beautiful people.

"So I won't be here much longer," she said. "I'll be moving on soon. Any time now, you know. I feel lots of good things coming. Like really good vibrations, you know?"

Her situation was ineffably sad, and Tony could think of nothing to say that would make a difference to her. "Uh . . . well . . . I sure wish you all the luck in the world," he said stupidly. He edged past her, through the door.

The gleam of vitality vanished from her eyes, and she was suddenly desperately posing again, shoulders back, chest out. But her face was still weary and drawn. Her belly was still straining at the waistband of her shorts. And her hips were still too big for girlish games. "Hey," she said, "if you're ever in the mood for some wine and, you know, a little conversation. . . ."

"Thank you," he said.

"I mean, feel free to stop by when you're not, you know, on duty."

"I might do that," he lied. Then, because he felt he had sounded insincere and didn't want to leave her without anything, he said, "You've got pretty legs."

That was true, but she didn't know how to accept a compliment, gracefully. She grinned and put her hands on her breasts and said, "It's usually my boobs that get all the attention."

"Well . . . I'll be seeing you," he said, turning away from her and heading toward the car.

After a few steps, he glanced back and saw that she was standing in the open door, head cocked to one side, far away from him and Las Palmeras Apartments, listening to those faint whispering voices that were trying to explain the meaning of her life.

As Tony got into the car, Frank said, "I thought she got her claws into you. I was about ready to call up a SWAT team to rescue you."

Tony didn't laugh. "It's sad."

"What?"

"Lana Haverby."

"You kidding me?"

"The whole situation."

"She's just a dumb broad," Frank said. "But what did you think about Bobby buying the Jag?"

"If he hasn't been robbing banks, there's only one way he could get hold of that kind of cash."

"Dope," Frank said.

"Cocaine, grass, maybe PCP."

"It gives us a whole new place to start looking for the little bastard," Frank said. "We can go out on the street and start putting some muscle on the known dealers, guys who've taken falls for selling junk. Make it hot for them, and if they've got a lot to lose and they know where Bobby is, they'll give him to us on a silver platter."

"Meanwhile," Tony said, "I'd better call in."

He wanted a DMV check on a black Jaguar registered to Juan Mazquezza. If they could get a license number for the hot sheet, then looking for Bobby's wheels would be part of every uniformed officer's daily duties.

That didn't mean they would find him right away. In any other city, if a man was wanted as badly as Bobby was wanted, he would not be able to live in the open for a long time. He would be spotted or tracked down in a few weeks at most. But Los Angeles was not like other cities; at least in terms of land area, it was bigger than any other urban center in the nation. L.A. was spread over nearly five hundred square miles. It covered half again as much land as all the boroughs of New York City, ten times more than all of Boston, and almost half as much as the state of Rhode Island. Counting the illegal aliens, which the Census Bureau did not do, the population of the entire metropolitan area was approaching nine million. In this vast maze of streets, alleyways, freeways, hills, and canyons, a clever fugitive could live in the open for many months, going about his business as boldly and unconcernedly as any ordinary citizen.

Tony switched on the radio, which they had left off all morning, called Communications, and asked for the DMV check on Juan Mazquezza and his Jaguar.

The woman handling their frequency had a soft appealing voice. After she took Tony's requests, she informed him that a call had been out for him and Frank the past two hours. It was now 11:45. The Hilary Thomas case was open again, and they were needed at her Westwood house, where other officers had answered a call at 9:30.

Racking the microphone, Tony looked at Frank and said, "I knew it! Dammit, I knew she wasn't lying about the whole thing."

"Don't preen your feathers yet," Frank said disagreeably. "Whatever this new development is, she's probably making it up like she made up all the rest of it."

"You never give up, do you?"

"Not when I know I'm right."

A few minutes later, they pulled up in front of the Thomas house. The circular driveway was filled with two press cars, a station wagon for the police laboratory, and a black-and-white.

As they got out of their car and started across the lawn, a uniformed officer came out of the house and walked toward them. Tony knew him; his name was Warren Prewitt. They met him halfway to the front door.

"You guys answered this call last night?" Prewitt asked.

"That's right," Frank said.

"What is it, do you work twenty-four hours a day?"

"Twenty-six," Frank said.

Tony said, "How's the woman?"

"Shaken up," Prewitt said.

"Not hurt?"

"Some bruises on her throat."

"Serious?"

"No."

"What happened?" Frank said.

Prewitt capsulized the story that Hilary Thomas had told him earlier.

"Any proof that she's telling the truth?" Frank asked.

"I heard how you feel about this case," Prewitt said. "But there is proof."

"Like what?" Frank asked.

"He got into the house last night through a study window. A very smart job it was, too. He taped up the glass so she wouldn't hear it breaking."

"She could have done that herself," Frank said.

"Broken her own window?" Prewitt asked.

"Yeah. Why not?" Frank said.

"Well," Prewitt said, "she wasn't the one who bled all the hell over the place."

"How much blood?" Tony asked.

"Not a whole lot, but not a whole little," Prewitt said. "There's some on the hall floor, a big bloody handprint on the wall up there, drops of blood on the stairs, another smeared print on the downstairs foyer wall, and traces of blood on the doorknob."

"Human blood?" Frank asked.

Prewitt blinked at him. "Huh?"

"I'm wondering if it's a fake, a hoax."

"Oh, for Christ's sake!" Tony said.

"The boys from the lab didn't get here till about forty-five minutes ago," Prewitt said. "They haven't said anything yet. But I'm sure it's human blood. Besides, three of the neighbors saw the man running away."

"Ahhh," Tony said softly.

Frank scowled at the lawn at his feet, as if he were trying to wither the grass.

"He left the house all doubled up," Prewitt said. "He was holding his stomach and shuffling kind of hunched over, which fits in with Miss Thomas's statement that she stabbed him twice in the midsection."

"Where'd he go?" Tony asked.

"We have a witness who saw him climb into a gray Dodge van two blocks south of here. He drove away."

"Got a license number?"

"No," Prewitt said. "But the word's out. There's a want on the van."

Frank Howard looked up. "You know, maybe this attack isn't related to the story she fed us last night. Maybe she cried wolf last night—and then this morning she really was attacked."

"Doesn't that strike you as just a bit too coincidental?" Tony asked exasperatedly.

"Besides, it must be related," Prewitt said. "She swears it was the same man."

Frank met Tony's stare and said, "But it can't be Bruno Frye. You know what Sheriff Laurenski said."

"I never insisted it was Frye," Tony said. "Last night, I figured she was attacked by someone who resembled Frye."

"She insisted—"

"Yeah, but she was scared and hysterical," Tony said. "She wasn't thinking clearly, and she mistook the look-alike for the real thing. It's understandable."

"And you tell me *I'm* building a case on coincidences," Frank said disgustedly.

At that moment Officer Gurney, Prewitt's partner, came out of the house and called to him! "Hey, they found him. The man she stabbed!"

Tony, Frank, and Prewitt hurried to the front door.

"HQ just phoned," Gurney said. "A couple of kids on skateboards found him about twenty-five minutes ago."

"Where?"

"Way the hell down on Sepulveda. In some supermarket parking lot. He was lying on the ground beside his van."

"Dead?"

"As a doornail."

"Did he have any ID?" Tony asked.

"Yeah," Gurney said. "It's just like the lady told us. He's Bruno Frye."

•

Cold.

Air conditioning thrummed in the walls. Rivers of icy air gushed from two vents near the ceiling.

Hilary was wearing a sea-green autumn dress, not of a light summery fabric, but not heavy enough to ward off a chill. She hugged herself and shivered.

Lieutenant Howard stood at her left side, still looking somewhat embarrassed. Lieutenant Clemenza was on her right.

The room didn't feel like part of a morgue. It was more like a cabin in a spaceship. She could easily imagine that the bone-freezing cold of deep space lay just beyond the gray walls. The steady humming of the air conditioning could be the distant roar of rocket engines. They were standing in front of a window that looked into another room, but she would have preferred to see endless blackness and far-away stars beyond the thick glass. She almost wished she were on a long inter-galactic voyage instead of in a morgue, waiting to identify a man she had killed.

I killed him, she thought.

Those words, ringing in her mind, seemed to make her even colder than she had been a second ago.

She glanced at her watch.

3:18.

"It'll be over in a minute," Lieutenant Clemenza said reassuringly.

Even as Clemenza spoke, a morgue attendant brought a wheeled litter into the room on the other side of the window. He positioned it squarely in front of the glass. A body lay on the cart, hidden by a sheet. The attendant pulled the shroud off the dead man's face, halfway down his chest, then stepped out of the way.

Hilary looked at the corpse and felt dizzy.

Her mouth went dry.

Frye's face was white and still, but she had the insane feeling that at any moment he would turn his head toward her and open his eyes.

"Is it him?" Lieutenant Clemenza asked.

"It's Bruno Frye," she said weakly.

"But is it the man who broke into your house and attacked you?" Lieutenant Howard asked.

"Not this stupid routine again," she said. "Please."

"No, no," Clemenza said, "Lieutenant Howard doesn't doubt your story any more, Miss Thomas. You see, we already know that man is Bruno Frye. We've established that much from the ID he was carrying. What we need to hear from you is that he was the man who attacked you, the man you stabbed."

The dead mouth was unexpressive now, neither frowning nor smiling, but she could remember the evil grin into which it had curved.

"That's him," she said. "I'm positive. I've been positive all along. I'll have nightmares for a long time."

Lieutenant Howard nodded to the morgue attendant beyond the window, and the man covered the corpse.

Another absurd but chilling thought struck her: What if it sits up on the cart and throws the sheet off?

"We'll take you home now," Clemenza said.

She walked out of the room ahead of them, miserable because she had killed a man—but thoroughly relieved and even delighted that he was dead.

•

They took her home in the unmarked police sedan. Frank drove, and Tony sat up front. Hilary Thomas sat in the back, shoulders drawn up a bit, arms crossed, as if she was cold on such a warm late-September day.

Tony kept finding excuses to turn around and speak to her. He didn't want to take his eyes off her. She was so lovely that she made him feel as he sometimes did in a great museum, when he stood before a particularly exquisite painting done by one of the old masters.

She responded to him, even gave him a couple of smiles, but she wasn't in the mood for light conversation. She was wrapped up in her own thoughts, mostly staring out the side window, mostly silent.

When they pulled into the circular driveway at her place and stopped in front of the door, Frank Howard turned to her and said, "Miss Thomas . . . I . . . well . . . I owe you an apology."

Tony was not startled by the admission, but he was somewhat surprised by the sincere note of contrition in Frank's voice and the supplicatory expression on his face; meekness and humility were not exactly Frank's strongest suits.

Hilary Thomas also seemed surprised. "Oh . . . well . . . I suppose you were only doing your job."

"No," Frank said. "That's the problem. I wasn't doing my job. At least I wasn't doing it well."

"It's over now," she said.

"But will you accept my apologies?"

"Well . . . of course," she said uncomfortably.

"I feel very bad about the way I treated you."

"Frye won't be bothering me any more," she said. "So I guess that's all that really matters."

Tony got out of the car and opened her door. She could not get out by herself because the rear doors of the sedan had no inside handles, a deterrent to escape-minded prisoners. Besides, he wanted to accompany her to the house.

"You may have to testify at a coroner's inquest," he said as they approached the house.

"Why? When I stabbed him, Frye was in my place, against my wishes. He was threatening my life."

"Oh, there's no doubt it's a simple case of self-defense," Tony said quickly. "If you have to appear at an inquest, it'll just be a formality. There's no chance in the world that any sort of charges will be brought or anything like that."

She unlocked the front door, opened it, turned to him, smiled radiantly. "Thank you for believing in me last night, even after what the Napa County Sheriff said."

"We'll be checking into him," Tony said. "He's got some explaining to do. If you're interested, I'll let you know what his excuse is."

"I *am* curious," she said.

"Okay. I'll let you know."

"Thank you."

"It's no bother."

She stepped into the house.

He didn't move.

She looked back at him.

He smiled stupidly.

"Is there anything else?" she asked.

"As a matter of fact, yes."

"What?"

"One more question."

"Yes?"

He had never felt so awkward with a woman before.

"Would you have dinner with me Saturday?"

"Oh," she said. "Well . . . I don't think I can."

"I see."

"I mean, I'd like to."

"You would?"

"But I really don't have much time for a social life these days," she said.

"I see."

"I've just gotten this deal with Warner Brothers, and it's going to keep me busy day and night."

"I understand," he said.

He felt like a high school boy who had just been turned down by the popular cheerleader.

"It was very nice of you to ask," she said.

"Sure. Well . . . good luck with Warner Brothers."

"Thank you."

"I'll let you know about Sheriff Laurenski."

"Thank you."

He smiled, and she smiled.

He turned away, started toward the car, and heard the door of the house close behind him. He stopped and looked back at it.

A small toad hopped out of the shrubbery, onto the stone footpath in front of Tony. It sat in the middle of the walk and peered up at him, its eyes rolled way back to achieve the necessary angle, its tiny green-brown chest rapidly expanding and contracting.

Tony looked at the toad and said, "Did I give up too easily?"

The little toad made a peeping-croaking sound.

"What have I got to lose?" Tony asked.

The toad peeped-croaked again.

"That's the way I look at it. I've got nothing to lose."

He stepped around the amphibian cupid and rang the bell. He could sense Hilary Thomas looking at him through the one-way peephole lens, and when she opened the door a second later, he spoke before she could. "Am I terribly ugly?"

"What?"

"Do I look like Quasimodo or something?"

"Really, I—"

"I don't pick my teeth in public," he said.

"Lieutenant Clemenza—"

"Is it because I'm a cop?"

"What?"

"You know what some people think?"

"What do some people think?"

"They think cops are socially unacceptable."

"Well, I'm not one of those people."

"You're not a snob?"

"No. I just—"

"Maybe you turned me down because I don't have a lot of money and don't live in Westwood."

"Lieutenant, I've spent most of my life without money, and I haven't always lived in Westwood."

"Then I wonder what's wrong with me," he said, looking down at himself in mock bewilderment.

She smiled and shook her head. "Nothing's wrong with you, Lieutenant."

"Thank God!"

"Really, I said no for just one reason. I don't have time for—"

"Miss Thomas, even the President of the United States manages to take a night off now and then. Even the head of General Motors has leisure time. Even the Pope. Even God rested the seventh day. No one can be busy all the time."

"Lieutenant—"

"Call me Tony."

"Tony, after what I've been through the last two days, I'm afraid I wouldn't be a barrel of laughs."

"If I wanted to go to dinner with a barrel of laughs, I'd take a bunch of monkeys."

She smiled again, and he wanted to take her beautiful face in his hands and kiss it all over.

She said, "I'm sorry. But I need to be alone for a few days."

"That's exactly what you don't need after the sort of experience you've had. You need to get out, be among people, get your spirits up. And I'm not the only one who thinks so." He turned and pointed to the stone footpath behind him. The toad was still there. It had turned around to look at them.

"Ask Mr. Toad," Tony said.

"Mr. Toad?"

"An acquaintance of mine. A very wise person." Tony stooped down and stared at the toad. "Doesn't she need to get out and enjoy herself, Mr. Toad?"

It blinked slow heavy lids and made its funny little sound right on cue.

"You're absolutely correct," Tony told it. "And don't you think I'm the one she should go out with?"

"*Scree-ooak,*" it said.

"And what will you do to her if she turns me down again?"

"*Scree-ooak, scree-ooak.*"

"Ahhh," Tony said, nodding his head in satisfaction as he stood up.

"Well, what did he say?" Hilary asked, grinning. "What will he do to me if I won't go out with you—give me warts?"

Tony looked serious. "Worse than that. He tells me he'll get into the walls of your house, work his way up to your bedroom, and croak so loudly every night that you won't be able to sleep until you give in."

She smiled. "Okay. I give up."

"Saturday night?"

"All right."

"I'll pick you up at seven."

"What should I wear?"

"Be casual," he said.

"See you Saturday at seven."

He turned to the toad and said, "Thank you, my friend."

It hopped off the walk, into the grass, then into the shrubbery.

Tony looked at Hilary. "Gratitude embarrasses him."

She laughed and closed the door.

Tony walked back to the car and got in, whistling happily.

As Frank drove away from the house, he said, "What was that all about?"

"I got a date," Tony said.

"With her?"

"Well, not with her sister."

"Lucky stiff."

"Lucky toad."

"Huh?"

"Private joke."

When they had gone a couple of blocks, Frank said, "It's after four o'clock. By the time we get this heap back to the depot and check out for the day, it'll be five o'clock."

"You want to quit on time for once?" Tony asked.

"Not much we can do about Bobby Valdez until tomorrow anyway."

"Yeah," Tony said. "Let's be reckless."

A few blocks farther on, Frank said, "Want to have a drink after we check out?"

Tony looked at him in amazement. That was the first time in their association that Frank had suggested hanging out together after hours.

"Just a drink or two," Frank said. "Unless you have something planned—"

"No. I'm free."

"You know a bar?"

"The perfect place. It's called The Bolt Hole."

"It's not around HQ, is it? Not a place where a lot of cops go?"

"So far as I know, I'm the only officer of the law who patronizes it. It's on Santa Monica Boulevard, out near Century City. Just a couple of blocks from my apartment."

"Sounds good," Frank said. "I'll meet you there."

They rode the rest of the way to the police garage in silence— somewhat more companionable silence than that in which they had worked before, but silence nonetheless.

What does he want? Tony wondered. Why has that famous Frank Howard reserve finally broken down?

•

At 4:30, the Los Angeles medical examiner ordered a limited autopsy on the body of Bruno Gunther Frye. If at all possible, the corpse was to be opened only in the area of the abdominal wounds, sufficient to determine if those two punctures had been the sole cause of death.

The medical examiner would not perform the autopsy himself, for he had to catch a 5:30 flight to San Francisco in order to keep a speaking engagement. The chore was assigned to a pathologist on his staff.

The dead man waited in a cold room with other dead men, on a cold cart, motionless beneath a white shroud.

•

Hilary Thomas was exhausted. Every bone ached dully; every joint seemed enflamed. Every muscle felt as if it had been put through a blender at high speed and then reconstituted. Emotional strain could have precisely the same physiological effect as strenuous physical labor.

She was also jumpy, much too tense to be able to refresh with a nap. Each time the big house made a normal settling noise, she wondered if the sound was actually the squeak of a floorboard under the weight of an intruder. When the softly sighing wind brushed a palm frond or a pine branch against a window, she imagined someone was stealthily cutting the glass or prying at a window lock. But when there was a long period of perfect quiet, she sensed something sinister in the silence. Her nerves were worn thinner than the knees of a compulsive penitent's trousers.

The best cure she had ever found for nervous tension was a good book. She looked through the shelves in the study and chose James Clavell's most recent novel, a massive story set in the Orient. She poured a glass of Dry Sack on the rocks, settled down in the deep brown armchair, and began to read.

Twenty minutes later, when she was just beginning to lose herself thoroughly in Clavell's story, the telephone rang. She got up and answered it. "Hello."

There was no response.

"Hello?"

The caller listened for a few seconds, then hung up.

Hilary put down the receiver and stared at it thoughtfully for a moment.

Wrong number?

Must have been.

But why didn't he say so?

Some people just don't know any better, she told herself. They're rude.

But what if it wasn't a wrong number. What if it was . . . something else.

Stop looking for goblins in every shadow! she told herself angrily. Frye's dead. It was a bad thing, but it's over and done with. You deserve a rest, a couple of days to collect your nerves and wits. But then you've got to stop looking over your shoulder and get on with your life. Otherwise, you'll end up in a padded room.

She curled up in the armchair again, but she caught a chill that brought goosebumps to her arms. She went to the closet and got a blue and green knitted afghan, returned to the chair, and draped the blanket over her legs.

She sipped the Dry Sack.

She started reading Clavell again.

In a while, she forgot about the telephone call.

•

After signing out for the day, Tony went home and washed his face, changed from his suit into jeans and a checkered blue shirt. He put on a thin tan jacket and walked two blocks to The Bolt Hole.

Frank was already there, sitting in a back booth, still in his suit and tie, sipping Scotch.

The Bolt Hole—or simply The Hole, as regular customers referred to it—was that rare and vanishing thing: an ordinary neighborhood bar. During the past two decades, in response to a continuously fracturing and subdividing culture, the American tavern industry, at least that part of it in cities and suburbs, had indulged in a frenzy of specialization. But The Hole had successfully bucked the trend. It wasn't a gay bar. It wasn't a singles' bar or a swingers' bar. It wasn't a bar patronized primarily by bikers or truckers or show business types or off-duty policemen or account executives; its clientele was a mixture, representative of the community. It wasn't a topless go-go bar. It wasn't a rock and roll bar or a country and western bar. And, thank God, it wasn't a sports bar with one of those six-foot television screens and Howard Cosell's voice in quadraphonic sound. The Hole had nothing more to offer than pleasantly low lighting, cleanliness, courtesy, comfortable stools and booths, a jukebox that wasn't turned too loud, hot dogs and hamburgers served from the minuscule kitchen, and good drinks at reasonable prices.

Tony slid into the booth, facing Frank.

Penny, a sandy-haired waitress with pinchable cheeks and a dimpled chin, stopped by the table. She ruffled Tony's hair and said, "What do you want, Renoir?"

"A million in cash, a Rolls-Royce, eternal life, and the acclaim of the masses," Tony said.

"What'll you settle for?"

"A bottle of Coors."

"That we can provide," she said.

"Bring me another Scotch," Frank said. When she went to the bar to get their drinks, Frank said, "Why'd she call you Renoir?"

"He was a famous French painter."

"So?"

"Well, I'm a painter, too. Neither French nor famous. It's just Penny's way of teasing me."

"You paint pictures?" Frank asked.

"Certainly not houses."

"How come you never mentioned it?"

"I made a few observations about fine art a time or two," Tony said. "But you greeted the subject with a marked lack of interest. In fact, you couldn't have shown less enthusiasm if I'd wanted to debate the fine points of Swahili grammar or discuss the process of decomposition in dead babies."

"Oil paintings?" Frank asked.

"Oils. Pen and ink. Watercolors. A little bit of everything, but mostly oils."

"How long you been at it?"

"Since I was a kid."

"Have you sold any?"

"I don't paint to sell."

"What do you do it for?"

"My own satisfaction."

"I'd like to see some of your work."

"My museum has odd hours, but I'm sure a visit can be arranged."

"Museum?"

"My apartment. There's not much furniture in it, but it's chockfull of paintings."

Penny brought their drinks.

They were silent for a while, and then they talked for a few minutes about Bobby Valdez, and then they were silent again.

There were about sixteen or eighteen people in the bar. Several of them had ordered sandwiches. The air was filled with the mouth-watering aroma of sizzling ground sirloin and chopped onions.

Finally, Frank said, "I suppose you're wondering why we're here like this."

"To have a couple of drinks."

"Besides that." Frank stirred his drink with a swizzle stick. Ice cubes rattled softly. "There are a few things I have to say to you."

"I thought you said them all this morning, in the car, after we left Vee Vee Gee."

"Forget what I said then."

"You had a right to say it."

"I was full of shit," Frank said.

"No, maybe you had a point."

"I tell you, I was full of shit."

"Okay," Tony said. "You were full of shit."

Frank smiled. "You could have argued with me a bit more."

"When you're right, you're right," Tony said.

"I was wrong about the Thomas woman."

"You already apologized to her, Frank."

"I feel like I should apologize to you."

"Not necessary."

"But you saw something there, saw she was telling the truth. I didn't even get a whiff of that. I was off on the wrong scent altogether. Hell, you even pushed my nose in it, and I couldn't pick up the right smell."

"Well, sticking strictly to nasal imagery, you might say you couldn't get the scent because your nose was so far out of joint."

Frank nodded glumly. His broad face seemed to sag into the melancholy mask of a bloodhound. "Because of Wilma. My nose is out of joint because of Wilma."

"Your ex-wife?"

"Yeah. You hit it right on the head this morning when you said I've been a woman-hater."

"Must have been bad, what she did to you."

"No matter what she did," Frank said, "that's no excuse for what I've let happen to me."

"You're right."

"I mean, you can't hide from women, Tony."

"They're everywhere," Tony agreed.

"Christ, you know how long it's been since I slept with a woman?"

"No."

"Ten months. Since she left me, since four months before the divorce came through."

Tony couldn't think of anything to say. He didn't feel he knew Frank well enough to engage in an intimate discussion of his sex life, yet it was obvious that the man badly needed someone to listen and care.

"If I don't get back in the swim pretty soon," Frank said, "I might as well go away and be a priest."

Tony nodded. "Ten months sure is a long time," he said awkwardly.

Frank didn't respond. He stared into his Scotch as he might have stared into a crystal ball, trying to see his future. Clearly, he wanted to talk about Wilma and the divorce and where he should go from here, but he didn't want to feel that he was forcing Tony to listen to his trouble. He had a lot of pride. He wanted to be coaxed, cajoled, drawn out with questions and murmured sympathy.

"Did Wilma find another man or what?" Tony asked, and knew immediately that he had gone to the heart of the matter much too quickly.

Frank was not ready to talk about that part of it, and he pretended not to hear the question. "What bothers me is the way I'm screwing up in my work. I've always been damned good at what I do. Just about perfect, if I say so myself. Until the divorce. Then I turned sour on women, and pretty soon I went sour on the job, too." He took a long pull on his Scotch. "And what the hell's going on with that damned crazy Napa County Sheriff? Why would he lie to protect Bruno Frye?"

"We'll find out sooner or later," Tony said.

"You want another drink?"

"Okay."

Tony could see that they were going to be sitting in The Bolt Hole for a long while. Frank wanted to talk about Wilma, wanted to get rid of all the poison that had been building up in him and eating at his heart for nearly a year, but he was only able to let it out a drop at a time.

•

It was a busy day for Death in Los Angeles. Many died of natural causes, of course, and therefore were not required by law to come under a coroner's probing scalpel. But the medical examiner's office had nine others with which to deal. There were two traffic fatalities in an accident certain to involve charges of criminal negligence. Two men were dead of gunshot wounds. One child had apparently been beaten to death by a mean-tempered drunken father. A woman had drowned in her own swimming pool, and two young men had died of what appeared to be drug overdoses. And there was Bruno Frye.

At 7:10 Thursday evening, hoping to catch up on the backlog of work, a pathologist at the city morgue completed a limited autopsy on the body of Bruno Gunther Frye, male, Caucasian, age forty. The doctor did not find it necessary to dissect the corpse beyond the general area of the two abdominal traumata, for he was swiftly able to determine that the deceased definitely had perished from those injuries and no other. The upper wound was not critical; the knife tore muscle tissue and grazed a lung. But the lower wound was a mess; the blade ripped open the stomach, pierced the pyloric vein, and damaged the pancreas, among other things. The victim had died of massive internal bleeding.

The pathologist sewed up the incisions he had made as well as the two crusted wounds. He sponged blood and bile and specks of tissue from the repaired stomach and the huge chest.

The dead man was transferred from the autopsy table (which still bore traces of red-brown gore in the stainless-steel blood gutters) to a cart. An attendant pushed the cart to a refrigerated room where other bodies, already cut open and explored and sewn up again, now waited patiently for their ceremonies and their graves.

After the attendant left, Bruno Frye lay silent and motionless, content in the company of the dead as he had never been in the company of the living.

•

Frank Howard was getting drunk. He had taken off his suit jacket and his tie, had opened the first two buttons of his shirt. His hair was in disarray because he kept running his fingers through it. His eyes were bloodshot, and his broad face was doughy. He slurred some of his words, and every once in a while he repeated himself, stressing a point so often that Tony had to gently nudge him on, as if bumping a phonograph needle out of a bad groove. He was downing two glasses of Scotch to one of Tony's beers.

The more he drank, the more he talked about the women in his life. The closer he got to being completely smashed, the closer he got to the central agony of his life: the loss of two wives.

During his second year as a uniformed officer with the LAPD, Frank Howard had met his first wife, Barbara Ann. She was a salesgirl working the jewelry counter in a downtown department store, and she helped him choose a gift for his mother. She was so charming, so petite, so pretty and dark-eyed, that he couldn't resist asking for a date, even though he was certain she would turn him down. She accepted. They were married seven months later. Barbara Ann was a planner; long before the wedding, she worked out a detailed agenda for their first four years together. She would continue to work at the department store, but they would not spend one penny of her earnings. All of her money would go into a savings account that would later be used to make a down payment on a house. They would try to save as much as they could from his salary by living in a safe, clean, but inexpensive studio apartment. They would sell his Pontiac because it was a gas hog, and because they would be living close enough to the store for Barbara Ann to walk to work; her Volkswagen would be sufficient to get him to and from divisional HQ, and his equity in his car would start the house fund. She had even planned a day-by-day menu for the first six months, nourishing meals prepared within a tight budget. Frank loved this stern accountant streak in her, partly because it seemed so out of character. She was a light-hearted, cheerful woman, quick to laugh, sometimes even giddy, impulsive in matters not financial, and a wonderful bedmate, always eager to make love and damned good at it. She was not an accountant in matters of the flesh; she never planned their love-making; it was usually sudden and surprising and passionate. But she planned that they would buy a house only after they'd acquired at least forty percent of the purchase price. And she knew exactly how many rooms it should have and what size each room should be; she drew up a floor plan of the ideal place, and she kept it in a dresser drawer, taking it out now and then to stare at it and dream. She wanted children a great deal, but she planned not to have them until she was secure in her own house. Barbara Ann planned for just about every eventuality—except cancer. She contracted a virulent form of lymph cancer, which was diagnosed two years and two days after she married Frank, and three months after that, she was dead.

Tony sat in the booth at The Bolt Hole, with a beer getting warm in front of him, and he listened to Frank Howard with the growing realization that this was the first time the man had shared his grief with anyone. Barbara Ann had died in 1958, twenty-two years ago, and in all the time since, Frank had not expressed to anyone the pain he had felt while watching her waste away and die. It was a pain that had never dwindled; it burned within him now as fiercely as it had then. He drank more Scotch and searched for words to describe his agony; and Tony was amazed at the sensitivity and depth of feeling that had been so well-concealed behind the hard Teutonic face and those usually expressionless blue eyes.

Losing Barbara Ann had left Frank weak, disconnected, miserable, but he had sternly repressed the tears and the anguish because he had been afraid that if he gave in to them he would not be able to regain control. He had sensed self-destructive impulses in himself: a terrible thirst for booze that he had never experienced prior to his wife's death; a tendency to drive much too fast and recklessly, though he had previously been a cautious driver. To improve his state of mind, to save himself from himself, he had submerged his pain in the demands of his job, had given his life to the LAPD, trying to forget Barbara Ann in long hours of police work and study. The loss of her left an aching hole in him that would never be filled, but in time he managed to plate over that hole with an obsessive interest in his work and with total dedication to the Department.

For nineteen years he survived, even thrived, on the monotonous regimen of a workaholic. As a uniformed officer, he could not extend his working hours, so he went to school five nights a week and Saturdays, until he earned a Bachelor of Science in Criminology. He used his degree and his superb service record to climb into the ranks of the plainclothes detectives, where he could labor well beyond his scheduled tour of duty each day without screwing up a dispatcher's roster. During his ten- and twelve- and fourteen-hour workdays, he thought of nothing else but the cases to which he had been assigned. Even when he wasn't on the job, he thought about current investigations to the exclusion of just about everything else, pondered them while standing in the shower and while trying to fall asleep at night, mulled over new evidence while eating his early breakfasts and his solitary late-night dinners. He read almost nothing but criminology textbooks and case studies of criminal types. For nineteen years he was a cop's cop, a detective's detective.

In all that time, he never got serious about a woman. He didn't have time for dating, and somehow it didn't seem right to him. It wasn't fair to Barbara Ann. He led a celibate's life for weeks, then indulged in a few nights of torrid release with a series of paid partners. In a way he could not fully understand, having sex with a hooker was not a betrayal of Barbara Ann's memory, for the exchange of cash for services made it strictly a business transaction and not a matter of the heart in even the slightest regard.

And then he met Wilma Compton.

Leaning back against the booth in The Bolt Hole, Frank seemed to choke on the woman's name. He wiped one hand across his clammy face, pushed spread fingers through his hair, and said, "I need another double Scotch." He made a great effort to articulate each syllable, but that only made him sound more thoroughly drunk than if he had slurred and mangled his words.

"Sure," Tony said. "Another Scotch. But we ought to get a bite of something, too."

"Not hungry," Frank said.

"They make excellent cheeseburgers," Tony said. "Let's get a couple of those and some French fries."

"No. Just Scotch for me."

Tony insisted, and finally Frank agreed to the burger but not the fries.

Penny took the food order, but when she heard Frank wanted another Scotch, she wasn't sure that was a good idea.

"I didn't drive here," Frank assured her, again stressing each sound in each word. "I came in a taxi 'cause I intended to get stupid drunk. I'll go home in a taxi, too. So please, you dimpled little darling, bring me another of those delicious double Scotches."

Tony nodded at her. "If he can't get a cab later, I'll take him home."

She brought new drinks for both of them. A half-finished beer stood in front of Tony, but it was warm and flat, and Penny took it away.

Wilma Compton.

Wilma was twelve years younger than Frank, thirty-one when he first met her. She was charming, petite, pretty, and dark-eyed. Slender legs. Supple body. Exciting swell of hips. A tight little ass. A pinched waist and breasts a shade too full for her size. She wasn't quite as lovely or quite as charming or quite as petite as Barbara Ann had been. She didn't have Barbara Ann's quick wit or Barbara Ann's industrious nature or Barbara Ann's compassion. But on the surface, at least, she bore enough resemblance to the long-dead woman to stir Frank's dormant interest in romance.

Wilma was a waitress at a coffee shop where policemen often ate lunch. The sixth time she waited on Frank, he asked for a date, and she said yes. On their fourth date, they went to bed. Wilma had the same hunger and energy and willingness to experiment that had made Barbara Ann a wonderful lover. If at times she seemed totally concerned with her own gratification and not at all interested in his, Frank was able to convince himself that her selfishness would pass, that it was merely the result of her not having had a satisfying relationship in a long time. Besides, he was proud that he could arouse her so easily, so completely. For the first time since he'd slept with Barbara Ann, love was a part of his lovemaking, and he'd thought he perceived the same emotion in Wilma's response to him. After they had been sleeping together for two months, he asked her to marry him. She said no, and thereafter she no longer wanted to date him; the only time he could see her and talk to her was when he stopped at the coffee shop.

Wilma was admirably forthright about her reasons for refusing him.

She wanted to get married; she was actively looking for the right man, but the right man had to have a substantial bankroll and a damned good job. A cop, she said, would never make enough money to provide her with the lifestyle and the security she wanted. Her first marriage had failed largely because she and her husband had always been arguing about bills and budgets. She had discovered that worries about finances could burn the love out of a relationship, leaving only an ashy shell of bitterness and anger. That had been a terrible experience, and she had made up her mind never to go through it again. She didn't rule out marrying for love, but there had to be financial security as well. She was afraid she sounded hard, but she could not endure the kind of pain she had endured before. She got all shaky-voiced and teary-eyed when she spoke of it. She would not, she said, risk the unbearably sad and depressing dissolution of another love affair because of a lack of money.

Strangely, her determination to marry for money did not decrease Frank's respect for her or dampen his ardor. Because he had been lonely for so long, he was eager to continue their relationship, even if he had to wear the biggest pair of rose-colored glasses ever made in order to maintain the illusion of romance. He revealed his financial situation to her, virtually begged her to look at his savings account passbook and short-term certificates of deposit which totaled nearly thirty-two thousand dollars. He told her what his salary was and carefully explained that he would be able to retire fairly young with a fine pension, young enough to use some of their savings to start a small business and earn even more money. If security was what she wanted, he was her man.

Thirty-two thousand dollars and a police pension were not sufficient for Wilma Compton. "I mean," she said, "it's a good little piece of change, but then you don't own a house or anything, Frank." She fingered the savings account passbooks for a long moment, as if receiving sexual pleasure from them, but then she handed them back and said, "Sorry, Frank. But I want to shoot for something better than this. I'm still young, and I look five years younger than I really am. I have some time yet, a little more time to look around. And I'm afraid that even thirty-two thousand isn't a big bankroll these days. I'm afraid it might not be enough to get us through some crisis. And I won't go into something with you if there's a chance it could . . . get hateful . . . and mean . . . like it did the last time I was married."

He was crushed.

"Christ, I was acting like such a fool!" Frank wailed, pounding one fist into the table to emphasize his foolishness. "I had made up my mind that she was exactly like Barbara Ann, something special, someone rare and precious. No matter what she did, no matter how crude she was or how coarse or how unfeeling, I made excuses for her. Lovely excuses. Dandy, elaborate, creative excuses. Stupid. I was stupid, stupid, dumb as a jackass. Jesus!"

"What you did was understandable," Tony said.

"It was stupid."

"You were alone a long, long time," Tony said. "You had such a wonderful two years with Barbara Ann that you thought you'd never have anything half as good again, and you didn't want to settle for less. So you shut out the world. You convinced yourself that you didn't need anyone. But we all need someone, Frank. We all need people to care about. A hunger for love and comradeship is as natural to our species as the requirement for food and water. So the need built up inside of you all those years, and when you saw someone who resembled Barbara Ann, when you saw Wilma, you couldn't keep that need bottled up any longer. Nineteen years of wanting and needing came bubbling out of you all at once. You were bound to act kind of crazy. It would have been nice if Wilma had turned out to be a good woman who deserved what you had to offer. But you know, actually, it's surprising someone like Wilma didn't get her claws into you years ago."

"I was a sap."

"No."

"An idiot."

"No, Frank. You were human," Tony said. "That's all. Just human like the rest of us."

Penny brought the cheeseburgers.

Frank ordered another double Scotch.

"You want to know what made Wilma change her mind?" Frank asked. "You want to know why she finally agreed to marry me?"

"Sure," Tony said. "But why don't you eat your burger first."

Frank ignored the sandwich. "My father died and left me everything. At first it looked like maybe thirty thousand bucks, but then I discovered the old man had collected a bunch of five- and ten-thousand dollar life insurance policies over the past thirty years. After taxes, the estate amounted to ninety thousand dollars."

"I'll be damned."

"With what I had already," Frank said, "that windfall was enough for Wilma."

"Maybe you'd have been better off if your father had died poor," Tony said.

Frank's red-rimmed eyes grew watery, and for a moment he looked as if he was about to weep. But he blinked rapidly and held back the tears. In a voice laden with despair, he said, "I'm ashamed to admit it, but when I found out how much money was in the estate, I stopped caring about my old man dying. The insurance policies turned up just one week after I buried him, and the moment I found them I thought, *Wilma.* All of a sudden I was so damned happy I couldn't stand still. As far as I was concerned, my dad might as well have been dead twenty years. It makes me sick to my stomach to think how I behaved. I mean, my dad and I weren't really close, but I owed him a lot more grieving than I gave. Jesus, I was one selfish son of a bitch, Tony."

"It's over, Frank. It's done," Tony said. "And like I said, you were a bit crazy. You weren't exactly responsible for your actions."

Frank put both hands over his face and sat that way for a minute, shaking but not crying. Finally, he looked up and said, "So when she saw I had almost a hundred and twenty-five thousand dollars, Wilma wanted to marry me. In eight months, she cleaned me out."

"This is a community property state," Tony said. "How could she get more than half of what you had?"

"Oh, she didn't take anything in the divorce."

"What?"

"Not one penny."

"Why?"

"It was all gone by then."

"Gone?"

"Poof!"

"She spent it?"

"Stole it," Frank said numbly.

Tony put down his cheeseburger, wiped his mouth with a napkin. "Stole it? How?"

Frank was still quite drunk, but suddenly he spoke with an eerie clarity and precision. It seemed important to him that this indictment of her, more than anything else in his story, should be clearly understood. She had left him nothing but his indignation, and now he wanted to share that with Tony. "As soon as we got back from our honeymoon, she announced she was taking over the bookkeeping. She was going to attend to all our banking business, watch over our investments, balance our checkbook.

She signed up for a course in investment planning at a business school, and she worked out a detailed budget for us. She was very adamant about it, very businesslike, and I was really pleased because she seemed so much like Barbara Ann."

"You'd told her that Barbara Ann had done those things?"

"Yeah. Oh, Jesus, yeah. I set myself up to be picked clean. I sure did."

Suddenly, Tony wasn't hungry any more.

Frank pushed one shaky hand through his hair. "See, there wasn't any way I could have suspected her. I mean, she was so good to me. She learned to cook my favorite things. She always wanted to hear about my day when I got home, and she listened with such interest. She didn't want a lot of clothes or jewelry or anything. We went out to dinner and to the movies now and then, but she always said it was a waste of money; she said she was just as happy staying home with me and watching TV together or just talking. She wasn't in any hurry to buy a house. She was so . . . easy-going. She gave me massages when I came home stiff and sore. And in bed . . . she was fabulous. She was perfect. Except . . . except . . . all the time she was cooking and listening and massaging and fucking my brains out, she was . . ."

"Bleeding your joint bank accounts."

"Of every last dollar. All except ten thousand that was in a long-term certificate of deposit."

"And then just walked out?"

Frank shuddered. "I came home one day, and there was a note from her. It said, 'If you want to know where I am, call this number and ask for Mr. Freyborn.' Freyborn was a lawyer. She'd hired him to handle the divorce. I was stunned. I mean, there was never any indication. . . . Anyway, Freyborn refused to tell me where she was. He said it would be a simple case, easily settled because she didn't want alimony or anything else from me. She didn't want a penny, Freyborn said. She just wanted out. I was hit hard. Real hard. Jesus, I couldn't figure out what I'd done. For a while, I nearly went crazy trying to figure out where I went wrong. I thought maybe I could change, learn to be a better person, and win her back. And then . . . two days later, when I needed to write a check, I saw the account was down to three dollars. I went to the bank and then to the savings and loan company, and after that I knew why she didn't want a penny. She'd taken all the pennies already."

"You didn't let her get away with it," Tony said.

Frank slugged down some Scotch. He was sweating. His face was pasty and sheet-white. "At first, I was just kind of dumb and . . . I don't know . . . suicidal, I guess. I mean, I didn't try to kill myself, but I didn't care if I lived either. I was in a daze, a kind of trance."

"But eventually you snapped out of that."

"Part way. I'm still a little numb. But I came part of the way out of it," Frank said. "Then I was ashamed of myself. I was ashamed of what I'd let her do to me. I was such a sap, such a dumb son of a bitch. I didn't want anyone to know, not even my attorney."

"That's the first purely stupid thing you did," Tony said. "I can understand the rest of it, but that—"

"Somehow, it seemed to me that if I let everyone know how Wilma conned me, then everyone would think that every word I'd ever said about Barbara Ann was wrong, too. I was afraid people would get the idea that Barbara Ann had been conning me just like Wilma, and it was important to me, more important than anything else in the world, that Barbara Ann's memory be kept clean. I know it sounds a little crazy now, but that's how I looked at it then."

Tony didn't know what to say.

"So the divorce went through smooth as glass," Frank said. "There weren't any long discussions about the details of the settlement. In fact, I never got to see Wilma again except for a few minutes in court, and I haven't talked to her since the morning of the day she walked out."

"Where is she now? Do you know?"

Frank finished his Scotch. When he spoke his voice was different, soft, almost a whisper, not as if he was trying to keep the rest of the story secret from other customers in The Hole, but as if he no longer had sufficient strength to speak in a normal tone of voice. "After the divorce went through, I got curious about her. I took out a small loan against that certificate of deposit she'd left behind, and I hired a private investigator to find out where she was and what she was doing. He turned up a lot of stuff. Very interesting stuff. She got married again just nine days after our divorce was final. Some guy named Chuck Pozley down in Orange County. He owns one of those electronic game parlors in a shopping center in Costa Mesa. He's worth maybe seventy or eighty thousand bucks. The way it looks, Wilma was seriously thinking about marrying him just when I inherited all the money from my dad. So what she did, she married me, milked me dry, and then went to this Chuck Pozley with my money. They used some of her capital to open two more of those game parlors, and it looks like they'll do real well."

"Oh, Jeez," Tony said.

This morning he had known almost nothing at all about Frank Howard, and now he knew almost everything. More than he really wanted to know. He was a good listener; that was both his blessing and his curse. His previous partner, Michael Savatino, often told him that he was a superior detective largely because people liked and trusted him and were willing to talk to him about almost anything. And the reason they were willing to talk to him, Michael said, was because he was a good listener. And a good listener, Michael said, was a rare and wonderful thing in a world of self-interest, self-promotion, and self-love. Tony listened willingly and attentively to all sorts of people because, as a painter fascinated by hidden patterns, he was seeking the overall pattern of human existence and meaning. Even now, as he listened to Frank, he thought of a quote from Emerson that he had read a long time ago: *The Sphinx must solve her own riddle. If the whole of history is in one man, it is all to be explained from individual experience.* All men and women and children were fascinating puzzles, great mysteries, and Tony was seldom bored by their stories.

Still speaking so softly that Tony had to lean forward to hear him, Frank said, "Pozley knew what Wilma had in mind for me. It looks like they were probably seeing each other a couple of days a week while I was at work. All the time she was playing the perfect wife, she was stealing me blind and fucking this Pozley. The more I thought about it, the madder I got, until finally I decided to tell my attorney what I should have told him in the first place."

"But it was too late?"

"That's about what it comes down to. Oh, I could have initiated some sort of court action against her. But the fact that I hadn't accused her of theft earlier, during the divorce proceedings, would have weighed pretty heavily against me. I'd have spent most of the money I had left on lawyers' fees, and I'd probably have lost the suit anyway. So I decided to put it behind me. I figured I'd lose myself in my work, like I'd done after Barbara Ann died. But I was torn up a whole lot worse than I realized. I couldn't do my job right any more. Every woman I had to deal with . . . I don't know. I guess I just . . . just saw Wilma in all women. If I had the slightest excuse, I got downright vicious with women I had to question, and then before long I was getting too rough with *every* witness, both men and women. I started losing perspective, overlooking clues a child would spot. . . . I had a hell of a falling out with my partner, and so here I am." His voice sank lower by the second, and he gave up the struggle for clarity; his words began to get mushy. "After Barbara Ann died, at least I had my work. At least I had somethin'. But Wilma took everythin'. She took my money and my self-respec', and she even took my ambition. I juss can't seem to care 'bout nothin' any more." He slid out of the booth and stood up, swaying like a toy clown that had springs for ankles. "S'cuse me. Gotta go pee." He staggered across the tavern to the men's room door, giving an exaggerated wide berth to everyone he encountered on the way.

Tony sighed and closed his eyes. He was weary, both in body and soul.

Penny stopped by the table and said, "You'd be doing him a favor if you took him home now. He's going to feel like a half-dead goat in the morning."

"What's a half-dead goat feel like?"

"A lot worse than a healthy goat, and a whole lot worse than a dead one," she said.

Tony paid the tab and waited for his partner. After five minutes, he picked up Frank's coat and tie and went looking for him.

The men's room was small: one stall, one urinal, one sink. It smelled strongly of pine-scented disinfectant and vaguely of urine.

Frank was standing at a graffiti-covered wall, his back to the door when Tony entered. He was pounding his open palms against the wall above his head, both hands at once, making loud slapping sounds that reverberated in the narrow high-ceilinged room. BAM-BAM-BAM-BAM-BAM! The noise wasn't audible in the barroom because of the dull roar of conversation and the music, but in here it hurt Tony's ears.

"Frank?"

BAM-BAM-BAM-BAM-BAM-BAM-BAM!

Tony went to him, put a hand on his shoulder, pulled him gently away from the wall, and turned him around.

Frank was weeping. His eyes were bloodshot and filled with tears. Big tears streamed down his face. His lips were puffy and loose; his mouth quivered with grief. But he was crying soundlessly, neither sobbing nor whimpering, his voice stuck far back in his throat.

"It's okay," Tony said. "Everything will be all right. You don't need Wilma. You're better off without her. You've got friends. We'll help you get over this, Frank, if you'll just let us. I'll help. I care. I really do care, Frank."

Frank closed his eyes. His mouth sagged down, and he sobbed, but still in eerie silence, making noise only when he sucked in a wheezy breath. He reached out, seeking support, and Tony put an arm around him.

"Wanna go home," Frank said mushily. "I juss wanna go home."

"All right. I'll take you home. Just hold on."

With arms around each other, like old buddies from the war, they left The Bolt Hole. They walked two and a half blocks to the apartment complex where Tony lived and climbed into Tony's Jeep station wagon.

They were halfway to Frank's apartment when Frank took a deep breath and said, "Tony . . . I'm afraid."

Tony glanced at him.

Frank was hunched down in his seat. He seemed small and weak; his clothes looked too big for him. Tears shone on his face.

"What are you afraid of?" Tony asked.

"I don't wanna be alone," Frank said, weeping thinly, shaking from the effects of too much liquor, but shaking from something else as well, some dark fear.

"You aren't alone," Tony said.

"I'm afraid of . . . dyin' alone."

"You aren't alone, and you aren't dying, Frank."

"We all get old . . . so fast. And then. . . . I want someone to be there."

"You'll find someone."

"I want someone to remember and care."

"Don't worry," Tony said lamely.

"It scares me."

"You'll find someone."

"Never."

"Yes. You will."

"Never. Never," Frank said, closing his eyes and leaning his head against the side window.

By the time they got to Frank's apartment house, he was sleeping like a child. Tony tried to wake him. But Frank would not come fully to his senses. Stumbling, mumbling, sighing heavily, he allowed himself to be half-walked, half-carried to the door of the apartment. Tony propped him against the wall beside the front door, held him up with one hand, felt through his pockets, found the key. When they finally reached the bedroom, Frank collapsed on the mattress in a loose-limbed heap and began to snore.

Tony undressed him down to his shorts. He pulled back the covers, rolled Frank onto the bottom sheet, pulled the top sheet and the blanket over him. Frank just snuffled and snored.

In the kitchen, in a junk drawer beside the sink, Tony found a pencil, a pad of writing paper, and a roll of Scotch tape. He wrote a note to Frank and taped it to the refrigerator door.

> *Dear Frank,*
> *When you wake up in the morning, you're going to remember every-*
> *thing you told me, and you're probably going to be a little embar-*
> *rassed. Don't worry. What you told me will stay strictly between us.*
> *And tomorrow I'll tell you some outrageously embarrassing secrets of*
> *my own, so then we'll be even. After all, cleaning the soul is one thing*
> *friends are for.*
>
> *Tony.*

He locked the door on his way out.

Driving home, he thought about poor Frank being all alone, and then he realized that his own situation was not markedly better. His father was still alive, but Carlo was sick a lot these days and probably would not live more than five years, ten at the most. Tony's brothers and sisters were spread all over the country, and none of them was really close in spirit either. He had a great many friends, but it was not just friends that you wanted by you when you were old and dying. He knew what Frank had meant. When you were on your deathbed, there were only certain hands that you could hold and from which you could draw courage: the hands of your spouse, your children, or your parents. He realized that he was building the kind of life that, when complete, might well be a hollow temple of loneliness. He was thirty-five, still young, but he had never truly given much serious thought to marriage. Suddenly, he had the feeling that time was slipping through his fingers. The years went by so very fast. It seemed only last year that he had been twenty-five, but a decade was gone.

Maybe Hilary Thomas is the one, he thought as he pulled into the parking slot in front of his apartment. She's special. I can see that. Very special. Maybe she'll think I'm someone special, too. It could work out for us. Couldn't it?

For a while he sat in the Jeep, staring at the night sky, thinking about Hilary Thomas and about getting old and dying alone.

•

At 10:30, when Hilary was deeply involved in the James Clavell novel, just as she was finishing a snack of apples and cheese, the telephone rang.

"Hello?"

There was only silence on the other end of the line.

"Who's there?"

Nothing.

She slammed the receiver down. That's what they told you to do when you got a threatening or obscene phone call. Just hang up. Don't encourage the caller. Just hang up quickly and sharply. She had given him a real pain in the ear, but that didn't make her feel a lot better.

She was sure it wasn't a wrong number. Not twice in one night with no apology either time. Besides, there had been a menacing quality in that silence, an unspoken threat.

Even after she had been nominated for the Academy Award, she had never felt the need for an unlisted number. Writers were not celebrities in the same sense that actors and even directors were. The general public never remembered or cared who earned the screenplay credit on a hit picture. Most writers who got unlisted numbers did it because it seemed prestigious; unlisted meant the harried scribbler was so busy with so many important projects that he had no time for even the rare unwanted call. But she didn't have an ego problem like that, and leaving her name in the book was just as anonymous as taking it out.

Of course, maybe that was no longer true. Perhaps the media reports about her two encounters with Bruno Frye had made her an object of general interest where her two successful screenplays had not. The story of a woman fighting off a would-be rapist and killing him the second time— that might very well fascinate a certain kind of sick mind. It might make some animal out there eager to prove he could succeed where Bruno Frye had failed.

She decided to call the telephone company business office first thing in the morning and ask for a new, unlisted number.

•

At midnight, the city morgue was, as the medical examiner himself had once described it, quiet as a tomb. The dimly lighted hallway was silent. The laboratory was dark. The room full of corpses was cold and lightless and still except for the insect hum of the blowers that pumped chill air through the wall vents.

As Thursday night changed to Friday morning, only one man was on duty in the morgue. He was in a small chamber adjacent to the M.E.'s private office. He was sitting in a spring-backed chair at an ugly metal and walnut-veneer desk. His name was Albert Wolwicz. He was twenty-nine years old, divorced, and the father of one child, a daughter named Rebecca. His wife had won custody of Becky. They both lived in San Diego now. Albert didn't mind working the (you should forgive the expression) graveyard shift. He did a little filing, then just sat and listened to the radio for a while, then did a bit more filing, then read a few chapters of a really good Stephen King novel about vampires on the loose in New England; and if the city remained cool all night, if the uniformed bulls and the meat wagon boys didn't start running in stretchers from gang fights or freeway accidents, it would be sweet duty all the way through to quitting time.

At ten minutes past midnight, the phone rang.

Albert picked it up. "Morgue."

Silence.

"Hello," Albert said.

The man on the other end of the line groaned in agony and began to cry.

"Who is this?"

Weeping, the caller could not respond.

The tortured sounds were almost a parody of grief, an exaggerated and hysterical sobbing that was the strangest thing Albert had ever heard. "If you'll tell me what's wrong, maybe I can help."

The caller hung up.

Albert stared at the receiver for a moment, finally shrugged and put it down.

He tried to pick up where he'd left off in the Stephen King novel, but he kept thinking he heard something shuffling through the doorway behind him. He turned around half a dozen times, but there was never anyone (or anything) there.

chapter four

Friday morning.

Nine o'clock.

Two men from Angels' Hill Mortuary of West Los Angeles arrived at the city morgue to claim the body of Bruno Gunther Frye. They were working in association with the Forever View Funeral Home in the town of St. Helena, where the deceased had lived. One man from Angels' Hill signed the necessary release, and both men transferred the corpse from cold storage to the back of a Cadillac hearse.

•

Frank Howard did not appear to have a hangover. His complexion did not have that after-the-binge sallowness; he was ruddy and healthy-looking. His blue eyes were clear. Confession apparently was every bit as good for the soul as the proverb promised.

At first in the office, then in the car, Tony sensed the awkwardness he had anticipated, and he did his best to make Frank feel comfortable. In time, Frank seemed to realize that nothing had changed for the worse between them; indeed, the partnership was working far better than it had during the past three months. By mid-morning, they had established a degree of rapport that would make it possible for them to learn to function together almost as a single organism. They still did not interact with the perfect harmony that Tony had experienced with Michael Savatino, but now there did not seem to be any obstacles to the development of precisely that sort of deep relationship. They needed some time to adjust to each other, a few more months, but eventually they would share a psychic bond that would make their job immeasurably easier than it had been in the past.

Friday morning, they worked on leads in the Bobby Valdez case. There were not many trails to follow, and the first two led nowhere.

The Department of Motor Vehicles report on Juan Mazquezza was the first disappointment. Apparently, Bobby Valdez had used a phony birth certificate and other false ID to obtain a valid driver's license under the name Juan Mazquezza. But the last address the DMV could provide was the one from which Bobby had moved last July, the Las Palmeras Apartments on La Brea Avenue. There were two other Juan Mazquezzas in the DMV files. One was a nineteen-year-old boy who lived in Fresno. The other Juan was a sixty-seven-year-old man in Tustin. They both owned automobiles with California registrations, but neither of them had a Jaguar. The Juan Mazquezza who had lived on La Brea Avenue had never registered a car, which meant that Bobby had bought the Jaguar using yet another phony name. Evidently, he had a source for forged documents of extremely high quality.

Dead end.

Tony and Frank returned to the Vee Vee Gee Laundry and questioned the employees who had worked with Bobby when he'd been using the Mazquezza name. They hoped that someone would have kept in touch with him after he quit his job and would know where he was living now. But everyone said Juan had been a loner; no one knew where he'd gone.

Dead end.

After they left Vee Vee Gee, they went to lunch at an omelet house that Tony liked. In addition to the main dining room, the restaurant had an open-air brick terrace where a dozen tables stood under blue- and white-striped umbrellas. Tony and Frank ate salads and cheese omelets in the warm autumn breeze.

"You doing anything tomorrow night?" Tony asked.

"Me?"

"You."

"No. Nothing."

"Good. I've arranged something."

"What?"

"A blind date."

"For me?"

"You're half of it."

"Are you serious?"

"I called her this morning."

"Forget it," Frank said.

"She's perfect for you."

"I hate match-making."

"She's a gorgeous woman."

"Not interested."

"And sweet."

"I'm not a kid."

"Who said you were?"

"I don't need you to fix me up with someone."

"Sometimes a guy does that for a friend. Doesn't he?"

"I can find my own dates."

"Only a fool would turn down this lady."

"Then I'm a fool."

Tony sighed. "Suit yourself."

"Look, what I said last night at The Bolt Hole . . ."

"Yeah?"

"I wasn't looking for sympathy."

"Everybody needs some sympathy now and then."

"I just wanted you to understand why I've been in such a foul mood."

"And I do understand."

"I didn't mean to give you the impression that I'm a jerk, that I'm a sucker for the wrong kind of woman."

"You didn't give me that impression at all."

"I've never broken down like that before."

"I believe it."

"I've never . . . cried like that."

"I know."

"I guess I was just tired."

"Sure."

"Maybe it was all that liquor."

"Maybe."

"I drank a lot last night."

"Quite a lot."

"The liquor made me sentimental."

"Maybe."

"But now I'm all right."

"Who said you weren't?"

"I can get my own dates, Tony."

"Whatever you say."

"Okay?"

"Okay."

They concentrated on their cheese omelets.

There were several large office buildings nearby, and dozens of secretaries in bright dresses paraded past on the sidewalk, going to lunch.

Flowers ringed the restaurant terrace and perfumed the sun-coppered air.

The noise on the street was typically that of L.A. It wasn't the incessant barking of brakes and screaming of horns that you heard in New York or Chicago or most other cities. Just the hypnotic grumble of engines. And the air-cutting *whoosh* of passing cars. A lulling noise. Soothing. Like the tide on the beach. Made by machines but somehow natural, primal. Also subtly and inexpressibly erotic. Even the sounds of the traffic conformed to the city's subconscious subtropical personality.

After a couple of minutes of silence, Frank said, "What's her name?"

"Who?"

"Don't be a smartass."

"Janet Yamada."

"Japanese?"

"Does she sound Italian?"

"What's she like?"

"Intelligent, witty, good-looking."

"What's she do?"

"Works at city hall."

"How old is she?"

"Thirty-six, thirty-seven."

"Too young for me?"

"You're only forty-five, for God's sake."

"How'd you come to know her?"

"We dated for a while," Tony said.

"What went wrong?"

"Nothing. We just discovered we make better friends than lovers."

"You think I'll like her?"

"Positive."

"And she'll like me?"

"If you don't pick your nose or eat with your hands."

"Okay," Frank said. "I'll go out with her."

"If it's going to be an ordeal for you, maybe we should just forget it."

"No. I'll go. It'll be okay."

"You don't have to do it just to please me."

"Give me her phone number."

"I don't feel right about this," Tony said. "I feel like I've forced you into something."

"You haven't forced me."

"I think I should call her and cancel the arrangements," Tony said.

"No, listen, I—"

"I shouldn't try to be a matchmaker. I'm lousy at it."

"Dammit, I *want* to go out with her!" Frank said.

Tony smiled broadly. "I know."

"Have I just been manipulated?"

"You manipulated yourself."

Frank tried to scowl, but couldn't. He grinned instead. "Want to double-date Saturday night?"

"No way. You've got to stand on your own, my friend."

"And besides," Frank said knowingly, "you don't want to share Hilary Thomas with anyone else."

"Exactly."

"You really think it can work with you two?"

"You make it sound like we're planning to get married. It's just a date."

"But even for a date, won't it be . . . awkward?"

"Why should it be?" Tony asked.

"Well, she's got all that money."

"That's a male chauvinist remark if I ever heard one."

"You don't think that'll make it difficult?"

"When a *man* has some money, does he have to limit his dating to women who have an equal amount of money?"

"That's different."

"When a king decides to marry a shopgirl, we think it's too romantic for words. But when a queen wants to marry a shopboy, we think she's letting herself be played for a fool. Classic double standard."

"Well . . . good luck."

"And to you as well."

"Ready to go back to work?"

"Yeah," Tony said. "Let's find Bobby Valdez."

"Judge Crater might be easier."

"Or Amelia Earhart."

"Or Jimmy Hoffa."

•

Friday afternoon.

One o'clock.

The body lay on an embalming table at Angels' Hill Mortuary in West Los Angeles. A tag wired to the big toe on the right foot identified the deceased as Bruno Gunther Frye.

A death technician prepared the body for shipment to Napa County. He swabbed it down with a long-lasting disinfectant. The intestines and other soft abdominal organs were pulled out of the dead man through the only available natural body opening and discarded. Because of the stab wounds and the autopsy that had taken place the previous night, there was not much unclotted blood or other fluids remaining in the corpse, but those last few dollops were forced out nonetheless; embalming fluid took their place.

The technician whistled a Donny and Marie Osmond hit while he labored over the dead man.

The Angels' Hill Mortuary was not responsible for any cosmetic work on the corpse. That would be handled by the mortician in St. Helena. The Angels' Hill technician merely tucked the sightless eyes shut forever and sewed up the lips with a series of tight interior stitches which froze the wide mouth in a vague eternal smile. It was a neat job; none of the sutures would be visible to the mourners—if there were any mourners.

Next, the deceased was wrapped in an opaque white shroud and put into a cheap aluminum coffin that met minimum construction and seal standards set by the state for the conveyance of a dead body by any and all means of public transportation. In St. Helena, it would be transferred to a more impressive casket, one that would be chosen by the family or friends of the loved one.

At 4:00 Friday afternoon, the body was taken to the Los Angeles International Airport and put into the cargo hold of a California Airways propjet destined for Monterey, Santa Rosa, and Sacramento. It would be taken off the plane at the second stop.

At 6:30 Friday evening, in Santa Rosa, there was no one from Bruno Frye's family at the small airport. He had no relatives. He was the last of his line. His grandfather had brought only one child into the world, a lovely daughter named Katherine, and she had produced no children at all. Bruno was adopted. He never had married.

Three people waited on the Tarmac behind the small terminal, and two of them were from the Forever View Funeral Home. Mr. Avril Thomas Tannerton was the owner of Forever View, which served St. Helena and the surrounding communities in that part of the Napa Valley. He was forty-three, good-looking, slightly pudgy but not fat, with lots of reddish-blond hair, a scattering of freckles, lively eyes, and an easy warm smile that he had difficulty suppressing. He had come to Santa Rosa with his twenty-four-year-old assistant, Gary Olmstead, a slightly-built man who seldom talked more than the dead with whom he worked. Tannerton made you think of a choirboy, a veneer of genuine piety over a core of good-natured mischievousness; but Olmstead had a long, mournful, ascetic face perfectly suited to his profession.

The third man was Joshua Rhinehart, Bruno Frye's local attorney and executor of the Frye estate. He was sixty-one years old, and he had the looks that would have contributed to a successful career as a diplomat or politician. His hair was thick and white, swept back from brow and temples, not chalk-white, not yellow-white, but a lustrous silver-white. A broad forehead. A long proud nose. A strong jaw and chin. His coffee-brown eyes were quick and clear.

The body of Bruno Frye was transferred from the aircraft to the hearse, then driven back to St. Helena. Joshua Rhinehart followed in his own car.

Neither business nor personal obligations had required Joshua to make this trip to Santa Rosa with Avril Tannerton. Over the years, he had done quite a lot of work for Shade Tree Vineyards, the company that had been wholly owned by the Frye family for three generations, but he had long ago ceased to need the income from that account, and in fact it had become considerably more trouble than it was worth. He continued to handle the Frye family's affairs largely because he still remembered the time, thirty-five years ago, when he had been struggling to build a practice in rural Napa County and had been helped immeasurably by Katherine Frye's decision to give him all the family's legal business. Yesterday, when he heard that Bruno was dead, he hadn't grieved at all. Neither Katherine nor her adopted son had ever inspired affection, and they most certainly had not encouraged the special emotional ties of friendship. Joshua accompanied Avril Tannerton to the Santa Rosa airport only because he wanted to be in a position to manage the arrival of the corpse in case any reporters showed up and tried to turn the event into a circus. Although Bruno had been an unstable man, a very sick man, perhaps even a profoundly evil man, Joshua was determined that the funeral would be carried out with dignity. He felt he owed the dead man that much. Besides, for most of his life, Joshua was a stalwart supporter and promoter of the Napa Valley, championing both its quality of life and its magnificent wine, and he did not want to see the fabric of the entire community stained by the criminal acts of one man.

Fortunately, there had not been a single reporter at the airport.

They drove back to St. Helena through creeping shadows and dying light, east from Santa Rosa, across the southern end of the Sonoma Valley, into the five-mile-wide Napa Valley, then north in the purple-yellow gloaming. As he followed the hearse, Joshua admired the countryside, something he had done with ever-increasing pleasure for the last thirty-five years. The looming mountain ridges were thick with pine and fir and birch, lighted only along their crests by the westering sun, already out of sight; those ridges were ramparts, Joshua thought, great walls keeping out the corrupting influences of a less civilized world than that which lay within. Below the mountains the rolling hills were studded with black-trunked oaks and covered with long dry grass that, in the daylight, looked as blond and soft as cornsilk; but now in the gathering dusk which leeched away its color, the grass shimmered in dark waves, awash in the ebb and glow of a gentle breeze. Beyond the boundaries of the small quaint towns, endless vineyards sprang up on some of the hills and on nearly all of the rich flatland. In 1880, Robert Louis Stevenson had written of the Napa Valley: "One corner of land after another is tried with one kind of grape after another. This is a failure; that is better; a third is best. So, bit by bit, they grope about for their Clos Vougeot and Lafite . . . and the wine is bottled poetry." When Stevenson had been honeymooning in the valley and writing *Silverado Squatters*, there had been fewer than four thousand acres in vines. By the coming of the Great Plague—Prohibition—in 1920, there had been ten thousand acres producing viniferous grapes. Today, there were thirty thousand acres bringing forth grapes that were far sweeter and less acidic than those grown anywhere else in the world, as much productive land as in all of the Sonoma Valley, which was twice as large as the Napa. Tucked in among the vineyards were the great wineries and houses, some of them converted from abbeys and monasteries and Spanish-style missions, others built along clean modern lines. Thank God, Joshua thought, only a couple of the newer wineries had opted for the sterile factory look that was an insult to the eye and a blight upon the valley. Most of man's handiwork either complemented or at least did not intrude upon the truly dazzling natural beauty of his unique and idyllic place. As he followed the hearse toward Forever View, Joshua saw lights come on in the windows of the houses, soft yellow lights that brought a sense of warmth and civilization to the encroaching night. The wine *is* bottled poetry, Joshua thought, and the land from which it comes is God's greatest work of art; my land; my home; how lucky I am to be here when there are so many less charming, less pleasant places in which I might have wound up.

Like in an aluminum coffin, dead.

Forever View stood a hundred yards back from the two-lane highway, just south of St. Helena. It was a big white colonial-style house with a circular driveway, marked by a tasteful white and green hand-painted sign. As darkness fell, a single white spotlight came on automatically, softly illuminating the sign; and a low row of electric carriage lamps marked the circular driveway with a curve of amber light.

There were no reporters waiting at Forever View either. Joshua was pleased to see that the Napa County press evidently shared his strong aversion to unnecessary bad publicity.

Tannerton drove the hearse around to the rear of the huge white house. He and Olmstead slid the coffin onto a cart and wheeled it inside.

Joshua joined them in the mortician's workroom.

An effort had been made to give the chamber an airy cheerful ambience. The ceiling was covered with prettily textured acoustical tile. The walls were painted pale blue, the blue of a robin's egg, the blue of a baby's blanket, the blue of new life. Tannerton touched a wall switch, and lilting music came from stereo speakers, bright soaring music, nothing somber, nothing heavy.

To Joshua, at least, the place reeked of death in spite of everything that Avril Tannerton had done to make it cosy. The air bore traces of the pungent fumes from embalming fluid, and there was a sweet cover-up aerosol scent of carnations that only reminded him of funeral bouquets. The floor was glossy white ceramic tile, freshly scrubbed, a bit slippery for anyone not wearing rubber-soled shoes; Tannerton and Gary Olmstead were wearing them, but Joshua was not. At first, the tile gave an impression of openness and cleanliness, but then Joshua realized the floor was grimly utilitarian; it had to have a stainproof surface that would resist the corroding effects of spilled blood and bile and other even more noxious substances.

Tannerton's clients, the relatives of the deceased, would never be brought into this room, for the bitter truth of death was too obvious here.

In the front of the house, where the viewing chambers were decorated with heavy wine-red velvet drapes and plush carpets and dark wood paneling and brass lamps, where the lighting was low and artfully arranged, the phrases "passed away" and "called home by God" could be taken seriously; in the front rooms, the atmosphere encouraged a belief in heaven and the ascendance of the spirit. But in the tile-floored workroom with the lingering stink of embalming fluid and the shiny array of mortician's instruments lined up on enamel trays, death seemed depressingly clinical and unquestionably final.

Olmstead opened the aluminum coffin.

Avril Tannerton folded back the plastic shroud, revealing the body from the hips up.

Joshua looked down at the waxy yellow-gray corpse and shivered. "Ghastly."

"I know this is a trying time for you," Tannerton said in practiced mournful tones.

"Not at all," Joshua said. "I won't be a hypocrite and pretend grief. I knew very little about the man, and I didn't particularly like what I did know. Ours was strictly a business relationship."

Tannerton blinked. "Oh. Well . . . then perhaps you would prefer us to handle the funeral arrangements through one of the deceased's friends."

"I don't think he had any," Joshua said.

They stared down at the body for a moment, silent.

"Ghastly," Joshua said again.

"Of course," Tannerton said, "no cosmetic work has been done. Absolutely none. If I could have gotten to him soon after death, he'd look much better."

"Can you . . . do anything with him?"

"Oh, certainly. But it won't be easy. He's been dead a day and a half, and though he's been kept refrigerated—"

"Those wounds," Joshua said thickly, staring at the hideously scarred abdomen with morbid fascination. "Dear God, she really cut him."

"Most of that was done by the coroner," Tannerton said. "This small slit is a stab wound. And this one."

"The pathologist did a good job with his mouth," Olmstead said appreciatively.

"Yes, didn't he?" Tannerton said, touching the sealed lips of the corpse. "It's unusual to find a coroner with an aesthetic sense."

"Rare," Olmstead said.

Joshua shook his head. "I still find it hard to believe."

"Five years ago," Tannerton said, "I buried his mother. That's when I met him. He seemed a little . . . strange. But I figured it was the stress and the grief. He was such an important man, such a leading figure in the community."

"Cold," Joshua said. "He was an extremely cold and self-contained man. Vicious in business. Winning a battle with a competitor wasn't always enough for him; if at all possible, he preferred to utterly destroy the other fellow. I've always thought he was capable of cruelty and physical violence. But attempted rape? Attempted murder?"

Tannerton looked at Joshua and said, "Mr. Rhinehart, I've often heard it said that you don't mince words. You've got a reputation, a much admired reputation, for saying exactly what you think and to hell with the cost. But . . ."

"But what?"

"But when you're speaking of the dead, don't you think you ought to—"

Joshua smiled. "Son, I'm a cantankerous old bastard and not entirely admirable. Far from it! As long as truth is my weapon, I don't mind hurting the feelings of the living. Why, I've made children cry, and I've made kindly gray-haired grandmothers weep. I have little compassion for fools and sons of bitches when they're alive. So why should I show more respect than that for the dead?"

"I'm just not accustomed to—"

"Of course, you're not. Your profession requires you to speak well of the deceased, regardless of who he might have been and what heinous things he might have done. I don't hold that against you. It's your job."

Tannerton couldn't think of anything to say. He closed the lid of the coffin.

"Let's settle on the arrangements," Joshua said. "I'd like to get home and have my dinner—if I have any appetite left when I leave here." He sat down on a high stool beside a glass-fronted cabinet that contained more tools of the mortician's trade.

Tannerton paced in front of him, a freckled, mop-haired bundle of energy. "How important is it to you to have the usual viewing?"

"Usual viewing?"

"An open casket. Would you find it offensive if we avoided that?"

"I hadn't really given it a thought," Joshua said.

"To be honest with you, I don't know how . . . presentable the deceased can be made to look," Tannerton said. "The people at Angels' Hill didn't give him quite a full enough look when they embalmed him. His face appears to be somewhat drawn and shrunken. I am not pleased. I am definitely not pleased. I could attempt to pump him up a bit, but patchwork like that seldom looks good. As for cosmetology . . . well . . . again, I wonder if too much time has passed. I mean, he apparently was in the hot sun for a couple of hours after he died, before he was found. And then it was eighteen hours in cold storage before the embalming was done. I can certainly make him look a great deal better than he does now. But as for bringing the glow of life back to his face. . . . You see, after all that he's been through, after the extremes of temperature, and after this much time, the skin texture has changed substantially; it won't take makeup and powder at all well. I think perhaps—"

Beginning to get queasy, Joshua interrupted. "Make it a closed casket."

"No viewing?"

"No viewing."

"You're sure?"

"Positive."

"Good. Let me see. . . . Will you want him buried in one of his suits?"

"Is it necessary, considering the casket won't be open?"

"It would be easier for me if I just tucked him into one of our burial gowns."

"That'll be fine."

"White or a nice dark blue?"

"Do you have something in polka dots?"

"Polka dots?"

"Or orange and yellow stripes?"

Tannerton's ever-ready grin slipped from beneath his dour funeral director expression, and he struggled to force it out of sight again. Joshua suspected that, privately, Avril was a fun-loving man, the kind of hail-fellow-well-met who would make a good drinking buddy; but he seemed to feel that his public image required him to be somber and humorless at all times. He was visibly upset when he slipped up and allowed the private Avril to appear when only the public man ought to be seen. He was, Joshua thought, a likely candidate for an eventual schizophrenic breakdown.

"Make it the white gown," Joshua said.

"What about the casket? What style would—"

"I'll leave that to you."

"Very well. Price range?"

"Might as well have the best. The estate can afford it."

"The rumor is he must have been worth two or three million."

"Probably twice that," Joshua said.

"But he really didn't live like it."

"Or die like it," Joshua said.

Tannerton thought about that for a moment, then said, "Any religious services?"

"He didn't attend church."

"Then shall I assume the minister's role?"

"If you wish."

"We'll have a short graveside service," Tannerton said. "I'll read something from the Bible, or perhaps just a simple inspirational piece, something nondenominational."

They agreed on a time for burial: Sunday at two o'clock in the afternoon. Bruno would be laid to rest beside Katherine, his adoptive mother, in the Napa County Memorial Park.

As Joshua got up to leave, Tannerton said, "I certainly hope you've found my services valuable thus far, and I assure you I'll do everything in my power to make the rest of this go smoothly."

"Well," Joshua said, "you've convinced me of one thing. I'm going to draw up a new will tomorrow. When my times comes, I sure as hell intend to be cremated."

Tannerton nodded. "We can handle that for you."

"Don't rush me, son. Don't rush me."

Tannerton blushed. "Oh, I didn't mean to—"

"I know, I know. Relax."

Tannerton cleared his throat uncomfortably. "I'll . . . uh . . . show you to the door."

"No need. I can find it myself."

Outside, behind the funeral home, the night was very dark and deep. There was only one light, a hundred-watt bulb above the rear door. The glow reached only a few feet into the velveteen blackness.

In the late afternoon, a breeze had sprung up, and with the coming of the night, it had grown into a gusty wind. The air was turbulent and chilly; it hissed and moaned.

Joshua walked to his car, which lay beyond the meager semicircle of frosty light, and as he opened the door he had the peculiar feeling he was being watched. He glanced back at the house, but there were no faces at the windows.

Something moved in the gloom. Thirty feet away. Near the three-car garage. Joshua sensed rather than saw it. He squinted, but his vision was not what it had once been; he couldn't discern anything unnatural in the night.

Just the wind, he thought. Just the wind stirring through the trees and bushes or pushing along a discarded newspaper, a piece of dry brush.

But then it moved again. He saw it this time. It was crouched in front of a row of shrubs leading out from the garage. He could not see any detail. It was just a shadow, a lighter purple-black smudge on the blue-black cloth of the night, as soft and lumpy and undefined as all the other shadows—except that this one moved.

Just a dog, Joshua thought. A stray dog. Or maybe a kid up to some mischief.

"Is someone there?"

No reply.

He took a few steps away from his car.

The shadow-thing scurried back ten or twelve feet, along the line of shrubbery. It stopped in an especially deep pool of darkness, still crouching, still watchful.

Not a dog, Joshua thought. Too damned big for a dog. Some kid. Probably up to no good. Some kid with vandalism on his mind.

"Who's there?"

Silence.

"Come on now."

No answer. Just the whispering wind.

Joshua started toward the shadow among shadows, but he was suddenly arrested by the instinctive knowledge that the thing was dangerous. Horrendously dangerous. Deadly. He experienced all of the involuntary animal reactions to such a threat: a shiver up his spine; his scalp seemed to crawl and then tighten; his heart began to pound; his mouth went dry; his hands curled into claws; and his hearing seemed more acute than it had been a minute ago. Joshua hunched over and drew up his bulky shoulders, unconsciously seeking a defensive posture.

"Who's there?" he repeated.

The shadow-thing turned and crashed through the shrubs. It ran off across the vineyards that bordered Avril Tannerton's property. For a few seconds, Joshua could hear the steadily diminishing clamor of its flight, the receding *thud-thud-thud* of heavy running footsteps and the fading wheeze as it gasped for breath. Then the wind was the only sound in the night.

Looking over his shoulder a couple of times, he returned to his car. He got in, closed the door, locked it.

Already, the encounter began to seem unreal, increasingly dreamlike. Was there actually someone in the darkness, waiting, watching? Had there been something dangerous out there, or had it been his imagination? After spending half an hour in Avril Tannerton's ghoulish workshop, a man could be expected to jump at strange noises and start looking for monstrous creatures in the shadows. As Joshua's muscles relaxed, as his heart slowed, he began to think he had been a fool. The threat he had sensed so strongly seemed, in retrospect, to be a phantom, a vagary of the night and wind.

At worst, it had been a kid. A vandal.

He started the car and drove home, surprised and amused by the effect Tannerton's workroom had had upon him.

•

Saturday evening, promptly at seven o'clock, Anthony Clemenza arrived at Hilary's Westwood house in a blue Jeep station wagon.

Hilary went out to meet him. She was wearing a sleek emerald-green silk dress with long tight sleeves and a neckline cut low enough to be enticing but not cheap. She hadn't been on a date in more than fourteen months, and she nearly had forgotten how to dress for the ritual of courtship; she had spent two hours choosing her outfit, as indecisive as a schoolgirl. She accepted Tony's invitation because he was the most interesting man she'd met in a couple of years—and also because she was trying her best to overcome her tendency to hide from the rest of the world. She had been stung by Wally Topelis's assessment of her; he had warned her that she was using the virtue of self-reliance as an excuse to hide from people, and she had recognized the truth in what he'd said.

She avoided making friends and finding lovers, for she was afraid of the pain that only friends and lovers could inflict with their rejections and betrayals. But at the same time that she was protecting herself from the pain, she was denying herself the pleasure of good relationships with good people who would not betray her. Growing up with her drunken violent parents, she had learned that displays of affection were usually followed by sudden outbursts of rage and anger and unexpected punishment.

She was never afraid to take chances in her work and in business matters; now it was time to bring the same spirit of adventure to her personal life. As she walked briskly toward the blue Jeep, swinging her hips a little, she felt tense about taking the emotional risks that the mating dance entailed, but she also felt fresh and feminine and considerably happier than she had in a long time.

Tony hurried around to the passenger's side and opened the door. Bending low, he said, "The royal carriage awaits."

"Oh, there must be some mistake. I'm not the queen."

"You look like a queen to me."

"I'm just a lowly serving girl."

"You're a great deal prettier than the queen."

"Better not let her hear you say that. She'll have your head for sure."

"Too late."

"Oh?"

"I've already lost my head over you."

Hilary groaned.

"Too saccharine?" he asked.

"I need a bite of lemon after that one."

"But you liked it."

"Yes, I admit I did. I guess I'm a sucker for flattery," she said, getting into the Jeep in a swirl of green silk.

As they drove down toward Westwood Boulevard, Tony said, "You're not offended?"

"By what?"

"By this buggy?"

"How could I be offended by a Jeep? Does it talk? Is it liable to insult me?"

"It's not a Mercedes."

"A Mercedes isn't a Rolls. And a Rolls isn't a Toyota."

"There's something very Zen about that."

"If you think I'm a snob, why'd you ask me out?"

"I don't think you're a snob," he said. "But Frank says we'll be awkward with each other because you've got more money than I have."

"Well, based on my experience with him, I'd say Frank's judgments of other people are not to be trusted."

"He has his problems," Tony agreed as he turned left onto Wilshire Boulevard. "But he's working them out."

"I will admit this isn't a car you see many of in L.A."

"Usually, women ask me if it's my second car."

"I don't really care if it is or isn't."

"They say that in L.A. you are what you drive."

"Is that what they say? Then you're a Jeep. And I'm a Mercedes. We're cars, not people. We should be going to the garage for an oil change, not to a restaurant for dinner. Does that make sense?"

"No sense at all," Tony said. "Actually, I got a Jeep because I like to go skiing three or four weekends every winter. With this jalopy, I know I'll always be able to get through the mountain passes, no matter how bad the weather gets."

"I've always wanted to learn to ski."

"I'll teach you. You'll have to wait a few weeks. But it won't be long until there's snow at Mammoth."

"You seem pretty sure we'll still be friends a few weeks from now."

"Why wouldn't we be?" he asked.

"Maybe we'll get into a fight tonight, first thing, at the restaurant."

"Over what?"

"Politics."

"I think all politicians are power-hungry bastards too incompetent to tie their own shoelaces."

"So do I."

"I'm a Libertarian."

"So am I—sort of."

"Short argument."

"Maybe we'll fight over religion."

"I was raised a Catholic. But I'm not much of anything any more."

"Me either."

"We don't seem to be good at arguing."

"Well," she said, "maybe we're the kind of people who fight over little things, inconsequential matters."

"Such as?"

"Well, since we're going to an Italian restaurant, maybe you'll love the garlic bread, and I'll hate it."

"And we'll fight over that?"

"That or the fettucini or the manicotti."

"No. Where we're going, you'll love everything," he said. "Wait and see."

He took her to Savatino's Ristorante on Santa Monica Boulevard. It was an intimate place, seating no more than sixty and somehow appearing to seat only half that number; it was cozy, comfortable, the kind of restaurant in which you could lose track of time and spend six hours over dinner if the waiters didn't nudge you along. The lighting was soft and warm. The recorded opera—leaning heavily to the voices of Gigli and Caruso and Pavarotti—was played loud enough to be heard and appreciated, but not so loud that it intruded on conversation. There was a bit too much decor, but one part of it, a spectacular mural, was, Hilary thought, absolutely wonderful. The painting covered an entire wall and was a depiction of the most commonly perceived joys of the Italian lifestyle: grapes, wine, pasta, dark-eyed women, darkly handsome men, a loving and rotund *nonna*, a group of people dancing to the music of an accordionist, a picnic under olive trees, and much more. Hilary had never seen anything remotely like it, for it was neither entirely realistic nor stylized nor abstract nor impressionistic, but an odd stepchild of surrealism, as if it were a wildly inventive collaboration between Andrew Wyeth and Salvador Dali.

Michael Savatino, the owner, who turned out to be an ex-policeman, was irrepressibly jolly, hugging Tony, taking Hilary's hand and kissing it, punching Tony lightly in the belly and recommending pasta to fatten him up, insisting they come into the kitchen to see the new cappuccino machine. As they came out of the kitchen, Michael's wife, a striking blonde named Paula, arrived, and there was more hugging and kissing and complimenting. At last, Michael linked arms with Hilary and escorted her and Tony to a corner booth. He told the captain to bring two bottles of Biondi-Santi's Brunello di Montelcino, waited for the wine, and uncorked it himself. After glasses had been filled and toasts made, he left them, winking at Tony to show his approval, seeing Hilary notice the wink, laughing at himself, winking at her.

"He seems like such a nice man," she said when Michael had gone.

"He's some guy," Tony said.

"You like him a great deal."

"I love him. He was a perfect partner when we worked homicide together."

They fell smoothly into a discussion of policework and then screenwriting. He was so easy to talk to that Hilary felt she had known him for years. There was absolutely none of the awkwardness that usually marred a first date.

At one point, he noticed her looking at the wall mural. "Do you like the painting?" he asked.

"It's superb."

"Is it?"

"Don't you agree?"

"It's pretty good," he said.

"Better than pretty good. Who did it? Do you know?"

"Some artist down on his luck," Tony said. "He painted it in exchange for fifty free dinners."

"Only fifty? Michael got a bargain."

They talked about films and books and music and theater.

The food was nearly as good as the conversation. The appetizer was light; it consisted of two stubby crèpes, one filled with unadulterated ricotta cheese, the other with a spicy concoction of shaved beef, onions, peppers, mushrooms, and garlic. Their salads were huge and crisp, smothered in sliced raw mushrooms. Tony selected the entrée, Veal Savatino, a *specialita* of the house, incredibly tender white-white veal with a thin brown sauce, pearl onions, and grilled strips of zucchini. The cappuccino was excellent.

When she finished dinner and looked at her watch, Hilary was amazed to see that it was ten minutes past eleven.

Michael Savatino stopped by the table to bask in their praise, and then he said to Tony, "That's number twenty-one."

"Oh, no. Twenty-three."

"Not by my records."

"Your records are wrong."

"Twenty-one," Michael insisted.

"Twenty-three," Tony said. "And it ought to be numbers twenty-three and twenty-four. It was two meals, after all."

"No, no," Michael said. "We count by the visit, not by the number of meals."

Perplexed, Hilary said, "Am I losing my mind, or does this conversation make no sense at all?"

Michael shook his head, exasperated with Tony. To Hilary he said, "When he painted the mural, I wanted to pay him in cash, but he wouldn't accept it. He said he'd trade the painting for a few free dinners. I insisted on a hundred free visits. He said twenty-five. We finally settled on fifty. He undervalues his work, and that makes me angry as hell."

"Tony painted that mural?" she asked.

"He didn't tell you?"

"No."

She looked at Tony, and he grinned sheepishly.

"That's why he drives that Jeep," Michael said. "When he wants to go up in the hills to work on a nature study, the Jeep will take him anywhere."

"He said he had it because he likes to go skiing."

"That too. But mostly, it's to get him into the hills to paint. He should be proud of his work. But it's easier to pull teeth from an alligator than it is to get him to talk about his painting."

"I'm an amateur," Tony said. "Nothing's more boring than an amateur dabbler running off at the mouth about his 'art.'"

"That mural is not the work of an amateur," Michael said.

"Definitely not," Hilary agreed.

"You're my friends," Tony said, "so naturally you're too generous with your praise. And neither of you has the qualifications to be an art critic."

"He's won two prizes," Michael told Hilary.

"Prizes?" she asked Tony.

"Nothing important."

"Both times he won best of the show," Michael said.

"What shows were these?" Hilary asked.

"No big ones," Tony said.

"He dreams about making a living as a painter," Michael said, "but he never does anything about it."

"Because it's only a dream," Tony said. "I'd be a fool if I seriously thought I could make it as a painter."

"He never really tried," Michael told Hilary.

"A painter doesn't get a weekly paycheck," Tony said. "Or health benefits. Or retirement checks."

"But if you only sold two pieces a month for only half what they're worth, you'd make more than you get as a cop," Michael said.

"And if I sold nothing for a month or two months or six," Tony said, "then who would pay the rent?"

To Hilary, Michael said, "His apartment's crammed full of paintings, one stacked on the other. He's sitting on a fortune, but he won't do anything about it."

"He exaggerates," Tony told her.

"Ah, I give up!" Michael said. "Maybe you can talk some sense into him, Hilary." As he walked away from their table, he said, "Twenty-one."

"Twenty-three," Tony said.

Later, in the Jeep, as he was driving her home, Hilary said, "Why don't you at least take your work around to some galleries and see if they'll handle it?"

"They won't."

"You could at least ask."

"Hilary, I'm not really good enough."

"That mural was excellent."

"There's a big difference between restaurant murals and fine art."

"That mural was fine art."

"Again, I've got to point out that you aren't an expert."

"I buy paintings for both pleasure and investment."

"With the aid of a gallery director for the investment part?" he asked.

"That's right. Wyant Stevens in Beverly Hills."

"Then he's the expert, not you."

"Why don't you show some of your work to him?"

"I can't take rejection."

"I'll bet he won't reject you."

"Can we not talk about my painting?"

"Why?"

"I'm bored."

"You're difficult."

"And bored," he said.

"What shall we talk about?"

"Well, why don't we talk about whether or not you're going to invite me in for brandy."

"Would you like to come in for brandy?"

"Cognac?"

"That's what I have."

"What label?"

"Remy Martin."

"The best." He grinned. "But, gee, I don't know. It's getting awfully late."

"If you don't come in," she said, "I'll just have to drink alone." She was enjoying the silly game.

"Can't let you drink alone," he said.

"That's one sign of alcoholism."

"It certainly is."

"If you don't come in for a brandy with me, you'll be starting me on the road to problem drinking and complete destruction."

"I'd never forgive myself."

Fifteen minutes later, they were sitting side by side on the couch, in front of the fireplace, watching the flames and sipping Remy Martin.

Hilary felt slightly light-headed, not from the cognac but from being next to him—and from wondering if they were going to go to bed together. She had never slept with a man on the first date. She was usually wary, reluctant to commit herself to an affair until she had spent a couple of weeks—sometimes a couple of months—evaluating the man. More than once she had taken so long to make up her mind that she had lost men who might have made wonderful lovers and lasting friends. But in just one evening with Tony Clemenza, she felt at ease and perfectly safe with him. He was a damned attractive man. Tall. Dark. Rugged good looks. The inner authority and self-confidence of a cop. Yet gentle. Really surprisingly gentle. And sensitive. So much time had passed since she'd allowed herself to be touched and possessed, since she'd used and been used and shared. How could she have let so much time pass? She could easily imagine herself in his arms, naked beneath him, then atop him, and as those lovely images filled her mind, she realized that he was probably having the same sweet thoughts.

Then the telephone rang.

"Damn!" she said.

"Someone you don't want to hear from?"

She turned and looked at the phone, which was a walnut box model that stood on a corner desk. It rang, rang.

"Hilary?"

"I'll bet it's him," she said.

"Him who?"

"I've been getting these calls. . . ."

The strident ringing continued.

"What calls?" Tony asked.

"The last couple of days, someone's been calling and then refusing to speak when I answer. It's happened six or eight times."

"He doesn't say anything at all?"

"He just listens," she said. "I think it's some nut who was turned on by the newspaper stories about Frye."

The insistent bell made her grit her teeth.

She stood up and hesitantly approached the phone.

Tony went with her. "You have a listed number?"

"I'm getting a new one next week. It'll be unlisted."

They reached the desk and stood looking at the phone. It rang again and again and again.

"It's him," she said. "Who else would let it ring that long?"

Tony snatched up the receiver. "Hello?"

The caller didn't respond.

"Thomas residence," Tony said. "Detective Clemenza speaking."

Click.

Tony put the phone down and said, "He hung up. Maybe I scared him off for good."

"I hope so."

"It's still a good idea to get an unlisted number."

"Oh, I'm not going to change my mind about that."

"I'll call the telephone company service department first thing Monday morning and tell them the LAPD would appreciate a speedy job."

"Can you do that?"

"Sure."

"Thank you, Tony." She hugged herself. She felt cold.

"Try not to worry about it," he said. "Studies show that the kind of creep who makes threatening phone calls usually gets all his kicks that way. The call itself usually satisfies him. He usually isn't the violent type."

"Usually?"

"Almost never."

She smiled thinly. "That's still not good enough."

The call had spoiled any chance that the night might end in a shared bed. She was no longer in the mood for seduction, and Tony sensed the change.

"Would you like me to stay a while longer, just to see if he calls again?"

"That's sweet of you," she said. "But I guess you're right. He's not dangerous. If he was, he'd come around instead of just calling. Anyway, you scared him off. He probably thinks the police are here just waiting for him."

"Did you get your pistol back?"

She nodded. "I went downtown yesterday and filled out the registration form like I should have done when I moved into the city. If the guy on the phone *does* come around, I can plink him legally now."

"I really don't think he'll bother you again tonight."

"I'm sure you're right."

For the first time all evening, they were awkward with each other.

"Well, I guess I'd better be going."

"It is late," she agreed.

"Thank you for the cognac."

"Thank you for a wonderful dinner."

At the door he said, "Doing anything tomorrow night?"

She was about to turn him down when she remembered how good she had felt sitting beside him on the sofa. And she thought of Wally Topelis's warning about becoming a hermit. She smiled and said, "I'm free."

"Great. What would you like to do?"

"Whatever you want."

He thought about it for a moment. "Shall we make a whole day of it?"

"Well . . . why not?"

"We'll start with lunch. I'll pick you up at noon."

"I'll be ready and waiting."

He kissed her lightly and affectionately on the lips. "Tomorrow," he said.

"Tomorrow."

She watched him leave, then closed and locked the door.

•

All day Saturday, morning and afternoon and evening, the body of Bruno Frye lay alone in the Forever View Funeral Home, unobserved and unattended.

Friday night, after Joshua Rhinehart had left, Avril Tannerton and Gary Olmstead had transferred the corpse to another coffin, an ornate brass-plated model with a plush velvet and silk interior. They tucked the dead man into a white burial gown, put his arms straight out at his sides, and pulled a white velvet coverlet up to the middle of his chest. Because the condition of the flesh was not good, Tannerton did not want to expend any energy trying to make the corpse presentable. Gary Olmstead thought there was something cheap and disrespectful about consigning a body to the grave without benefit of makeup and powder. But Tannerton persuaded him that cosmetology offered little hope for Bruno Frye's shrunken yellow-gray countenance.

"And anyway," Tannerton had said, "you and I will be the last people in this world to lay eyes on him. When we shut this box tonight, it'll never be opened again."

At 9:45 Friday night, they had closed and latched the lid of the casket. That done, Olmstead went home to his wan little wife and his quiet and intense young son. Avril went upstairs; he lived above the rooms of the dead.

Early Saturday morning, Tannerton left for Santa Rosa in his silver-gray Lincoln. He took an overnight bag with him, for he didn't intend to return until ten o'clock Sunday morning. Bruno Frye's funeral was the only one that he was handling at the moment. Since there was to be no viewing, he hadn't any reason to stay at Forever View; he wouldn't be needed until the service on Sunday.

He had a woman in Santa Rosa. She was the latest of a long line of women; Avril thrived on variety. Her name was Helen Virtillion. She was a good-looking woman in her early thirties, very lean, taut, with big firm breasts which he found endlessly fascinating.

A lot of women were attracted to Avril Tannerton, not in spite of what he did for a living but because of it. Of course, some were turned off when they discovered he was a mortician. But a surprising number were intrigued and even excited by his unusual profession.

He understood what made him desirable to them. When a man worked with the dead, some of the mystery of death rubbed off on him. In spite of his freckles and his boyish good looks, in spite of his charming smile and his great sense of fun and his open-hearted manner, some women felt he was nonetheless mysterious, enigmatic. Unconsciously, they thought they could not die so long as they were in his arms, as if his services to the dead earned him (and those close to him) special dispensation. That atavistic fantasy was similar to the secret hope shared by many women who married doctors because they were subconsciously convinced that their spouses could protect them from all of the microbial dangers of this world.

Therefore, all day Saturday, while Avril Tannerton was in Santa Rosa making love to Helen Virtillion, the body of Bruno Frye lay alone in an empty house.

Sunday morning, two hours before sunrise, there was a sudden rush of movement in the funeral home, but Tannerton was not there to notice.

The overhead lights in the windowless workroom were switched on abruptly, but Tannerton was not there to see.

The lid of the sealed casket was unlatched and thrown back. The workroom was filled with screams of rage and pain, but Tannerton was not there to hear.

•

At ten o'clock Sunday morning, as Tony stood in his kitchen drinking a glass of grapefruit juice, the telephone rang. It was Janet Yamada, the woman who had been Frank Howard's blind date last night.

"How'd it go?" he asked.

"It was wonderful, a wonderful night."

"Really?"

"Sure. He's a doll."

"Frank is a doll."

"You said he might be kind of cold, difficult to get to know, but he wasn't."

"He wasn't?"

"And he's so romantic."

"Frank?"

"Who else?"

"Frank Howard is romantic?"

"These days you don't find many men who have a sense of romance," Janet said. "Sometimes it seems like romance and chivalry were thrown out the window when the sexual revolution and the women's rights movement came in. But Frank still helps you on with your coat and opens doors for you and pulls your chair out and everything. He even brought me a bouquet of roses. They're beautiful."

"I thought you might have trouble talking to him."

"Oh, no. We have a lot of the same interests."

"Like what?"

"Baseball, for one thing."

"That's right! I forgot you like baseball."

"I'm an addict."

"So you talked baseball all night."

"Oh, no," she said. "We talked about a lot of other things. Movies—"

"Movies? Are you trying to tell me Frank is a film buff?"

"He knows the old Bogart pictures almost line by line. We traded favorite bits of dialogue."

"I've been talking about film for three months, and he hasn't opened his mouth," Tony said.

"He hasn't seen a lot of recent pictures, but we're going to a show tonight."

"You're seeing him again?"

"Yeah. I wanted to call and thank you for fixing me up with him," she said.

"Am I one hell of a matchmaker, or am I one hell of a matchmaker?"

"I also wanted to let you know that even if it doesn't work out, I'll be gentle with him. He told me about Wilma. What a rotten thing! I wanted you to know that I'm aware she put a couple of cracks in him, and I won't ever hit him too hard."

Tony was amazed. "He told you about Wilma the first night he met you?"

"He said he used to be unable to talk about it, but then you showed him how to handle his hostility."

"Me?"

"He said after you helped him accept what had happened, he could talk about it without pain."

"All I did was sit and listen when he wanted to get it off his chest."

"He thinks you're a hell of a great guy."

"Frank's a damned good judge of people, isn't he?"

Later, feeling good about the excellent impression that Frank had made on Janet Yamada, optimistic about his own chances for a little romance, Tony drove to Westwood to keep his date with Hilary. She was waiting for him; she came out of the house as he pulled into the driveway. She looked crisp and lovely in black slacks, a cool ice-blue blouse, and a lightweight blue corduroy blazer. As he opened the door for her, she gave him a quick, almost shy kiss on the cheek, and he got a whiff of fresh lemony perfume.

It was going to be a good day.

•

Exhausted from a nearly sleepless night in Helen Virtillion's bedroom, Avril Tannerton got back from Santa Rosa shortly before ten o'clock Sunday morning.

He did not look inside the coffin.

With Gary Olmstead, Tannerton went to the cemetery and prepared the gravesite for the two o'clock ceremony. They erected the equipment that would lower the casket into the ground. Using flowers and a lot of cut greenery, they made the site as attractive as possible.

At 12:30 back at the funeral home, Tannerton used a chamois cloth to wipe the dust and smudged fingerprints from Bruno Frye's brass-plated casket. As he ran his hand over the rounded edges of the box, he thought of the magnificent contours of Helen Virtillion's breasts.

He did not look inside the coffin.

At one o'clock, Tannerton and Olmstead loaded the deceased into the hearse.

Neither of them looked inside the coffin.

At one-thirty they drove to the Napa County Memorial Park. Joshua Rhinehart and a few local people followed in their own cars. Considering that it was for a wealthy and influential man, the funeral procession was embarrassingly small.

The day was clear and cool. Tall trees cast stark shadows across the road, and the hearse passed through alternating bands of sunlight and shade.

At the cemetery, the casket was placed on a sling above the grave, and fifteen people gathered around for the brief service. Gary Olmstead took up a position beside the flower-concealed control box that operated the sling and would cause it to lower the deceased into the ground. Avril stood at the front of the grave and read from a thin book of nondenominational inspirational verses. Joshua Rhinehart was at the mortician's side. The other twelve people flanked the open grave. Some of them were grape growers and their wives. They had come because they had sold their harvests to Bruno Frye's winery, and they considered their attendance at his funeral to be a business obligation. The others were Shade Tree Vineyards executives and their wives, and their reasons for being present were no more personal than those of the growers. Nobody wept.

And nobody had the opportunity or the desire to look into the coffin.

Tannerton finished reading from his small black book. He glanced at Gary Olmstead and nodded.

Olmstead pushed a button on the control box. The powerful little electric motor hummed. The casket was lowered slowly and smoothly into the gaping earth.

•

Hilary could not remember another day that was as much fun as that first full day with Tony Clemenza.

For lunch, they went to the Yamashiro Skyroom, high in the Hollywood Hills. The food at Yamashiro was uninspiring, even ordinary, but the ambience and the stunning view made it a fine place for an occasional light lunch or dinner. The restaurant, an authentic Japanese palace, had

once been a private estate. It was surrounded by ten acres of lovely orna-
mental gardens. From its mountaintop perch, Yamashiro offered a breath-
taking view of the entire Los Angeles basin. The day was so clear that
Hilary could see all the way to Long Beach and Palos Verdes.

After lunch, they went to Griffith Park. For an hour, they walked
through part of the Los Angeles Zoo, where they fed the bears, and where
Tony did hilarious imitations of the animals. From the zoo they went to a
special afternoon performance of the dazzling Laserium hologram show
in the Griffith Park Observatory.

Later, they passed an hour on Melrose Avenue, between Doheny Drive
and La Cienega Boulevard, prowling through one fascinating antique shop
after another, not buying, just browsing, chatting with the proprietors.

When the cocktail hour arrived, they drove to Malibu for Mai Tais at
Tonga Lei. They watched the sun set into the ocean and relaxed to the
rhythmic roar of breaking waves.

Although Hilary had been an Angeleno for quite some time, her
world had been composed only of her work, her house, her rose garden,
her work, the film studios, her work, and the few fancy restaurants in
which the motion picture and television crowd gathered to do business.
She had never been to the Yamashiro Skyroom, the zoo, the laser show,
the Melrose antique shops, or Tonga Lei. It was all new to her. She felt
like a wide-eyed tourist—or, more accurately, like a prisoner who had just
finished serving a long, long sentence, most of it in solitary confinement.

But it was not just where they went that made the day special. None
of it would have been half as interesting or as much fun if she'd been with
someone other than Tony. He was so charming, so quick-witted, so full of
fun and energy, that he made the bright day brighter.

After slowly sipping two Mai Tais each, they were starving. They
drove back to Sepulveda and went north into the San Fernando Valley to
have dinner at Mel's landing, another place with which she was not familiar. Mel's was unpretentious and moderately priced, and it offered some
of the freshest and tastiest seafood she had ever eaten.

As she and Tony ate Mel's steamed clams and discussed other favorite
places to eat, Hilary found that he knew ten times as many as she did. Her
knowledge did not extend much beyond that handful of expensive dining
spots that served the movers and shakers of the entertainment industry.
The out-of-the-way eateries, the hole-in-the-wall cafés with surprising
house specialties, the small mom-and-pop restaurants with plainly served
but delicious food—all of that was one more aspect of the city about

which she had never taken time to learn. She saw that she had become rich without ever discovering how to use and fully enjoy the freedom that her money could provide.

They ate too many of Mel's clams and then too much red snapper with too many Malaysian shrimp. They also drank too much white wine.

Considering how much they consumed, it was amazing, Hilary thought, that they had so much time between mouthfuls for conversation. But they never stopped talking. She was usually reticent on the first few dates with a new man, but not with Tony. She wanted to hear what he thought about everything, from *Mork and Mindy* to Shakespearean drama, from politics to art. People, dogs, religion, architecture, sports, Bach, fashions, food, women's liberation, Saturday morning cartoons—it seemed urgent and vital that she know what he thought about those and a million other subjects. She also wanted to tell him what she thought about all those things, and she wanted to know what he thought of what she thought, and pretty soon she was telling him what she thought of what he thought of what she thought. They chattered as if they had just learned that God was going to strike everyone in the world deaf and dumb at sunrise. Hilary was drunk, not on wine, but on the fluidity and intimacy of their conversation; she was intoxicated by communication, a potent brew for which she had built up little tolerance over the years.

By the time he took her home and agreed to come in for a nightcap, she was certain they would go to bed together. She wanted him very much; the thought of it made her warm and tingly. She knew he wanted her. She could see the desire in his eyes. They needed to let dinner settle a bit, and with that in mind, she poured white crème de menthe on the rocks for both of them.

They were just sitting down when the telephone rang.

"Oh, no," she said.

"Did he bother you after I left last night?"

"No."

"This morning?"

"No."

"Maybe that's not him."

They both went to the phone.

She hesitated, then picked it up. "Hello?"

Silence.

"Damn you!" she said, and she slammed the receiver down so hard that she wondered if she'd cracked it.

"Don't let him rattle you."

"I can't help it," she said.

"He's just a slimy little creep who doesn't know how to deal with women. I've seen others like him. If he ever got a chance to make it with a woman, if a woman offered herself to him on a silver platter, he'd run away screaming in terror."

"He still scares me."

"He's no threat. Come back to the couch. Sit down. Try to forget about him."

They returned to the sofa and sipped their crème de menthe in silence for a minute or two.

At last, she softly said, "Damn."

"You'll have an unlisted number by tomorrow afternoon. Then he won't be able to bother you any more."

"But he sure spoiled this evening. I was so mellow."

"I'm still enjoying myself."

"It's just that . . . I'd figured on more than just drinks in front of the fireplace."

He stared at her. "Had you?"

"Hadn't you?"

His smile was special because it was not merely a configuration of the mouth; it involved his whole face and his expressive dark eyes; it was the most genuine and by far the most appealing smile that she had ever seen. He said, "I've got to admit I had hopes of tasting more than the crème de menthe."

"Damn the phone."

He leaned over and kissed her. She opened her mouth to him, and for a brief sweet moment their tongues met. He pulled back and looked at her, put his hand against her face as if he was touching delicate porcelain. "I think we're still in the mood."

"If the phone rings again—"

"It won't."

He kissed her on the eyes, then on the lips, and he put one hand gently on her breast.

She leaned back, and he leaned into her. She put her hand on his arm and felt the muscles bunched beneath his shirt.

Still kissing her, he stroked her soft throat with his fingertips, then began to unbutton her blouse.

Hilary put her hand on his thigh, where the muscles were also tense beneath his slacks. Such a lean hard man. She slid her hand up to his groin and felt the huge steeliness and fierce heat of his erection. She thought of him entering her and moving hotly within her, and a thrill of anticipation made her shiver.

He sensed her excitement and paused in the unbuttoning of her blouse to lightly trace the swell of her breasts where they rose above the cups of her bra. His fingers seemed to leave cool trails on her warm skin; she could feel the lingering ghost of his touch as clearly as she could feel the touch itself.

The telephone rang.

"Ignore it," he said.

She tried to do as he said. She put her arms around him and slid down on the couch and pulled him on top of her. She kissed him hard, crushing her lips against his, licking, sucking.

The phone rang and rang.

"Damn!"

They sat up.

It rang, rang, rang.

Hilary stood.

"Don't," Tony said. "Talking to him hasn't helped. Let me handle it another way and see what happens."

He got up from the couch and went to the corner desk. He lifted the receiver, but he didn't say anything. He just listened.

Hilary could tell from his expression that the caller had not spoken.

Tony was determined to wait him out. He looked at his watch.

Thirty seconds passed. A minute. Two minutes.

The battle of nerves between the two men was strangely like a childish staring contest, yet there was nothing childish about it. It was eerie. Goosebumps popped up on her arms.

Two and a half minutes.

It seemed like an hour.

Finally, Tony put down the phone. "He hung up."

"Without saying anything?"

"Not a word. But he hung up first, and I think that's important. I figured if I gave him a dose of his own medicine he wouldn't like it. He thinks he's going to frighten you. But you're expecting the call, and you just listen like he does. At first, he thinks you're only being cute, and he's sure he can outwait you. But the longer you're silent, the more he starts to wonder if you aren't up to some trick. Is there a tap on your phone? Are you stalling so the police can trace the call? Is it even you who picked up the phone? He thinks about that, starts to get scared, and hangs up."

"*He's* scared? Well, that's a nice thought," she said.

"I doubt that he'll get up the nerve to call back. At least not until you've changed numbers tomorrow. And then he'll be too late."

"Nevertheless, I'll be on edge until the man from the phone company's done his job."

Tony held out his arms, and she moved into his embrace. They kissed again. It was still extraordinarily sweet and good and right, but the sharp edge of unrestrained passion could no longer be felt. Both of them were unhappily aware of the difference.

They returned to the couch, but only to drink their crème de menthe and talk. By twelve-thirty in the morning, when he had to go home, they had decided to spend the following weekend on a museum binge. Saturday, they'd go to the Norton Simon Museum in Pasadena to look at the German expressionist paintings and the Renaissance tapestry. Then they would spend most of Sunday at the J. Paul Getty Museum, which boasted a collection of art richer than any other in the world. Of course, in between the museums, they would eat a lot of good food, share a lot of good talk, and (they ardently hoped) pick up where they had left off on the couch.

At the front door, as he was leaving, Hilary suddenly couldn't bear to wait five days to see him again. She said, "What about Wednesday?"

"What about it?"

"Doing anything for dinner?"

"Oh, I'll probably fry up a batch of eggs that are just getting stale in the refrigerator."

"All that cholesterol's bad for you."

"And maybe I'll cut the mold off the bread, make some toast. And I should finish the fruit juice I bought two weeks ago."

"You poor dear."

"The bachelor's life."

"I can't let you eat stale eggs and moldy toast. Not when I make such a terrific tossed salad and filet of sole."

"A nice light supper," he said.

"We don't want to get bloated and sleepy."

"Never know when you might have to move fast."

She grinned. "Precisely."

"See you Wednesday."

"Seven?"

"Seven sharp."

They kissed, and he walked away from the door, and a cold night wind rushed in where he had been, and then he was gone.

Half an hour later, upstairs, in bed, Hilary's body ached with frustration. Her breasts were full and taut; she longed to feel his hands on them, his fingers gently stroking and massaging. She could close her eyes and feel his lips on her stiffening nipples. Her belly fluttered as she pictured him braced above her on his powerful arms, and then she above him, moving in slow sensuous circles. Her sex was moist and warm, ready, waiting. She tossed and turned for almost an hour before she finally got up and took a sedative.

As sleep crept over her, she held a drowsy dialogue with herself.

Am I falling in love?

—No. Of course not.

Maybe. Maybe I am.

—No. Love's dangerous.

Maybe it'll work with him.

—Remember Earl and Emma.

Tony's different.

—You're horny. That's all it is. You're just horny.

That, too.

She slept, and she dreamed. Some of the dreams were golden and fuzzy about the edges. In one of them she was naked with Tony, lying in a meadow where the grass felt like feathers, high above the world, a meadow atop a towering pillar of rock, and the warm wind was cleaner than sunshine, cleaner than the electric current of a lightning bolt, cleaner than anything in the world.

But she had nightmares, too. In one of them, she was in the old Chicago apartment, and the walls were closing in, and when she looked up she saw there was no ceiling, and Earl and Emma were staring down at her, their faces as big as God's face, grinning down at her as the walls closed in, and when she opened the door to run out of the apartment, she collided with an enormous cockroach, a monstrous insect bigger than she was, and it obviously intended to eat her alive.

●

At three o'clock in the morning, Joshua Rhinehart woke, grunting and tussling briefly with the tangled sheets. He'd drunk a bit too much wine with dinner, which was most unusual for him. The buzz was gone, but his bladder was killing him; however, it was not merely the call of nature that had disturbed his sleep. He'd had a horrible dream about Tannerton's workroom. In that nightmare, several dead men—all of them duplicates of Bruno Frye—had risen up from their caskets and from the porcelain and stainless steel embalming tables; he had run into the night behind Forever View, but they had come after him, had searched the shadows for him, moving jerkily, calling his name in their flat dead voices.

He lay on his back in the darkness, staring at the ceiling which he could not see. The only sound was the nearly inaudible purr of the electronic digital clock on the nightstand.

Before his wife's death three years ago, Joshua had seldom dreamed. And he'd never had a nightmare. Not once in fifty-eight years. But after Cora passed away, all of that changed. He dreamed at least once or twice a week now, and more often than not the dream was a bad one. Many of them had to do with losing something terribly important but indescribable, and there always ensued a frantic but hopeless search for that which he had lost. He didn't need a fifty-dollar-an-hour psychiatrist to tell him that those dreams were about Cora and her untimely death. He still had not adjusted to life without her. Perhaps he never would. The other nightmares were filled with walking dead men who often looked like him, symbols of his own mortality; but tonight they all bore a striking resemblance to Bruno Frye.

He got out of bed, stretched, yawned. He shuffled to the bathroom without turning on a lamp.

A couple of minutes later, on his way back to bed, he stopped at the window. The panes were cold to the touch. A stiff wind pressed against the glass and made mewling sounds like an animal that wanted to be let inside. The valley was still and dark except for the lights of the wineries. He could see the Shade Tree Vineyards to the north, farther up in the hills.

Suddenly, his eye was caught by a fuzzy white dot just south of the winery, a single smudge of light in the middle of a vineyard, approximately where the Frye house stood. Lights in the Frye house? There wasn't supposed to be anyone there. Bruno had lived alone. Joshua squinted, but without his glasses, everything at a distance tended to grow hazier the harder he tried to focus on it. He couldn't tell if the light was at the Frye place or at one of the administration buildings between the house and the main winery complex. In fact, the longer he stared the less he was sure that it was a light he was watching; it was faint, lambent; it might only be a reflection of moonlight.

He went to the nightstand and, not wanting to turn on a lamp and spoil his night vision, he felt for his glasses in the dark. Before he found them, he knocked over an empty water glass.

When he got back to the window and looked up into the hills again, the mysterious light was gone. Nevertheless, he stood there for a long while, a vigilant guardian. He was executor of the Frye estate, and it was his duty to preserve it for final distribution in accordance with the will. If burglars and vandals were stripping the house, he wanted to know about it. For fifteen minutes, he waited and watched, but the light never returned.

At last, convinced that his weak eyes had deceived him, he went back to bed.

•

Monday morning, as Tony and Frank pursued a series of possible leads on Bobby Valdez, Frank talked animatedly about Janet Yamada. Janet was so pretty. Janet was so intelligent. Janet was so understanding. Janet was this, and Janet was that. He was a bore on the subject of Janet Yamada, but Tony allowed him to gush and ramble. It was good to see Frank talking and acting like a normal human being.

Before checking out their unmarked police sedan and getting on the road, Tony and Frank had spoken to two men on the narcotics squad, Detectives Eddie Quevedo and Carl Hammerstein. The word from those two specialists was that Bobby Valdez was most likely selling either cocaine or PCP to support himself while he pursued his unpaid vocation as a rapist. The biggest money in the L.A. drug market was currently in those two illegal but extremely popular substances. A dealer could still make a fortune in heroin or grass, but those were no longer the most lucrative commodities in the underground pharmacy. According to the narcs, if Bobby was involved in drug traffic, he had to be a pusher, selling directly to users, a man at the lower end of the production and marketing structure. He was virtually penniless when he got out of prison last April, and he needed substantial capital to become either a manufacturer or an importer of narcotics. "What you're looking for is a common street hustler," Quevedo had told Tony and Frank. "Talk to other hustlers." Hammerstein had said, "We'll give you a list of names and addresses. They're all guys who've taken falls for dealing drugs. Most of them are probably dealing again; we just haven't caught them at it yet. Put on a little pressure. Sooner or later, you'll find one of them who's run into Bobby on the street and knows where he's holed up." There were twenty-four names on the list that Quevedo and Hammerstein had given them.

Three of the first six men were not at home. The other three swore they didn't know Bobby Valdez or Juan Mazquezza or anyone else with the face in the mug shots.

The seventh name on the list was Eugene Tucker, and he was able to help them. They didn't even have to lean on him.

Most black men were actually one shade of brown or another, but Tucker was truly black. His face was broad and smooth and as black as tar. His dark brown eyes were far lighter than his skin. He had a bushy black beard that was salted with curly white hairs, and that touch of frosting was the only thing about him, other than the whites of his eyes, that was not very, very dark. He even wore black slacks and a black shirt. He was stocky, with a big chest and bigger arms, and his neck was as thick as a wharf post. He looked as if he snapped railroad ties in two for exercise—or maybe just for fun.

Tucker lived in a high-rent townhouse in the Hollywood Hills, a roomy place that was sparsely but tastefully furnished. The living room had only four pieces in it: a couch, two chairs, a coffee table. No end tables or fancy storage units. No stereo. No television set. There weren't even any lamps; at night, the only light would come from the ceiling fixture. But the four pieces that he did have were of remarkably high quality, and each item perfectly accented the others. Tucker had a taste for fine Chinese antiques. The couch and chairs, which recently had been reupholstered in jade-green velvet, were all made of hand-carved rosewood, a hundred years old, maybe twice that, immensely heavy and well-preserved, matchless examples of their period and style. The low table was also rosewood with a narrow inlaid ivory border. Tony and Frank sat on the couch, and Eugene Tucker perched on the edge of a chair opposite them.

Tony ran one hand along the rosewood arm of the couch and said, "Mr. Tucker, this is marvelous."

Tucker raised his eyebrows. "You know what it is?"

"I don't know the precise period," Tony said. "But I'm familiar enough with Chinese art to know this is definitely not a reproduction that you picked up on sale at Sears."

Tucker laughed, pleased that Tony knew the value of the furniture. "I know what you're thinking," he said good-naturedly. "You're wondering how an ex-con, just two years out of the stir, can afford all this. A twelve-hundred-dollar-a-month townhouse. Chinese antiques. You're wondering if maybe I've gotten back into the heroin trade or some allied field of endeavor."

"In fact," Tony said, "that's not what I'm asking myself at all. I *am* wondering how the devil you've done it. But I know it's not from selling junk."

Tucker smiled. "How can you be so sure?"

"If you were a drug dealer with a passion for Chinese antiques," Tony said, "you'd simply furnish the entire house at a single crack, instead of a piece or two at a time. You are clearly into something that earns a lot of bread, but not nearly as much as you'd make distributing dope like you used to do."

Tucker laughed again and applauded approvingly. He turned to Frank and said, "Your partner is perceptive."

Frank smiled. "A regular Sherlock Holmes."

To Tucker, Tony said, "Satisfy my curiosity. What do you do?"

Tucker leaned forward, suddenly frowning, raising one granite fist and shaking it, looking huge and mean and very dangerous. When he spoke he snarled: "I design dresses."

Tony blinked.

Collapsing back in his chair, Tucker laughed again. He was one of the happiest people Tony had ever seen. "I design women's clothes," he said. "I really do. My name's already beginning to be known in the California design community, and some day it'll be a household word. I promise you."

Intrigued, Frank said, "According to our information, you did four years of an eight-year sentence for wholesaling heroin and cocaine. How'd you go from that to making women's clothes?"

"I used to be one mean son of a bitch," Tucker said. "And those first few months in prison, I was even meaner than usual. I blamed society for everything that happened to me. I blamed the white power structure. I blamed the whole world, but I just wouldn't put any blame on myself. I thought I was a tough dude, but I hadn't really grown up yet. You aren't a man until you accept responsibility for your life. A lot of people never do."

"So what turned you around?" Frank asked.

"A little thing," Tucker said. "Man, sometimes it amazes me how such a little thing can change a person's life. With me, it was a TV show. On the six o'clock news, one of the L.A. stations did a five-part series about black success stories in the city."

"I saw it," Tony said. "More than five years ago, but I still remember it."

"It was fascinating stuff," Tucker said. "It was an image of the black man you never get to see. But at first, before the series began, everybody in the slammer figured it would be one big laugh. We figured the reporter would spend all his time asking the same idiot question: 'Why can't all these poor black folks work hard and become rich Las Vegas headliners like Sammy Davis, Jr.?' But they didn't talk to any entertainers or sports stars."

Tony remembered that it had been a striking piece of journalism, especially for television, where news—and especially the human interest stories on the news—had as much depth as a teacup. The reporters had interviewed black businessmen and businesswomen who had made it to the top, people who had started out with nothing and eventually had become millionaires. Some in real estate. One in the restaurant business. One with a chain of beauty shops. About a dozen people. They all agreed that it was harder to get rich if you were black, but they also agreed that it was not as hard as they thought when they started out, and that it was easier in Los Angeles than in Alabama or Mississippi or even Boston or New York. There were more black millionaires in L.A. than in the rest of California *and* the other forty-nine states combined. In Los Angeles, almost everyone was living in the fast lane; the typical Southern Californian did not merely accommodate himself to change but actively sought it and reveled in it. This atmosphere of flux and constant experimentation drew a lot of marginally sane and even insane people into the area, but it also attracted some of the brightest and most innovative minds in the country, which was why so many new cultural and scientific and industrial developments originated in the region. Very few Southern Californians had the time or patience for outmoded attitudes, one of which was racial prejudice. Of course, there was bigotry in L.A. But whereas a landed white family in Georgia might require six or eight generations to overcome its prejudice toward blacks, that same metamorphosis of attitudes often transpired in one generation of a Southern California family. As one of the black businessmen on the TV news report had said, "The Chicanos have been the niggers of L.A. for quite some time now." But already that was changing, too. The Hispanic culture was regarded with ever-increasing respect, and the browns were creating their own success stories. Several people interviewed on that news special had offered the same explanation for the unusual fluidity of Southern California's social structures and for the eagerness with which people there accepted change; it was, they said, partly because of geology. When you were living on some of the worst fault lines in the world, when the earth could quake and move and *change* under your feet without warning, did that awareness of impermanence have a subconscious influence on a person's attitudes toward less cataclysmic kinds of change? Some of those black millionaires thought it did, and Tony tended to agree with them.

"There were about a dozen rich black people on that program," Eugene Tucker said. "A lot of guys in the slammer with me just hooted at the TV and called them all Uncle Toms. But I started thinking. If some people on that show could make it in a white world, why couldn't I? I was just as clever and smart as any of them, maybe even smarter than some. It was a completely new image of a black man to me, a whole new idea, like a light bulb going on in my head. Los Angeles was my home. If it really offered a better chance, why hadn't I taken advantage of it? Sure, maybe some of those people had to act like Uncle Toms on their way to the top. But when you've made it, when you've got that million in the bank, you're nobody's man but your own." He grinned. "So I decided to get rich."

"Just like that," Frank said, impressed.

"Just like that."

"The power of positive thinking."

"Realistic thinking," Tucker corrected.

"Why dress designing?" Tony asked.

"I took aptitude tests that said I'd do well in design work or any aspect of the art business. So I tried to decide what I'd most enjoy designing. Now, I've always liked to choose the clothes my girlfriends wear. I like to go shopping with them. And when they wear an outfit I've picked, they get more compliments than when they wear something they chose themselves. So I hooked up with a university program for inmates, and I studied design. Took a lot of business courses, too. When I was finally paroled, I worked for a while at a fast food restaurant. I lived in a cheap rooming house and kept my expenses down. I drew some designs, paid seamstresses to sew up samples, and started hawking my wares. It wasn't easy at first. Hell, it was damned hard! Every time I got an order from a shop, I walked it to the bank and borrowed money against it to complete the dresses. Man, I was clawing to hold on. But it got better and better. It's pretty good now. In a year, I'll open my own shop in a good area. And eventually you'll see a sign in Beverly Hills that says 'Eugene Tucker.' I promise you."

Tony shook his head. "You're a remarkable man."

"Not particularly," Tucker said. "I'm just living in a remarkable place and a remarkable time."

Frank was holding the manila envelope that contained the mug shots of Bobby "Angel" Valdez. He tapped it against his knee and looked at Tony and said, "I think maybe we've come to the wrong place this time."

"It sure looks that way," Tony said.

Tucker slid forward on his chair. "What was it you wanted?"

Tony told him about Bobby Valdez.

"Well," Tucker said, "I don't move in the circles I once did, but I'm not completely out of touch either. I donate fifteen or twenty hours of my time every week to Self-Pride. That's a city-wide anti-drug campaign. I feel sort of like I've got debts to pay, you know? A Self-Pride Volunteer spends about half his time talking to kids, the other half working on an information-gathering program, sort of like TIP. You know about TIP?"

"Turn in Pushers," Tony said.

"Right. They have a number you can call and give anonymous tips about neighborhood drug dealers. Well, we don't wait for people to call us at Self-Pride. We canvas those neighborhoods where we know pushers work. We go door to door, talk to parents and kids, pump them for anything they know. We build up dossiers on dealers until we feel we've really got the goods, then we turn the dossiers over to the LAPD. So if this Valdez is dealing, there's a chance I'll know at least a little something about him."

Frank said, "I have to agree with Tony. You are rather remarkable."

"Hey, look, I don't deserve any pats on the back for my work at Self-Pride. I wasn't asking for congratulations. In my day I created a lot of junkies out of kids who might have done right if I hadn't been there to steer them wrong. It's going to take me a long, long time to help enough kids to balance the equation."

Frank took the photographs out of the envelope and gave them to Tucker.

The black man looked at each of the three shots. "I know the little bastard. He's one of about thirty guys we're building files on right now."

Tony's heartbeat accelerated a bit in anticipation of the chase to come.

"Only he doesn't use the name Valdez," Tucker said.

"Juan Mazquezza?"

"Not that either. I think he calls himself Ortiz."

"Do you know where we can find him?"

Tucker stood up. "Let me call the information center at Self-Pride. They might have an address on him."

"Terrific," Frank said.

Tucker started toward the kitchen to use the phone in there, stopped, looked back at them. "This might take a few minutes. If you'd like to pass the time looking at my designs, you can go into the study." He pointed to a set of double doors that opened off the living room.

"Sure," Tony said. "I'd like to see them."

He and Frank went into the study and found that it was even more sparsely furnished than the living room. There was a large expensive drawing table with its own lamp. A high stool with a padded seat and a spring back stood in front of the table, and beside the stool there was an artist's supply cabinet on wheels. Near one of the windows, a department store mannequin posed with head tilted coyly and shiny-smooth arms spread wide; bolts of bright cloth lay at its plastic feet. There were no shelves or storage cabinets; stacks of sketches and drawing tablets and draftsman's tools were lined up on the floor along one wall. Obviously, Eugene Tucker was confident that eventually he would be able to furnish the entire townhouse with pieces as exquisite as those in the living room, and in the meantime, regardless of the inconvenience, he did not intend to waste money on cheap temporary furniture.

Quintessential California optimism, Tony thought.

Pencil sketches and a few full-color renditions of Tucker's work were thumbtacked to one wall. His dresses and two-piece suits and blouses were tailored yet flowing, feminine yet not frilly. He had an excellent sense of color and a flair for the kind of detail that made a piece of clothing special. Every one of the designs was clearly the work of a superior talent.

Tony still found it somewhat difficult to believe that the big hard-bitten black man designed women's clothes for a living. But then he realized that his own dichotomous nature was not so different from Tucker's. During the day, he was a homicide detective, desensitized and hardened by all of the violence he saw, but at night, he was an artist, hunched over a canvas in his apartment-studio, painting, painting, painting. In a curious way, he and Eugene were brothers under the skin.

Just as Tony and Frank were looking at the last of the sketches, Tucker returned from the kitchen. "Well, what do you think?"

"Wonderful," Tony said. "You've got a terrific feeling for color and line."

"You're really good," Frank said.

"I know," Tucker said, and he laughed.

"Does Self-Pride have a file on Valdez?" Tony asked.

"Yes. But he calls himself Ortiz, like I thought. Jimmy Ortiz. From what we've been able to gather, he deals strictly in PCP. I know I'm not on solid ground when I start pointing the finger at other people . . . but so far as I'm concerned, a PCP dealer is the lowest kind of bastard in the drug trade. I mean, PCP is *poison*. It rots the brain cells faster than anything else. We don't have enough information in our file to turn it over to the police, but we're working on it."

"Address?" Tony asked.

Tucker handed him a slip of paper on which the address had been noted in neat handwriting. "It's a fancy apartment complex one block south of Sunset, just a couple of blocks from La Cienega."

"We'll find it," Tony said.

"Judging from what you've told me about him," Tucker said, "and from what we've learned about him at Self-Pride, I'd say this guy isn't the kind who's ever going to knuckle down and rehabilitate himself. You'd better put this one away for a long, long time."

"We're sure going to try," Frank said.

Tucker accompanied them to the front door, then outside, where the patio deck in front of the townhouse offered a wide view of Los Angeles in the basin below. "Isn't it gorgeous?" Tucker asked. "Isn't it something?"

"Quite a view," Tony said.

"Such a big, big, beautiful city," Tucker said with pride and affection, as if he had created the megalopolis himself. "You know, I just heard that the bureaucrats back in Washington made a study of mass transit possibilities for L.A. They were determined to ram some system or other down our throats, but they were stunned to find out it would cost at least one hundred billion dollars to build a rapid transit railway network that would handle only ten or twelve percent of the daily commuter crush. They still don't understand how vast the West is." He was rhapsodizing now, his broad face alight with pleasure, his strong hands tossing off one gesture after another. "They don't realize that the meaning of L.A. is space—space and mobility and freedom. This is a city with elbow room. Physical and emotional elbow room. Psychological elbow room. In L. A., you have a chance to be almost anything you want to be. Here, you can take your future out of the hands of other people and shape it yourself. It's fantastic. I love it. God, I love it!"

Tony was so impressed with the depth of Tucker's feeling for the city that he revealed his own secret dream. "I've always wanted to be an artist, to make a living with my art. I paint."

"Then why are you a cop?" Tucker asked.

"It's a steady paycheck."

"Screw steady paychecks."

"I'm a good cop. I like the work well enough."

"Are you a good artist?"

"Pretty good, I think."

"Then take the leap," Tucker said. "Man, you are living on the edge of the Western world, on the edge of possibility. Jump. Jump off. It's one hell of a thrill, and it's so damned far to the bottom that you'll never crash into anything hard or sharp. In fact, you'll probably find exactly the same thing I found. It's not like falling down at all. You'll feel like you're falling *up!*"

Tony and Frank followed the brick wall to the driveway, past a jade-plant hedge that had thick juicy leaves. The unmarked sedan was parked in the shade of a large date palm.

As Tony opened the door on the passenger's side, Tucker called to him from the patio deck, "Jump! Just jump off and fly!"

"He's some character," Frank said as he drove away from the town-house.

"Yeah," Tony said, wondering what it felt like to fly.

As they headed for the address that Tucker had given them, Frank talked a little about the black man and then a lot about Janet Yamada. Still mulling over Eugene Tucker's advice, Tony gave his partner only half his attention. Frank didn't notice that Tony was distracted. When he was talking about Janet Yamada, he really didn't attempt to carry on a conversation; he delivered a soliloquy.

Fifteen minutes later, they found the apartment complex where Jimmy Ortiz lived. The parking garage was underground, guarded by an iron gate that opened only to an electronic signal, so they couldn't see if there was a black Jaguar on the premises.

The apartments were on two levels, in randomly set wings, with open staircases and walkways. The complex was structured around an enormous swimming pool and a lot of lush greenery. There was also a whirlpool spa. Two girls in bikinis and a hairy young man were sitting in the swirling water, drinking a martini lunch and laughing at one another's banter as tendrils of steam writhed up from the turbulent pool around them.

Frank stopped at the edge of the Jacuzzi and asked them where Jimmy Ortiz lived.

One of the girls said, "Is he that cute little guy with the mustache?"

"Baby face," Tony said.

"That's him," she said.

"Does he have a mustache now?"

"If it's the same guy," she said. "This one drives a terrific Jag."

"That's him," Frank said.

"I think he lives over there," she said, "in Building Four, on the second floor, all the way at the end."

"Is he home?" Frank asked.

No one knew.

At Building Four, Tony and Frank climbed the stairs to the second floor. An open-air balcony ran the length of the building and served the four apartments that faced onto the courtyard. Along the railing, opposite the first three doors, pots of ivy and other climbing plants had been set out to give the second level a pleasant green look like that enjoyed by ground-floor residents; but there were no plants in front of the end apartment.

The door was ajar.

Tony's eyes met Frank's. A worried look passed between them.

Why was the door ajar?

Did Bobby know they were coming?

They flanked the entrance. Waited. Listened.

The only sound came from the happy trio in the courtyard whirlpool.

Frank raised his eyebrows questioningly.

Tony pointed to the doorbell.

After a brief hesitation, Frank pressed it.

Inside, the chimes rang softly. *Bong-bing-bong.*

They waited for a response, eyes on the door.

Suddenly the air seemed perfectly still and oppressively heavy. Humid. Thick. Syrupy. Tony had trouble breathing it; he felt as if he were drawing a fluid into his lungs.

No one answered the bell.

Frank rang it again.

When there was still no response, Tony reached under his jacket and slipped his revolver from its shoulder holster. He felt weak. His stomach was bubbling acidly.

Frank took out his revolver, listened closely for sounds of movement inside, then finally pushed the door all the way open.

The foyer was deserted.

Tony leaned sideways to get a better look inside. The living room, of which he could see only a small part, was shadowy and still. The drapes were shut, and there were no lights burning.

Tony shouted, "Police!"

His voice echoed under the balcony roof.

A bird chirruped in an olive tree.

"Come out with your hands raised, Bobby!"

On the street, a car horn sounded.

In another apartment a phone rang, muffled but audible.

"Bobby!" Frank shouted. "You hear what he said? We're the police. It's all over now. So just come out of there. Come on! *Right now!*"

Down in the courtyard, the whirlpool bathers had grown very quiet.

Tony had the crazy notion that he could hear people in a dozen apartments as they crept stealthily to their windows.

Frank raised his voice even further: "We don't want to hurt you, Bobby!"

"Listen to him!" Tony shouted into the apartment. "Don't force us to hurt you. Come on out peacefully."

Bobby didn't respond.

"If he was in there," Frank said, "he'd at least tell us to go fuck ourselves."

"So what now?" Tony asked.

"I guess we go in."

"Jesus, I hate shit like this. Maybe we should call a backup team."

"He's probably not armed," Frank said.

"You're kidding."

"He doesn't have any prior arrests for carrying a gun. Except when he's after a woman, he's a sniveling little creep."

"He's a killer."

"Women. He's only dangerous to women."

Tony shouted again: "Bobby, this is your last chance! Now, dammit, come out of there nice and slow!"

Silence.

Tony's heart was hammering furiously.

"Okay," Frank said. "Let's get this over with."

"If memory serves me right, you went in first the last time we had to do something like this."

"Yeah. The Wilkie-Pomeroy case."

"Then I guess it's my turn," Tony said.

"I know you've been looking forward to this."

"Oh, yes."

"With all your heart."

"Which is now in my throat."

"Go get him, tiger."

"Cover me."

"The foyer's too narrow for me to give you good cover. I won't be able to see past you once you go in."

"I'll stay as low as possible," Tony said.

"Make like a duck. I'll try to look over you."

"Just do the best you can."

Tony's stomach was cramping up on him. He took a couple of deep breaths and tried to calm down. That trick had no effect other than to make his heart pound harder and faster than it had been doing. At last, he crouched and launched himself through the open door, the revolver held out in front of him. He scuttled across the slippery tile floor of the foyer and stopped at the brink of the living room, searching the shadows for movement, expecting to take a bullet right between the eyes.

The living room was dimly illuminated by thin strips of sunlight that found their way around the edges of the heavy drapes. As far as Tony could tell, all of the lumpy shapes were couches and chairs and tables. The place appeared to be full of big, expensive, and utterly tasteless Americanized Mediterranean furniture. A narrow shaft of sunlight fell across a red velvet sofa that had a large and thoroughly grotesque wrought-iron fleur-de-lis bolted to its imitation oak side.

"Bobby?"

No response.

A clock ticking somewhere.

"We don't want to hurt you, Bobby."

Only silence.

Tony held his breath.

He could hear Frank breathing.

Nothing else.

Slowly, cautiously, he stood.

No one shot at him.

He felt along the wall until he located a light switch. A lamp with a garish bullfight scene on its shade came on in one corner, and he could see that both the living room and the open dining area beyond it were deserted.

Frank came in behind him and motioned toward the door of the foyer closet.

Tony stepped back, out of the way.

Holding his revolver at gut-level, Frank gingerly opened the sliding door. The closet contained only a couple of lightweight jackets and several shoe boxes.

Staying away from each other in order to avoid making a single easy target of themselves, they crossed the living room. There was a liquor cabinet with ridiculously large black iron hinges; the glass in the cabinet doors was tinted yellow. A round coffee table was in the center of the room, a mammoth eight-sided thing with a useless copper-lined brazier in the middle of it. The sofa and high-backed chairs were upholstered in flame-red velvet with lots of gold fringe and black tassels. The drapes were flashy yellow and orange brocade. The carpet was a thick green shag. It was a singularly ugly place to live.

And, Tony thought, it's also an absurd place in which to die.

They walked through the dining area and looked into the small kitchen. It was a mess. The refrigerator door and a few of the cupboards were standing open. Cans and jars and boxes of food had been pulled off the shelves and dumped onto the floor. Some items appeared to have been thrown down in a rage. Several jars were broken; sharp fragments of glass sparkled in the garbage. A puddle of maraschino cherry juice lay like a pink-red amoeba on the yellow tiles; the bright red cherries gleamed in every corner. Chocolate dessert topping was splashed all over the electric stove. Cornflakes were scattered everywhere. And dill pickles. Olives. Dry spaghetti. Someone had used mustard and grape jelly to scrawl one word four times on the only blank wall in the kitchen:

Cocodrilos
Cocodrilos
Cocodrilos
Cocodrilos

They whispered:

"What is it?"

"Spanish."

"What's it mean?"

"Crocodiles."

"Why crocodiles?"

"I don't know."

"Creepy," Frank said.

Tony agreed. They had walked into a bizarre situation. Even though he could not understand what was happening, Tony knew there was great danger ahead. He wished he knew which door it would pop out of.

They looked in the den, which was as overfurnished as the other two rooms. Bobby wasn't hiding in there or in the den closet.

They moved warily back down the hall toward the two bedrooms and two baths. They didn't make a sound.

They didn't find anything out of the ordinary in the first bedroom and bathroom.

In the master bedroom, there was another mess. All of the clothes had been taken out of the closet and strewn about. They were piled on the floor, wadded into balls on the bed, draped over the dresser where they had fallen when thrown, and most if not all of them were badly damaged. Sleeves and collars had been stripped off shirts. Lapels had been torn from sports jackets and suit coats. The inseams of trousers had been ripped open. The person who had done all of that had been functioning in a blind rage, yet he had been surprisingly methodical and thorough in spite of his fury.

But who had done it?

Someone with a grudge against Bobby?

Bobby himself? Why would he mess up his own kitchen and destroy his own clothes?

What did crocodiles have to do with it?

Tony had the disturbing feeling that they were moving too fast through the apartment, that they were overlooking something important. An explanation for the strange things they'd discovered seemed to be hovering at the edge of his mind, but he could not reach out and grab it.

The door to the adjoining bath was closed. It was the only place they hadn't looked.

Frank trained his revolver on the door and watched it while he spoke to Tony. "If he didn't leave before we got here, he has to be in the bathroom."

"Who?"

Frank gave him a quick perplexed glance. "Bobby, of course. Who else?"

"You think he tore up his own place?"

"Well . . . what do you think?"

"We're missing something."

"Yeah? Like what?"

"I don't know."

Frank moved toward the bathroom door.

Tony hesitated, listening to the apartment.

The place was about as noisy as a tomb.

"*Somebody* must be in that bathroom," Frank said.

They took up positions flanking the door.

"Bobby! You hear me?" Frank shouted. "You can't stay in there forever. Come out with your hands raised!"

Nobody came out.

Tony said, "Even if you're not Bobby Valdez, no matter who you are, you've got to come out of there."

Ten seconds. Twenty. Thirty.

Frank took hold of the knob and twisted it slowly until the bolt slipped out of its slot with a soft snick. He pushed the door open and convulsively threw himself back against the wall to get out of the way of any bullets or knives or other indications that he was unwelcome.

No gunfire. No movement.

The only thing that came out of the bathroom was a really terrible stench. Urine. Excrement.

Tony gagged. "Jesus!"

Frank put one hand over his mouth and nose.

The bathroom was deserted. The floor was puddled with bright yellow urine, and feces was smeared over the commode and sink and clear glass shower door.

"What in the name of God is going on here?" Frank asked through his fingers.

One Spanish word was printed twice in feces on the bathroom wall.

Cocodrilos
Cocodrilos

Tony and Frank swiftly retreated to the center of the bedroom, stepping on torn shirts and ruined suits. But now that the bathroom door had been opened, they could not escape the odor without leaving the room altogether, so they went into the hallway.

"Whoever did this really hates Bobby," Frank said.

"So you no longer think Bobby did it to himself?"

"Why would he? It doesn't make sense. Christ, this is about as weird as they come. The hairs are up on the back of my neck."

"Spooky," Tony agreed.

His stomach muscles were still painfully cramped with tension, and his heart was thumping only slightly slower than it had been when they'd first crept into the apartment.

They were both silent for a moment, listening for the footsteps of ghosts.

Tony watched a small brown spider as it climbed the corridor wall.

Finally Frank put his gun away and took out his handkerchief and wiped his sweat-streaked face.

Tony holstered his own revolver and said, "We can't just leave it like this and put a stakeout on the place. I mean, we've gone too far for that. We've found too much that needs explaining."

"Agreed," Frank said. "We'll have to call for assistance, get a warrant, and run a thorough search."

"Drawer by drawer."

"What do you think we'll find?"

"God knows."

"I saw a phone in the kitchen," Frank said.

Frank led the way down the hall to the living room, then around the corner, into the kitchen. Before Tony could follow him across the threshold from the dining area, Frank said, "Oh, Jesus," and tried to back out of the kitchen.

"What's the matter?"

Even as Tony spoke, something cracked loudly.

Frank cried out and fell sideways and clutched at the edge of a counter, trying to stay on his feet.

Another sharp crack slammed through the apartment, echoing from wall to wall, and Tony realized it was gunfire.

But the kitchen had been deserted!

Tony reached for his revolver, and he had the peculiar feeling he was moving in slow-motion while the rest of the world rushed past in frantic double time.

The second shot took Frank in the shoulder and spun him around. He crashed down into the mess of maraschino cherry juice and dry spaghetti and cornflakes and glass.

As Frank dropped out of the way, Tony was able to see beyond him for the first time, and he spotted Bobby Valdez. He was wriggling out of the cupboard space under the sink, a spot they hadn't thought to investigate because it looked too small to conceal a man. Bobby was squirming and slithering out of there like a snake from a tight hole. Only his legs were still under the sink; he was on his side, pulling himself out with one arm, holding a .32 pistol in his other hand. He was naked. He looked sick. His eyes were huge, wild, dilated, sunken in rings of puffy dark flesh. His face was shockingly pale, his lips bloodless. Tony took in all of those details in a fraction of a second, with senses sharpened by a flood of adrenaline.

Frank was just hitting the floor, and Tony was still reaching for his revolver when Bobby fired a third time. The bullet whacked into the edge of the archway. An explosion of plaster chips stung Tony's face.

He threw himself backward and down, twisting as he went, struck the floor too hard with his shoulder, gasped in pain, and rolled out of the dining area, out of the line of fire. He scrambled behind a chair in the living room and finally got his gun out of its holster.

Perhaps six or seven seconds had passed since Bobby had fired the first shot.

Someone was saying, "Jesus, Jesus, Jesus, Jesus," in a quivering, high-pitched voice.

Suddenly, Tony realized he was listening to himself. He bit his lip and fought off an attack of hysteria.

He now knew what had been bothering him; he knew what they had overlooked. Bobby Valdez was selling PCP, and that should have told them something when they saw the state of the apartment. They should have remembered that pushers were sometimes stupid enough to use what they sold. PCP, also called angel dust, was an animal tranquilizer that had a fairly predictable effect upon horses and bulls. But when people took the stuff, their reactions ranged from placid trances to weird hallucinations to unexpected fits of rage and violence. As Eugene Tucker said, PCP was poison; it literally ate away at brain cells, rotted the mind. Supercharged on PCP, bursting with perverse energy, Bobby had smashed up his kitchen and had done all the other damage in the apartment. Pursued by fierce but imaginary crocodiles, desperately seeking refuge from their snapping jaws, he had squirmed into the cupboard under the sink and had pulled the doors shut. Tony hadn't thought to look in the cupboard because he hadn't realized they were stalking a raving lunatic. They had searched the apartment with caution, prepared for the moves that might be expected of a mentally-disturbed rapist and incidental killer, but unprepared for the bizarre actions of a gibbering madman. The mindless destruction evident in the kitchen and master bedroom, the apparently senseless writing on the walls, the disgusting mess in the bathroom—all of those were familiar indications of PCP-induced hysteria. Tony never served on the narcotics squad, but, nevertheless, he felt he should have recognized those signs. If he had interpreted them properly, he most likely would have checked under the sink, as well as anywhere else conceivably big enough for a man to hide, even if the quarters would be brutally uncomfortable; for it was not uncommon for a person on an extremely ugly PCP trip to surrender totally to his paranoia and try to hide from a hostile world, especially in cramped, dark, womblike places. But he and Frank misinterpreted the clues, and now they were up to their necks in trouble.

Frank had been shot twice. He was badly hurt. Maybe dying. Maybe dead.

No!

Tony tried to push that thought out of his mind as he cast about for a way to seize the initiative from Bobby.

In the kitchen Bobby began to scream in genuine terror. *"Hay muchos cocodrilos!"*

Tony translated: *There are many crocodiles!*

"Cocodrilos! Cocodrilos! Cocodrilos! Ah! Ah! Ahhhhh!" His repeated cry of alarm swiftly degenerated into a wordless wail of agony.

He sounds as if he's really being eaten alive, Tony thought, shivering.

Still screaming, Bobby rushed out of the kitchen. He fired the .32 into the floor, apparently trying to kill one of the crocodiles.

Tony crouched behind the chair. He was afraid that, if he stood up and took aim, he would be cut down before he could pull the trigger.

Doing a frantic little jig, trying to keep his bare feet out of the mouths of the crocodiles, Bobby fired into the floor once, twice.

Six shots so far, Tony thought. Three in the kitchen, three here. How many in the clip? Eight? Maybe ten.

Bobby fired again, twice, three times. One of the bullets ricocheted off something.

Nine shots had been fired. One more to go.

"Cocodrilos!"

The tenth shot boomed deafeningly in the enclosed space, and again the bullet ricocheted with a sharp whistle.

Tony stood up from his hiding place. Bobby was less than ten feet away. Tony held the service revolver in both hands, the muzzle lined up on the naked man's hairless chest. "Okay, Bobby. Be cool. It's all over."

Bobby seemed surprised to see him. Clearly, he was so deeply into his PCP hallucinations that he didn't remember seeing Tony in the kitchen archway less than a minute ago.

"Crocodiles," Bobby said urgently, in English this time.

"There are no crocodiles," Tony said.

"Big ones."

"No. There aren't any crocodiles."

Bobby squealed and jumped and whirled and tried to shoot at the floor, but his pistol was empty.

"Bobby," Tony said.

Whimpering, Bobby turned and looked at him.

"Bobby, I want you to lay face-down on the floor."

"They'll get me," Bobby said. His eyes were bulging out of his head; the dark irises were rimmed with wide circles of white. He was trembling violently. "They'll eat me."

"Listen to me, Bobby. Listen carefully. There are no crocodiles. You're hallucinating them. It's all inside your head. You hear me?"

"They came out of the toilets," Bobby said shakily. "And out of the shower drains. And the sink drain, too. Oh, man, they're big. They're real big. And they're all trying to bite off my cock." His fear began to turn to anger; his pale face flushed, and his lips pulled back from his teeth in a wolflike snarl. "I won't let them. I won't let them bite off my cock. I'll kill all of them!"

Tony was frustrated by his inability to get through to Bobby, and his frustration was exacerbated by the knowledge that Frank might be bleeding to death, getting weaker by the second, in desperate need of immediate medical attention. Deciding to enter into Bobby's dark fantasy in order to control it, Tony spoke in a soft and reassuring voice: "Listen to me. All of those crocodiles have crawled back into the toilets and the drains. Didn't you see them going? Didn't you hear them sliding down the pipes and out of the building? They saw that we'd come to help you, and they knew they were outnumbered. Every one of them has gone away."

Bobby stared at him with glassy eyes that were less than human.

"They've all gone away," Tony said.

"Away?"

"None of them can hurt you now."

"Liar."

"No. I'm telling the truth. All of the crocodiles have gone down the—"

Bobby threw his empty pistol.

Tony ducked under it.

"You rotten cop son of a bitch."

"Hold it, Bobby."

Bobby started toward him.

Tony backstepped away from the naked man.

Bobby didn't walk around the chair. He angrily pushed it aside, knocked it over, even though it was quite heavy.

Tony remembered that a man in an angel dust rage often exhibited superhuman strength. It was not uncommon for four or five burly policemen to have difficulty restraining one puny PCP junkie. There were several medical theories about the cause of this freakish increase in physical power, but no theory was of any help to an officer confronted by a raging man with the strength of five or six. Tony figured he probably wouldn't be able to subdue Bobby Valdez with anything less than the revolver, even though he was philosophically opposed to using that ultimate force.

"I'm gonna kill you," Bobby said. His hands were curled into claws. His face was bright red, and spittle formed at one corner of his mouth.

Tony put the big octagonal coffee table between them. "Stop right there, dammit!"

He didn't want to have to kill Bobby Valdez. In all his years with the LAPD, he had shot only three men in the line of duty, and on every occasion he had pulled the trigger strictly in self-defense. None of those three men had died.

Bobby started around the coffee table.

Tony circled away from him.

"Now, I'm the crocodile," Bobby said, grinning.

"Don't make me hurt you."

Bobby stopped and grabbed hold of the coffee table and tipped it up, over, out of the way, and Tony backed into a wall, and Bobby rushed him, shouting something unintelligible, and Tony pulled the trigger, and the bullet tore through Bobby's left shoulder, spinning him around, driving him to his knees, but incredibly, he got up again, his left arm all bloody and hanging uselessly at his side, and, screaming in anger rather than agony, he ran to the fireplace and picked up a small brass shovel and threw it, and Tony ducked, and then suddenly Bobby was rushing at him with an iron poker raised high, and the damned thing caught Tony across the thigh, and he yelped as pain flashed up his hip and down his leg, but the blow wasn't hard enough to break bones, and he didn't collapse, but he did drop down as Bobby swung it again, at his head this time, with more power behind it this time, and Tony fired up into the naked man's chest, at close range, and Bobby was flung backwards with one last wild cry, and he crashed into a chair, then fell to the floor, gushing blood like a macabre fountain, twitched, gurgled, clawed at the shag carpet, bit his own wounded arm, and finally was perfectly still.

Gasping, shaking, cursing, Tony holstered his revolver and stumbled to a telephone he'd spotted on one of the end tables. He dialed 0 and told the operator who he was, where he was, and what he needed. "Ambulance first, police second," he said.

"Yes, sir," she said.

He hung up and limped into the kitchen.

Frank Howard was still sprawled on the floor, in the garbage. He had managed to roll onto his back, but he hadn't gotten any farther.

Tony knelt beside him.

Frank opened his eyes. "You hurt?" he asked weakly.

"No," Tony said.

"Get him?"

"Yeah."

"Dead?"

"Yeah."

"Good."

Frank looked terrible. His face was milk-white, greasy with sweat. The whites of his eyes had an unhealthy yellowish cast that had not been there before, and the right eye was badly bloodshot. There was a hint of blue in his lips. The right shoulder and sleeve of his suit coat were soaked with blood. His left hand was clamped over his stomach wound, but a lot of blood had leaked from under his pale fingers; his shirt and the upper part of his trousers were wet and sticky.

"How's the pain?" Tony asked.

"At first, it was real bad. Couldn't stop screaming. But it's starting to get better. Just kind of a dull burning and thumping now."

Tony's attention had been focused so totally on Bobby Valdez that he hadn't heard Frank's screams.

"Would a tourniquet on your arm help at all?"

"No. The wound's too high. In the shoulder. There's no place to put a tourniquet."

"Help's on the way," Tony said. "I phoned in."

Outside, sirens wailed in the distance. It was too soon to be an ambulance or a black-and-white responding to his call. Someone must have phoned the police when the shooting started.

"That'll be a couple of uniforms," Tony said. "I'll go down and meet them. They'll have a pretty good first aid kit in the cruiser."

"Don't leave me."

"But if they've got a first aid kit—"

"I need more than first aid. Don't leave me," Frank repeated pleadingly.

"Okay."

"Please."

"Okay, Frank."

They were both shivering.

"I don't want to be alone," Frank said.

"I'll stay right here."

"I tried to sit up," Frank said.

"You just lay there."

"I couldn't sit up."

"You're going to be okay."

"Maybe I'm paralyzed."

"Your body's taken a hell of a shock, that's all. You've lost some blood. Naturally, you're weak."

The sirens moaned into silence outside of the apartment complex.

"The ambulance can't be far behind," Tony said.

Frank closed his eyes, winced, groaned.

"You'll be okay, buddy."

Frank opened his eyes. "Come to the hospital with me."

"I will."

"Ride in the ambulance with me."

"I don't know if they'll let me."

"Make them."

"All right. Sure."

"I don't want to be alone."

"Okay," Tony said. "I'll make them let me in the damned ambulance even if I have to pull a gun on them to do it."

Frank smiled thinly, but then a flash of pain burned the smile off his face. "Tony?"

"What is it, Frank?"

"Would you . . . hold my hand?"

Tony took his partner's right hand. The right shoulder was the one that had taken the bullet, and Tony thought Frank would have no use of that extremity, but the cold fingers closed around Tony's hand with surprising strength.

"You know what?" Frank asked.

"What?"

"You should do what he says."

"What who says?"

"Eugene Tucker. You should jump off. Take a chance. Do what you really want with your life."

"Don't worry about me. You've got to save your energy for getting better."

Frank grew agitated. He shook his head. "No, no, no. You've got to listen to me. This is important . . . what I'm trying to tell you. Damned important."

"Okay," Tony said quickly. "Relax. Don't strain yourself."

Frank coughed, and a few bubbles of blood appeared on his bluish lips.

Tony's heart was working like a runaway triphammer. Where was the goddamned ambulance? What the hell was taking the lousy bastards so long?

Frank's voice had a hoarse note in it now, and he was forced to pause repeatedly to draw breath. "If you want to be a painter . . . then do it. You're still young enough . . . to take a chance."

"Frank, please, for God's sake, save your strength."

"*Listen to me!* Don't waste any more . . . time. Life's too goddamned short . . . to fiddle away any of it."

"Stop talking like that. I've got a lot of years ahead, and so do you."

"They go by so fast . . . so fucking fast. It's no time at all."

Frank gasped. His fingers tightened their already firm grip on Tony's hand.

"Frank? What's wrong?"

Frank didn't say anything. He shuddered. Then he began to cry.

Tony said, "Let me see about that first aid kit."

"Don't leave me. I'm afraid."

"I'll only be gone a minute."

"Don't leave me." Tears streamed down his cheeks.

"Okay. I'll wait. They'll be here in a few seconds."

"Oh, Jesus," Frank said miserably.

"But if the pain's getting worse—"

"I'm not . . . in much pain."

"Then what's wrong? Something's wrong."

"I'm just embarrassed. I don't want anyone . . . to know."

"Know what?"

"I just . . . lost control. I just . . . I . . . peed in my pants."

Tony didn't know what to say.

"I don't want to be laughed at," Frank said.

"Nobody's going to laugh at you."

"But, Jesus, I peed . . . in my pants . . . like a baby."

"With all this other mess on the floor, who's going to notice?"

Frank laughed, wincing at the pain the laughter caused, and he squeezed Tony's hand even harder.

Another siren. A few blocks away. Approaching rapidly.

"The ambulance," Tony said. "It'll be here in a minute."

Frank's voice was getting thinner and weaker by the second. "I'm scared, Tony."

"Please, Frank. Please, don't be scared. I'm here. Everything's going to be all right."

"I want . . . someone to remember me," Frank said.

"What do you mean?"

"After I'm gone . . . I want someone to remember I was here."

"You'll be around a long time yet."

"Who's going to remember me?"

"I will," Tony said thickly. "I'll remember you."

The new siren was only a block away, almost on top of them.

Frank said, "You know what? I think . . . maybe I will make it. The pain's gone all of a sudden."

"Is it?"

"That's good, isn't it?"

"Sure."

The siren cut out as the ambulance stopped with a squeal of brakes almost directly below the apartment windows.

Frank's voice was getting so weak that Tony had to lean close to hear it. "Tony . . . hold me." His grip on Tony's hand slackened. His cold fingers opened. "Hold me, please. Jesus. Hold me, Tony. Will you?"

For an instant, Tony was worried about complicating the man's wounds, but then he knew intuitively that it no longer mattered. He sat down on the floor in the garbage and blood. He put an arm under Frank and lifted him into a sitting position. Frank coughed weakly, and his left hand slid off his belly; the wound was revealed, a hideous and unrepairable hole from which intestines bulged. From the moment Bobby first pulled the trigger, Frank had begun to die; he had never had a hope of survival.

"Hold me."

Tony took Frank into his arms as best he could, held him, held him as a father would hold a frightened child, held him and rocked gently, crooned softly, reassuringly. He kept crooning even after he knew that Frank was dead, crooning and slowly rocking, gently and serenely rocking, rocking.

•

At four o'clock Monday afternoon, the telephone company serviceman arrived at Hilary's house. She showed him where the five extensions were located. He was just about to begin work on the kitchen phone when it rang.

She was afraid that it was the anonymous caller again. She didn't want to answer it, but the serviceman looked at her expectantly, and on the fifth ring she overcame her fear, snatched up the receiver. "Hello?"

"Hilary Thomas?"

"Yes."

"This is Michael Savatino. Savatino's Ristorante?"

"Oh, I don't need reminding. I won't forget you or your wonderful restaurant. We had a perfect dinner."

"Thank you. We try very hard. Listen, Miss Thomas—"

"Please call me Hilary."

"Hilary, then. Have you heard from Tony yet today?"

Suddenly she was aware of the tension in his voice. She *knew*, almost as a clairvoyant might know, that something awful had happened to Tony. For a moment she was breathless, and fuzzy darkness closed in briefly at the edges of her vision.

"Hilary? Are you there?"

"I haven't heard from him since last night. Why?"

"I don't want to alarm you. There was some trouble—"

"Oh, God."

"—but Tony wasn't hurt."

"Are you sure?"

"Just a few bruises."

"Is he in the hospital?"

"No, no. He's really all right."

The knot of pressure in her chest loosened a bit.

"What kind of trouble?" she asked.

In a few sentences, Michael told her about the shooting.

It could have been Tony who died. She felt weak.

"Tony's taking it hard," Michael said. "Very hard. When he and Frank first started working together, they didn't get along well. But things have improved. The past few days, they got to know each other better. In fact they'd gotten fairly close."

"Where's Tony now?"

"His apartment. The shooting was at eleven-thirty this morning. He's been at his apartment since two. I was with him until a few minutes ago. I wanted to stay, but he insisted I go to the restaurant as usual. I wanted him to come with me, but he wouldn't. He won't admit it, but he needs someone right now."

"I'll go to him," she said.

"I was hoping you'd say that."

Hilary freshened up and changed clothes. She was ready to leave fifteen minutes before the repairman had finished with the phones, and she never endured a longer quarter-hour.

In the car, on the way to Tony's place, she recalled how she had felt in that dark moment when she'd thought Tony was seriously hurt, perhaps dead. She nearly had been sick to her stomach. An intolerable sense of loss had filled her.

Last night, in bed, awaiting sleep, she had argued with herself about whether or not she loved Tony. Could she possibly love anyone after the physical and psychological torture she had suffered as a child, after what she had learned about the ugly duplicitous nature of most other human beings? And could she love a man she'd known for only a few days? The argument still wasn't settled. But now she knew that she dreaded losing Tony Clemenza in a way and to a degree that she had never feared losing anyone else in her life.

At his apartment complex, she parked beside the blue Jeep.

He lived upstairs in a two-story building. Glass wind chimes were hung from the balcony near one of the other apartments; they sounded melancholy in the late-afternoon breeze.

When he answered the door, he wasn't surprised to see her. "I guess. Michael called you."

"Yes. Why didn't you?" she asked.

"He probably told you I'm a total wreck. As you can see, he exaggerates."

"He's concerned about you."

"I can handle it," he said, forcing a smile. "I'm okay."

In spite of his attempt to play down his reaction to Frank Howard's death, she saw the haunted look in his face and the bleak expression in his eyes.

She wanted to hug him and console him, but she was not very good with people in ordinary circumstances, let alone in a situation like this. Besides, she sensed that he had to be ready for consolation before she dared offer it, and he was not.

"I'm coping," he insisted.

"Can I come in anyway?"

"Oh. Sure. Sorry."

He lived in a one-bedroom bachelor apartment, but the living room, at least, was large and airy. It had a high ceiling and a row of big windows in the north wall.

"Good northern light for a painter," Hilary said.

"That's why I rented the place."

It looked more like a studio than like a living room. A dozen of his eye-catching paintings hung on the walls. Other canvases were standing on the floor, leaning against the walls, stacks of them in some places, sixty or seventy in all. Two easels held works in progress. There were also a large drawing table, stool, and artist's supply cabinet. Tall shelves were jammed full of oversized art books. The only concessions to ordinary living room decor were two short sofas, two end tables, two lamps, a coffee table—all of which were arranged to form a cozy conversation corner. Although its arrangement was peculiar, the room had great warmth and livability.

"I've decided to get drunk," Tony said as he closed the door. "Very drunk. Totally smashed. I was just pouring my first drink when you rang. Would you like something?"

"What are you drinking?" she asked.

"Bourbon on the rocks."

"Make it the same for me."

While he was in the kitchen preparing drinks, she took a closer look at his paintings. Some of them were ultra-realistic; in these the detail was so fine, so brilliantly observed, so flawlessly rendered that, in terms of re-alism, the paintings actually transcended mere photography. Several of the canvases were surrealistic, but in a fresh and commanding style that was not at all reminiscent of Dalí, Ernst, Miró, or Tanguy. They were closer to the work of René Magritte than to anything else, especially the Magritte of *The Domain of Arnheim* and *Ready-Made Bouquet*. But Magritte had never used such meticulous detail in his paintings, and it was this realer than real quality in Tony's visions that made the surrealistic el-ements especially striking and unique.

He returned from the kitchen with two glasses of bourbon, and as she accepted her drink she said, "Your work is so fresh and exciting."

"Is it?"

"Michael is right. Your paintings will sell as fast as you can create them."

"It's nice to think so. Nice to dream about."

"If you'd only give them a chance—"

"As I said before, you're very kind, but you're not an expert."

He was not at all himself. His voice was drab, wooden. He was dull, washed out, depressed.

She needled him a bit, hoping to bring him to life. "You think you're so smart," she said. "But you're dumb. When it comes to your own work, you're dumb. You're blind to the possibilities."

"I'm just an amateur."

"Bullshit."

"A fairly *good* amateur."

"Sometimes you can be so damned infuriating," she said.

"I don't want to talk about art," he said.

He switched on the stereo: Beethoven interpreted by Ormandy. Then he went to one of the sofas in the far corner of the room.

She followed him, sat beside him. "What *do* you want to talk about?"

"Movies," he said.

"Do you really?"

"Maybe books."

"Really?"

"Or theater."

"What you really want to talk about is what happened to you today."

"No. That's the last thing."

"You *need* to talk about it, even if you don't want to."

"What I need to do is forget all about it, wipe it out of my mind."

"So you're playing turtle," she said. "You think you can pull your head under your shell and close up tight."

"Exactly," he said.

"Last week, when I wanted to hide from the whole world, when you wanted me to go out with you instead, you said it wasn't healthy for a person to withdraw into himself after an upsetting experience. You said it was best to share your feelings with other people."

"I was wrong," he said.

"You were right."

He closed his eyes, said nothing.

"Do you want me to leave?" she asked.

"No."

"I will if you want me to. No hard feelings."

"Please stay," he said.

"All right. What shall we talk about?"

"Beethoven and bourbon."

"I can take a hint," she said.

They sat silently side by side on the sofa, eyes closed, heads back, listening to the music, sipping the bourbon, as the sunlight turned amber and then muddy orange beyond the large windows. Slowly, the room filled up with shadows.

•

Early Monday evening, Avril Tannerton discovered someone had broken into Forever View. He made that discovery when he went down to the cellar, where he had a lavishly equipped woodworking shop; he saw that one of the panes in a basement window had been carefully covered with masking tape and then broken to allow the intruder to reach the latch. It was a much smaller-than-average window, hinged at the top, but even a fairly large man could wriggle through it if he was determined.

Avril was certain there was no stranger in the house at the moment. Furthermore, he knew the window hadn't been broken Friday night, for he would have noticed it when he spent an hour in his workshop, doing fine sanding on his latest project—a cabinet for his three hunting rifles and two shotguns. He didn't believe anyone would have the nerve to smash the window in broad daylight or when he, Tannerton, was at home, as he had been the previous night, Sunday; therefore, he concluded that the break-in must have occurred Saturday night, while he was at Helen Virtillion's place in Santa Rosa. Except for the body of Bruno Frye, Forever View had been deserted on Saturday. Evidently, the burglar had known the house was unguarded and had taken advantage of the opportunity.

Burglar.

Did that make sense?

A burglar?

He didn't think anything had been stolen from the public rooms on the first floor or from his private quarters on the second level. He was positive he would have noticed evidence of a theft almost immediately upon his return Sunday morning. Besides, his guns were still in the den, and so was his extensive coin collection; certainly, those things would be prime targets for a thief.

In his woodworking shop, to the right of the broken cellar window, there were a couple of thousand dollars' worth of high-quality hand and power tools. Some of them were hanging neatly from a pegboard wall, and others were nestled in custom racks he had designed and built for them. He could tell at a glance that nothing was missing.

Nothing stolen.

Nothing vandalized.

What sort of burglar broke into a house just to have a look at things?

Avril stared at the pieces of glass and masking tape on the floor, then up at the violated window, then around the cellar, pondering the situation, until suddenly he realized that, indeed, something had been taken. Three fifty-pound bags of dry mortar mix were gone. Last spring, he and Gary Olmstead had torn out the old wooden porch in front of the funeral home; they'd built up the ground with a couple truckloads of topsoil, had terraced it quite professionally, and had put down a new brick veranda. They had also torn up the cracked and canted concrete sidewalks and had replaced them with brick. At the end of the five-week-long chore, they found themselves with three extra bags of mortar mix, but they didn't return them for a refund because Avril intended to construct a large patio behind the house next summer. Now those three bags of mix were gone.

That discovery, far from answering his questions, only contributed to the mystery. Amazed and perplexed, he stared at the spot where the bags had been stacked.

Why would a burglar ignore expensive rifles, valuable coins, and other worthwhile loot in favor of three relatively inexpensive bags of dry mortar mix?

Tannerton scratched his head. "Strange," he said.

•

After sitting quietly beside Hilary in the gathering darkness for fifteen minutes, after listening to Beethoven, after sipping two or three ounces of bourbon, and after Hilary replenished their drinks, Tony found himself talking about Frank Howard. He didn't realize he was going to open up to her until he had already begun speaking; he seemed to hear himself suddenly in mid-sentence, and then the words poured out. For half an hour, he spoke continuously, pausing only for an occasional sip of bourbon, recalling his first impression of Frank, the initial friction between them, the tense and the humorous incidents on the job, that boozy evening at The Bolt Hole, the blind date with Janet Yamada, and the recent understanding and affection that he and Frank had found for each other. Finally, when he began to recount the events in Bobby Valdez's apartment, he spoke hesitantly, softly. When he closed his eyes he could see that garbage- and blood-spattered kitchen as vividly as he could see his own living room when his eyes were open. As he tried to tell Hilary what it had been like to hold a dying friend in his arms, he began to tremble. He was terribly cold, frigid in his flesh and bones, icy in his heart. His teeth chattered. Slouched on the sofa, deep in purple shadow, he shed his first tears for Frank Howard, and they felt scalding hot on his chilled skin.

As he wept, Hilary took his hand; then she held him in much the same way that he had held Frank. She used her small cocktail napkin to dry his face. She kissed his cheeks, his eyes.

At first, she offered only consolation, and that was all he sought; but without either of them consciously striving to alter the embrace, the quality of it began to change. He put his arms around her, and it was no longer entirely clear who was holding and comforting whom. His hands moved up and down her sleek back, up and down, and he marveled at the exquisite contours; he was excited by the firmness and strength and suppleness of her body beneath the blouse. Her hands roamed over him, too, stroking and squeezing and admiring his hard muscles. She kissed the corners of his mouth, and he eagerly returned those kisses full on her lips. Their quick tongues met, and the kiss became hot, fiercely hot and liquid; it left them breathing harder than they had been when their lips first touched.

Simultaneously, they realized what was happening, and they froze, uncomfortably reminded of the dead friend for whom mourning had just begun. If they gave each other what they so badly needed and wanted, it might be like giggling at a funeral. For a moment, they felt that they were on the verge of committing a thoughtless and thoroughly blasphemous act.

But their desire was so strong that it overcame their doubts about the propriety of making love on this night of all nights. They kissed tentatively, then hungrily, and it was as sweet as ever. Her hands moved demandingly over him, and he responded to her touch, then she to his. He realized it was good and right for them to seek joy together. Making love now was not an act of disrespect toward the dead; it was a reaction to the unfairness of death itself. Their unquenchable desire was the result of many things, one of which was a profound animal need to prove that they were alive, fully and unquestionably and exuberantly alive.

By unspoken agreement, they got up from the couch and went to the bedroom.

Tony switched on a lamp in the living room as they walked out; that light spilled through the open doorway and was the only thing that illuminated the bed. Soft penumbral light. Warm and golden light. The light seemed to love Hilary, for it didn't merely fall dispassionately upon her as it did upon the bed and upon Tony; it caressed her, lovingly accented the milky bronze shade of her flawless skin, added luster to her raven-black hair, and sparkled in her big eyes.

They stood beside the bed, embracing, kissing, and then he began to undress her. He unbuttoned her blouse, slipped it off. He unhooked her bra; she shrugged out of it and let it fall to the floor. Her breasts were beautiful—round and full and upswept. The nipples were large and erect; he bent to them, kissed them. She took his head in her hands, lifted his face to hers, found his mouth with hers. She sighed. His hands trembled with excitement as he unbuckled her belt, unsnapped and unzipped her jeans. They slid down her long legs, and she stepped out of them, already having stepped out of her shoes.

Tony went to his knees before her, intending to pull off her panties, and he saw a four-inch-long welt of scar tissue along her left side. It began at the edge of her flat belly and curved around to her back. It was not the result of surgery; it wasn't the thin line that even a moderately neat doctor would leave. Tony had seen old, well-healed bullet and knife wounds before, and even though the light was not bright, he was sure that this mark had been caused by either a gun or a blade. A long time ago, she had been hurt badly. The thought of her enduring so much pain stirred in him a desire to protect and shelter her. He had a hundred questions about the scar, but this wasn't the right time to ask them. He tenderly kissed the welt of puckered skin, and he felt her stiffen. He sensed that the scar embarrassed her. He wanted to tell her it didn't detract from her beauty or desirability, and that, in fact, this single minor flaw only emphasized her otherwise incredible physical perfection.

The way to reassure her was with actions, not words. He pulled down her panties, and she stepped out of them. Slowly, slowly, he moved his hands up her gorgeous legs, over the lovely curves of her calves, over the smooth thighs. He kissed her glossy black pubic bush, and the hairs bristled crisply against his face. As he stood, he cupped her firm buttocks in both hands, gently kneaded the taut flesh, and she moved against him, and their lips met again. The kiss lasted either a few seconds or a few minutes, and when it ended, Hilary said, "Hurry."

As she pulled back the covers and got into bed, Tony stripped off his own clothes. Nude, he stretched out beside her and took her in his arms.

They explored each other with their hands, endlessly fascinated by textures and shapes and angles and sizes and degrees of resiliency, and his erection throbbed as she fondled it.

After a while, but long before he actually entered her, he felt strangely as if he were melting into her, as if they were becoming one creature, not physically or sexually so much as spiritually, blending together through some sort of truly miraculous psychic osmosis. Overwhelmed by the warmth of her, excited by the promise of her magnificent body, but most deeply affected by the unique murmurs and movements and actions and reactions that made her Hilary and nobody but Hilary, Tony felt as if he had taken some new and exotic drug. His perceptions seemed to extend beyond the range of his own senses, so that he felt almost as if he were seeing through Hilary's eyes as well as through his own, feeling with his hands *and* her hands, tasting her mouth with his but also tasting his mouth with hers. Two minds, meshed. Two hearts, synchronized.

Her hot kisses made him want to taste every part of her, every delicious inch, and he did, arriving, at long last, at the warm juncture of her thighs. He spread her elegant legs and licked the moist center of her, opened those secret folds of flesh with his tongue, found the hidden nubble that, when softly flicked, caused her to gasp with pleasure.

She began to moan and writhe under the loving lash.

"Tony!"

He made love to her with his tongue and teeth and lips.

She arched her back, clutched the sheets with both hands, thrashed ecstatically.

As she raised herself, he slipped his hands under her, grabbed her rump, held her to him.

"Oh, Tony! Yes, yes!"

She was breathing deeply, rapidly. She tried to pull away from him when the pleasure became too intense, but then a moment later she thrust herself at him, begging for more. Eventually, she began to quiver all over, and those shallow tremors swiftly grew into wonderful wrenching shudders of pure delight. She gasped for breath and tossed her head and cried out deliriously, rode the wave within her, came and came again, lithe muscles contracting, relaxing, contracting, relaxing, until finally she was exhausted. She collapsed, and sighed.

He raised his head, kissed her fluttering belly, then moved up to tease her nipples with his tongue.

She reached down between them and gripped the iron hardness of him. Suddenly, as she anticipated this final joining, this complete union, she was filled with a new erotic tension.

He opened her with his fingers, and she released him from her hand, and he guided himself into her.

"Yes, yes, yes," she said as he filled her up. "My lovely Tony. Lovely, lovely, lovely Tony."

"You're beautiful."

It had never been sweeter for him. He braced himself above her on his fully-extended arms, looked down at her exquisite face. Their eyes locked, and after a moment it seemed that he was no longer merely staring at her, but into her, through her eyes, into the essence of Hilary Thomas, into her soul. She closed her eyes, and a moment later he closed his, and he discovered that the extraordinary bond was not destroyed when the gaze was broken.

Tony had made love to other women, but he had never been as close to any of them as he was to Hilary Thomas. Because this coupling was so special, he wanted to make it last a long time, wanted to bring her to the edge with him, wanted to take the plunge together. But this time he did not have the kind of control that usually marked his love-making. He was rushing toward the brink and could do nothing to stop himself. It was not just that she was tighter and slicker and hotter than other women he had known; it was not merely some trick of well-trained vaginal muscles; it was not that her perfect breasts drove him wild or that her silken skin was far silkier than that of any other women in his experience. All of those things were true, but it was the fact that she was special to him, extraordinarily special in a way that he had not yet even fully defined, that made being with her unbearably exciting.

She sensed his onrushing orgasm, and she put her hands on his back, pulled him down. He didn't want to burden her with his full weight, but she seemed unaware of it. Her breasts squashed against his chest as he settled onto her. She lifted her hips and ground her pelvis against him, and he thrust harder and faster. Incredibly, she started to come again just as he began to spurt uncontrollably. She held him close, held him tight, repeatedly whispering his name as he erupted and erupted within her, thickly and forcefully and endlessly within her, in the deepest and darkest reaches of her. As he emptied himself, a tremendous tide of tenderness and affection and aching need swept through him, and he knew that he would never be able to let her go.

•

Afterwards, they lay side by side on the bed, holding hands, heartbeats gradually easing.

Hilary was physically and emotionally wrung out by the experience. The number and startling power of her climaxes had shaken her. She'd never felt anything quite like it. Each orgasm had been a bolt of lightning, striking to the core of her, jolting through every fiber, an indescribably thrilling current. But Tony had given her a great deal more than sexual pleasure; she had felt something else, something new to her, something splendid and powerful that was beyond words.

She was aware that some people would say the word "love" perfectly described her feelings, but she wasn't ready to accept that disturbing definition. For a long, long time, since her childhood, the words "love" and "pain" had been inextricably linked in Hilary's mind. She couldn't believe that she was in love with Tony Clemenza (or he with her), dared not believe it, for if she were to do so, she would make herself vulnerable, leave herself defenseless.

On the other hand, she had difficulty believing that Tony would knowingly hurt her. He wasn't like Earl, her father. He wasn't like anyone she had ever known before. There was a tenderness about him, a quality of mercy, that made her feel that she would be perfectly safe in his hands. Perhaps she ought to take a chance with him. Maybe he was the one man who was worth the risk.

But then she realized how she would feel if their luck together went sour after she had put everything on the line for him. That would be a hard blow. She didn't know if she would bounce back from that one.

A problem.

No easy solution.

She didn't want to think about it right now. She just wanted to lay beside him, basking in the glow that they had created together.

She began to remember their lovemaking, the erotic sensations that had left her weak, some of which still lingered warmly in her flesh.

Tony rolled onto his side and faced her. He kissed her throat, her cheek. "A penny for your thoughts."

"They're worth more than that," she said.

"A dollar."

"More than that."

"A hundred dollars?"

"Maybe a hundred thousand."

"Expensive thoughts."

"Not thoughts, really. Memories."

"Hundred-thousand-dollar memories?"

"Mmmmmm."

"Of what?"

"Of what we did a few minutes ago."

"You know," he said, "you surprised me. You seem so proper and pure—almost angelic—but you've got a wonderfully bawdy streak in you."

"I can be bawdy," she admitted.

"Very bawdy."

"You like my body?"

"It's a beautiful body."

For a while, they talked mostly nonsense, lovers' talk, murmuring dreamily. They were so mellow that everything seemed amusing to them.

Then, still speaking softly, but with a more serious note in his voice, Tony said, "You know, of course, I'm not ever going to let go of you."

She sensed that he was prepared to make a commitment if he could determine that she was ready to do likewise. But that was the problem. She wasn't ready. She didn't know if she would ever be ready. She wanted him. Oh, Jesus, how she wanted him! She couldn't think of anything more exciting or rewarding than the two of them living together, enriching each other's lives with their separate talents and interests. But she dreaded the disappointment and pain that would come if he ever stopped wanting her. She had put all of those terrible years in Chicago with Earl and Emma behind her, but she could not so easily disregard the lessons she had learned in that tenement apartment so long ago. She was afraid of commitment.

Looking for a way to avoid the implied question in his statement, hoping to keep the conversation frivolous, she said, "You're *never* going to let go of me?"

"Never."

"Won't it be awkward for you, trying to do police work with me in hand?"

He looked into her eyes, trying to determine if she understood what he had said.

Nervously, she said, "Don't hurry me, Tony. I need time. Just a little time."

"Take all the time you want."

"Right now I'm so happy that I just want to be silly. It's not the right time to be serious."

"So I'll try to be silly," he said.

"What shall we talk about?"

"I want to know all about you."

"That sounds serious, not silly."

"Tell you what. You be half-serious, and I'll be half-silly. We'll take turns at it."

"All right. First question."

"What's your favorite breakfast food?"

"Cornflakes," she said.

"Your favorite lunch?"

"Cornflakes."

"Your favorite dinner?"

"Cornflakes."

"Wait a minute," he said.

"What's wrong?"

"I figure you were serious about breakfast. But then you slipped in two silly responses in a row."

"I *love* cornflakes."

"Now you owe me two serious answers."

"Shoot."

"Where were you born?"

"Chicago."

"Raised there?"

"Yes."

"Parents?"

"I don't know who my parents are. I was hatched from an egg. A duck egg. It was a miracle. You must have read all about it. There's even a Catholic church in Chicago named after the event. Our Lady of the Duck Egg."

"Very silly indeed."

"Thank you."

"Parents?" he asked again.

"That's not fair," she said. "You can't ask the same thing twice."

"Who says?"

"I say."

"Is it that horrible?"

"What?"

"Whatever your parents did."

She tried to deflect the question. "Where'd you get the idea they did something horrible?"

"I've asked you about them before. I've asked you about your childhood, too. You've always avoided those questions. You were very smooth, very clever about changing the subject. You thought I didn't notice, but I did."

He had the most penetrating stare she'd ever encountered. It was almost frightening.

She closed her eyes so that he couldn't see into her.

"Tell me," he said.

"They were alcoholics."

"Both of them?"

"Yeah."

"Bad?"

"Oh, yeah."

"Violent?"

"Yeah."

"And?"

"And I don't want to talk about it now."

"It might be good for you."

"No. Please, Tony. I'm happy. If you make me talk about . . . them . . . then I won't be happy any more. It's been a beautiful evening so far. Don't spoil it."

"Sooner or later, I want to hear about it."

"Okay," she said. "But not tonight."

He sighed. "All right. Let's see. . . . Who's your favorite television personality?"

"Kermit the Frog."

"Who's your favorite human television personality?"

"Kermit the Frog," she said.

"I said *human* this time."

"To me, he seems more human than anyone else on TV."

"Good point. What about the scar?"

"Does Kermit have a scar?"

"I mean your scar."

"Does it turn you off?" she asked, again trying to deflect the question.

"No," he said. "It just makes you more beautiful."

"Does it?"

"It does."

"Mind if I check you out on my lie detector?"

"You have a lie detector here?"

"Oh, sure," she said. She reached down and took his flaccid prick in her hand. "My lie detector works quite simply. There's no chance of getting an inaccurate reading. We just take the main plug"—she squeezed his organ—"and we insert it in socket B."

"Socket B?"

She slid down on the bed and took him into her mouth. In seconds, he swelled into pulsing, rigid readiness. In a few minutes, he was barely able to restrain himself.

She looked up and grinned. "You weren't lying."

"I'll say it again. You're a surprisingly bawdy wench."

"You want my body again?"

"I want your body again."

"What about my mind?"

"Isn't that part of the package?"

She took the top this time, settled onto him, moved back and forth, side to side, up and down. She smiled at him as he reached for her jiggling breasts, and after that she was not aware of single movements or individual strokes; everything blurred into a continuous, fluid, superheated motion that had no beginning and no end.

At midnight, they went to the kitchen and prepared a very late dinner, a cold meal of cheese and leftover chicken and fruit and chilled white wine. They brought everything back to the bedroom and ate a little, fed each other a little, then lost interest in the food before they'd eaten much of anything.

They were like a couple of teenagers, obsessed with their bodies and blessed with apparently limitless stamina. As they rocked in rhythmic ecstasy, Hilary was acutely aware that this was not merely a series of sex acts in which they were engaged; this was an important ritual, a profound ceremony that was cleansing her of long-nurtured fears. She was entrusting herself to another human being in a way she would have thought impossible only a week ago, for she was putting her pride out of the way, prostrating herself, offering herself up to him, risking rejection and humiliation and degradation, with the fragile hope that he would not misuse her. And he did not. A lot of the things they did might have been degrading with the wrong partner, but with Tony each act was exhalting, uplifting, glorious. She was not yet able to tell him that she loved him, not with words, but she was saying the same thing when, in bed, she begged him to do whatever he wanted with her, leaving herself no protection, opening herself completely, until, finally, kneeling before him, she used her lips and tongue to draw one last ounce of sweetness from his loins.

Her hatred for Earl and Emma was as strong now as it had been when they were alive, for it was their influence that made her unable to express her feelings to Tony. She wondered what she would have to do to break the chains that they had put on her.

For a while, she and Tony lay in bed, holding each other, saying nothing because nothing needed to be said.

Ten minutes later, at four-thirty in the morning, she said, "I should be getting home."

"Stay."

"Are you capable of doing more?"

"God, no! I'm wiped out. I just want to hold you. Sleep here," he said.

"If I stay, we won't sleep."

"Are *you* capable of doing more?"

"Unfortunately, dear man, I'm not. But I've got things to do tomorrow, and so have you. And we're much too excited and too full of each other to get any rest so long as we're sharing a bed. We'll keep touching like this, talking like this, resisting sleep like this."

"Well," he said, "we've got to learn to spend the night together. I mean, we're going to be spending a lot of them in the same bed, don't you think?"

"Many, many," she said. "The first night's the worst. We'll adjust when the novelty wears off. I'll start wearing curlers and cold cream to bed."

"And I'll start smoking cigars and watching Johnny Carson."

"Such a shame," she said.

"Of course, it'll take a bit of time for the freshness to wear off."

"A bit," she agreed.

"Like fifty years."

"Or sixty."

They delayed her leaving for another fifteen minutes, but finally she got up and dressed. Tony pulled on a pair of jeans.

In the living room, as they walked toward the door, she stopped and stared at one of his paintings and said, "I want to take six of your best pieces to Wyant Stevens in Beverly Hills and see if he'll handle you."

"He won't."

"I want to try."

"That's one of the best galleries."

"Why start at the bottom?"

He stared at her, but he seemed to be seeing someone else. At last, he said, "Maybe I should jump."

"Jump?"

He told her about the impassioned advice he had received from Eugene Tucker, the black ex-convict who was now designing dresses.

"Tucker is right," she said. "And this isn't even a jump. It's only a little hop. You're not quitting your job with the police department or anything. You're just testing the waters."

Tony shrugged. "Wyant Stevens will turn me down cold, but I guess I don't lose anything by giving him the chance to do it."

"He won't turn you down," she said. "Pick out half a dozen paintings you feel are most representative of your work. I'll try to get us an appointment with Wyant either later today or tomorrow."

"You pick them out right now," he said. "Take them with you. When you get a chance to see Stevens, show them to him."

"But I'm sure he'll want to meet you."

"If he likes what he sees, then he'll want to meet me. And if he does like it, I'll be happy to go see him."

"Tony, really—"

"I just don't want to be there when he tells you it's good work but only that of a gifted amateur."

"You're impossible."

"Cautious."

"Such a pessimist."

"Realist."

She didn't have time to look at all of the sixty canvases that were stacked in the living room. She was surprised to learn that he had more than fifty others stored in closets, as well as a hundred pen and ink drawings, nearly as many watercolors, and countless preliminary pencil sketches. She wanted to see all of them, but only, when she was well-rested and fully able to enjoy them. She chose six of the twelve pieces that hung on the living room walls. To protect the paintings, they carefully wrapped them in lengths of an old sheet, which Tony tore apart for that purpose.

He put on a shirt and shoes, helped her carry the bundles to her car, where they stashed them in the trunk.

She closed and locked the trunk, and they looked at each other, neither of them wanting to say goodbye.

They were standing at the edge of a pool of light cast by a twenty-foot-high sodium-vapor lamp. He kissed her chastely.

The night was chilly and silent. There were stars.

"It'll be dawn before long," he said.

"Want to sing 'Two Sleepy People' with me?"

"I'm a lousy singer," he said.

"I doubt it." She leaned against him. "Judging from my experience, you're excellent at everything you do."

"Bawdy."

"I try to be."

They kissed again, and then he opened the driver's door for her.

"You're not going to work today?" she asked.

"No. Not after . . . Frank. I have to go in and write up a report, but that'll take only an hour or so. I'm taking a few days. I've got a lot of time coming to me."

"I'll call you this afternoon."

"I'll be waiting," he said.

She drove away from there on empty early-morning streets. After she had gone a few blocks, her stomach began to growl with hunger, and she remembered that she didn't have the fixings for breakfast at home. She'd intended to do her grocery shopping after the man from the telephone company had gone, but then she'd heard from Michael Savatino and had rushed to Tony's place. She turned left at the next corner and went to an all-night market to pick up eggs and milk.

•

Tony figured Hilary wouldn't need any more than ten minutes to get home on the deserted streets, but he waited fifteen minutes before he called to find out if she had made the trip safely. Her phone didn't ring. All he got was a series of computer sounds—the beeps and buzzes that comprised the language of smart machines—then a few clicks and snaps and pops, then the hollow ghostly hissing of a missed connection. He hung up, dialed once more, being careful to get every digit right, but again the phone would not ring.

He was certain that the new unlisted number he had for her was correct. When she had given it to him, he had double-checked to be sure he'd gotten it right. And she read it off a carbon copy of the telephone company work order, which she had in her purse, so there wasn't any chance she was mistaken about it.

He dialed the operator and told her his problem. She tried to ring the number for him, but she couldn't get through, either.

"Is it off the hook?" he asked.

"It doesn't seem to be."

"What can you do?"

"I'll report the number out of order," she said. "Our service department will take care of it."

"When?"

"Does this number belong to either an elderly person or an invalid?"

"No," he said.

"Then it falls under normal service procedures," she said. "One of our servicemen will look into it sometime after eight o'clock this morning."

"Thank you."

He put down the receiver. He was sitting on the edge of the bed. He stared pensively at the rumpled sheets where Hilary had lain, looked at the slip of paper on which her new number was written.

Out of order?

He supposed it was possible that the serviceman had made a mistake when he'd switched Hilary's phones yesterday afternoon. Possible. But not probable. Not very likely at all.

Suddenly, he thought of the anonymous caller who had been bothering her. A man who did that sort of thing was usually weak, ineffectual, sexually stunted; almost without exception, he was incapable of having a normal relationship with a woman, and he was generally too introverted and frightened to attempt rape. Usually. Almost without exception. Generally. But was it conceivable that this crank was the one out of a thousand who *was* dangerous?

Tony put one hand on his stomach. He was beginning to feel queasy.

If bookmakers in Las Vegas had been taking bets on the likelihood of Hilary Thomas becoming the target of two unconnected homicidal maniacs in less than a week, the odds against would have been astronomical. On the other hand, during his years with the Los Angeles Police Department, Tony had seen the improbable happen again and again; and long ago he had learned to expect the unexpected.

He thought of Bobby Valdez. Naked. Crawling out of that small kitchen cabinet. Eyes wild. The pistol in his hand.

Outside the bedroom window, even though first light still had not touched the eastern sky, a bird cried. It was a shrill cry, rising and falling and rising again as the bird swooped from tree to tree in the courtyard; it sounded as if it was being pursued by something very fast and very hungry and relentless.

Sweat broke out on Tony's brow.

He got up from the bed.

Something was happening at Hilary's place. Something was wrong. Terribly wrong.

•

Because she stopped at the all-night market to buy milk, eggs, butter, and a few other items, Hilary didn't get home until more than half an hour after she left Tony's apartment. She was hungry and pleasantly weary. She was looking forward to a cheese omelet with a lot of finely chopped parsley—and then at least six uninterrupted hours of deep, deep sleep. She was far too tired to bother putting the Mercedes in the garage; she parked in the circular driveway.

The automatic lawn sprinklers sprayed water over the dark grass, making a cool hissing-whistling sound. A breeze rustled the palm fronds overhead.

She let herself into the house by the front entrance. The living room was pitch-black. But having anticipated a late return, she had left the foyer light burning when she'd gone out. Inside, she held the bag of groceries in one arm, closed and double-locked the door.

She switched on the living room ceiling light and took two steps out of the foyer before she realized that the place had been destroyed. Two table lamps were smashed, the shades torn to shreds. A glass display case lay in thousands of sharp pieces on the carpet; and the expensive limited-edition porcelains that had been in it were ruined; they were reduced to worthless fragments, thrown down on the stone hearth and ground underfoot. The sofa and armchairs were ripped open; chunks of foam and wads of cotton padding material were scattered all over the floor. Two wooden chairs, which apparently had been smashed repeatedly against one wall, were now only piles of kindling, and the wall was scarred. The legs were broken off the lovely little antique corner desk; all of the drawers were pulled from it and the bottoms knocked out of them. Every painting was still where she'd put it, but each hung in unrepairable ribbons. Ashes had been scooped out of the fireplace and smeared over the beautiful Edward Fields carpet. Not a single piece of furniture or decoration had been overlooked; even the fireplace screen had been kicked apart, and all of the plants had been jerked out of their pots and torn to bits.

Hilary was dazed at first, but then her shock gave way to anger at the vandals. "Son of a bitch," she said between clenched teeth.

She had passed many happy hours personally choosing every item in the room. She spent a small fortune on them, but it wasn't the cost of the wreckage that disturbed her; most of it was covered by insurance. However, there was sentimental value that could not be replaced, for these were the first really nice things that she had ever owned, and it hurt to lose them. Tears shimmered at the corners of her eyes.

Numb, disbelieving, she walked farther into the rubble before she realized that she might be in danger. She stopped, listened. The house was silent.

An icy shiver raced up her spine, and for one horrible instant she thought she felt someone's breath against the nape of her neck.

She whirled, looked behind her.

No one was there.

The foyer closet, which had been closed when she'd come into the house, was still closed. For a moment, she stared at it expectantly, afraid that it would open. But if anyone had been hiding in there, waiting for her to arrive, he would have come out by now.

This is absolutely crazy, she thought. It can't happen again. It just can't. That's preposterous. Isn't it?

There was a noise behind her.

With a soft cry of alarm, she turned and threw up her free arm to fend off the attacker.

But there was no attacker. She was still alone in the living room.

Nevertheless, she was convinced that what she had heard was not something so innocent as a naturally settling beam or floorboard. She knew she was not the only person in the house. She sensed another presence.

The noise again.

In the dining room.

A snapping. A tinkling. Like someone taking a step on broken glass or shattered china.

Then another step.

The dining room lay beyond an archway, twenty feet from Hilary. It was as black as a grave in there.

Another step: *tinkle-snap*.

She started to back up, cautiously retreating from the source of the noise, edging toward the front door, which now seemed a mile away. She wished she hadn't locked it.

A man moved out of the perfect darkness of the dining room, into the penumbral area beneath the archway, a big man, tall, and broad in the shoulders. He paused in the gloom for a second, then stepped into the brightly lit living room.

"No!" Hilary said.

Stunned, she stopped backing toward the door. Her heart leapt, and her mouth went dry, and she shook her head back and forth, back and forth: no, no, no.

He was holding a large and wickedly sharp knife. He grinned at her. It was Bruno Frye.

•

Tony was thankful that the streets were empty, for he couldn't have tolerated any delay. He was afraid he was already too late.

He drove hard and fast, north on Santa Monica, then west on Wilshire, putting the Jeep up to seventy miles an hour by the time he reached the first downslope just outside the Beverly Hills city limits, engine screaming, windows and loose dashboard knobs vibrating tinnily. At the bottom of the hill, the traffic light was red. He didn't brake. He pressed the horn in warning and flew through the intersection. He slammed across a shallow drainage channel in the street, a broad depression that was almost unnoticeable at thirty-five miles an hour, but at his speed it felt like a yawning ditch beneath him; for a fraction of a second he actually was airborne, thumping his head into the roof in spite of the restraining harness that he wore. The Jeep came back to the pavement with a bang, a many-voiced chorus of rattles and clanks, and a sharp bark of tortured rubber. It began to slue to the left, its rear end sliding around with a blood-chilling screech, smoke curling up from the protesting tires. For an electrifying instant, he thought he was going to lose control, but then abruptly the wheel was his again, and he was more than halfway up the next hill without realizing how he'd gotten there.

His speed was down to forty miles an hour, and he got it back up to sixty. He decided not to push it beyond that. He only had a short distance to go. If he wrapped the Jeep around a streetlamp or rolled it over and killed himself, he wouldn't be able to do Hilary any good.

He was still not obeying the rules of the road. He went much too fast and wide on what few turns there were, swinging out into the east-bound lanes, again thankful that there were no oncoming cars. The traffic signals were all against him, a perverse twist of fate, but he ignored every one of them. He wasn't worried about getting a ticket for speeding or reckless driving. If stopped, he would flash his badge and take the uniformed officers along with him to Hilary's place. But he hoped to God he wasn't given a chance to pick up those reinforcements, for it would mean stopping, identifying himself, and explaining the emergency. If they pulled him over, he would lose at least a minute.

He had a hunch that a minute might be the difference between life and death for Hilary.

•

As she watched Bruno Frye coming through the archway, Hilary thought she must be losing her mind. The man was dead. *Dead!* She had stabbed him twice, had seen his blood. She had seen him in the morgue, too, cold and yellow-gray and lifeless. An autopsy had been performed. A death certificate had been signed. *Dead men don't walk.* Nevertheless, he was back from the grave, walking out of the dark dining room, the ultimate uninvited guest, a large knife in one gloved hand, eager to finish what he had started last week; and it simply was not possible that he could be there.

Hilary closed her eyes and willed him to be gone. But a second later, when she forced herself to look again, he was still there.

She was unable to move. She wanted to run, but all of her joints—hips, knees, ankles—were rigid, locked, and she didn't have the strength to make them move. She felt weak, as frail as an old, old woman; she was sure that, if she somehow managed to unlock her joints and take a step, she would collapse.

She couldn't speak, but, inside, she was screaming.

Frye stopped less than fifteen feet from her, one foot in a cotton snowdrift of stuffing that had been torn from one of the ruined armchairs. He was pasty-faced, shaking violently, obviously on the edge of hysteria.

Could a dead man be hysterical?

She had to be out of her mind. *Had* to be. Stark raving mad. But she knew she wasn't.

A ghost? But she didn't believe in ghosts. And besides, wasn't a spirit supposed to be insubstantial, transparent, or at least translucent? Could an apparition be as solid as this walking dead man, as convincingly and terrifyingly *real* as he was?

"Bitch," he said. "You stinking bitch!"

His hard, low-pitched, gravelly voice was unmistakable.

But, Hilary thought crazily, his vocal cords already should have started to rot. His throat should be blocked with putrescence.

She felt high-pitched laughter building in her, and she struggled to control it. If she began to laugh, she might never stop.

"You killed me," he said menacingly, still teetering on the brink of hysteria.

"No," she said. "Oh, no. No."

"You did!" he screamed, brandishing the knife. "You killed me! Don't lie about it. I know. Don't you think I know? Oh, Jesus! I feel so strange, so alone, all alone, so empty." There was genuine spiritual agony mixed up with his rage. "So empty and scared. And it's all because of you."

He slowly crossed the few yards that separated him from her, stepping carefully through the rubble.

Hilary could see that this dead man's eyes were not blank or filmed with milky cataracts. These eyes were blue-gray and very much alive—and brimming with cold, cold anger.

"This time you'll stay dead," Frye said as he approached. "You won't come back this time."

She tried to retreat from him, took one hesitant step, and her legs almost buckled. But she didn't fall. She had more strength left than she had thought.

"This time," Frye said, "I'm taking every precaution. I'm not giving you a chance to come back. I'm going to cut your fuckin' heart out."

She took another step, but it didn't matter; she could not escape. She wouldn't have time to reach the door and throw off both locks. If she tried that, he would be on her in a second, ramming the knife down between her shoulders.

"Pound a stake through your fuckin' heart."

If she ran for the stairs and tried to get to the pistol in her bedroom, she surely wouldn't be as lucky as she had been the last time. This time he would catch her before she made it to the second floor.

"I'll cut your goddamned head off."

He loomed over her, within arm's reach.

She had nowhere to run, nowhere to hide.

"Gonna cut out your tongue. Stuff your fuckin' mouth full of garlic. Stuff it full of garlic so you can't sweet-talk your way back from hell."

She could hear her own thunderous heartbeat. She couldn't breathe because of the intensity of her fear.

"Cut your fuckin' eyes out."

She froze again, unable to move an inch.

"Gonna cut your eyes out and crush them so you can't see your way back."

Frye raised the knife high above his head. "Cut your hands off so you can't feel your way back from hell."

The knife hung up there for an eternity as terror distorted Hilary's sense of time. The wicked point of the weapon drew her gaze, nearly hypnotizing her.

"No!"

Sharp slivers of light glinted on the cutting edge of the poised blade.

"Bitch."

And then the knife started down, straight at her face, light flashing off the steel, down and down and down in a long, smooth, murderous arc.

She was holding the bag of groceries in one arm. Now, without pausing to think about what she must do, in one quick and instinctive move, she grabbed the bag with both hands and thrust it out, up, in the way of the descending knife, trying desperately to block the killing blow.

The blade rammed through the groceries, puncturing a carton of milk.

Frye roared in fury.

The dripping bag was knocked out of Hilary's grasp. It fell to the floor, spilling milk and eggs and scallions and sticks of butter.

The knife had been torn from the dead man's hand. He stopped to retrieve it.

Hilary ran toward the stairs. She knew that she had only delayed the inevitable. She had gained two or three seconds, no more than that, not nearly enough time to save herself.

The doorbell rang.

Surprised, she stopped at the foot of the stairs and looked back.

Frye stood up with the knife in hand.

Their eyes met; Hilary could see a flicker of indecision in his.

Frye moved toward her, but with less confidence than he had exhibited before. He glanced nervously toward the foyer and the front door.

The bell rang again.

Holding on to the bannister, backing up the steps, Hilary yelled for help, screamed at the top of her voice.

Outside, a man shouted: "Police!"

It was Tony.

"Police! Open this door!"

Hilary couldn't imagine why he had come. She had never been so glad to hear anyone's voice as she was to hear his, now.

Frye stopped when he heard the word "police," looked up at Hilary, then at the door, then at her again, calculating his chances.

She kept screaming.

Glass exploded with a bang that caused Frye to jump in surprise, and sharp pieces rang discordantly on a tile floor.

Although she couldn't see into the foyer from her position on the steps, Hilary knew that Tony had smashed the narrow window beside the front door.

"Police!"

Frye glared at her. She had never seen such hatred as that which twisted his face and gave his eyes a mad shine.

"Hilary!" Tony said.

"I'll be back," Frye told her.

The dead man turned away from her and ran across the living room, toward the dining room, apparently intending to slip out of the house by way of the kitchen.

Sobbing, Hilary dashed down the few steps she had climbed. She rushed to the front door, where Tony was calling her through the small broken windowpane.

•

Holstering his service revolver, Tony returned from the rear lawn, stepped into the brightly-lit kitchen.

Hilary was standing by the utility island in the center of the room. There was a knife on the counter, inches from her right hand.

As he closed the door he said, "There's no one in the rose garden."

"Lock it," she said.

"What?"

"The door. Lock it."

He locked it.

"You looked everywhere?" she asked.

"Every corner."

"Along both sides of the house?"

"Yes."

"In the shrubbery?"

"Every bush."

"Now what?" she asked.

"I'll call in to HQ, get a couple of uniforms out here to write up a report."

"It won't do any good," she said.

"You never can tell. A neighbor might have seen someone lurking here earlier. Or maybe somebody spotted him running away."

"Does a dead man have to run away? Can't a ghost just vanish when it wants to?"

"You don't believe in ghosts?"

"Maybe he wasn't a ghost," she said. "Maybe he was a walking corpse. Just your ordinary, everyday, run-of-the-mill walking corpse."

"You don't believe in zombies, either."

"Don't I?"

"You're too level-headed for that."

She closed her eyes and shook her head. "I don't know what I believe any more."

Her voice contained a tremor that disturbed him. She was on the verge of a collapse.

"Hilary . . . are you sure of what you saw?"

"It was *him*."

"But how could it be?"

"It was Frye," she insisted.

"You saw him in the morgue last Thursday."

"Was he dead then?"

"Of course he was dead."

"Who said?"

"The doctors. Pathologists."

"Doctors have been known to be wrong."

"About whether or not a person is dead?"

"You read about it in the papers every once in a while," she said. "They decide a man has kicked the bucket; they sign the death certificate; and then the deceased suddenly sits up on the undertaker's table. It happens. Not often. I admit it's not an everyday occurrence. I know it's pretty much a one in a million kind of thing."

"More like one in ten million."

"But it *does* happen."

"Not in this case."

"I *saw* him! Here. Right here. Tonight."

He went to her, kissed her on the cheek, took her hand, which was ice-cold. "Listen, Hilary, he's dead. Because of the stab wounds you inflicted, Frye lost half the blood in his body. They found him in a huge pool of it. He lost all that blood, and then he lay in the hot sun, unattended, for a few hours. He simply couldn't have lived through that."

"Maybe he could."

Tony lifted her hand to his lips, kissed her pale fingers. "No," he said quietly but firmly. "Frye would have had to die from such a blood loss."

Tony figured that she was suffering from mild shock, which was somehow responsible for a temporary short circuit of her senses, a brief confusion of memories. She just was getting this attack mixed up with the one last week. In a minute or two, when she regained control of herself, everything would clear up in her mind, and she would realize that the man who had been here tonight had not been Bruno Frye. All he had to do was stroke her a little bit, speak to her in a measured voice, and answer all her questions and wild suppositions as reasonably as possible, until she was her normal self again.

"Maybe Frye wasn't dead when they found him in that supermarket parking lot," she said. "Maybe he was just in a coma."

"The coroner would have discovered it when he did the autopsy."

"Maybe he didn't do the autopsy."

"If he didn't, another doctor on his staff did."

"Well," Hilary said, "maybe they were especially busy that day—a lot of bodies all at once or something like that—and they decided just to fill out a quick report without actually doing the work."

"Impossible," Tony said. "The medical examiner's office has the highest professional standards imaginable."

"Can't we at least check on it?" she asked.

He nodded. "Sure. We can do that. But you're forgetting that Frye must have passed through the hands of at least one mortician. Probably two. What little blood was left in him must have been drained out and replaced with embalming fluid."

"Are you sure?"

"He had to be either embalmed or cremated to be shipped to St. Helena. It's the law."

She considered that for a moment, then said, "But what if this *is* one of those bizarre cases, the one in ten million? What if he *was* mistakenly pronounced dead? What if the coroner *did* fudge on the autopsy? And what if Frye sat up on the embalmer's table, just as the mortician was starting to work on him?"

"You're grasping at straws, Hilary. Surely you can see that if anything like that happened, we'd know about it. If a mortician found himself in possession of a dead body that turned out not to be dead after all, that turned out to be a virtually bloodless man urgently in need of medical attention, then that mortician would get him to the nearest hospital in one hell of a hurry. He'd also call the coroner's office. Or the hospital would call. We'd know about it immediately."

She thought about what he had said. She stared at the kitchen floor and chewed on her lower lip. Finally, she said, "What about Sheriff Laurenski up there in Napa County?"

"We haven't been able to get a response out of him yet."

"Why not?"

"He's dodging our inquiries. He won't take our calls or return them."

"Well, doesn't that tell you that there's more to this than meets the eye?" she asked. "There's some sort of conspiracy, and the Napa sheriff is part of it."

"What sort of conspiracy did you have in mind?"

"I . . . don't know."

Still speaking softly and calmly, still certain that she would eventually respond to his gentle and reasonable arguments, Tony said, "A conspiracy between Frye and Laurenski and maybe even Satan himself? A conspiracy to cheat Death out of his due? An evil conspiracy to come back from the grave? A conspiracy to somehow live forever? None of that makes sense to me. Does it make sense to you?"

"No," she said irritably. "It doesn't make the slightest bit of sense."

"Good. I'm glad to hear that. If you said it did, I'd be worried about you."

"But, dammit, something highly unusual is happening here. Something extraordinary. And it seems to me that Sheriff Laurenski must be a part of it. After all, he protected Frye last week, actually lied for him. And now he's avoiding you because he doesn't have an acceptable explanation for his actions. Doesn't that seem like suspicious behavior to you? Doesn't he seem like a man who is up to his neck in some sort of conspiracy?"

"No," Tony said. "To me, he just seems like a very badly embarrassed policeman. For an officer of the law, he committed a damned serious error. He covered for a local big shot because he thought the man couldn't possibly be involved in rape and attempted murder. He couldn't get hold of Frye last Wednesday night, but he pretended that he had. He was totally convinced that Frye wasn't the man we wanted. But he was wrong. And now he's thoroughly ashamed of himself."

"Is that what you think?" she asked.

"That's what everyone at HQ thinks."

"Well, it's not what I think."

"Hilary—"

"I saw Bruno Frye tonight!"

Instead of gradually coming to her senses, as he had hoped she would do, she was getting worse, retreating further into this dark fantasy of walking dead men and strange conspiracies. He decided to get tough with her.

"Hilary, you didn't see Bruno Frye. He wasn't here. Not tonight. He's dead. Dead and buried. This was another man who came after you tonight. You're in mild shock. You're confused. That's perfectly understandable. However—"

She pulled her hand out of his and stepped back from him. "I am not confused. Frye was here. And he said he'd be back."

"Just a minute ago, you admitted your story doesn't make any sense at all. Didn't you?"

Reluctantly, she said, "Yes. That's what I said. It doesn't make sense. *But it happened!*"

"Believe me, I've seen how a sudden shock can affect people," Tony said. "It distorts perceptions and memories and—"

"Are you going to help me or not?" she asked.

"Of course I'm going to help you."

"How? What will we do?"

"For starters, we'll report the break-in and the assault."

"Isn't that going to be terribly awkward?" she asked sourly. "When I tell them that a dead man tried to kill me, don't you suppose they'll decide to commit me for a few days, until they can complete a psychiatric evaluation? You know me a hell of a lot better than anyone else, and even you think I'm crazy."

"I don't think you're crazy," he said, dismayed by her tone of voice. "I think you're distraught."

"Damn."

"It's understandable."

"Damn."

"Hilary, listen to me. When the responding officers get here, you won't say a word to them about Frye. You'll calm down, get a grip on yourself—"

"I've *got* a grip on myself!"

"—and you'll try to recall exactly what the assailant looked like. If you settle your nerves, if you give yourself half a chance, I'm sure you'll be surprised by what you'll remember. When you're calm, collected, more rational about this, you'll realize that he wasn't Bruno Frye."

"He was."

"He might have resembled Frye, but—"

"You're acting just like Frank Howard did the other night," she said angrily.

Tony was patient. "The other night, at least, you were accusing a man who was *alive*."

"You're just like everyone else I've ever trusted," she said, her voice cracking.

"I want to help you."

"Bullshit."

"Hilary, don't turn away from me."

"You're the one who turned away first."

"I care about you."

"Then show it!"

"I'm here, aren't I? What more proof do you need?"

"Believe me," she said. "That's the best proof."

He saw that she was profoundly insecure, and he supposed she was that way because she had had very bad experiences with people she had loved and trusted. Indeed, she must have been brutally betrayed and hurt, for no ordinary disappointment would have made her as sensitive as she was now. Still suffering from those old emotional wounds, she now demanded fanatical trust and loyalty. The moment he showed doubts about her story, she began to withdraw from him, even though he wasn't impugning her veracity. But, dammit, he knew it wasn't healthy to play along with her delusion; the best thing he could do for her was gently coax her back to reality.

"Frye was here tonight," she insisted. "Frye and nobody else. But I won't tell the police that."

"Good," he said, relieved.

"Because I'm not going to call the police."

"What?"

Without explaining, she turned away from him and walked out of the kitchen.

As he followed her through the wrecked dining room, Tony said, "You have to report this."

"I don't have to do anything."

"Your insurance company won't pay if you haven't filed a police report."

"I'll worry about that later," she said, leaving the dining room, entering the living room.

He trailed her as she weaved through the debris in the front room, heading toward the stairs. "You're forgetting something," he said.

"What's that?"

"I'm a detective."

"So?"

"So now that I'm aware of this situation, it's my duty to report it."

"So report it."

"Part of the report will be a statement from you."

"You can't force me to cooperate. I won't."

As they reached the foot of the stairs, he grabbed her by the arm. "Wait a minute. Please wait."

She turned and faced him. Her fear had been driven out by anger. "Let go of me."

"Where are you going?"

"Upstairs."

"What are you going to do?"

"Pack a suitcase and go to a hotel."

"You can stay at my place," he said.

"You don't want a crazy woman like me staying overnight," she said sarcastically.

"Hilary, don't be this way."

"I might go berserk and kill you in your sleep."

"I don't think you're crazy."

"Oh, that's right. You think I'm just confused. Maybe a little dotty. But not dangerous."

"I'm only trying to help you."

"You've got a funny way of doing it."

"You can't live in a hotel forever."

"I'll come home once he's been caught."

"But if you don't make a formal complaint, no one's even going to be looking for him."

"I'll be looking for him."

"You?"

"Me."

Now Tony was angry. "What game are you going to play—Hilary Thomas, Girl Detective?"

"I might hire private investigators."

"Oh, really?" he asked scornfully, aware that he might alienate her further with this approach, but too frustrated to be patient any longer.

"Really," she said. "Private investigators."

"Who? Philip Marlowe? Jim Rockford? Sam Spade?"

"You can be a sarcastic son of a bitch."

"You're forcing me to be. Maybe sarcasm will snap you out of this."

"My agent happens to know a first-rate firm of private detectives."

"I tell you, this isn't their kind of work."

"They'll do anything they're paid to do."

"Not anything."

"They'll do this."

"It's a job for the LAPD."

"The police will only waste their time looking for known burglars, known rapists, known—"

"That's a very good, standard, effective investigative technique," Tony said.

"But it won't work this time."

"Why? Because the assailant was an ambulatory dead man?"

"That's right."

"So you think maybe the police should spend their time looking for known *dead* rapists and burglars?"

The look she gave him was a withering mixture of anger and disgust.

"The way to break this case," she said, "is to find out how Bruno Frye could have been stone-cold dead last week—and alive tonight."

"Will you listen to yourself, for God's sake?"

He was concerned for her. This stubborn irrationality frightened him.

"I know what I said," she told him. "And I also know what I saw. And it wasn't just that I *saw* Bruno Frye in this house a little while ago. I heard him, too. He had that distinct, unmistakable, guttural voice. It was him. No one else. I saw him, and I heard him threatening to cut off my head and stuff my mouth full of garlic, as if he thought I was some sort of vampire or something."

Vampire.

That word jolted Tony because it made such a startling and incredible connection with several things that had been found last Thursday in Bruno Frye's gray Dodge van, strange items about which Hilary couldn't possibly know anything, items that Tony had forgotten until this morning. A chill swept through him.

"Garlic?" he asked. "Vampires? Hilary, what are you talking about?"

She pulled out of his grasp and hurried up the stairs.

He ran after her. "What's this about vampires?"

Climbing the steps, refusing to look at Tony or answer his questions, Hilary said, "Isn't this some swell story I've got to tell? I was assaulted by a walking dead man who thought *I* was a vampire. Oh, wow! Now you're absolutely positive that I've lost my mind. Call the little white chuckle wagon! Get this poor lady into a straitjacket before she hurts herself! Put her in a nice padded room real quick! Lock the door and throw away the key!"

In the second-floor hallway, a few feet from the top of the stairs, as Hilary was heading toward a bedroom door, Tony caught up with her. He grabbed her arm again.

"Let go, dammit!"

"Tell me what he said."

"I'm going to a hotel, and then I'm going to work this thing out on my own."

"I want to know every word he said."

"There's nothing you can do to stop me," she told him. "Now let me go."

He shouted in order to get through to her. "I have to know what he said about vampires, dammit!"

Her eyes met his. Apparently she recognized the fear and confusion in him, for she stopped trying to pull away. "What's so damned important?"

"The vampire thing."

"Why?"

"Frye apparently was obsessed with the occult."

"How do you know that?"

"We found some things in that van of his."

"What things?"

"I don't remember all of it. A deck of tarot cards, a Ouija board, more than a dozen crucifixes—"

"I didn't see anything about that in the newspapers."

"We didn't make a formal press release out of it," Tony said. "Besides, by the time we searched the van and inventoried its contents and were prepared to consider a release, all of the papers had published their first-day stories, and the reporters had filed their followups. The case just didn't have enough juice to warrant squeezing third-day coverage out of it. But let me tell you what else was in that van. Little linen bags of garlic taped above all the doors. Two wooden stakes with very sharp points. Half a dozen books about vampires and zombies and other varieties of the so-called 'living dead.'"

Hilary shuddered. "He told me he was going to cut out my heart and pound a stake through it."

"Jesus."

"He was going to cut out my eyes, too, so I wouldn't be able to find my way back from hell. That's how he put it. Those were his words. He was afraid that I was going to return from the dead after he killed me. He was raving like a lunatic. But then again, *he* returned from the grave, didn't he?" She laughed harshly, without a note of humor, but with a trace of hysteria. "He was going to cut off my hands, so I couldn't feel my way back."

Tony felt sick when he thought of how close that man had come to fulfilling those threats.

"It *was* him," Hilary said. "You see? It was Frye."

"Could it have been make-up?"

"What?"

"Could it have been someone made-up to look like Frye?"

"Why would anyone do that?"

"I don't know."

"What would he have to gain?"

"I don't know."

"You accused me of grabbing at straws. Well, this isn't even a straw you're grabbing at. It's just a mirage. It's nothing."

"But could it have been another man in make-up?" Tony persisted.

"Impossible. There isn't any make-up that convincing at close range. And the body was the same as Frye's. The same height and weight. The same bone structure. The same muscles."

"But if it was someone in make-up, imitating Frye's voice—"

"That would make it easy for you," she said coldly. "A clever impersonation, no matter how bizarre and unexplainable, is easier to accept than my story about a dead man walking. But you mentioned his voice, and that's another hole in your theory. No one could mimic that voice. Oh, an excellent impressionist might get the low pitch and the phrasing and the accent just right, but he wouldn't be able to re-create that awful rasping, crackling quality. You could only talk like that if you had an abnormal larynx or screwed-up vocal cords. Frye was born with a malformed voice box. Or he suffered a serious throat injury when he was a child. Maybe both. Anyway, that was Bruno Frye who spoke to me tonight, not a clever imitation. I'd bet every cent I have on it."

Tony could see that she was still angry, but he was no longer so sure that she was hysterical or even mildly confused. Her dark eyes were sharply focused. She spoke in clipped and precise sentences. She looked like a woman in complete control of herself.

"But Frye is dead," Tony said weakly.

"He was here."

"How could he have been?"

"As I said, that's what I intend to find out."

Tony had walked into a strange room, a room of the mind, which was constructed of impossibilities. He half-remembered something from a Sherlock Holmes story. Holmes had expressed the view to Watson that, in detection, once you had eliminated all the possibilities except one, that which was left, no matter how unlikely or absurd, must be the truth.

Was the impossible possible?

Could a dead man walk?

He thought of the inexplicable tie between the threats the assailant had made and the items found in Bruno Frye's van. He thought of Sherlock Holmes, and finally he said, "All right."

"All right what?" she asked.

"All right, maybe it was Frye."

"It was."

"Somehow . . . some way . . . God knows how . . . but maybe he did survive the stabbing. It seems utterly impossible, but I guess I've got to consider it."

"How wonderfully open-minded of you," she said. Her feathers were still ruffled. She was not going to forgive him easily.

She pulled away from him again and entered the master bedroom.

He followed her.

He felt slightly numb. Sherlock Holmes hadn't said anything about the effects of living with the disturbing thought that nothing was impossible.

She got a suitcase out of the closet, put it on the bed, and started filling it with clothes.

Tony went to the bedside phone and picked up the receiver. "Line's dead. He must have cut the wires outside. We'll have to use a neighbor's phone to report this."

"I'm not reporting it."

"Don't worry," he said. "All that's changed. I'll support your story now."

"It's too late for that," she said sharply.

"What do you mean?"

She didn't answer. She took a blouse off a hanger with such a sudden tug that the hanger clattered to the closet floor.

He said, "You're not still planning to hide out in a hotel and hire private investigators."

"Oh, yes. That's exactly what I'm planning to do," she said, folding the blouse.

"But I've said I believe you."

"And *I* said it's too late for that. Too late to make any difference."

"Why are you being so difficult?"

Hilary didn't respond. She placed the folded blouse in the suitcase and returned to the closet for other pieces of clothing.

"Listen," Tony said, "all I did was express a few quite reasonable doubts. The same doubts that anyone would have in a situation like this. In fact, the same doubts that you would have expressed if *I'd* been the one who'd said he'd seen a dead man walking. If our roles were reversed, I'd expect you to be skeptical. I wouldn't be furious with you. Why are you so damned touchy?"

She came back from the closet with two more blouses and started to fold one of them. She wouldn't look at Tony. "I trusted you . . . with everything," she said.

"I haven't violated any trust."

"You're like everyone else."

"What happened at my apartment earlier—wasn't that kind of special?"

She didn't answer him.

"Are you going to tell me that what you felt tonight—not just with your body, but with your heart, your mind—are you going to tell me that was no different from what you feel with every man?"

Hilary tried to freeze him out. She kept her eyes on her work, put the second blouse in the suitcase, began to fold the third. Her hands were trembling.

"Well, it was special for me," Tony said, determined to thaw her. "It was perfect. Better than I ever thought it could be. Not just the sex. The being together. The sharing. You got inside me like no woman ever has before. You took away a piece of me when you left my place last night, a piece of my soul, a piece of my heart, a piece of something vital. For the rest of my life, I'm not going to feel like a whole man except when I'm with you. So if you think I'm going to just let you walk away, you're in for a big surprise. I'll put up one hell of a fight to hold on to you, lady."

She had stopped folding the blouse. She was just standing with it in her hands, staring down at it.

Nothing in his entire life had seemed half so important as knowing what she was thinking at that moment.

"I love you," he said.

Still looking at the blouse, she responded to him in a tremulous voice. "Are commitments ever kept? Are promises between two people ever kept? Promises like this? When someone says, 'I love you,' does he ever really mean it? If my parents could gush about love one minute, then beat me black and blue a minute later, who the hell can I trust? You? Why should I? Isn't it going to end in disappointment and pain? Doesn't it always end that way? I'm better off alone. I can take good care of myself. I'll be all right. I just don't want to be hurt any more. I'm sick of being hurt. Sick to death of it! I'm not going to make commitments and take risks. I can't. I just can't."

Tony went to her, gripped her by the shoulders, forced her to look at him. Her lower lip quivered. Tears gathered in the corners of her beautiful eyes, but she held them back.

"You feel the same thing for me that I feel for you," he said. "I know it. I feel it. I'm sure of it. You're not turning your back on me because I had some doubts about your story. That doesn't really have anything to do with it. You're turning your back on me because you're falling in love, and you are absolutely terrified of that. Terrified because of your parents. Because of what they did to you. Because of all the beatings you took. Because of a lot of other things you haven't even told me about yet. You're running from your feelings for me because your rotten childhood left you emotionally crippled. But you love me. You do. And you know it."

She couldn't speak. She shook her head: no, no, no.

"Don't tell me it isn't true," he said. "We need each other, Hilary. I need you because all my life I've been afraid to take risks with *things*— money, my career, my art. I've always been open to people, to changing relationships, but never to changing circumstances. With you, because of you, for the very first time, I'm willing to take a few tentative steps away from the security of being on the public payroll. And now, when I think seriously about painting for a living, I don't start feeling guilty and lazy, like I used to. I don't always hear Papa's lectures about money and responsibility and the cruelty of fate, like I used to. When I dream of a life as an artist, I no longer automatically start reliving all the financial crises our family endured, the times we were without enough food, the times we were almost without a roof over our heads. I'm finally able to put that behind me. I'm not yet strong enough to quit my job and take the plunge. God, no. Not yet. But because of you, I can now envision myself as a full-time painter, seriously anticipate it, which is something I couldn't do a week ago."

Tears were streaming down her face now. "You're so good," she said. "You're a wonderful, sensitive artist."

"And you need me every bit as much as I need you," he said. "Without me, you're going to build that shell a little thicker, a little harder. You're going to wind up alone and bitter. You have always been able to take risks with *things*—money, your career. But you haven't been able to take chances with people. You see? We're opposites in that respect. We complement each other. We can teach each other so much. We can help each other grow. It's like we were each only half a person—and now we've found our missing halves. I'm yours. You're mine. We've been knocking around all our lives, groping in the dark, trying to find each other."

Hilary dropped the yellow blouse that she had intended to pack in the suitcase, and she threw her arms around him.

Tony hugged her, kissed her salty lips.

For a minute or two they just held each other. Neither of them could speak.

At last he said, "Look in my eyes."

She raised her head.

"You've got such dark eyes."

"Tell me," he said.

"Tell you what?"

"What I want to hear."

She kissed the corners of his mouth.

"Tell me," he said.

"I . . . love you."

"Again."

"I love you, Tony. I do. I really do."

"Was that so difficult?"

"Yeah. For me it was."

"It'll get easier the more often you say it."

"I'll make sure to practice a lot," she said.

She was smiling and weeping at the same time.

Tony was aware of a growing tightness, like a rapidly expanding bubble, in his chest, as if he quite literally were bursting with happiness. In spite of the sleepless night just passed, he was full of energy, wide awake, keenly aware of the special woman in his arms—her warmth, her sweet curves, her deceptive softness, the resiliency of her mind and flesh, the fading scent of her perfume, the pleasant animal odor of clean hair and skin.

He said, "Now that we've found each other, everything will be all right."

"Not until we know about Bruno Frye. Or whoever he is. Whatever he is. Nothing will be all right until we know he's definitely dead and buried, once and for all."

"If we stick together," Tony said, "we'll come through safe and sound. He's not going to get his hands on you so long as I'm around. I promise you that."

"And I trust you. But . . . just the same . . . I'm scared of him."

"Don't be scared."

"I can't help it," she said. "Besides, I think it's probably smart to be scared of him."

Tony thought of the destruction downstairs, thought of the sharp wooden stakes and the little bags of garlic that had been found in Frye's van, and he decided that Hilary was right. It was smart to be scared of Bruno Frye.

A walking dead man?

She shivered, and Tony caught it from her.

part two

THE LIVING AND
THE LIVING DEAD

Goodness speaks in a whisper.
Evil shouts.
> —a Tibetan proverb

Goodness shouts.
Evil whispers.
> —a Balinese proverb

chapter five

Tuesday morning, for the second time in eight days, Los Angeles was rocked by a middle-register earthquake. It hit as high as 4.6 on the Richter Scale as measured at Cal Tech, and it lasted twenty-three seconds.

There was no major damage, and most Angelenos spoke of the tremor only to make jokes. There was the one about the Arabs repossessing part of the country for failure to pay oil debts. And that night, on television, Johnny Carson would say that Dolly Parton had caused the seismic disturbance by getting out of bed too suddenly. To new residents, however, those twenty-three seconds hadn't been the least bit funny, and they couldn't believe that they would ever become blasé about the earth moving under their feet. A year later, of course, they would be making their own jokes about other tremors.

Until the really big one.

A never-spoken, deeply subconscious fear of the big one, the quake to end all quakes, was what made Californians joke about the smaller jolts and shocks. If you dwelt upon the possibility of cataclysm, if you thought about the treachery of the earth for too long, you would be paralyzed with fear. Life must go on regardless of the risks. After all, the big one might not come for a hundred years. Perhaps never. More people died in those snowy, sub-zero Eastern winters than in California quakes. It was as dangerous to live in Florida's hurricane country and on the tornado-stricken plains of the Midwest as it was to build a house on the San Andreas fault. And with every nation on the planet acquiring or seeking to acquire nuclear weapons, the fury of the earth seemed less frightening than the petulant anger of men. To put the quake threat in perspective,

Californians made light of it, found humor in the potential disaster, and pretended that living on unstable ground had no effect on them.

But that Tuesday, as on all other days when the earth moved noticeably, more people than usual would exceed the speed limit on the freeways, hurrying to work or to play, hurrying home to families and friends, to lovers; and none of them would be consciously aware that he was living at a somewhat faster pace than he had on Monday. More men would ask their wives for divorces than on a day without a quake. More wives would leave their husbands than had done so the previous day. More people would decide to get married. A greater than usual number of gamblers would make plans to go to Las Vegas for the weekend. Prostitutes would enjoy substantial new business. And there most likely would be a marked increase in sexual activity between husbands and wives, between unwed lovers, and between inexperienced teenagers making their first clumsy experimental moves. Uncontestable proof of this erotic aspect of seismic activity did not exist. But over the years, at several zoos, many sociologists and behavioral psychologists had observed primates—gorillas, chimpanzees, and orangutans—engaging in an abnormal amount of frenzied coupling in the hours following large- and middle-sized earthquakes; and it was reasonable to assume that, at least in the matter of primal reproductive organs, man was not a great deal different from his primitive cousins.

Most Californians smugly believed that they were perfectly adjusted to life in earthquake country; but in ways of which they were not aware, the psychological stress continued to shape and change them. Fear of the impending catastrophe was an everpresent whisper that propagandized the subconscious mind, a very influential whisper that molded people's attitudes and characters more than they would ever know.

Of course, it was just one whisper among many.

•

Hilary wasn't surprised by the police response to her story, and she tried not to let it upset her.

Less than five minutes after Tony placed the call from a neighbor's home, approximately thirty-five minutes before the morning earthquake, two uniformed officers in a black-and-white arrived at Hilary's house, lights flashing, no siren. With typical, bored, professional dispatch and courtesy, they duly recorded her version of the incident, located the point at which the house had been breached by the intruder (a study window again), made a general listing of the damage in the living room and the dining room, and gathered the other information required for the proper completion of a crime report. Because Hilary had said that the assailant had worn gloves, they decided not to bother calling for a lab man and a fingerprint search.

They were intrigued by her contention that the man who attacked her was the same man she thought she had killed last Thursday. Their interest had nothing to do with a desire to determine if she was correct in her identification of the culprit; they made up their minds about that as soon as they heard her story. So far as they were concerned, there was no chance whatsoever that the assailant could have been Bruno Frye. They asked her to repeat her account of the attack several times, and they frequently interrupted with questions; but they were only trying to determine if she was genuinely mistaken, hysterical and confused, or lying. After a while, they decided that she was slightly mixed up due to shock, and that her confusion was exacerbated by the intruder's resemblance to Bruno Frye.

"We'll work from this description you've given us," one of them said.

"But we can't put an APB on a dead man," said the other. "I'm sure you understand that."

"It was Bruno Frye," Hilary said doggedly.

"Well, there's just no way we can go with that, Miss Thomas."

Although Tony supported her story as best he could without having seen the assailant, his arguments and his position with the Los Angeles Police Department made little or no impression on the uniformed officers. They listened politely, nodded a lot, but were not swayed.

Twenty minutes after the morning earthquake, Tony and Hilary stood at the front door and watched the black-and-white police cruiser as it pulled out of the driveway.

Frustrated, she said, "Now what?"

"Now you'll finish packing that suitcase, and we'll go to my apartment. I'll call the office and have a chat with Harry Lubbock."

"Who's he?"

"My boss. Captain Lubbock. He knows me pretty damned well, and we respect each other. Harry knows I don't go out on a limb unless I've thoroughly tested it first. I'll ask him to take another look at Bruno Frye, get some deeper background on the man. And Harry can put more pressure on Sheriff Laurenski than he's done so far. Don't worry. One way or another, I'll get some action."

But forty-five minutes later, in Tony's kitchen, when he placed the call, he could not get any satisfaction from Harry Lubbock. The captain listened to everything that Tony had to say, and he didn't doubt that Hilary *thought* she had seen Bruno Frye, but he couldn't find any justification for launching an investigation of Frye in conjunction with a crime that had been committed days after the man's death. He was not prepared to consider the one-in-ten-million chance that the coroner had been wrong and that Frye miraculously had survived massive blood loss, an autopsy, and subsequent refrigeration in the morgue. Harry was sympathetic, soft-spoken, and endlessly patient, but it was clear that he thought Hilary's observations were unreliable, her perceptions distorted by terror and hysteria.

Tony sat down beside her, on one of the three breakfast bar stools, and told her what Lubbock had said.

"Hysteria!" Hilary said. "God, I'm sick of that word! Everyone thinks I panicked. Everyone's so damned sure I was reduced to a blubbering mess. Well, of all the women I know, I'm the one least likely to lose my head in a situation like that."

"I agree with you," Tony said. "I'm just telling you how Harry sees it."

"Damn."

"Exactly."

"And your support didn't mean a thing?"

Tony grimaced. "He thinks that, because of what happened to Frank, I'm not entirely myself."

"So he's saying *you're* hysterical."

"Just upset. A little confused."

"Is that really what he said?"

"Yeah."

Remembering that Tony had used those same words to describe her when he'd first heard her story about a walking dead man, she said, "Maybe you deserved that."

"Maybe I did."

"What did Lubbock say when you told him about the threats—the stake through the heart, the mouth full of garlic, all of that stuff?"

"He agreed it was a striking coincidence."

"Just that? Just a coincidence?"

"For the time being," Tony said, "that's how he's going to look at it."

"Damn."

"He didn't say it straight out, but I'm pretty sure he thinks that, last week some time, I told you what was found in Frye's van."

"But you didn't."

"You know I didn't, and I know I didn't. But I suppose that's the way it's going to look to everyone else."

"But I thought you said that you and Lubbock were close, that there was a lot of mutual respect."

"We are, and there is," Tony replied. "But like I told you, he thinks I'm not myself right now. He figures I'll get my head on straight in a few days or a week, when the shock of my partner's death subsides. He thinks then I'll change my mind about supporting your story. I'm sure I won't because I *know* you weren't aware of the occult books and bric-a-brac in Frye's van. And I've got a hunch, too, a very strong hunch that Frye somehow *has* come back. God knows how. But I need more than a hunch to sway Harry, and I can't blame him for being skeptical."

"In the meantime?"

"In the meantime, the homicide squad has no interest in the case. It doesn't come under our jurisdiction. It'll be handled like any other break-in and attempted assault by a person or persons unknown."

Hilary frowned. "Which means not much of anything will be done."

"Unfortunately, I'm afraid that's true. There's almost nothing the police *can* do with a complaint like this one. This sort of thing is usually solved, if ever, a long way down the line, when they catch the guy in the act, breaking and entering another house or assaulting another woman, and he confesses to a lot of old, unsolved cases."

Hilary got up from the stool and began to pace in the small kitchen. "Something strange and frightening is happening here. I can't wait a week for you to convince Lubbock. Frye said he'd be back. He's going to keep trying to kill me until one of us is dead—permanently and irrevocably dead. He could pop up anytime, anywhere."

"You won't be in danger if you stay here until we can puzzle this out," Tony said, "or at least until we come up with something that'll convince Harry Lubbock. You'll be safe here. Frye—if it is Frye—won't know where to find you."

"How can you be sure of that?" she asked.

"He's not omniscient."

"Isn't he?"

Tony scowled. "Wait a minute now. You aren't going to tell me that he has supernatural powers or second sight or something like that."

"I'm not going to tell you that, and I'm not going to rule it out either," she said. "Listen, once you've accept the fact that Frye is somehow alive, how can you rule out *anything?* I might even start believing in gnomes and goblins and Santa Claus. But what I meant was—maybe he simply followed us here."

Tony raised his eyebrows. "Followed us from your house?"

"It's a possibility."

"No. It isn't."

"Are you positive?"

"When I arrived at your place, he ran away."

She stopped pacing, stood in the middle of the kitchen, hugging herself. "Maybe he hung around the neighborhood, just watching, waiting to see what we'd do and where we'd go."

"Highly unlikely. Even if he did stay nearby after I got there, he sure as hell split when he saw the police cruiser pull up."

"You can't assume that," Hilary said. "At best, we're dealing with a madman. At worst, we're confronting the unknown, something so far beyond our understanding that the danger is incalculable. Whichever the case, you can't expect Frye to reason and behave like an ordinary man. Whatever he may be, he's most definitely *not* ordinary."

Tony stared at her for a moment, then wearily wiped one hand across his face. "You're right."

"So are you positive we weren't followed here?"

"Well . . . I didn't look for a tail," Tony said. "It never occurred to me."

"Me either. Until just now. So as far as we know, he might be outside, watching the apartment, right this very minute."

That idea disturbed Tony. He stood up. "But he'd have to be pretty damned bold to pull a stunt like that."

"He *is* bold!"

Tony nodded. "Yeah. You're right again." He stood for a moment, thinking, then walked out of the kitchen.

She followed him. "Where are you going?"

He crossed the living room toward the front door. "You stay here while I have a look around."

"Not a chance," Hilary said firmly. "I'm coming along with you."

He stopped with his hand on the door. "If Frye is out there, keeping a watch on us, you'll be a whole lot safer staying here."

"But what if I wait for you—and then it's not you who comes back?"

"It's broad daylight out there," Tony said. "Nothing's going to happen to me."

"Violence isn't restricted to darkness," Hilary said. "People get killed in broad daylight all the time. You're a policeman. You know that."

"I have my service revolver. I can take care of myself."

She shook her head. She was adamant. "I'm not going to sit here biting my nails. Let's go."

Outside, they stood by the balcony railing and looked down at the vehicles in the apartment complex parking lot. There were not many of them at that time of day. Most people had gone to work more than an hour ago. In addition to the blue Jeep that belonged to Tony, there were seven cars. Bright sunshine sparkled on the chrome and transformed some of the windshields into mirrors.

"I think I recognize all of them," Tony said. "They belong to people who live here."

"Positive?"

"Not entirely."

"See anybody in any of them?"

He squinted. "I can't tell with the sun shining on the glass."

"Let's take a closer look," she said.

Down in the parking area, they found the cars were empty. There wasn't anyone hanging around who didn't belong.

"Of course," Tony said, "even as bold as he is, it's not likely that he'd stand a watch right on our doorstep. And since there's only one driveway in and out of these apartments, he could keep an eye on us from a distance."

They walked out of the walled complex, onto the sidewalk, and looked north, then south along the tree-shaded street. It was a neighborhood of garden apartments and townhouses and condominiums, nearly all of which lacked adequate parking; therefore, even at that hour of a weekday morning, a lot of cars were lined up along both curbs.

"You want to check them out?" Hilary asked.

"It's a waste of time. If he has binoculars, he'll be able to watch this driveway from four blocks away. We'd have to walk four blocks in each direction, and even then, he could just pull out and drive away."

"But if he does, then we'll spot him. We won't be able to stop him, of course, but at least we'll know for sure that he followed us. And we'll know what he's driving."

"Not if he's two or three blocks from us when he splits," Tony said. "We wouldn't be close enough to be sure it was him. And he might just get out of his car and take a walk, then come back after we've gone."

To Hilary, the air seemed leaden; she found it somewhat taxing to draw a deep breath. The day was going to be very hot, especially for the end of September; and it would be a humid day, too, especially for Los Angeles, where the air was nearly always dry. The sky was high and clear and gas flame–blue. Already, wriggling ghost snakes of heat were rising from the pavement. High-pitched, musical laughter sailed on the light breeze; children were playing in the swimming pool at the townhouse development across the street.

On such a day as this, it was difficult to maintain a belief in the living dead.

Hilary sighed and said, "So how do we find out if he's here, watching us?"

"There's no way to be sure."

"I was afraid you'd say that."

Hilary looked down the street, which was mottled with shadow and light. Horror cloaked in sunshine. Terror hiding against a backdrop of beautiful palm trees and bright stucco walls and Spanish-tile roofs. "Paranoia Avenue," she said.

"Paranoia *City* until this is over."

They turned away from the street and walked back across the macadam parking area in front of his apartment building.

"Now what?" she asked.

"I think we both need to get some sleep."

Hilary had never been so weary. Her eyes were grainy and sore from lack of rest; the strong sunlight stung them. Her mouth felt fuzzy and tasted like cardboard; there was an unpleasant film of tartar on her teeth, and her tongue seemed to be coated with a furry mold. She ached in every bone and muscle and sinew, from her toes to the top of her head, and it didn't help to realize that at least half of the way she felt was the consequence of emotional rather than physical exhaustion.

"I *know* we need to sleep," she said. "But do you really think you can?"

"I know what you mean. I'm tired as hell, but my mind's racing. It's not going to shut off easily."

"There's a question or two I'd like to ask the coroner," she said. "Or whoever performed the autopsy. Maybe when I get some answers I'll be able to take a nap."

"Okay," Tony said. "Let's lock up the apartment and go to the morgue right now."

A few minutes later, when they drove away in Tony's blue Jeep, they watched for a tail, but they were not followed. Of course, that didn't mean Frye wasn't sitting in one of those parked cars along that tree-lined street. If he had followed them from Hilary's house earlier, he didn't need to trail after them now, for he already knew the location of their lair.

"What if he breaks in while we're gone?" Hilary asked. "What if he's hiding in there, waiting, when we come back?"

"I've got two locks on my door," Tony said. "One of them is the best deadbolt money can buy. He'd have to chop down the door. The only other way is to break one of the windows that faces on the balcony. If he's waiting in there when we come back, we'll know it long before we set foot inside."

"What if he finds another way in?"

"There isn't one," Tony said. "To get in through any of the other windows, he'd have to climb to the second floor on a sheer wall, and he'd have to do it right out in the open where he'd be sure to be seen. Don't worry. Home base is safe."

"Maybe he can pass through a door. You know," she said shakily. "Like a ghost. Or maybe he can turn into smoke and drift through a keyhole."

"You don't believe garbage like that," Tony said.

She nodded. "You're right."

"He doesn't have any supernatural powers. He had to break a windowpane to get into your house last night."

They headed downtown through heavy traffic.

Her bone-deep weariness undermined her usually strong mental defenses against the pernicious disease of self-doubt, leaving her uncharacteristically vulnerable. For the first time since seeing Frye walk out of the dining room, she began to wonder if she truly had seen what she thought she had seen.

"Am I crazy?" she asked Tony.

He glanced at her, then back at the street. "No. You're not crazy. You saw something. You didn't wreck the house all by yourself. You didn't just imagine that the intruder looked like Bruno Frye. I'll admit I thought that's what you were doing at first. But now I know you aren't confused."

"But . . . a walking dead man? Isn't that too much to accept?"

"It's just as difficult to accept the other theory—that two unassociated maniacs, both suffering from the same unique set of delusions, both obsessed with a psychotic fear of vampires, attacked you in one week. In fact, I think it's a little easier to believe that Frye is somehow alive."

"Maybe you caught it from me."

"Caught what?"

"Insanity."

He smiled. "Insanity isn't like the common cold. You can't spread it with a cough—or a kiss."

"Haven't you heard of a 'shared psychosis'?"

Braking for a traffic light, he said, "Shared psychosis? Isn't that a social welfare program for underprivileged lunatics who can't afford psychoses of their own?"

"Jokes at a time like this?"

"Especially at a time like this."

"What about mass hysteria?"

"It's not one of my favorite pastimes."

"I mean, maybe that's what's happening here."

"No. Impossible," he said. "There's only two of us. That's not enough to make a mass."

She smiled. "God, I'm glad you're here. I'd hate to be fighting this thing alone."

"You'll never be alone again."

She put one hand on his shoulder.

They reached the morgue at quarter past eleven.

•

At the coroner's office, Hilary and Tony learned from the secretary that the chief medical examiner had not performed the autopsy on the body of Bruno Frye. Last Thursday and Friday, he had been in San Francisco on a speaking engagement. The autopsy had been left to an assistant, another doctor on the M. E.'s staff.

That bit of news gave Hilary hope that there would be a simple solution to the mystery of Frye's return from the grave. Perhaps the assistant assigned to the job had been a slacker, a lazy man who, free of his boss's constant supervision, had skipped the autopsy and filed a false report.

That hope was dashed when she met Ira Goldfield, the young doctor in question. He was in his early thirties, a handsome man with piercing blue eyes and a lot of tight blond curls. He was friendly, energetic, bright, and obviously too interested in his work and too dedicated to it to do less than a perfect job.

Goldfield escorted them to a small conference room that smelled of pine-scented disinfectant and cigarette smoke. They sat at a rectangular table that was covered with half a dozen medical reference books, pages of lab reports, and computer print-outs.

"Sure," Goldfield said. "I remember that one. Bruno Graham . . . no . . . Gunther. Bruno Gunther Frye. Two stab wounds, one of them just a little worse than superficial, the other very deep and fatal. Some of the best developed abdominal muscles I've ever seen." He blinked at Hilary and said, "Oh yes. . . . You're the woman who . . . stabbed him."

"Self-defense," Tony said.

"I don't doubt that for a second," Goldfield assured him. "In my professional opinion, it's highly unlikely that Miss Thomas could have initiated a successful assault against that man. He was huge. He'd have brushed her away as easily as one of us might turn aside a small child." Goldfield looked at Hilary again. "According to the crime report and the newspaper accounts that I read, Frye attacked you without realizing you were carrying a knife."

"That's right. He thought I was unarmed."

Goldfield nodded. "It had to be that way. Considering the disparity in body sizes, that's the only way you could have taken him without being seriously injured yourself. I mean, the biceps and triceps and forearms on that man were truly astounding. Ten or fifteen years ago, he could have entered body building competitions with considerable success. You were damned lucky, Miss Thomas. If you hadn't surprised him, he could have broken you in half. Almost literally in half. And easily, too." He shook his head, still impressed with Frye's body. "What was it you wanted to ask me about him?"

Tony looked at her, and she shrugged. "It seems rather pointless now that we're here."

Goldfield looked from one of them to the other, a vague, encouraging smile of curiosity on his handsome face.

Tony cleared his throat. "I agree with Hilary. It seems pointless . . . now that we've met you."

"You came in looking so somber and mysterious," Goldfield said pleasantly. "You pricked my interest. You can't keep me hanging like this."

"Well," Tony said, "we came here to find out if there actually had been an autopsy."

Goldfield didn't understand. "But you knew that before you asked to see me. Agnes, the M.E.'s secretary, must have told you . . ."

"We wanted to hear it from you," Hilary said.

"I still don't get it."

"We knew that an autopsy report had been filed," Tony said. "But we didn't know for certain that the work had been done."

"But now that we've met you," Hilary said quickly, "we have no doubt about it."

Goldfield cocked his head. "You mean to say . . . you thought I filed a fake report without bothering to cut him open?" He didn't seem to be offended, just amazed.

"We thought there might be an outside chance of it," Tony admitted. "A long shot."

"Not in *this* M.E.'s jurisdiction," Goldfield said. "He's a tough old SOB. He keeps us in line. If one of us didn't do his job, the old man would crucify him." It was obvious from Goldfield's affectionate tone that he greatly admired the chief medical examiner.

Hilary said, "Then there's no doubt in your mind that Bruno Frye was . . . dead?"

Goldfield gaped at her as if she had just asked him to stand on his head and recite a poem. "Dead? Why, of course he was dead!"

"You did a complete autopsy?" Tony asked.

"Yes. I cut him—" Goldfield stopped abruptly, thought for a second or two, then said, "No. It wasn't a complete autopsy in the sense you probably mean. Not a medical school dissection of every part of the body. It was an extremely busy day here. A lot of incoming. And we were short-handed. Anyway, there wasn't any need to open Frye all the way up. The stab wound in the lower abdomen was decisive. No reason to open his chest and have a look at his heart. Nothing to be gained by weighing a lot of organs and poking around in his cranium. I did a very thorough exterior examination, and then I opened the two wounds further, to establish the extent of the damage and to be certain that at least one of them had been the cause of death. If he hadn't been stabbed in your house, while attacking you . . . if the circumstances of his death had been less clear, I might have done more with him. But it was clear there wasn't going to be any criminal charges brought in the case. Besides, I am absolutely positive that the abdominal wound killed him."

"Is it possible he was only in a very deep coma when you examined him?" Hilary asked.

"Coma? My God, no! Jesus, no!" Goldfield stood up and paced the length of the long narrow room. "Frye was checked for pulse, respiration, pupil activity, and even brainwaves. The man was indisputably dead, Miss Thomas." He returned to the table and looked down at them. "Dead as stone. When I saw him, there wasn't enough blood in his body to sustain even the barest threshold of life. There was advanced lividity, which means that the blood still in his tissues had settled to the lowest point of the body—the lowest corresponding, in this case, to the position in which he'd been when he'd died. At those places, the flesh was somewhat distended and purple. There's no mistaking that and no overlooking it."

Tony pushed his chair back and stood. "My apologies for wasting your time, Dr. Goldfield."

"And I'm sorry for suggesting you might not have done your job well enough," Hilary said as she got to her feet.

"Hold on now," Goldfield said. "You can't just leave me standing here in the dark. What's this all about?"

She looked at Tony. He seemed as reluctant as she was to discuss walking dead men with the doctor.

"Come on," Goldfield said. "Neither of you strikes me as stupid. You had your reasons for coming here."

Tony said, "Last night, another man broke into Hilary's house and attempted to kill her. He bore a striking resemblance to Bruno Frye."

"Are you serious?" Goldfield asked.

"Oh, yes," Hilary said. "Very serious."

"And you thought—"

"Yes."

"God, it must have been a shock to see him and think he'd come back!" Goldfield said. "But all I can tell you is that the resemblance must be coincidental. Because Frye is dead. I've never seen a man any deader than he was."

They thanked Goldfield for his time and patience, and he escorted them out to the reception area.

Tony stopped at the desk and asked Agnes, the secretary, for the name of the funeral home that had claimed Frye's body.

She looked through the files and said, "It was Angels' Hill Mortuary."

Hilary wrote down the address.

Goldfield said, "You don't still think—"

"No," Tony said. "But on the other hand, we've got to pursue every lead. At least, that's what they taught me at the police academy."

Eyes hooded, frowning, Goldfield watched them as they walked away.

•

At Angels' Hill Mortuary, Hilary waited in the Jeep while Tony went inside to talk to the mortician who had handled the body of Bruno Frye. They had agreed that he would be able to obtain the information faster if he went in alone and used his LAPD identification.

Angels' Hill was a big operation with a fleet of hearses, twelve roomy viewing chapels, and a large staff of morticians and technicians. Even in the business office, the lighting was indirect and relaxing, and the colors were somber yet rich, and the floor was covered with plush wall-to-wall carpet. The decor was meant to convey a hushed appreciation for the mystery of death; but to Tony, all it conveyed was a loud and clear statement about the profitability of the funeral business.

The receptionist was a cute blonde in a gray skirt and maroon blouse. Her voice was soft, smooth, whispery, but it did not contain even a slight hint of sexual suggestiveness or invitation. It was a voice that had been carefully trained to project consolation, heartfelt solace, respect, and low-key but genuine concern. Tony wondered if she used the same cool funeral tone when she cried encouragement to her lover in bed, and that thought chilled him.

She located the file on Bruno Frye and found the name of the technician who had worked on the body. "Sam Hardesty. I believe Sam is in one of the preparation rooms at the moment. We've had a couple of recent admissions," she said, as if she were working in a hospital rather than a mortuary. "I'll see if he can spare you a few minutes. I'm not sure how far along he is in the treatment. If he can get free, he'll meet you in the employees' lounge."

She took Tony to the lounge to wait. The room was small but pleasant. Comfortable chairs were pushed up against the walls. There were ashtrays and all kinds of magazines. A coffee machine. A soda machine. A bulletin board covered with notices about bowling leagues and garage sales and car pools.

Tony was leafing through a four-page mimeographed copy of the *Angels' Hill Employee News* when Sam Hardesty arrived from one of the preparation rooms. Hardesty looked unnervingly like an automobile mechanic. He was wearing a rumpled white jumpsuit that zipped up the front; there were several small tools (the purpose of which Tony did not want to know) clipped to Hardesty's breast pocket. He was a young man, in his late twenties, with long brown hair and sharp features.

"Detective Clemenza?"

"Yes."

Hardesty held out his hand, and Tony shook it with some reluctance, wondering what it had touched just moments ago.

"Suzy said you wanted to talk to me about one of the accounts." Hardesty had been trained by the same voice coach who had worked with Suzy, the blond receptionist.

Tony said, "I understand you were responsible for preparing Bruno Frye's body for shipment to Santa Rosa last Thursday."

"That's correct. We were cooperating with a mortuary up in St. Helena."

"Would you please tell me exactly what you did with the corpse after you picked it up at the morgue?"

Hardesty looked at him curiously. "Well, we brought the deceased here and treated him."

"You didn't stop anywhere between the morgue and here?"

"No."

"From the moment the body was consigned to you until you relinquished it at the airport, was there ever a time when it was alone?"

"Alone? Only for a minute or two. It was a rush job because we had to put the deceased aboard a Friday afternoon flight. Say, can you tell me what this is all about? What are you after?"

"I'm not sure," Tony said. "But maybe if I ask enough questions I'll find out. Did you embalm him?"

"Certainly," Hardesty said. "We had to because he was being shipped on a public conveyance. The law requires us to hook out the soft organs and embalm the deceased before putting him on a public conveyance."

"Hook out?" Tony asked.

"I'm afraid it's not very pleasant," Hardesty said. "But the intestines and stomach and certain other organs pose a real problem for us. Filled with decaying waste as they are, those parts of the body tend to deteriorate a great deal faster than other tissues. To prevent unpleasant odors and embarrassingly noisy gas accumulations at the viewing, and for ideal preservation of the deceased even after burial, it's necessary to remove as many of those organs as we can. We use a sort of telescoping instrument with a retractable hook on one end. We insert it in the anal passage and—"

Tony felt the blood drain out of his face, and he quickly raised one hand to halt Hardesty. "Thank you. I believe that's all I've got to hear. I get the picture."

"I warned you it wasn't particularly pleasant."

"Not particularly," Tony agreed. Something seemed to be stuck in his throat. He coughed into his hand. It was still down there. It would probably be down there until he got out of this place. "Well," he said to Hardesty, "I think you've told me everything I needed to know."

Frowning thoughtfully, Hardesty said, "I don't know what you're looking for, but there *was* one peculiar thing connected with the Frye assignment."

"What's that?"

"It happened two days after we shipped the deceased to Santa Rosa," Hardesty said. "It was Sunday afternoon. The day before yesterday. Some guy called up and wanted to talk to the technician who handled Bruno Frye. I was here because my days off are Wednesday and Thursday, so I took the call. He was very angry. He accused me of doing a quick and sloppy job on the deceased. That wasn't true. I did the best work I could under the circumstances. But the deceased had lain in the hot sun for a few hours, and then he'd been refrigerated. And there were those stab wounds and the coroner's incisions. Let me tell you, Mr. Clemenza, the flesh was not in very good condition when I received the deceased. I mean, you couldn't expect him to look lifelike. Besides, I wasn't responsible for cosmetic work. That was taken care of by the funeral director up there in St. Helena. I tried to tell this guy on the phone that it wasn't my fault, but he wouldn't let me get a word in edgewise."

"Did he give his name?" Tony asked.

"No. He just got angrier and angrier. He was screaming at me and crying, carrying on like a lunatic. He was in real agony. I thought he must be a relative of the deceased, someone half out of his mind with grief. That's why I was so patient with him. But then, when he got really hysterical, he told me that *he* was Bruno Frye."

"He did what?"

"Yeah. He said *he* was Bruno Frye and that some day he might just come back down here and tear me apart because of what I'd done to him."

"What else did he say?"

"That was it. As soon as he started with that kind of stuff, I knew he was a nut, so I hung up on him."

Tony felt as if he had just been given a transfusion of icewater; he was cold inside as well as out.

Sam Hardesty saw that he was shocked. "What's wrong?"

"I was just wondering if three people are enough to make it mass hysteria."

"Huh?"

"Was there anything peculiar about this caller's voice?"

"How'd you know that?"

"A very deep voice?"

"He rumbled," Hardesty said.

"And gravelly, coarse?"

"That's right. You know him?"

"I'm afraid so."

"Who is he?"

"You wouldn't believe me if I told you."

"Try me," Hardesty said.

Tony shook his head. "Sorry. This is confidential police business."

Hardesty was disappointed; the tentative smile on his face slipped away.

"Well, Mr. Hardesty, you've been a great help. Thank you for your time and trouble."

Hardesty shrugged. "It wasn't anything."

It was something, Tony thought. Something indeed. But I sure as hell don't know what it means.

In the short hall outside the employees' lounge, they went in different directions, but after a few steps Tony turned and said, "Mr. Hardesty?"

Hardesty stopped, looked back. "Yes?"

"Answer a personal question?"

"What is it?"

"What made you decide to do . . . this kind of work?"

"My favorite uncle was a funeral director."

"I see."

"He was a lot of fun. Especially with kids. He loved kids. I wanted to be like him," Hardesty said. "You always had the feeling that Uncle Alex knew some enormous, terribly important secret. He did a lot of magic tricks for us kids, but it was more than that. I always thought that what he did for a living was very magical and mysterious, too, and that it was because of his work that he'd learned something nobody else knew."

"Have you found his secret yet?"

"Yes," Hardesty said. "I think maybe I have."

"Can you tell me?"

"Sure. What Uncle Alex knew, and what I've come to learn, is that you've got to treat the dead with every bit as much concern and respect as you do the living. You can't just put them out of mind, bury them and forget about them. The lessons they taught us when they were alive are still with us. All the things they did to us and for us are still in our minds, still shaping and changing us. And because of how they've affected us, we'll have certain influences on people who will be alive long after we're dead. So in a way, the dead never really die at all. They just go on and on. Uncle Alex's secret was just this: The dead are people, too."

Tony stared at him for a moment, not certain what he should say. But then the question came unbidden: "Are you a religious man, Mr. Hardesty?"

"I wasn't when I started doing this work," he said. "But I am now. I certainly am now."

"Yes, I suppose you are."

Outside, when Tony got behind the wheel of the Jeep and pulled the driver's door shut, Hilary said, "Well? Did he embalm Frye?"

"Worse than that."

"What's worse than that?"

"You don't want to know."

He told her about the telephone call that Hardesty had received from the man claiming to be Bruno Frye.

"Ahhh," she said softly. "Forget what I said about shared psychoses. This is proof!"

"Proof of what? That Frye's alive? He can't be alive. In addition to other things too disgusting to mention, he was embalmed. No one can sustain even a deep coma when his veins and arteries are full of embalming fluid instead of blood."

"But at least that phone call is proof that something out of the ordinary is happening."

"Not really," Tony said.

"Can you take this to your captain?"

"There's no point in doing that. To Harry Lubbock, it'll look like nothing more sinister than a crank call, a hoax."

"But the *voice!*"

"That won't be enough to convince Harry."

She sighed. "So what's next?"

"We've got to do some heavy thinking," Tony said. "We've got to examine the situation from every angle and see if there's something we've missed."

"Can we think at lunch?" she asked. "I'm starved."

"Where do you want to eat?"

"Since we're both rumpled and wrung out, I suggest some place dark and private."

"A back booth at Casey's Bar?"

"Perfect," she said.

As he drove to Westwood, Tony thought about Hardesty and about how, in one way, the dead were not really dead at all.

•

Bruno Frye stretched out in the back of the Dodge van and tried to get some sleep.

The van was not the one in which he had driven to Los Angeles last week. That vehicle had been impounded by the police. By now it had been claimed by a representative of Joshua Rhinehart, who was executor of the Frye estate and responsible for the proper liquidation of its assets. This van wasn't gray, like the first one, but dark blue with white accent lines. Frye had paid cash for it yesterday morning at a Dodge dealership on the outskirts of San Francisco. It was a handsome machine.

He had spent nearly all of yesterday on the road and had arrived in Los Angeles last night. He'd gone straight to Katherine's house in Westwood.

She was using the name Hilary Thomas this time, but he knew she was Katherine.

Katherine.

Back from the grave again.

The rotten bitch.

He had broken into the house, but she hadn't been there. Then she'd finally come home just before dawn, and he'd almost gotten his hands on her. He still couldn't figure out why the police had shown up.

During the past four hours, he'd driven by her house five times, but he hadn't seen anything important. He didn't know if she was there or not.

He was confused. Mixed up. And frightened. He didn't know what he should do next, didn't know how he should go about locating her. His thoughts were becoming increasingly strange, fragmented, difficult to control. He felt intoxicated, dizzy, disjointed, even though he hadn't drunk anything.

He was tired. So very tired. No sleep since Sunday night. And not much then. If he could just get caught up on his sleep, he would be able to think clearly again.

Then he could go after the bitch again.

Cut off her head.

Cut out her heart. Put a stake through it.

Kill her. Kill her once and for all.

But first, sleep.

He stretched out on the floor of the van, thankful for the sunlight that streamed through the windshield, over the front seats, and into the cargo hold. He was scared to sleep in the dark.

A crucifix lay nearby.

And a pair of sharp wooden stakes.

He had filled small linen bags with garlic and had taped one over each door.

Those things might protect him from Katherine, but he knew they would not ward off the nightmare. It would come to him now as it always did when he slept, as it had all his life, and he would wake with a scream caught in the back of his throat. As always, he would not be able to recall what the dream had been about. But upon waking, he would hear the whispers, the loud but unintelligible whispers, and he would feel something moving on his body, all over his body, on his face, trying to get into his mouth and nose, some horrible *thing;* and during the minute or two that it would take for those sensations to fade away, he would ardently wish that he were dead.

He dreaded sleep, but he needed it.

He closed his eyes.

•

As usual, the lunchtime din in the main dining room at Casey's Bar was very nearly deafening.

But in the other part of the restaurant, behind the oval bar, there were several sheltered booths, each of which was enclosed on three sides like a big confessional, and in these the distant dining room roar of conversation was tolerable; it acted as a background screen to insure even greater privacy than was afforded by the cozy booths themselves.

Halfway through lunch, Hilary looked up from her food and said, "I've got it."

Tony put down his sandwich. "Got what?"

"Frye must have a brother."

"A brother?"

"It explains everything."

"You think you killed Frye last Thursday—and then his brother came after you last night?"

"Such a likeness could only be found in brothers."

"And the voice?"

"They could have inherited the same voice."

"Maybe a low-pitched voice could be inherited," Tony said. "But that special gravelly quality you described? Could that be inherited, too?"

"Why not?"

"Last night you said the only way a person could get such a voice was to suffer a serious throat injury or be born with a deformed larynx."

"So I was wrong," she said. "Or maybe both brothers were born with the same deformity."

"A million-to-one shot."

"But not impossible."

Tony sipped his beer, then said, "Maybe brothers could share the same body type, the same facial features, the same color eyes, the same voice. But could they also share precisely the same set of psychotic delusions?"

She took a taste of her own beer while she thought about that. Then: "Severe mental illness is a product of environment."

"That's what they used to think. They're not entirely sure of that any more."

"Well, for the sake of my theory, suppose that psychotic behavior *is* a product of environment. Brothers would have been raised in the same house by the same parents—in exactly the same environment. Isn't it conceivable that they could develop identical psychoses?"

He scratched his chin. "Maybe. I remember. . . ."

"What?"

"I took a university course in abnormal psychology as part of a study program in advanced criminology," Tony said. "They were trying to teach us how to recognize and deal with various kinds of psychopaths. The idea was a good one. If a policeman can identify the specific type of mental illness when he first encounters an irrational person, and if he has at least a little understanding of how that type of psychopath thinks and reacts, then he's got a much better chance of handling him quickly and safely. We saw a lot of films of mental patients. One of them was an incredible study of a mother and daughter who were both paranoid schizophrenics. They suffered from the same delusions."

"So there!" Hilary said excitedly.

"But it was an extremely rare case."

"So is this."

"I'm not sure, but maybe it was the only one of its type they'd ever found."

"But it *is* possible."

"Worth thinking about, I guess."

"A brother. . . ."

They picked up their sandwiches and began to eat again, each of them staring thoughtfully at his food.

Suddenly, Tony said, "Damn! I just remembered something that shoots a big hole in the brother theory."

"What?"

"I assume you read the newspaper accounts last Friday and Saturday."

"Not all of them," she said. "It's sort of . . . I don't know . . . sort of embarrassing to read about yourself as victim. I got through one article; that was enough."

"And you don't remember what was in that article?"

She frowned, trying to figure out what he was talking about, and then she knew. "Oh, yeah. Frye didn't have a brother."

"Not a brother or a sister. Not anyone. He was the sole heir to the vineyards when his mother died, the last member of the Frye family, the end of his line."

Hilary didn't want to abandon the brother idea. That explanation was the only one that made sense of the recent bizarre events. But she couldn't think of a way to hold on to the theory.

They finished their food in silence.

At last Tony said, "We can't keep you hidden from him forever. And we can't just sit around and wait for him to find you."

"I don't like the idea of being bait in a trap."

"Anyway, the answer isn't here in L.A."

She nodded. "I was thinking the same thing."

"We've got to go to St. Helena."

"And talk with Sheriff Laurenski."

"Laurenski and anyone else who knew Frye."

"We might need several days," she said.

"Like I told you, I've got a lot of vacation time and sick leave built up. A few weeks of it. And for the first time in my life, I'm not particularly anxious to get back to work."

"Okay," she said. "When do we leave?"

"The sooner the better."

"Not today," she said. "We're both too damned tired. We need sleep. Besides, I want to drop your paintings off with Wyant Stevens. I've got to make arrangements for an insurance adjuster to put a price on the damage at my place, and I want to tell my house cleaning service to straighten up the wreckage while I'm gone. And if I'm not going to talk to the peo-

ple at Warner Brothers about *The Hour of the Wolf* this week, then I've at
least got to make excuses—or tell Wally Topelis what excuses he should
make for me."

"I've got to fill out a final report on the shooting," Tony said. "I was
supposed to do that this morning. And they'll want me for the inquest, of
course. There's always an inquest when a policeman is killed—or when he
kills someone else. But they shouldn't have scheduled the inquest any
sooner than next week. If they did, I can probably get them to postpone it."

"So when do we leave for St. Helena?"

"Tomorrow," he said. "Frank's funeral is at nine o'clock. I want to go
to that. So let's see if there's a flight leaving around noon."

"Sounds good to me."

"We've got a lot to do. We'd better get moving."

"One other thing," Hilary said. "I don't think we should stay at your
place tonight."

He reached across the table and took her hand. "I'm sure he can't get
to you there. If he tries, you've got me, and I've got my service revolver.
He may be built like Mr. Universe, but a gun is a good equalizer."

She shook her head. "No. Maybe it would be all right. But I wouldn't
be able to sleep there, Tony. I'd be awake all night, listening for sounds at
the door and windows."

"Where do you want to stay?"

"After we've run our errands this afternoon, let's pack for the trip,
leave your apartment, make sure we're not followed, and check in to a
room at a hotel near the airport."

He squeezed her hand. "Okay. If that'll make you feel better."

"It will."

"I guess it's better to be safe than sorry."

•

In St. Helena, at 4:10 Tuesday afternoon, Joshua Rhinehart put down his
office phone and leaned back in his chair, pleased with himself. He had
accomplished quite a lot in the past two days. Now he swiveled around to
look out the window at the far mountains and the nearer vineyards.

He had spent nearly all of Monday on the telephone, dealing with
Bruno Frye's bankers, stockbrokers, and financial advisers. There had
been many lengthy discussions about how the assets ought to be managed
until the estate was finally liquidated, and there had been more than a little debate about the most profitable ways to dispose of those assets when

the time came for that. It had been a long, dull patch of work, for there had been a large number of savings accounts of various kinds, in several banks, plus bond investments, a rich portfolio of common stocks, real estate holdings, and much more.

Joshua spent Tuesday morning and the better part of the afternoon arranging, by telephone, for some of the most highly-respected art appraisers in California to journey to St. Helena for the purpose of cataloging and evaluating the varied and extensive collections that the Frye family had accumulated over six or seven decades. Leo, the patriarch, Katherine's father, now dead for forty years, had begun simply, with a fascination for elaborately hand-carved wooden spigots of the sort often used on beer and wine barrels in some European countries. Most of them were in the form of heads, the gaping or gasping or laughing or weeping or howling or snarling heads of demons, angels, clowns, wolves, elves, fairies, witches, gnomes, and other creatures. At the time of his death, Leo owned more than two thousand of those spigots. Katherine had shared her father's interest in collecting while he was alive, and after his death she had made collecting the central focus of her life. Her interest in acquiring beautiful things became a passion, and the passion eventually became a mania. (Joshua remembered how her eyes had gleamed and how she had chattered breathlessly each time that she had shown him a new purchase; he knew there had been something unhealthy about her desperate rush to fill every room and closet and drawer with lovely things, but then the rich always had been permitted their eccentricities and manias, so long as they caused no harm to anyone else.) She bought enameled boxes, turn-of-the-century landscape paintings, Lalique crystal, stained glass lamps and windows, antique cameo lockets, and many other items, not so much because they were excellent investments (which they were) but because she wanted them, needed them as a junkie always needed another fix. She stuffed her enormous house with these displays, spent countless hours just cleaning, polishing, and caring for everything. Bruno contained that tradition of almost frantic acquisition, and now both houses—the one Leo built in 1918, and the one Bruno had built five years ago—were crammed full of treasures. On Tuesday, Joshua called art galleries and prestige auction houses in San Francisco and Los Angeles, and all of them were eager to send their appraisers, for there were many fat commissions to be earned from the disposition of the Frye collections. Two men from San Francisco and two from Los Angeles were arriving Saturday morning; and, certain that they would require several days to catalogue the Frye holdings, Joshua made reservations for them at a local inn.

By 4:10 Tuesday afternoon, he was beginning to feel that he was on top of the situation; and for the first time since he was informed of Bruno's death, he was getting a fix on how long it would take him to fulfill his obligations as executor. Initially, he had worried that the estate would be so complicated that he would be tangled up in it for years, or at least for several months. But now that he had reviewed the will (which he had drawn up five years ago), and now that he had discovered where Bruno's capable financial advisers had led the man, he was confident that the entire matter could be resolved in a few weeks. His job was made easier by three factors that were seldom present in multimillion-dollar estate settlements: First, there were no living relatives to contest the will or make other problems; second, the entire after-tax net was left to a single charity clearly named in the will; third, for a man of such wealth, Bruno Frye had kept his investments simple, presenting his executor with a reasonably neat balance sheet of easily understood debits and credits. Three weeks would see the end of it. Four at most.

Since the death of his wife, Cora, three years ago, Joshua was acutely conscious of the brevity of life, and he jealously guarded this time. He didn't want to waste one precious day, and he felt that every minute he spent bogged down in the Frye estate was definitely a minute wasted. Of course, he would receive an enormous fee for his legal services, but he already had all the money he would ever need. He owned substantial real estate in the valley, including several hundred acres of prime grape-producing land which was managed for him and which supplied grapes to two big wineries that could never get enough of them. He had thought, briefly, of asking the court to relieve him of his duties; one of Frye's banks would have taken on the job with great pleasure. He also considered turning the work over to Ken Gavins and Roy Genelli, the two sharp young attorneys who he had taken on as partners seven years ago. But his strong sense of loyalty had kept him from taking the easy way out. Because Katherine Frye had given him his start in the Napa Valley thirty-five years ago, he felt he owed her the time it would take to personally preside over the orderly and dignified dissolution of the Frye family empire.

Three weeks.

Then he could spend more time on the things he enjoyed: reading good books, swimming, flying the new airplane that he'd bought, learning to cook new dishes, and indulging in an occasional weekend in Reno. Ken and Roy handled most of the law firm's business these days, and they did a damned good job of it. Joshua hadn't plunged into full retirement yet, but he sat on the edge of it a lot, dangling his legs in a big pool of leisure time that he wished he had found and used when Cora was still alive.

At 4:20, content with his progress on the Frye estate and soothed by the magnificent view of the autumn valley beyond his window, he got up from his chair and went out to the reception area. Karen Farr was pounding the hell out of an IBM Selectric II, which would have responded equally well to a feather touch. She was a slip of a girl, pale and blue-eyed and soft-voiced, but she attacked every chore with tremendous energy and strength.

"I am about to treat myself to an early whiskey," Joshua told her. "When people call and ask for me, please tell them I am in a disgraceful drunken condition and cannot come to the phone."

"And they'll all say, 'What? Again?'"

Joshua laughed. "You're a lovely and charming young woman, Miss Farr. Such a delightfully quick mind and tongue for such a mere wisp of a lass."

"And such a lot of malarkey you've got for a man who isn't even Irish. Go and have your whiskey. I'll keep the bothersome hordes away."

In his office again, he opened the corner bar, put ice in a glass, added a generous measure of Jack Daniel's Black Label. He had taken only two sips of the brew when someone knocked on his office door.

"Come in."

Karen opened the door. "There's a call—"

"I thought I was permitted to have my drink in peace."

"Don't be a grouch," she said.

"It's part of my image."

"I told him you weren't in. But then when I heard what he wanted, I thought maybe you should talk to him. It's weird."

"Who is it?"

"A Mr. Preston from the First Pacific United Bank in San Francisco. It's about the Frye estate."

"What's so weird?"

"You better hear it from him," she said.

Joshua sighed. "Very well."

"He's on line two."

Joshua went to his desk, sat down, picked up the phone, and said, "Good afternoon, Mr. Preston."

"Mr. Rhinehart?"

"Speaking. What can I do for you?"

"The business office at Shade Tree Vineyards informs me that you're the executor of the Frye estate."

"That's correct."

"Are you aware that Mr. Bruno Frye maintained accounts at our main office here in San Francisco?"

"The First Pacific United? No, I wasn't aware of that."

"A savings account, a checking account, and a safe-deposit box," Preston said.

"He had several accounts in several banks. He kept a list of them. But yours wasn't on the list. And I haven't run across any passbooks or canceled checks from your bank."

"I was afraid of that," Preston said.

Joshua frowned. "I don't understand. Are there problems with his accounts at Pacific United?"

Preston hesitated, then said, "Mr. Rhinehart, did Mr. Frye have a brother?"

"No. Why do you ask?"

"Did he ever employ a look-alike?"

"I beg your pardon?"

"Did he ever have need for a double, someone who could pass for him on fairly close inspection?"

"Are you pulling my leg, Mr. Preston?"

"I know it's a rather strange question. But Mr. Frye was a wealthy man. These days, what with terrorism on the rise and all sorts of crazies on the loose, wealthy people often have to hire bodyguards, and sometimes—not often; I admit it's rare; but in certain special cases—they even find it necessary to employ look-alikes for security reasons."

"With all due respect for your fair city," Joshua said, "let me point out that Mr. Frye lived here in the Napa Valley, not in San Francisco. We don't have that sort of crime here. We have a much different lifestyle from that which you . . . enjoy. Mr. Frye had no need for a double, and I'm certain he did not have one. Mr. Preston, what on earth is this all about?"

"We only just discovered that Mr. Frye was killed last Thursday," Preston said.

"So?"

"It is the opinion of our attorneys that the bank can in no way be held responsible."

"For what?" Joshua asked impatiently.

"As executor of the estate, it was your duty to inform us that our depositor had died. Until we received that notice—or learned of it third-hand, as we did—we had absolutely no reason to consider the account frozen."

"I'm aware of that." Slumped in his chair, staring wistfully at the glass of whiskey on his desk, afraid that Preston was about to tell him something that would disturb his rosy complacency, Joshua decided that a bit of curmudgeonly gruffness might speed the conversation along. He said, "Mr. Preston, I know that business is conducted slowly and carefully in a bank, which is fitting for an institution handling other people's hard-earned money. But I wish you could find your way clear to get to the point quickly."

"Last Thursday, half an hour before our closing time, a few hours *after* Mr. Frye was killed in Los Angeles, a man who resembled Mr. Frye entered our main branch. He had Mr. Frye's personalized checks. He wrote a check to cash, reducing that account to one hundred dollars."

Joshua sat up straight. "How much did he get?"

"Six thousand from checking."

"Ouch."

"Then he presented his passbook and withdrew all but five hundred from the savings account."

"And how much was that?"

"Another twelve thousand."

"Eighteen thousand dollars altogether?"

"Yes. Plus whatever he might have taken from the safe-deposit box."

"He hit that, too?"

"Yes. But of course, we don't know what he might have gotten out of it," Preston said. Then he added hopefully: "Perhaps nothing."

Joshua was amazed. "How could your bank release such a substantial sum in cash without requiring identification?"

"We did require it," Preston said. "And you've got to understand that he looked like Mr. Frye. For the past five years, Mr. Frye has come in two or three times every month; each time he has deposited a couple of thousand dollars in his checking. That made him noticeable. People remembered him. Last Thursday, our teller recognized him and had no reason to be suspicious, especially since he had those personalized checks and his passbook and—"

"That's not identification," Joshua said.

"The teller asked for ID, even though she recognized him. That's our policy on large withdrawals, and she handled it all according to policy. The man showed her a valid California driver's license, complete with photograph, in the name of Bruno Frye. I assure you, Mr. Rhinehart, First Pacific United has not acted irresponsibly in this matter."

"Do you intend to investigate the teller?" Joshua asked.

"An investigation has already begun."

"I'm pleased to hear it."

"But I'm quite sure it won't lead anywhere," Preston said. "She's been with us for more than sixteen years."

"Is she the same woman who let him get to the safe deposit box?" Joshua asked.

"No. That's another employee. We're investigating her as well."

"This is a damned serious matter."

"You don't have to tell me," Preston said miserably. "In all my years in banking, I've never had it happen to me. Before I phoned you, I notified the authorities, the state and federal banking officials, and First Pacific United's attorneys."

"I believe I should come down there tomorrow and have a chat with your people."

"I wish you would."

"Shall we say ten o'clock?"

"Whenever it's convenient for you," Preston said. "I'll be at your disposal all day."

"Then let's make it ten o'clock."

"I'm terribly sorry about this. But of course, the loss is covered by federal insurance."

"Except for the contents of the safe deposit box," Joshua said. "No insurance covers that loss." That was the part of it that was giving Preston a bad case of the jitters, and they both knew it. "The box might have held more of value than the savings and checking accounts combined."

"Or it might very well have been empty before he got to it," Preston said quickly.

"I'll see you in the morning, Mr. Preston."

Joshua hung up and stared at the telephone.

Finally he sipped his whiskey.

A double for Bruno Frye? A dead ringer?

Suddenly, he remembered the light he had thought he'd seen in Bruno's house at three o'clock Monday morning. He'd spotted it on his way back to bed from the bathroom, but when he'd put on his glasses, there had been no light. He'd figured that his eyes had played a trick on him. But perhaps the light had been real. Perhaps the man who had looted those Pacific United accounts had been in Bruno's house, looking for something.

Joshua had been to the house yesterday, had taken a brisk five-minute tour to be certain everything was as it should be, and he had not noticed anything awry.

Why had Bruno kept secret bank accounts in San Francisco?

Was there a dead ringer, a double?

Who? And why?

Damn!

Evidently, overseeing the complete and final settlement of the Frye estate was not going to be as short and easy a job as he had thought.

•

At six o'clock Tuesday evening, as Tony swung the Jeep into the street that ran past his apartment building, Hilary felt more awake than she had all day. She had entered that peculiar second-wind state of grainy-eyed alertness that came after being awake for a day and a half. Suddenly, the body and the mind seemed to decide to make the best of this forced consciousness; and, by some chemical trick, the flesh and the spirit were renewed. She stopped yawning. Her vision, which had been blurry at the edges, grew clear again. The grinding weariness receded. But she knew it would be only a short-lived reprieval from exhaustion. In an hour or two, this surprising high would end in an abrupt and inevitable crash, not unlike the sudden descent from an amphetamine energy peak, and then she would be too drained even to stay on her feet.

She and Tony had successfully dealt with all of their business that needed tending to—the insurance adjuster, the house cleaning service, the police reports, and all the rest. The only thing that hadn't gone smoothly was the stop at the Wyant Stevens Gallery in Beverly Hills. Neither Wyant nor his assistant, Betty, was there, and the plump young woman in charge was reluctant to take possession of Tony's paintings. She didn't want the responsibility, but Hilary finally convinced her that she would not be sued if one of the canvases was marked or torn accidentally. Hilary had written a note to Wyant, explaining the artist's background, and then she and Tony had gone to the offices of Topelis & Associates to ask Wally to make excuses to Warner Brothers. Now the slate was clean. Tomorrow, after

Frank Howard's funeral, they would catch the 11:55 PSA flight that would take them to San Francisco in time to board a connecting commuter air shuttle to Napa.

And then a rented car to St. Helena.

And then they would be on Bruno Frye's home ground.

And then—what?

Tony parked the Jeep and switched off the engine.

Hilary said, "I forgot to ask if you managed to find a hotel room."

"Wally's secretary made reservations for me while you and Wally were huddling in his office."

"At the airport."

"Yes."

"Not twin beds, I hope."

"One kingsize."

"Good," she said. "I want you to hold me while I drift off to sleep."

He leaned over and kissed her.

They took twenty minutes to pack a pair of suitcases for him and to carry their four bags down to the Jeep. During that time, Hilary was on edge, fully expecting Frye to leap out of a shadow or step around a corner, grinning.

He didn't.

They drove to the airport by a roundabout route that was full of twists and turns. Hilary watched the cars behind them.

They were not followed.

They reached the hotel at 7:30. With a touch of old-fashioned chivalry that amused Hilary, Tony signed them in as husband and wife.

Their room was on the eighth floor. It was a restful place, done in shades of green and blue.

When the bellhop left, they stood by the bed, just holding each other for a minute, silently sharing their weariness and what strength they had left.

Neither of them felt capable of going out to dinner. Tony ordered from room service, and the operator said service would take about half an hour.

Hilary and Tony showered together. They soaped and rinsed each other with pleasure, but the pleasure wasn't really sexual. They were too tired for passion. The shared bath was merely relaxing, tender, sweet.

They ate club sandwiches and french fries.

They drank half a bottle of Gamay rosé by Robert Mondavi.

They talked only a little while.

They draped a bath towel over a lamp and left the lamp on for a nightlight because, for only the second time in her life, Hilary was afraid to sleep in the dark.

They slept.

Eight hours later, at 5:30 in the morning, she woke from a bad dream in which Earl and Emma had come back to life, just like Bruno Frye. All three of them pursued her down a dark corridor that grew narrower and narrower and narrower. . . .

She couldn't get back to sleep. She lay in the vague amber glow of the makeshift nightlight and watched Tony sleep.

At 6:30 he woke, turned toward her, blinked, touched her face, her breasts, and they made love. For a short while, she forgot about Bruno Frye, but later, as they dressed for Frank's funeral, the fear came back in a rush.

"Do you really think we should go to St. Helena?"

"We have to go," Tony said.

"But what's going to happen to us there?"

"Nothing," he said. "We'll be all right."

"I'm not so sure," she said.

"We'll find out what's going on."

"That's just it," she said uneasily. "I have the feeling we'd be better off not knowing."

•

Katherine was gone.

The bitch was gone.

The bitch was hiding.

Bruno had awakened in the blue Dodge van at 6:30 Tuesday evening, thrown from sleep by the nightmare he could never quite remember, threatened by wordless whispers. Something was crawling all over him, on his arms, on his face, in his hair, even underneath his clothes, trying to get inside his body, trying to scuttle inside through his ears and mouth and nostrils, something unspeakably filthy and evil. He screamed and clawed frantically at himself until he finally realized where he was; then the awful whispers slowly faded, and the imaginary crawling thing crept away. For a few minutes, he curled up on his side, in a tight fetal position, and he wept with relief.

An hour later, after eating at McDonald's, he had gone to Westwood.

He drove by her place half a dozen times, then parked up the street from it, in a pool of shadows between streetlamps. He watched her house all night.

She was gone.

He had the linen bags full of garlic and the sharp wooden stakes and the crucifix and the vial of holy water. He had the two very sharp knives and a small woodman's hatchet with which he could chop off her head. He had the courage and the will and the determination.

But she was gone.

When he first began to realize that she had skipped out and might not be back for days or weeks, he was furious. He cursed her, and he wept with frustration.

Then he gradually regained control of himself. He told himself that all was not lost. He would find her.

He had found her countless times before.

chapter six

Wednesday morning, Joshua Rhinehart made the short flight to San Francisco in his own Cessna Turbo Skylane RG. It was a honey of a plane with a cruising speed of 173 knots and a range of over one thousand miles.

He had begun taking flying lessons three years ago, shortly after Cora died. For most of his life, he had dreamed about being a pilot, but he had never found time to learn until he was fifty-eight years old. When Cora was taken from him so unexpectedly, he saw that he was a fool, a fool who thought that death was a misfortune that only befell other people. He had spent his life as if he possessed an infinite store of it, as if he could spend and spend, live and live, forever. He thought he would have all the time in the world to take those dreamed-about trips to Europe and the Orient, all the time in the world to relax and travel and have fun; therefore, he always put off the cruises and vacations, postponed them until the law practice was built, and then until the mortgages on their large real estate holdings were all paid, and then until the grape-growing business was firmly established, and then. . . . And then Cora suddenly ran out of time. He missed her terribly, and he still filled up with remorse when he thought of all the things that had been delayed too long. He and Cora had been happy with each other; in many ways, they had enjoyed an extremely good life together, an excellent life by most standards. They'd never wanted for anything—not food or shelter or a fair share of luxuries. There'd always been enough money. But never enough time. He could not help dwelling on what might have been. He could not bring Cora back, but at least he was determined to grab all of the joy he could get his hands on in his remaining years. Because he had never been a gregarious man, and because he felt that nine out of ten people were woefully ignorant and/or malicious, most of his pleasures were solitary pursuits; but, in spite of his preference for solitude, nearly all of those pleasures were less satisfying than they would have been if he'd been able to share them with Cora. Flying was one of the few exceptions to that rule. In his Cessna, high above the earth, he felt as if he'd been freed from all restraints, not just from the bonds of gravity, but from the chains of regret and remorse as well.

Refreshed and renewed by the flight, Joshua landed in San Francisco shortly after nine o'clock. Less than an hour later, he was at the First Pacific United Bank, shaking hands with Mr. Ronald Preston, with whom he had spoken on the phone Tuesday afternoon.

Preston was a vice-president of the bank, and his office was sumptuous. There was a lot of real leather upholstery and well-polished teak. It was a padded, plush, fat office.

Preston, on the other hand, was tall and thin; he looked brittle, breakable. He was darkly tanned and sported a neatly trimmed mustache. He talked too fast, and his hands flung off one quick gesture after another, like a short-circuiting machine casting off sparks. He was nervous.

He was also efficient. He had prepared a detailed file on Bruno Frye's accounts, with pages for each of the five years that Frye had done business with First Pacific United. The file contained a list of savings account deposits and withdrawals, another list of the dates on which Frye had visited his safe-deposit box, clear photocopies of the monthly checking account statements blown up from microfilm records, and similar copies of every check ever written on that account.

"At first glance," Preston said, "it might appear that I haven't given you copies of all the checks Mr. Frye wrote. But let me assure you that I have. There simply weren't many of them. A lot of money moved in and out of that account, but for the first three and a half years, Mr. Frye wrote only two checks a month. For the last year and a half, it's been three checks every month, and always to the same payees."

Joshua didn't bother to open the folder. "I'll look at these things later. Right now, I want to question the teller who paid out on the checking and savings accounts."

A round conference table stood in one corner of the room. Six comfortably padded captain's chairs were arranged around it. That was the place Joshua chose for the interrogations.

Cynthia Willis, the teller, was a self-assured and rather attractive black woman in her late thirties. She was wearing a blue skirt and a crisp white blouse. Her hair was neatly styled, her fingernails well-shaped and brightly polished. She carried herself with pride and grace, and she sat with her back very straight when Joshua directed her into the chair opposite him.

Preston stood by his desk, silently fretting.

Joshua opened the envelope he had brought with him and took from it fifteen snapshots of people who lived or had once lived in St. Helena. He spread them out on the table and said, "Miss Willis—"

"Mrs. Willis," she corrected him.

"I'm sorry. Mrs. Willis, I want you to look at each one of those photographs, and then you tell me which is Bruno Frye. But only after you've looked at them all."

She went through the batch of photos in a minute and picked two of them. "Both of these are him."

"Are you sure?"

"Positive," she said. "That wasn't much of a test. The other thirteen don't look like him at all."

She had done an excellent job, much better than he had expected. Many of the photographs were fuzzy, and some were taken in poor light. Joshua purposefully used bad pictures to make the identification more difficult than it otherwise might have been, but Mrs. Willis did not hesitate. And although she said the other thirteen didn't look like Frye, a few of them actually did, a little. Joshua had chosen a few people who resembled Frye, at least when the camera was slightly out of focus, but that ruse had not fooled Cynthia Willis; and neither had the trick of including two photographs of Frye, two headshots, each much different from the other.

Tapping the two snapshots with her index finger, Mrs. Willis said, "This was the man who came into the bank last Thursday afternoon."

"On Thursday morning," Joshua said, "he was killed in Los Angeles."

"I don't believe it," she said firmly. "There must be some mistake about that."

"I saw his body," Joshua told her. "We buried him up in St. Helena last Sunday."

She shook her head. "Then you must have buried someone else. You must have buried the wrong man."

"I've known Bruno Frye since he was five years old," Joshua said. "I couldn't be mistaken."

"And I know who I saw," Mrs. Willis said politely but stubbornly.

She did not glance at Preston. She had too much pride to tailor her answers to his measurements. She knew she was a good worker, and she had no fear of the boss. Sitting up even straighter than she had been sitting, she said, "Mr. Preston is entitled to his opinion. But, after all, he didn't see the man. I did. It was Mr. Frye. He's been coming in the bank two or three times a month for the past five years. He always makes at least a two-thousand-dollar deposit in checking, sometimes as much as three thousand, and always in cash. Cash. That's unusual. It makes him very memorable. That and the way he looks, all of those muscles and—"

"Surely he didn't always make his deposits at your window."

"Not always," she admitted. "But a lot of the time, he did. And I swear it was him who made those withdrawals last Thursday. If you know him at all, Mr. Rhinehart, you know that I wouldn't even have had to see Mr. Frye to know it was him. I would have recognized him blindfolded because of that strange voice of his."

"A voice can be imitated," Preston said, making his first contribution to the conversation.

"Not this one," Mrs. Willis said.

"It might be imitated," Joshua said, "but not easily."

"And those eyes," Mrs. Willis said. "They were almost as strange as his voice."

Intrigued by that remark, Joshua leaned toward her and said, "What about his eyes?"

"They were cold," she said. "And not just because of the blue-gray color. Very cold, hard eyes. And most of the time he didn't seem to be able to look straight at you. His eyes kept sliding away, as if he was afraid you'd see his thoughts or something. But then, that every great once in a while when he *did* look straight at you, those eyes gave you the feeling you were looking at . . . well . . . at somebody who wasn't altogether right in the head."

Ever the diplomatic banker, Preston quickly said, "Mrs. Willis, I'm sure that Mr. Rhinehart wants you to stick to the objective facts of the case. If you interject your personal opinions, that will only cloud the issue and make his job more difficult."

Mrs. Willis shook her head. "All I know is, the man who was here last Thursday had those same eyes."

Joshua was slightly shaken by that observation, for he, too, often thought that Bruno's eyes revealed a soul in torment. There had been a frightened, haunted look in that man's eyes—but also the hard, cold, murderous iciness that Cynthia Willis had noted.

For another thirty minutes, Joshua questioned her about a number of subjects, including: the man who had withdrawn Frye's money, the usual procedures she followed when dispensing large amounts of cash, the procedures she had followed last Thursday, the nature of the ID that the imposter had presented, her home life, her husband, her children, her employment record, her current financial condition, and half a dozen other things. He was tough with her, even gruff when he felt that would help his cause. Unhappy at the prospect of spending extra weeks on the Frye estate because of this new development, anxious to find a quick solution to the mystery, he was searching for a reason to accuse her of complicity in the looting of the Frye accounts, but in the end he found nothing. Indeed, by the time he was finished quizzing her, he had come to like her a great deal and to trust her as well. He even went so far as to apologize to her for his sometimes sharp and quarrelsome manner, and such an apology was extremely rare for him.

After Mrs. Willis returned to her teller's cage, Ronald Preston brought Jane Symmons into the room. She was the woman who had accompanied the Frye look-alike into the vault, to the safe-deposit box. She was a twenty-seven-year-old redhead with green eyes, a pug nose, and a querulous disposition. Her whiny voice and peevish responses brought out the worst in Joshua; but the more curmudgeonly he became, the more querulous she grew. He did not find Jane Symmons to be as articulate as Cynthia Willis, and he did not like her as he did the black woman, and he did not apologize to her; but he was certain that she was as truthful as Mrs. Willis, at least about the matter at hand.

When Jane Symmons left the room, Preston said, "Well, what do you think?"

"It's not likely that either of them was part of any swindle," Joshua said.

Preston was relieved, but tried not to show it. "That's our assessment, too."

"But this man who's posing as Frye must bear an incredible likeness to him."

"Miss Symmons is a most astute young woman," Preston said. "If she said he looked exactly like Frye, the resemblance must, indeed, be remarkable."

"Miss Symmons is a hopeless twit," Joshua said grumpily. "If she were the only witness, I would be lost."

Preston blinked in surprise.

"However," Joshua continued, "your Mrs. Willis is keenly observant. And damned smart. And self-confident without being smug. If I were you, I'd make more of her than just a teller."

Preston cleared his throat. "Well . . . uh, what now?"

"I want to see the contents of that safe-deposit box."

"I don't suppose you have Mr. Frye's key?"

"No. He hasn't yet returned from the dead to give it to me."

"I thought perhaps it had turned up among his things since I talked to you yesterday."

"No. If the imposter used the key, I suppose he still has it."

"How did he get it in the first place?" Preston wondered. "If it was given to him by Mr. Frye, then that casts a different light on things. That would alter the bank's position. If Mr. Frye conspired with a look-alike to remove funds—"

"Mr. Frye could not have conspired. He was dead. Now shall we see what's in the box?"

"Without both keys, it'll have to be broken open."

"Please have that done," Joshua said.

Thirty-five minutes later, Joshua and Preston stood in the bank's secondary vault as the building engineer pulled the ruined lock out of the safe-deposit box and, a moment after that, slid the entire box out of the vault wall. He handed it to Ronald Preston, and Preston presented it to Joshua.

"Ordinarily," Preston said somewhat stiffly, "you would be escorted to one of our private cubicles, so that you could look through the contents without being observed. However, because there's a strong possibility you'll claim that some valuables were illegally removed, and because the bank might face a law suit on those charges, I must insist that you open the box in my presence."

"You haven't any legal right to insist on any such thing," Joshua said sourly. "But I have no intention of hitting your bank with a phony law suit, so I'll satisfy your curiosity right now."

Joshua lifted the lid of the safe-deposit box. A white envelope lay inside, nothing else, and he plucked it out. He handed the empty metal box to Preston and tore open the envelope. There was a single sheet of white paper bearing a dated, signed, typewritten note.

It was the strangest thing Joshua had ever read. It appeared to have been written by a man in a fever delirium.

> *Thursday, September 25*
> *To whom it may concern:*
> *My mother, Katherine Anne Frye, died five years ago, but she keeps coming back to life in new bodies. She has found a way to return from the grave, and she is trying to get me. She is currently living in Los Angeles, under the name Hilary Thomas.*
>
> *This morning, she stabbed me, and I died in Los Angeles. I intend to go back down there and kill her before she kills me again. Because if she kills me twice, I'll stay dead. I don't have her magic. I can't return from the grave. Not if she kills me twice.*
>
> *I feel so empty, so incomplete. She killed me, and I'm not whole any more.*
>
> *I'm leaving this note in case she wins again. Until I'm dead twice, this is my own little war, mine and no one else's. I can't come out in the open and ask for police protection. If I do that, everyone will know what I am, who I am. Everyone will know what I've been hiding all my life, and then they'll stone me to death. But if she gets me again, then it won't matter if everyone finds out what I am, because I'll already be dead twice. If she gets me again, then whoever finds this letter must take the responsibility for stopping her.*
>
> *You must cut off her head and stuff her mouth full of garlic. Cut out her heart and pound a stake through it. Bury her head and her heart in different church graveyards. She's not a vampire. But I think these things may work. If she is killed this way, she might stay dead. She comes back from the grave.*

Below the body of the letter, in ink, there was a fine forgery of Bruno Frye's signature. It had to be a forgery, of course. Frye was dead already when these lines were written.

The skin tingled on the back of Joshua's neck, and for some reason he thought of Friday night: walking out of Avril Tannerton's funeral home, stepping into the pitch-black night, being certain that something dangerous was nearby, sensing an evil presence in the darkness, a thing crouching and waiting.

"What is it?" Preston asked.

Joshua handed over the paper.

Preston read it and was amazed. "What in the world?"

"It must have been put in the box by the imposter who cleaned out the accounts," Joshua said.

"But why would he do such a thing?"

"Perhaps it's a hoax," Joshua said. "Whoever he is, he evidently enjoys a good ghost story. He knew we'd find out that he'd looted the checking and savings, so he decided to have some fun with us."

"But it's so . . . strange," Preston said. "I mean, you might expect a self-congratulatory note, something that would rub our faces in it. But this? It doesn't seem like the work of a practical joker. Although it's weird and doesn't always make sense, it seems so . . . *earnest*."

"If you think it's not merely a hoax, then what do you think?" Joshua asked. "Are you telling me Bruno Frye wrote this letter and put it in the safe-deposit box *after* he died?"

"Well . . . no. Of course not."

"Then what?"

The banker looked down at the letter in his hands. "Then I would say that this imposter, this man who looks so remarkably like Mr. Frye and talks like Mr. Frye, this man who carries a driver's license in Mr. Frye's name, this man who knew that Mr. Frye had accounts in First Pacific United—this man isn't just pretending to be Mr. Frye. He actually thinks he *is* Mr. Frye." He looked up at Joshua. "I don't believe that an ordinary thief with a prankster's turn of mind would compose a letter like this. There's genuine madness in it."

Joshua nodded. "I'm afraid I have to agree with you. But where did this doppelganger come from? Who is he? How long has he been around? Was Bruno aware that this man existed? Why would the look-alike share Bruno's obsessive fear and hatred of Katherine Frye? How could both men suffer from the same delusion—the belief that she had come back from the dead? There are a thousand questions. It truly boggles the mind."

"It certainly does," Preston said. "And I don't have any answers for you. But I do have one suggestion. This Hilary Thomas should be told that she may be in grave danger."

•

After Frank Howard's funeral, which was conducted with full police honors, Tony and Hilary caught the 11:55 flight from Los Angeles. On the way north, Hilary worked at being bubbly and amusing, for she could see that the funeral had depressed Tony and had brought back horrible memories of the Monday morning shootout. At first, he slumped in his seat, brooding, barely responding to her. But after a while, he seemed to become aware of her determination to cheer him up, and, perhaps because he didn't want her to feel that her effort was unappreciated, he found his lost smile and began to come out of his depression. They landed on time at San Francisco International Airport, but the two o'clock shuttle flight to Napa was now rescheduled for three o'clock because of minor mechanical difficulties.

With time to kill, they ate lunch in an airport restaurant that offered a view of the busy runways. The surprisingly good coffee was the only thing to recommend the place; the sandwiches were rubbery, and the french fries were soggy.

As the time approached for their departure for Napa, Hilary began to dread going. Minute by minute, she grew more apprehensive.

Tony noticed the change in her. "What's wrong?"

"I don't know exactly. I just feel like . . . well, maybe this is wrong. Maybe we're just rushing straight into the lion's den."

"Frye is down there in Los Angeles. He doesn't have any way of knowing that you're going to St. Helena," Tony said.

"Doesn't he?"

"Are you still convinced that it's supernatural, a matter of ghosts and ghouls and whatnot?"

"I'm not ruling out anything."

"We'll find a logical explanation in the end."

"Whether we do or not, I've got this feeling . . . this premonition."

"A premonition of what?"

"Of worse things to come," she said.

•

After a hurried but excellent lunch in the First Pacific United Bank's private executive dining room, Joshua Rhinehart and Ronald Preston met with federal and state banking officials in Preston's office. The bureaucrats were boring and poorly prepared and obviously ineffectual; but Joshua tolerated them, answered their questions, filled out their forms, for it was his duty to use the federal insurance system to recover the stolen funds for the Frye estate.

As the bureaucrats were leaving, Warren Sackett, an FBI agent, arrived. Because the money had been stolen from a federally-chartered financial institution, the crime was within the Bureau's jurisdiction.

Sackett—a tall, intense man with chiseled features—sat at the conference table with Joshua and Preston, and he elicited twice as much information as the covey of bureaucrats had done, in only half the time that those paper-pushers had required. He informed Joshua that a very detailed background check on him would be part of the investigation, but Joshua already knew that and had no reason to fear it. Sackett agreed that Hilary Thomas might be in danger, and he took the responsibility for informing the Los Angeles police of the extraordinary situation that had arisen, so that both the LAPD and the Los Angeles office of the FBI would be prepared to look after her.

Although Sackett was polite, efficient, and thorough, Joshua realized that the FBI was not going to solve the case in a few days—not unless the Bruno Frye imposter walked into their office and confessed. This was not an urgent matter to them. In a country plagued by various crackpot terrorist groups, organized crime families, and corrupt politicians, the resources of the FBI could not be brought fully to bear on an eighteen-thousand-dollar case of this sort. More likely than not, Sackett would be the only agent on it full-time. He would begin slowly, with background checks on everyone involved; and then he would conduct an exhaustive survey of banks in northern California, to see if Bruno Frye had any other secret accounts. Sackett wouldn't get to St. Helena for a day or two. And if he didn't come up with any leads in the first week or ten days, he might thereafter handle the case only on a part-time basis.

When the agent finished asking questions, Joshua turned to Ronald Preston and said, "Sir, I trust that the missing eighteen thousand will be replaced in short order."

"Well. . . ." Preston nervously fingered his prim little mustache. "We'll have to wait until the FDIC approves the claim."

Joshua looked at Sackett. "Am I correct in assuming the FDIC will wait until you can assure them that neither I nor any beneficiary of the estate conspired to withdraw that eighteen thousand dollars?"

"They might," Sackett said. "After all, this is a highly unusual case."

"But quite a lot of time could pass before you're able to give them such assurances," Joshua said.

"We wouldn't make you wait beyond a reasonable length of time," Sackett said. "At most, three months."

Joshua sighed. "I had hoped to settle the estate quickly."

Sackett shrugged. "Maybe I won't need three months. It could all break fast. You never know. In a day or two, I might even turn up this guy who's a dead ringer for Frye. Then I'd be able to give the FDIC an all-clear signal."

"But you don't expect to solve it that fast."

"The situation is so bizarre that I can't commit myself to deadlines," Sackett said.

"Damnation," Joshua said wearily.

A few minutes later, as Joshua crossed the cool marble-floored lobby on his way out of the bank, Mrs. Willis called to him. She was on duty at a teller's cage. He went to her, and she said, "You know what I'd do if I were you?"

"What's that?" Joshua asked.

"Dig him up. That man you buried. Dig him up."

"Bruno Frye?"

"You didn't bury Mr. Frye." Mrs. Willis was adamant; she pressed her lips together and shook her head back and forth, looking very stern. "No. If there's a double for Mr. Frye, he's not the one who's up walking around. The double is the one who's six feet under with a slab of granite for a hat. The real Mr. Frye was here last Thursday. I'd swear to that in any court. I'd stake my life on it."

"But if it wasn't Frye who was killed down in Los Angeles, then where is the real Frye now? Why did he run away? What in the name of God is going on?"

"I don't know about that," she said. "I only know what I saw. Dig him up, Mr. Rhinehart. I believe you'll find that you've buried the wrong man."

•

At 3:20 Wednesday afternoon, Joshua landed at the county airport just outside the town of Napa. With a population of forty-five thousand, Napa was far from being a major city, and in fact it partook of the wine country ambience to such an extent that it seemed smaller and cozier than it really was; but to Joshua, who was long accustomed to the rural peace of tiny St. Helena, Napa was as noisy and bothersome as San Francisco had been, and he was anxious to get out of the place.

His car was parked in the public lot by the airfield, where he had left it that morning. He didn't go home or to his office. He drove straight to Bruno Frye's house in St. Helena.

Usually, Joshua was acutely aware of the incredible natural beauty of the valley. But not today. Now he drove without seeing anything until the Frye property came into view.

Part of Shade Tree Vineyards, the Frye family business, occupied fertile black flat land, but most of it was spread over the gently rising foothills on the west side of the valley. The winery, the public tasting room, the extensive cellars, and the other company buildings—all fieldstone and redwood and oak structures that seemed to grow out of the earth—were situated on a large piece of level highland, near the westernmost end of the Frye property. All the buildings faced east, across the valley, toward vistas of seriated vines, and all of them were constructed with their backs to a one-hundred-sixty-foot cliff, which had been formed in a distant age when earth movement had sheered the side off the last foothill at the base of the more precipitously rising Mayacamas Mountains.

Above the cliff, on the isolated hilltop, stood the house that Leo Frye, Katherine's father, had built when he'd first come to the wine country in 1918. Leo had been a brooding Prussian type who had valued his privacy more than almost anything else. He looked for a building site that would provide a wide view of the scenic valley plus absolute privacy, and the clifftop property was precisely what he wanted. Although Leo was already a widower in 1918, and although he had only one small child and was not, at that time, contemplating another marriage, he nevertheless constructed a large twelve-room Victorian house on top of the cliff, a place with many bay windows and gables and a lot of architectural gingerbread. It overlooked the winery that he established, later, on the highland below, and there were only two ways to reach it. The first approach was by aerial tramway, a system comprised of cables, pulleys, electric motors, and one four-seat gondola that carried you from the lower station (a second-floor corner of the main winery building) to the upper station (somewhat to the north of the house on the clifftop). The second approach was by way of a double-switchback staircase fixed to the face of the cliff. Those three hundred and twenty steps were meant to be used only if the aerial tramway broke down—and then only if it was not possible to wait until repairs were made. The house was not merely private; it was remote.

As Joshua turned from the public road onto a very long private drive that led to the Shade Tree winery, he tried to recall everything he knew about Leo Frye. There was not much. Katherine had seldom spoken of her father, and Leo had not left a great many friends behind.

Because Joshua hadn't come to the valley until 1945, a few years after Leo's death, he'd never met the man, but he'd heard just enough tales about him to form a picture of the sort of mind that hungered for the excessive privacy embodied in that clifftop house. Leo Frye had been cold, stern, somber, self-possessed, obstinate, brilliant, a bit of an egomaniac, and an iron-handed authoritarian. He was not unlike a feudal lord from a distant age, a medieval aristocrat who preferred to live in a well-fortified castle beyond the easy reach of the unwashed rabble.

Katherine had continued to live in the house after her father died. She raised Bruno in those high-ceilinged rooms, a world far removed from that of the child's contemporaries, a Victorian world of waist-high wainscoting and flowered wallpaper and crenelated molding and footstools and mantel clocks and lace tablecloths. Indeed, mother and son lived together until he was thirty-five years old, at which time Katherine died of heart disease.

Now, as Joshua drove up the long macadam lane toward the winery, he looked above the fieldstone and wood buildings. He raised his eyes to the big house that stood like a giant cairn atop the cliff.

It was strange for a grown man to live with his mother as long as Bruno had lived with Katherine. Naturally, there had been rumors, speculations. The consensus of opinion in St. Helena was that Bruno had little or no interest in girls, that his passions and affections were directed secretly toward young men. It was assumed that he satisfied his desires during his occasional visits to San Francisco, out of sight of his wine country neighbors. Bruno's possible homosexuality was not a scandal in the valley. Local people didn't spend a great deal of time talking about it; they didn't really care. Although St. Helena was a small town, it could claim more than a little sophistication; winemaking made it so.

But now Joshua wondered if the consensus of local opinion about Bruno had been wrong. Considering the extraordinary events of the past week, it was beginning to appear as if the man's secret had been much darker and infinitely more terrible than mere homosexuality.

Immediately after Katherine's funeral, deeply shaken by her death, Bruno had moved out of the house on the cliff. He took his clothes, as well as large collections of paintings, metal sculptures, and books, which he had acquired on his own; but he left behind everything that belonged to Katherine. Her clothes were left hanging in closets and folded in drawers. Her antique furniture, paintings, porcelains, crystals, music boxes, enameled boxes—all of those things (and much more) could have been sold at auction for a substantial sum. But Bruno insisted that every item be left exactly where Katherine had put it, undisturbed, untouched. He locked the windows, drew the blinds and drapes, closed and bolt-locked the exterior shutters on both the first and second floors, locked the doors, sealed the place tight, as if it were a vault in which he could preserve forever the memory of his adoptive mother.

When Bruno had rented an apartment and had begun to make plans for the construction of a new house in the vineyards, Joshua had tried to persuade him that it was foolish to leave the contents of the cliff house unattended. Bruno insisted that the house was secure and that its remoteness made it an unlikely target of burglars—especially since burglary was an almost unheard-of crime in the valley. The two approaches to the house—the switchback stairs and the aerial tramway—were deep in Frye property, behind the winery; and the tramway operated only with a key. Besides (Bruno had argued), no one but he and Joshua knew that a great many items of value remained in the old house. Bruno was adamant; Katherine's belongings must not be touched; and finally, reluctantly, unhappily, Joshua surrendered to his client's wishes.

To the best of Joshua's knowledge, no one had been in the cliff house for five years, not since the day that Bruno had moved out. The tramway was well-maintained, even though the only person who rode it was Gilbert Ulman, a mechanic employed to keep Shade Tree Vineyards' trucks and farm equipment in good shape; Gil also had the job of regularly inspecting and repairing the aerial tramway system, which required only a couple of hours a month. Tomorrow, or Friday at the latest, Joshua would have to take the cable car to the top of the cliff and open the house, every door and window, so that it could air out before the art appraisers arrived from Los Angeles and San Francisco on Saturday morning.

At the moment, Joshua was not the least bit interested in Leo Frye's isolated Victorian redoubt; his business was at Bruno's more modern and considerably more accessible house. As he drew near the end of the road that led to the winery's public parking lot, he turned left, onto an extremely narrow driveway that struck south through the sun-splashed vineyards. Vines crowded both sides of the cracked, raggedy-edged blacktop. The pavement led him down one hill, across a shallow glen, up another slope, and ended two hundred yards south of the winery, in a clearing, where Bruno's house stood with vineyards on all sides. It was a large, single-story, ranch-style, redwood and fieldstone structure shaded by one of the nine mammoth oak trees that dotted the huge property and gave the Frye company its name.

Joshua got out of the car and walked to the front door of the house. There were only a few high white clouds against the electric-blue sky. The air flowing down from the piney heights of the Mayacamas was crisp and fresh.

He unlocked the door, stepped inside, and stood in the foyer for a moment, listening. He wasn't sure what he expected to hear.

Maybe footsteps.

Or Bruno Frye's voice.

But there was only silence.

He went from one end of the house to the other in order to get to Frye's study. The decor was proof that Bruno had acquired Katherine's obsessive compulsion to collect and hoard beautiful things. On some walls, so many fine paintings were hung so close together that their frames touched, and no single piece could claim the eye in that exquisite riot of shape and color. Display cases stood everywhere, filled with art glass and bronze sculpture and crystal paperweights and pre-Columbian statuary. Every room contained far too much furniture, but each piece was a matchless example of its period and style. In the huge study, there were five or six hundred rare books, many of them limited editions that had been bound in leather; and there were a few dozen perfect little scrimshaw figures in a display case; and there were six terribly expensive and flawless crystal balls, one as small as an orange, one as large as a basketball, the others in various sizes between.

Joshua pulled back the drapes at the window, letting in a little light, switched on a brass lamp, and sat in a modern spring-backed office chair behind an enormous 18th-century English desk. From a jacket pocket he withdrew the strange letter that he had found in the safe-deposit box at the First Pacific United Bank. It was actually just a Xerox; Warren Sackett, the FBI agent, insisted on keeping the original. Joshua unfolded the copy and propped it up where he could see it. He turned to the low typing stand that was beside the desk, pulled it over his lap, rolled a clean sheet of paper into the typewriter, and quickly tapped out the first sentence of the letter.

My mother, Katherine Anne Frye, died five years ago, but she keeps coming back to life in new bodies.

He held the Xerox copy next to the sample and compared them. The type was the same. In both versions, the loop of the lower case "e" was completely filled in with ink because the keys hadn't been properly cleaned in quite a while. In both, the loop of the lower case "a" was partially occluded, and the lower case "d" printed slightly higher than any of the other characters. The letter had been typed in Bruno Frye's study, on Bruno Frye's machine.

The look-alike, the man who had impersonated Frye in that San Francisco bank last Thursday, apparently possessed a key to the house. But how had he gotten it? The most obvious answer was that Bruno had given it to him, which meant that the man was an employee, a hired double.

Joshua leaned back in the chair and stared at the Xerox of the letter, and other questions exploded like fireworks in his mind. Why had Bruno felt it necessary to hire a double? Where had he found such a remarkable look-alike? How long ago did the double start to work for him? Doing what? And how often had he, Joshua, spoken to this doppelganger, thinking the man was really Frye? Probably more than once. Perhaps more often than he'd spoken with the real Bruno. There was no way of knowing. Had the double been here, in the house, Thursday morning, when Bruno had died in Los Angeles? Most likely. After all, this was where he had typed the letter that he'd put in the safe-deposit box, so this must be where he had heard the news. But how had he learned about the death so quickly? Bruno's body had been found next to a public telephone. . . . Was it possible that Bruno's last act had been to call home and talk to his double? Yes. Possible. Even probable. The telephone company's records would have to be checked. But what had those two men said to each other as the one died? Could they conceivably share the same psychosis, the belief that Katherine had come back from the grave?

Joshua shuddered.

He folded the letter, returned it to his coat pocket.

For the first time, he realized how *gloomy* these rooms were—overstuffed with furniture and expensive ornaments, windows covered by heavy drapes, floors carpeted in dark colors. Suddenly, the place seemed far more isolated than Leo's clifftop retreat.

A noise. In another room.

Joshua froze as he was walking around the desk. He waited, listened. "Imagination," he said, trying to reassure himself.

He walked swiftly through the house to the front door, and he found that the noise had, indeed, been imaginary. He wasn't attacked. Nevertheless, when he stepped outside, closed the door, and locked it, he sighed with relief.

In the car, on his way to his office in St. Helena, he thought of more questions. Who actually had died in Los Angeles last week—Frye or his look-alike? Which of them had been at the First Pacific United Bank on Thursday—the real man or the imitation? Until he knew the answer to that, how could he settle the estate? He had countless questions but damned few answers.

When he parked behind his office a few minutes later, he realized that he would have to give serious consideration to Mrs. Willis's advice. Bruno Frye's grave might have to be opened to determine exactly who was buried in it.

•

Tony and Hilary landed in Napa, rented a car, and arrived at the headquarters of the Napa County Sheriff's Department by 4:20 Wednesday afternoon. The place was not somnolent like the county sheriff's offices you saw on television. A couple of young deputies and a pair of industrious clerical workers were busy with files and paperwork.

The sheriff's secretary-receptionist sat at a large metal desk, identified by a name plaque in front of her typewriter: MARSHA PELETRINO. She was a starched-looking woman with severe features, but her voice was soft, silky, and sexy. Likewise, her smile was far more pleasant and inviting than Hilary had expected.

When Marsha Peletrino opened the door between the reception area and Peter Laurenski's private office and announced that Tony and Hilary wanted to see him, Laurenski knew immediately who they were, and he didn't attempt to avoid them, as they thought he might. He came out of his office and awkwardly shook their hands. He seemed embarrassed. Clearly, he wasn't looking forward to explaining why he had provided a phony alibi for Bruno Frye last Wednesday night, but in spite of his unconcealed discomfort, he invited Tony and Hilary in for a chat.

Laurenski was somewhat of a disappointment for Hilary. He was not the sloppy, potbellied, cigar-chewing, easy to hate, small town, good old boy type that she had expected, not the sort of countrified power monger who would lie to protect a wealthy local resident like Bruno Frye. Laurenski was in his thirties, tall, blond, clean-cut, articulate, friendly, and apparently dedicated to his job, a good lawman. There was kindness in his eyes and a surprising gentleness in his voice; in some ways he reminded her of Tony. The Sheriff's Department's offices were clean and Spartan rooms where a lot of work got done, and the people who labored there with Laurenski, the deputies and civilians alike, were not patronage cronies but bright and busy public servants. After only one or two minutes with the sheriff, she knew there was not going to be any simple answer to the Frye mystery, no obvious and easily-exposed conspiracy.

In the sheriff's private office, she and Tony sat on a sturdy old railback bench that had been made comfortable with corduroy-covered foam pillows. Laurenski pulled up a chair and sat on it the wrong way, with his arms crossed on the backrest.

He disarmed Hilary and Tony by getting straight to the point and by being hard on himself.

"I'm afraid I've been less than professional about this whole thing," he said. "I've been dodging your department's phone calls."

"That's the reason we're here," Tony said.

"Is this an . . . official visit of some kind?" Laurenski asked, a bit puzzled.

"No," Tony said. "I'm here as a private citizen, not a policeman."

"We've had an extremely unusual and unsettling experience in the last couple of days," Hilary said. "Incredible things have happened, and we hope you'll have an explanation for them."

Laurenski raised his eyebrows. "Something more than Frye's attack on you?"

"We'll tell you about it," Tony said. "But first, we'd like to know why you haven't answered the LAPD."

Laurenski nodded. He was blushing. "I just didn't know what to say. I'd made a fool of myself by vouching for Frye. I guess I just hoped it would all blow away."

"And why did you vouch for him?" Hilary asked.

"It's just . . . you see . . . I really did think he was at home that night."

"You talked with him?" Hilary asked.

"No," Laurenski said. He cleared his throat. "You see, when the call came in that evening, it was taken by a night officer. Tim Larsson. He's one of my best men. Been with me seven years. A real go-getter. Well . . . when the Los Angeles police called about Bruno Frye, Tim thought he'd better call me and see if I wanted to handle it, since Frye was one of the county's leading citizens. I was at home that night. It was my daughter's birthday. As far as my family was concerned, that was a pretty special occasion, and for once I was determined not to let my work intrude on my private life. I have so little time for my kids. . . ."

"I understand," Tony said. "I have a hunch you do a good job here. And I'm familiar enough with police work to know that doing a good job requires a hell of a lot more than eight hours a day."

"More like twelve hours a day, six or seven days a week," the sheriff said. "Anyway, Tim called me that night, and I told him to handle it. You see, first of all, it sounded like such a ridiculous inquiry. I mean, Frye was an upstanding businessman, even a millionaire, for God's sake. Why would he throw it all away trying to rape someone? So I told Tim to look into it and get back to me as soon as he had something. As I said, he's a very competent officer. Besides, he knew Frye better than I did. Before he decided on a career in law enforcement, Tim worked for five years in the main office at Shade Tree Vineyards. During that time, he saw Frye just about every day."

"Then it was Officer Larsson who checked on Frye last Wednesday night," Tony said.

"Yes. He called me back at my daughter's birthday party. He said Frye was at home, not in Los Angeles. So I returned the call to the LAPD and proceeded to make a fool of myself."

Hilary frowned. "I don't understand. Are you saying that this Tim Larsson lied to you?"

Laurenski didn't want to have to answer that one. He got up and paced, staring at the floor, scowling. Finally he said, "I trust Tim Larsson. I always have trusted him. He's a good man. One of the best. But I just can't explain this."

"Did he have any reason to cover up for Frye?" Tony asked.

"You mean, were they buddies? No. Nothing like that. They weren't even friends. He'd only worked for Frye. And he didn't like the man."

"Did he claim to have seen Bruno Frye that night?" Hilary asked Laurenski.

"At the time," the sheriff said, "I just assumed he had seen him. But later, Tim said he figured he could identify Frye by phone and that there wasn't any need to run all the way out there in a patrol car to have a look-see. As you must know, Bruno Frye had a very distinct, very odd voice."

"So Larsson might have talked to someone who was covering for Frye, someone who could imitate his voice," Tony said.

Laurenski looked at him. "That's what Tim says. That's his excuse. But it doesn't fit. Who would it have been? Why would he cover for rape and murder? Where is he now? Besides, Frye's voice wasn't something that could be easily mimicked."

"So what do you think?" Hilary asked.

Laurenski shook his head. "I don't know what to think. I've been brooding about it all week. I want to believe my officer. But how can I? Something is going on here—but what? Until I can get a handle on it, I've laid Tim off without pay."

Tony glanced at Hilary, then back at the sheriff. "When you hear what we've got to tell you, I think you'll be able to believe Officer Larsson."

"However," Hilary said, "you still won't be able to make sense out of it. We're in deeper than you are, and we still don't know what's going on."

She told Laurenski about Bruno Frye being in her house Tuesday morning, five days after his death.

•

In his office in St. Helena, Joshua Rhinehart sat at his desk with a glass of Jack Daniel's Black Label and looked through the file that Ronald Preston had given him in San Francisco. It contained, among other things, clear photocopies of the monthly statements that had been blown up from microfilm records, plus similar copies of the front and back of every check Frye had written. Because Frye had kept the account a secret, tucked away in a city bank where he did no other business, Joshua was convinced that an examination of those records would yield clues to the solution of the dead ringer's identity.

During the first three and a half years that the account had been active, Bruno had written two checks each month, never more than that, never fewer. And the checks were always to the same people—Rita Yancy and Latham Hawthorne—names which meant nothing to Joshua.

For reasons not specified, Mrs. Yancy had received five hundred dollars a month. The only thing Joshua could deduce from the photocopies of those checks was that Rita Yancy must live in Hollister, California, for she deposited every one of them in a Hollister bank.

No two of the checks to Latham Hawthorne were for the same amount; they ranged from a couple of hundred dollars to five or six thousand. Apparently, Hawthorne lived in San Francisco, for all of his deposits were made at the same branch of the Wells Fargo Bank in that city. Hawthorne's checks were all endorsed with a rubber stamp that read:

> FOR DEPOSIT ONLY
> TO THE ACCOUNT OF:
> *Latham Hawthorne*
> ANTIQUARIAN BOOKSELLER
> &
> OCCULTIST

Joshua stared at that last word for a while. *Occultist*. It was obviously derived from the word "occult" and was intended by Hawthorne to describe his profession, or at least half of it, rare book dealing being the other half. Joshua thought he knew what the word meant, but he was not certain.

Two walls of his office were lined with law books and reference works. He had three dictionaries, and he looked up "occultist" in all of them. The first two did not contain the word, but the third gave him a definition that was pretty much what he had expected. An occultist was someone who believed in the rituals and supernatural powers of various "occult sciences"—including, but not limited to, astrology, palmistry, black magic, white magic, demonolatry, and Satanism. According to the dictionary, an occultist could also be someone who sold the paraphernalia required to engage in any of those odd pursuits—books, costumes, cards, magical instruments, sacred relics, rare herbs, pig-tallow candles, and the like.

In the five years between Katherine's death and his own demise, Bruno Frye had paid more than one hundred and thirty thousand dollars to Latham Hawthorne. There was nothing on any of the checks to indicate what he had received in return for all that money.

Joshua refilled his glass with whiskey and returned to his desk.

The file on Frye's secret bank accounts showed that he had written two checks a month for the first three and a half years, but then three checks a month for the past year and a half. One to Rita Yancy, one to Latham Hawthorne, as before. And now a third check to Dr. Nicholas W. Rudge. All of the checks to the doctor had been deposited in a San Francisco branch of the Bank of America, so Joshua assumed the physician lived in that city.

He placed a call to San Francisco Directory Assistance, then another to Directory Assistance in the 408 area code, which included the town of Hollister. In less than five minutes, he had telephone numbers for Hawthorne, Rudge, and Rita Yancy.

He called the Yancy woman first.

She answered on the second ring. "Hello?"

"Mrs. Yancy?"

"Yes."

"Rita Yancy?"

"That's right." She had a pleasant, gentle, melodic voice. "Who's this?"

"My name's Joshua Rhinehart. I'm calling from St. Helena. I'm the executor for the estate of the late Bruno Frye."

She didn't respond.

"Mrs. Yancy?"

"You mean he's dead?" she asked.

"You didn't know?"

"How would I know?"

"It was in the newspapers."

"I never read the papers," she said. Her voice had changed. It was not pleasant any more; it was hard and cold.

"He died last Thursday," Joshua said.

She was silent.

"Are you all right?" he asked.

"What do you want from me?"

"Well, as executor, one of my duties is to see that all of Mr. Frye's debts are paid before the estate is distributed to the heirs."

"So?"

"I discovered that Mr. Frye was paying you five hundred dollars a month, and I thought that might be installments on a debt of some sort."

She didn't answer him.

He could hear her breathing.

"Mrs. Yancy?"

"He doesn't owe me a penny," she said.

"Then he wasn't repaying a debt?"

"No," she said.

"Were you working for him in some capacity?"

She hesitated. Then: *click!*

"Mrs. Yancy?"

There wasn't any response. Just the hissing of the long distance line, a far-off crackle of static.

Joshua dialed her number again.

"Hello," she said.

"It's me, Mrs. Yancy. Evidently, we were cut off."

Click!

He considered calling her a third time, but he decided she would only hang up again. She wasn't handling herself well. Obviously, she had a secret, a secret she had shared with Bruno, and now she was trying to hide it from Joshua. But all she had done was feed his curiosity. He was more certain than ever that each of the people who were paid through the San Francisco bank account would have something to tell him that would help to explain the existence of a Bruno Frye look-alike.

If he could only get them to talk, he might settle the estate relatively quickly after all.

As he put the receiver down, he said, "You can't get away from me that easily, Rita."

Tomorrow, he would fly the Cessna down to Hollister and confront her in person.

Now he called Dr. Nicholas Rudge, got an answering service, and left a message, including both his home and office numbers.

On his third call, he struck paydirt, although not as much of it as he had hoped to find. Latham Hawthorne was at home and willing to talk. The occultist had a nasal voice and a trace of an upper-class British accent.

"I sold him quite a number of books," Hawthorne said in answer to a question from Joshua.

"Just books?"

"That's correct."

"That's a lot of money for books."

"He was an excellent customer."

"But a hundred and thirty thousand dollars?"

"Spread out over almost five years."

"Nevertheless—"

"And most of them were extremely rare books, you understand."

"Would you be willing to buy them back from the estate?" Joshua asked, trying to determine if the man was honest.

"Buy them back? Oh, yes, I'd be happy to do that. Most definitely."

"How much?"

"Well, I can't say exactly until I see them."

"Take a stab in the dark. How much?"

"You see, if the volumes have been abused—tattered and torn and marked and whatnot—then that's quite another story."

"Let's say they're spotless. How much would you offer?"

"If they're in the condition they were when I sold them to Mr. Frye, I'm prepared to offer you quite a bit more than he originally paid for them. A great many of the titles in his collection have appreciated in value."

"How much?" Joshua asked.

"You're a persistent man."

"One of my many virtues. Come on, Mr. Hawthorne. I'm not asking you to commit yourself to a binding offer. Just an estimate."

"Well, *if* the collection still contains every book that I sold him, and *if* they're all in prime condition . . . I'd say . . . allowing for my margin of profit, of course . . . around two hundred thousand dollars."

"You'd buy back the same books for seventy thousand more than he paid you?"

"As a rough estimate, yes."

"That's quite an increase in value."

"That's because of the area of interest," Hawthorne said. "More and more people come into the field every day."

"And what is the field?" Joshua asked. "What kind of books was he collecting?"

"Haven't you seen them?"

"I believe they're on bookshelves in his study," Joshua said. "Many of them are very old books, and a lot of them have leather bindings. I didn't realize there was anything unusual about them. I haven't taken time to look closely."

"They were occult titles," Hawthorne said. "I only sell books dealing with the occult in all its many manifestations. A high percentage of my wares are forbidden books, those that were banned by church or state in another age, those that have not been brought back into print by our modern and skeptical publishers. Limited edition items, too. I have more than two hundred steady customers. One of them is a San Jose gentleman who collects nothing but books on Hindu mysticism. A woman in Marin County has acquired an enormous library on Satanism, including a dozen obscure titles that have been published in no language but Latin. Another woman in Seattle has bought virtually every word ever printed about out-of-body experiences. I can satisfy any taste. I'm not merely polishing my ego when I say that I'm the most reputable and reliable dealer in occult literature in this country."

"But surely not all of your customers spend as much as Mr. Frye did."

"Oh, of course not. There are only two or three others like him, with his resources. But I've got a few dozen clients who budget approximately ten thousand dollars a year for their purchases."

"That's incredible," Joshua said.

"Not really," Hawthorne said. "These people feel that they are teetering on the edge of a great discovery, on the brink of learning some monumental secret, the riddle of life. Some of them are in pursuit of immortality. And some are searching for spells and rituals that will bring them tremendous wealth or unlimited power over others. Those are persuasive motivations. If they truly believe that just a little more forbidden knowledge will get them what they want, then they will pay virtually any price to obtain it."

Joshua swung around in his swivel chair and looked out the window. Low gray clouds were scudding in from the west, over the tops of the autumn-somber Mayacamas Mountains, bearing down on the valley.

"Exactly what aspect of the occult interested Mr. Frye?" Joshua asked.

"He collected two kinds of books loosely linked to the same general subject," Hawthorne said. "He was fascinated by the possibility of communicating with the dead. Séances, table knockings, spirit voices, ectoplasmic apparitions, amplification of ether recordings, automatic writing, that sort of thing. But his greatest interest, by far, lay in literature about the living dead."

"Vampires?" Joshua asked, thinking about the strange letter in the safe-deposit box.

"Yes," Hawthorne said. "Vampires, zombies, creatures of that sort. He couldn't get enough books on the subject. Of course, I don't mean that he was interested in horror novels and cheap sensationalism. He collected only serious nonfiction studies—and certain select esoterica."

"Such as?"

"Well, for instance . . . in the esoterica category . . . he paid six thousand dollars for the hand-written journal of Christian Marsden."

"Who is Christian Marsden?" Joshua asked.

"Fourteen years ago, Marsden was arrested for the murders of nine people in and around San Francisco. The press called him the Golden Gate Vampire because he always drank his victim's blood."

"Oh, yes," Joshua said.

"And he also dismembered his victims."

"Yes."

"Cut off their arms and legs and heads."

"Unfortunately, I remember him now. A gruesome case," Joshua said.

The dirty gray clouds were still rolling across the western mountains, moving steadily toward St. Helena.

"Marsden kept a journal during his year-long killing spree," Hawthorne said. "It's a curious piece of work. He believed that a dead man named Adrian Trench was trying to take over his body and come back to life through him. Marsden genuinely felt that he was in a constant, desperate struggle for control of his own flesh."

"So that when he killed, it wasn't really him killing, but this Adrian Trench."

"That's what he wrote in his journal," Hawthorne said. "For some reason he never explained, Marsden believed that the evil spirit of Adrian Trench required other people's blood to keep control of Marsden's body."

"A sufficiently screwy story to present to a court in a sanity hearing," Joshua said cynically.

"Marsden *was* sent to an asylum," Hawthorne said. "Six years later, he died there. But he wasn't faking insanity to escape a prison sentence. He actually believed that the spirit of Adrian Trench was trying to cast him out of his own body."

"Schizophrenic."

"Probably," Hawthorne agreed. "But I don't think we should rule out the possibility that Marsden was sane and that he was merely reporting a genuine paranormal phenomenon."

"Say again?"

"I'm suggesting that Christian Marsden might really have been possessed in some way or other."

"You don't mean that," Joshua said.

"To paraphrase Shakespeare—there are a great many things in heaven and earth that we do not and cannot understand."

Beyond the large office window, as the slate-colored bank of clouds continued to press into the valley, the sun sank westward, beyond the Mayacamas, and the autumn dusk came prematurely to St. Helena.

As he watched the light bleed slowly out of day, Joshua said, "Why did Mr. Frye want the Marsden journal so badly?"

"He believed he was living through an experience similar to Marsden's," Hawthorne said.

"You mean, Bruno thought some dead person was trying to take over his body?"

"No," Hawthorne said. "He didn't identify with Marsden, but with Marsden's victims. Mr. Frye believed that his mother—I think her name was Katherine—had come back from the dead in someone else's body and was plotting to kill him. He hoped that the Marsden journal would give him a clue about how to deal with her."

Joshua felt as if a large dose of ice-cold water had been injected into his veins. "Bruno never mentioned such a thing to me."

"Oh, he was quite secretive about it," Hawthorne said. "I'm probably the only person he ever revealed it to. He trusted me because I was sympathetic toward his interest in the occult. Even so, he only mentioned it once. He was quite passionate in his belief that she had returned from the dead, quite terrified of falling prey to her. But later, he was sorry that he had told me."

Joshua sat up straight in his chair, amazed, chilled. "Mr. Hawthorne, last week Mr. Frye attempted to kill a woman in Los Angeles."

"Yes, I know."

"He wanted to kill her because he thought that she was actually his mother hiding in a new body."

"Really? How interesting."

"Good God, sir! You knew what was going on in his mind. Why didn't you do something?"

Hawthorne remained cool and serene. "What would you have had me do?"

"You could have told the police! They could have questioned him, looked into the possibility that he needed medical attention."

"Mr. Frye hadn't committed a crime," Hawthorne said. "And beyond that, you're presuming he was crazy, and I make no such presumption."

"You're joking," Joshua said incredulously.

"Not at all. Perhaps Frye's mother did come back from the grave to get him. Maybe she even succeeded."

"For God's sake, that woman in Los Angeles was not his mother!"

"Maybe," Hawthorne said. "Maybe not."

Although Joshua was still sitting in his big office chair, and although the chair was still resting squarely on a solid floor, he felt curiously off balance. He had pictured Hawthorne as a rather cultured, mild-mannered, bookish fellow who had gotten into his unusual line of business largely because of the profits it offered. Now Joshua began to wonder if that image was altogether wrong. Maybe Latham Hawthorne was as strange as the merchandise he sold.

"Mr. Hawthorne, you're obviously a very efficient and successful businessman. You sound as if you're well-educated. You're far more articulate than most people I meet these days. Considering all of that, I find it difficult to believe that you put much credence in such things as séances and mysticism and the living dead."

"I scoff at nothing," Hawthorne said. "And in fact I think my willingness to believe is less surprising than your stubborn refusal to do so. I don't see how an intelligent man can *not* realize that there are many worlds beyond our own, realities beyond that in which we live."

"Oh, I believe the world is filled with mysteries and that we only partially perceive the nature of reality," Joshua said. "You'll get no argument from me on that. But I also think, in time, our perceptions will be sharpened and the mysteries all explained by scientists, by rational men working in their laboratories—not by superstitious cultists burning incense and chanting nonsense."

"I have no faith in scientists," Hawthorne said. "I'm a Satanist. I find my answers in that discipline."

"Devil worship?" Joshua asked. The occultist could still surprise him.

"That's a rather crude way of putting it. I believe in the Other God, the Dark Lord. His time is coming, Mr. Rhinehart." Hawthorne spoke calmly, pleasantly, as if he were discussing nothing more unusual or controversial than the weather. "I look forward to the day when He casts out Christ and all the lesser gods and takes the throne of the earth for His own. What a fine day that will be. All the devout of other religions will be enslaved or slaughtered. Their priests will be decapitated and fed to the dogs. Nuns will be ravished in the streets. Churches and mosques and synagogues and temples will be used for the celebration of black masses, and every person on the face of the earth will worship Him, and babies will be sacrificed on those altars, and Beelzebub will reign until the end of time. Soon, Mr. Rhinehart. There are signs and portents. Quite soon now. I look forward to it."

Joshua was at a loss for words. In spite of the madness that Hawthorne spouted, he sounded like a rational, reasonable man. He was not ranting or screaming. There was not even a vague trace of mania or hysteria in his voice. Joshua was more disturbed by the occultist's outward composure and surface gentleness than he would have been if Hawthorne had snarled and yelped and foamed at the mouth. It was like meeting a stranger at a cocktail party, talking with him for a while, getting to like him, and then suddenly realizing that he was wearing a latex mask, a clever false face, behind which lay the evil and grinning countenance of Death himself. A Halloween costume, but in reverse. The demon disguised as the ordinary man. Poe's nightmare come to life.

Joshua shivered.

Hawthorne said, "Could we arrange a meeting? I'm looking forward to having an opportunity to inspect the collection of books that Mr. Frye purchased from me. I can come up there almost any time. What day would be convenient for you?"

Joshua wasn't looking forward to meeting and doing business with this man. He decided to stall the occultist until the other appraisers had seen the books. Perhaps one of those men would understand the value of the collection and would make an equitable offer to the estate; then it wouldn't be necessary to traffic with Latham Hawthorne.

"I'll have to get back to you on that," Joshua said. "I've got a lot of other things to take care of first. It's a large and rather complex estate. It'll take quite a few weeks to get it all wrapped up."

"I'll be waiting for your call."

"Two more things before you hang up," Joshua said.

"Yes?"

"Did Mr. Frye say why he had such an obsessive fear of his mother?"

"I don't know what she did to him," Hawthorne said, "but he hated her with all his heart. I've never seen such raw, black hatred as when he spoke of her."

"I knew them both," Joshua said. "I never saw anything like that between them. I always thought he worshipped her."

"Then it must have been a secret hatred that he'd nurtured for a long, long time," Hawthorne said.

"But what could she have done to him?"

"As I said, he never told me. But there was something behind it, something so bad that he couldn't even bring himself to discuss it. You said there were two things you wanted to ask about. What's the other one?"

"Did Bruno mention a double?"

"Double?"

"A look-alike. Someone who could pass for him."

"Considering his size and his unusual voice, finding a double wouldn't be easy."

"Apparently, he managed to do it. I'm trying to find out why he thought it was necessary."

"Can't this look-alike tell you? He must know why he was hired."

"I'm having trouble locating him."

"I see," Hawthorne said. "Well, Mr. Frye never said a word about it to me. But it just occurred to me. . . ."

"Yes?"

"One reason he might need a double."

"What's that?" Joshua asked.

"To confuse his mother when she came back from the grave looking for him."

"Of course," Joshua said sarcastically. "How silly of me not to think of that."

"You misunderstand," Hawthorne said. "I know you're a skeptic. I'm not saying that she actually came back. I don't have enough information to make up my mind about that. But Mr. Frye was absolutely convinced that she *had* come back. He might have thought that hiring a double would provide him with some protection."

Joshua had to admit that Hawthorne's idea made more than a little sense. "What you're saying is that the easiest way to figure this out is to try to put myself in Frye's head, try to think like he did, like a paranoid schizophrenic."

"If he *was* a paranoid schizophrenic," Hawthorne said. "As I told you, I scoff at nothing."

"And I scoff at everything," Joshua said. "Well . . . thank you for your time and trouble, Mr. Hawthorne."

"No trouble. I'll be waiting for your call."

Don't hold your breath, Joshua thought.

After he put down the receiver, Joshua stood up, stepped to the big window, and stared out at the valley. The land was now settling into shadows under the gray clouds and the purple-blue edges of the oncoming darkness. Day seemed to be changing into night much too rapidly, and, as a sudden cold wind rattled the windowpanes, it also seemed to Joshua that autumn was giving way to winter with the same unnatural haste. The evening looked as if it belonged in gloomy, rainy January rather than early October.

In Joshua's mind, Latham Hawthorne's words spun like dark filaments of a black web on some monstrous spider's loom: *His time is coming, Mr. Rhinehart. There are signs and portents. Soon now. Quite soon.*

For the past fifteen years or so, the world had seemed to be rushing downhill with no brakes, totally out of control. A lot of strange people were out there. Like Hawthorne. And worse. Far worse. Many of them were political leaders, for that was the line of work that jackals often chose, seeking power over others; they had their hands on the controls of the planet, lunatic engineers in every nation, grinning maniacally as they pushed the machine toward derailment.

Are we living in the final days of the earth? Joshua wondered. Is Armageddon drawing near?

Bullshit, he told himself. You're just transferring your own intimations of mortality to your perception of the world, old man. You've lost Cora, and you're all alone, and you're suddenly aware of growing old and running out of time. Now you have the incredible, grand, egomaniacal notion that the entire world will go with you when you die. But the only doomsday drawing nigh is a very personal one, he told himself. The world will be here after you've gone. It'll be here a long, long time, he assured himself.

But he really wasn't certain of that. The air seemed to be full of ominous currents.

Someone knocked on the door. It was Karen Farr, his industrious young secretary.

"I didn't realize you were still here," Joshua said. He glanced at his watch. "Quitting time was almost an hour ago."

"I took a long lunch. I have a few things to catch up on."

"Work is an essential part of life, my dear. But don't spend all your time at it. Go home, You'll catch up tomorrow."

"I'll be finished in ten minutes," she said. "And just now two people came in. They want to see you."

"I don't have any appointments."

"They've come all the way from Los Angeles. His name's Anthony Clemenza, and the woman with him is Hilary Thomas. She's the one who was—"

"I know who she is," Joshua said, startled. "By all means, show them in."

He walked out from behind his desk and met the visitors in the middle of the room. There were awkward introductions, then Joshua saw to it that they were comfortably seated, offered drinks, poured Jack Daniel's for both of them, and pulled up a chair opposite the couch where they were seated side by side.

Tony Clemenza had an air about him that appealed to Joshua. He seemed pleasantly self-assured and competent.

Hilary Thomas radiated a brisk self-confidence and quiet competence much as Clemenza did. She was also achingly lovely.

For a moment, no one seemed to know what to say. They looked at one another in silent anticipation and then tentatively sipped their whiskey.

Joshua was the first to speak. "I've never put a lot of faith in such things as clairvoyance, but, by God, I'm having a little premonition right now. You haven't come all this way just to tell me about last Wednesday and Thursday, have you? Something's happened since then."

"A lot has happened," Tony said. "But none of it makes a whole hell of a lot of sense."

"Sheriff Laurenski sent us to see you," Hilary said.

"We hope you'll have some answers for us."

"I'm looking for answers myself," Joshua said.

Hilary tilted her head and looked curiously at Joshua. "I think maybe I'm having a premonition of my own," she said. "Something has happened here, too, hasn't it?"

Joshua took a sip of his whiskey. "If I were a superstitious man, I'd probably tell you that . . . somewhere out there . . . a dead man is walking around among the living."

Outside, the last light of day was snuffed from the sky. The coal-black night seized the valley beyond the window. A cold wind tried to find a way around the many panes of glass; it hissed and moaned. But a new warmth seemed to fill Joshua's office, for he and Tony and Hilary were drawn together by their shared knowledge of the incredible mystery of Bruno Frye's apparent resurrection.

•

Bruno Frye had slept in the back of the blue Dodge van, in a supermarket parking lot, until eleven o'clock that morning, when he had been awakened by a nightmare that resonated with fierce, threatening, yet meaningless whispers. For a while, he sat in the stuffy, dimly-lit cargo hold of the van, hugging himself, feeling so desperately alone and abandoned and afraid that he whimpered and wept as if he were a child.

I'm dead, he thought. Dead. The bitch killed me. Dead. The rotten, stinking bitch put a knife in my guts.

As his weeping gradually subsided, he had a peculiar and disturbing thought: But if I'm dead . . . how can I be sitting here now? How can I be alive and dead at the same time?

He felt his abdomen with both hands. There were no tender spots, no knife wounds, no scars.

Suddenly, his thoughts cleared. A gray fog seemed to lift from his mind, and for a minute everything shone with a multifaceted, crystalline light. He began to wonder if Katherine really had come back from the grave. Was Hilary Thomas only Hilary Thomas and not Katherine Anne Frye? Was he mad to want to kill her? And all the other women he had killed over the past five years—had they actually been new bodies in which Katherine had hidden? Or had they been real people, innocent women who hadn't deserved to die?

Bruno sat on the floor of the van, stunned, overwhelmed by this new perspective.

And the whispers that invaded his sleep every night, the awful whispers that terrified him . . .

Suddenly, he knew that, if only he concentrated hard enough, if only he searched diligently through his childhood memories, he would discover what the whispers were, what they meant. He remembered two heavy wooden doors that were set in the ground. He remembered Katherine opening those doors, pushing him into darkness beyond. He remembered her slamming and bolting the doors behind him, remembered steps that led down, down into the earth. . . .

No!

He clamped his hands over his ears as if he could block out unwanted memories as easily as he could shut out unpleasant noise.

He was dripping sweat. Shaking, shaking.

"No," he said. "No, no, no!"

For as long as he could remember, he had wanted to find out who was whispering in his nightmares. He had longed to discover what the whispers were trying to tell him, so that, perhaps, he could then banish them from his sleep forever. But now that he was on the verge of knowing, he found the knowledge more horrifying and devastating than the mystery had been, and, panic-stricken, he turned away from the hideous revelation before it could be delivered unto him.

Now the van was full of whispers again, sibilant voices, haunting susurrations.

Bruno cried out in fear and rocked back and forth on the floor.

Strange things were crawling on him again. They were trying to climb up his arms and chest and back. Trying to get to his face. Trying to squeeze between his lips and teeth. Trying to scurry up his nostrils.

Squealing, writhing, Bruno brushed them away, slapped at them, flailed at himself.

But the illusion was fed by darkness, and there was too much light in the van for the grotesque hallucinations to hold their substance. He could see there was nothing on him, and gradually the panic drained away, leaving him limp.

For several minutes, he just sat there, his back against the wall of the van, patting his sweaty face with a handkerchief, listening to his ragged breathing grow softer and softer.

Finally, he decided it was time to start looking for the bitch again. She was out there—waiting, hiding, somewhere in the city. He had to locate her and kill her before she found a way to kill him first.

The brief moment of mental clarity, the lightning flash of lucidity was gone as if it had never existed. He had forgotten the questions, the doubts. Once again, he was absolutely certain that Katherine had come back from the dead and that she must be stopped.

Later, after a quick lunch, he drove to Westwood and parked up the street from Hilary Thomas's house. He climbed into the cargo hold again and watched her place from a small, decorative porthole on the side of the Dodge.

A commercial van was parked in the circular driveway at the Thomas house. It was painted white with blue and gold lettering on the sides:

MAIDS UNLIMITED
WEEKLY CLEANING, SPRING CLEANING
& PARTIES
WE EVEN DO WINDOWS

Three women in white uniforms were at work in the house. They made a number of trips from the house to the van and back, carrying mops and brooms and vacuum sweepers and buckets and bundles of rags, bringing out plastic bags full of trash, taking in a machine for steam-cleaning carpets, bringing out fragments of the furniture that Frye had broken during his rampage in the pre-dawn hours of yesterday morning.

Although he watched all afternoon, he didn't get even one quick glimpse of Hilary Thomas, and he was convinced that she was not in the house. In fact, he figured that she wouldn't come back until she was positive that it was safe, until she knew he was dead.

"But I'm not the one who's going to die," he said aloud as he studied the house. "Do you hear me, bitch? I'll nail you first. I'll get you before you have a chance to get me. I'll cut off your fucking head."

At last, shortly after five o'clock, the maids brought out their equipment and loaded it into the back of their van. They locked up the house and drove away.

He followed them.

They were his only lead to Hilary Thomas. The bitch had hired them. They must know where she was. If he could get one of the maids alone and force her to talk, he would find out where Katherine was hiding.

Maids Unlimited was headquartered in a single-story stucco structure on a grubby side street, half a block off Pico. The van that Frye was following pulled into a lot beside the building and parked in a row of eight other vans that bore the company name in blue and gold lettering.

Frye drove past the line of identical white vans, went to the end of the block, swung around at the deserted intersection, and headed back the way he had come. He got there in time to see the three women going into the stucco building. None of them appeared to notice him or to realize that the Dodge was the same van that had been within sight of the Thomas house all day. He parked at the curb, across the street from the house-cleaning service, under the rustling fronds of a windstirred date palm, and he waited for one of those women to reappear.

During the next ten minutes, a lot of maids in white uniforms came out of Maids Unlimited, but none of them had been at Hilary Thomas's house that afternoon. Then he saw a woman he recognized. She came out of the building and went to a bright yellow Datsun. She was young, in her twenties, with straight brown hair that fell almost to her waist. She walked with her shoulders back, her head up, taking brisk, springy steps. The wind pasted the uniform to her hips and thighs and fluttered the hem above her pretty knees. She got in the Datsun and drove out of the lot, turned left, headed toward Pico.

Frye hesitated, trying to make up his mind if she was the best target, wondering if he should wait for one of the other two. But something felt right about this one. He started the Dodge and pulled away from the curb.

In order to camouflage himself, he tried to keep other traffic between the Dodge and the yellow Datsun. He trailed her from street to street as discreetly as possible, and she seemed utterly unaware that she was being followed.

Her home was in Culver City, just a few blocks from the MGM film studios. She lived in an old, beautifully detailed bungalow on a street of old, beautifully detailed bungalows. A few of the houses were shabby, in need of repairs, gray and sagging and mournful; but most of them were maintained with evident pride, freshly painted, with contrasting shutters, trim little verandas, an occasional stained glass window, a leaded glass door here and there, carriage lamps, and tile roofs. This wasn't a wealthy neighborhood, but it was rich in character.

The maid's house was dark when she arrived. She went inside and switched on lights in the front rooms.

Bruno parked the Dodge across the street, in shadows that were darker than the rest of the newly fallen night. He doused the headlamps, turned off the engine, and rolled down the window. The neighborhood was peaceful and nearly silent. The only sounds came from the trees, which responded to the insistent autumn wind, and from an occasional passing car, and from a distant stereo or radio that was playing swing music. It was a Benny Goodman tune from the Forties, but the title eluded Bruno; the brassy melody floated to him in fragments, at the whimsy of the wind. He sat behind the wheel of the van and waited, listened, watched.

By 6:40, Frye decided that the young woman had neither a husband nor a live-in boyfriend. If a man had shared the house with her, he most likely would have been home from work by this time.

Frye gave it another five minutes.

The Benny Goodman music stopped.

That was the only change.

At 6:45, he got out of the Dodge and crossed the street to her house.

The bungalow was on a narrow lot, much too close to its neighbors to suit Bruno's purpose. But at least there were a great many trees and shrubs along the property lines; they helped screen the front porch of the maid's house from the prying eyes of those who lived on both sides of her. Even so, he would have to move fast, get into the bungalow quickly and without causing a commotion, before she had a chance to scream.

He went up two low steps, onto the veranda. The floorboards squeaked a bit. He rang the bell.

She answered the door, smiling uncertainly. "Yes?"

A safety chain was fixed to the door. It was heavier and sturdier than most chains, but it was not one-tenth as effective as she probably thought it was. A man much smaller than Bruno Frye could have torn this one from its mountings with a couple of solid blows against the door. Bruno only needed to ram his massive shoulder into the barrier once, hard, just as she smiled and said, "Yes?" The door exploded inward, and splinters flew into the air, and part of the broken safety chain hit the floor with a sharp ringing sound.

He leaped inside and threw the door shut behind him. He was pretty sure that no one had seen him breaking in.

The woman was on her back, on the floor. The door had knocked her down. She was still wearing her white uniform. The skirt was up around her thighs. She had lovely legs.

He dropped to one knee beside her.

She was dazed. She opened her eyes and tried to look up at him, but she needed a moment to focus.

He put the point of the knife at her throat. "If you scream," he said, "I'll cut you wide open. Do you understand?"

Confusion vanished from her warm brown eyes, and fear replaced it. She began to tremble. Tears formed at the corners of her eyes, shimmered but didn't spill out.

Impatiently, he pricked her throat with the point of the blade, and a tiny bead of blood appeared.

She winced.

"No screaming," he said. "Do you hear me?"

With an effort, she said, "Yes."

"Will you be good?"

"Please. Please, don't hurt me."

"I don't want to hurt you," Frye said. "If you're quiet, if you're nice, if you cooperate with me, then I won't have to hurt you. But if you scream or try to get away from me, I'll cut you to pieces. You understand?"

In a very small voice, she said, "Yes."

"Are you going to be nice?"

"Yes."

"Do you live alone here?"

"Yes."

"No husband?"

"No."

"Boyfriend?"

"He doesn't live here."

"You expecting him tonight?"

"No."

"Are you lying to me?"

"It's the truth. I swear."

She was pale under her dusky complexion.

"If you're lying to me," he said, "I'll cut your pretty face to ribbons."

He raised the blade, put the point against her cheek.

She closed her eyes and shuddered.

"Are you expecting anyone at all?"

"No."

"What's your name?"

"Sally."

"Okay, Sally, I want to ask you a few questions, but not here, not like this."

She opened her eyes. Tears on the lashes. One trickling down her face. She swallowed hard. "What do you want?"

"I have some questions about Katherine."

She frowned. "I don't know any Katherine."

"You know her as Hilary Thomas."

Her frown deepened. "The woman in Westwood?"

"You cleaned her house today."

"But . . . I don't know her. I've never met her."

"We'll see about that."

"It's the truth. I don't know anything about her."

"Perhaps you know more than you think you do."

"No. Really."

"Come on," he said, working hard to keep a smile on his face and a friendly note in his voice. "Let's go into the bedroom where we can do this more comfortably."

Her shaking became worse, almost epileptic. "You're going to rape me, aren't you?"

"No, no."

"Yes, you are."

Frye was barely able to control his anger. He was angry that she was arguing with him. He was angry that she was so damned reluctant to move. He wished that he could ram the knife into her belly and cut the information out of her, but, of course, he couldn't do that. He wanted to know where Hilary Thomas was hiding. It seemed to him that the best way to get that information was to break this woman the way he might break a length of heavy wire: bend her repeatedly back and forth until she snapped, bend her one way with threats and another way with cajolery, alternate minor violence with friendliness and sympathy. He did not even consider the possibility that she might be willing to tell him everything she knew. To his way of thinking, she was employed by Hilary Thomas, therefore by Katherine, and was consequently part of Katherine's plot to kill him. This woman was not merely an innocent bystander. She was Katherine's handmaiden, a conspirator, perhaps even another of the living dead. He expected her to hide information from him and to give it up only grudgingly.

"I promise that I'm not going to rape you," he said softly, gently. "But while I question you, I want you to be flat on your back, so that it'll be harder for you to try to get up and run. I'll feel safer if you're on your back. So if you're going to have to lay down for a while, you might as well do it on a nice soft mattress rather than on a hard floor. I'm only thinking of your comfort, Sally."

"I'm comfortable here," she said nervously.

"Don't be silly," he said. "Besides, if someone comes up on the front porch to ring the bell . . . he might hear us and figure that something's wrong. The bedroom will be more private. Come on now. Come on. Upsy-daisy."

She got to her feet.

He held the knife on her.

They went into the bedroom.

•

Hilary was not much of a drinker, but she was glad that she had a glass of good whiskey as she sat on the couch in Joshua Rhinehart's office and listened to the attorney's story. He told her and Tony about the missing funds in San Francisco, about the dead ringer who had left the bizarre letter in the safe-deposit box—and about his own growing uncertainty as to the identity of the dead man in Bruno Frye's grave.

"Are you going to exhume the body?" Tony asked.

"Not yet," Joshua said. "There are a couple of things I've got to look into first. If they check out, I might get enough answers so that it's not really necessary to open the grave."

He told them about Rita Yancy in Hollister and about Dr. Nicholas Rudge in San Francisco, and he reconstructed his recent conversation with Latham Hawthorne.

In spite of the warm room and the heat of the whiskey, Hilary was chilled to the bone. "This Hawthorne sounds as if he belongs in an institution himself."

Joshua sighed. "Sometimes I think if we put all the crazies into institutions, there'd hardly be anyone left on the outside."

Tony leaned forward on the couch. "Do you believe that Hawthorne really didn't know about the look-alike?"

"Yes," Joshua said. "Curiously enough, I do believe him. He may be something of a nut about Satanism, and he may not be particularly moral in some areas, and he might even be somewhat dangerous, but he didn't strike me as a dissembler. Strange as it might seem, I think he's probably a generally truthful man in most matters, and I can't see that there's anything more to be learned from him. Perhaps Dr. Rudge or Rita Yancy will know something of more value. But enough of that. Now let me hear

from the two of you. What's happened? What's brought you all the way
to St. Helena?"

Hilary and Tony took turns recounting the events of the past few days.

When they finished, Joshua stared at Hilary for a moment, then
shook his head and said, "You've got a hell of a lot of courage, young
lady."

"Not me," she said. "I'm a coward. I'm scared to death. I've been
scared to death for days."

"Being scared doesn't mean you're a coward," Joshua said. "All brav-
ery is based on fear. Both the coward and the hero act out of terror and
necessity. The only difference between them is simply that the coward suc-
cumbs to his fear while the person with courage triumphs in spite of it. If
you were a coward, you would have run away for a month-long holiday in
Europe or Hawaii or some such place, and you'd have counted on time to
solve the Frye riddle. But you've come here, to Bruno's hometown, where
you might well expect to be in even more danger than you were in Los
Angeles. I don't admire much in this world, but I do admire your spunk."

Hilary was blushing. She looked at Tony, then down at her glass of
whiskey. "If I was brave," she said, "I'd stay in the city and set up a trap
for him, using myself for bait. I'm not really in much danger here. After
all, he's busy looking for me down in L.A. And there's no way that he can
find out where I've gone."

•

The bedroom.

From the bed Sally watched him with alert and fear-filled eyes.

He walked around the room, looking in drawers. Then he came back
to her.

Her throat was slender and taut. The bead of blood had dribbled
down the graceful arc of flesh to her collarbone.

She saw him looking at the blood, and she reached up with one hand,
touched it, stared at her stained fingers.

"Don't worry," he said. "It's only a scratch."

Sally's bedroom, at the rear of the neat little bungalow, was decorated
entirely in earth tones. Three walls were painted beige; the fourth was
covered with burlap wallpaper. The carpet was chocolate brown. The
bedspread and the matching drapes were a coffee and cream abstract pattern, restful swirls of natural shades that soothed the eye. The highly polished mahogany furniture gleamed where it was touched by the soft,

shaded, amber glow that came from one of the two copper-plated bedside lamps that stood on the nightstands.

She lay on the bed, on her back, legs together, arms at her sides, hands fisted. She was still wearing her white uniform; it was pulled down demurely to her knees. Her long chestnut-brown hair was spread out like a fan around her head. She was quite pretty.

Bruno sat on the edge of the bed beside her. "Where is Katherine?"

She blinked. Tears slid out of the corners of her eyes. She was weeping, but silently, afraid to shriek and wail and groan, afraid that the slightest sound would cause him to stab her.

He repeated the question: "Where is Katherine?"

"I told you, I don't know anyone named Katherine," she said. Her speech was halting, tremulous; each word required a separate struggle. Her sensual lower lip quivered as she spoke.

"You know who I mean," he said sharply. "Don't play games with me. She calls herself Hilary Thomas now."

"Please. Please . . . let me go."

He held the knife up to her right eye, the point directed at the widening pupil. "Where is Hilary Thomas?"

"Oh, Jesus," she said shakily. "Look, mister, there's some sort of mix-up. A mistake. You're making a big mistake."

"You want to lose your eye?"

Sweat popped out along her hairline.

"You want to be half blind?" he asked.

"I don't know where she is," Sally said miserably.

"Don't lie to me."

"I'm not lying. I swear I'm not."

He stared at her for a few seconds.

By now there was sweat on her upper lip, too, tiny dots of moisture.

He took the knife away from her eye.

She was visibly relieved.

He surprised her. He slapped her face with his other hand, hit her so hard that her teeth clacked together and her eyes rolled back in her head.

"Bitch."

There were a lot of tears now. She made soft, mewling sounds and shrank back from him.

"You must know where she is," he said. "She hired you."

"We work for her regularly. She just called in and asked for a special clean-up. She didn't say where she was."

"Was she at the house when you got there?"

"No."

"Was anyone at the house when you got there?"

"No."

"Then how'd you get in?"

"Huh?"

"Who gave you the key?"

"Oh. Oh, yeah," she said, brightening a bit as she saw a way out. "Her agent. A literary agent. We had to stop at his office first to get the key."

"Where's that?"

"Beverly Hills. You should go talk to her agent if you want to know where she is. That's who you should see. He'll know where you can find her."

"What's his name?"

She hesitated. "A funny name. I saw it written down . . . but I'm not sure I remember it exactly. . . ."

He held the knife up to her eye again.

"Topelis," she said.

"Spell it for me."

She did. "I don't know where Miss Thomas is. But that Mr. Topelis will know. He'll know for sure."

He took the knife away from her eye.

She had been rigid. She sagged a bit.

He stared down at her. Something stirred in the back of his mind, a memory, then an awful realization.

"Your hair," he said. "You've got dark hair. And your eyes. They're so dark."

"What's wrong?" she asked worriedly, suddenly sensing that she was not safe yet.

"You've got the same hair and eyes, the same complexion that she had," Frye said.

"I don't understand, I don't know what's happening here. You're scaring me."

"Did you think you could trick me?" He was grinning at her, pleased with himself for not being fooled by her clever ruse.

He knew. He *knew*.

"You figured I'd go off to see this Topelis," Bruno said, "and then you would have a chance to slip away."

"Topelis knows where she is. He knows. I don't. I really don't know anything."

"*I* know where she is now," Bruno said.

"If you know, then you can just let me go."

He laughed. "You changed bodies, didn't you?"

She stared at him. "What?"

"Somehow you got out of the Thomas woman and took control of this girl, didn't you?"

She wasn't crying any more. Her fear was burning so very brightly that it had seared away her tears.

The bitch.

The rotten bitch.

"Did you really think you could fool me?" he asked. He laughed again, delighted. "After everything you've done to me, how could you think I wouldn't recognize you?"

Terror reverberated in her voice. "I haven't done anything to you. You're not making sense. Oh, Jesus. Oh, my God, my God. What do you want from me?"

Bruno leaned toward her, put his face close to hers. He peered into her eyes and said, "You're in there, aren't you? You're in there, deep down in there, hiding from me, aren't you? Aren't you, Mother? I see you, Mother. I see you in there."

•

A few fat droplets of rain splattered on the mullioned window in Joshua Rhinehart's office.

The night wind moaned.

"I still don't understand why Frye chose me," Hilary said. "When I came up here to do research for that screenplay, he was friendly. He answered all my questions about the wine industry. We spent two or three hours together, and I never had a hint that he was anything but an ordinary businessman. Then a few weeks later, he shows up at my house with a knife. And according to that letter in the safe-deposit box, he thinks I'm his mother in a new body. Why me?"

Joshua shifted in his chair. "I've been looking at you and thinking. . . ."

"What?"

"Maybe he chose you because . . . well, you look just a bit like Katherine."

"You don't mean we've got another look-alike on our hands," Tony said.

"No," Joshua said. "The resemblance is only slight."

"Good," Tony said. "Another dead ringer would be too much for me to deal with."

Joshua got up, went to Hilary, put one hand under her chin, lifted her face, turned it left, then right. "The hair, the eyes, the dusty complexion," he said thoughtfully. "Yes, all of that's similar. And there are other things about your face that remind me vaguely of Katherine, little things, so minor that I can't really put my finger on them. It's only a passing resemblance. And she wasn't as attractive as you are."

As Joshua took his hand away from her chin, Hilary got up and walked to the attorney's desk. Mulling over what she had learned in the past hour, she stared down at the neatly arranged items on the desk: blotter, stapler, letter opener, paperweight.

"Is something wrong?" Tony asked.

The wind worked up into a brief squall. Another burst of raindrops snapped against the window.

She turned around, faced the men. "Let me summarize the situation. Let me see if I've got this straight."

"I don't think any of us has it straight," Joshua said, returning to his chair. "The whole damned tale is too twisted to be arranged in a nice straight line."

"That's what I'm leading up to," she said. "I think maybe I just found another twist."

"Go ahead," Tony said.

"So far as we can tell," Hilary said, "shortly after his mother's death, Bruno got the idea that she had come back from the grave. For nearly five years, he has been buying books about the living dead from Latham Hawthorne. For five years, he's been living in fear of Katherine. Finally, when he saw me, he decided I was the new body she was using. But why did it take him so long?"

"I'm not sure I follow," Joshua said.

"Why did he take five years to fixate on someone, five long years to select a flesh and blood target for his fears?"

Joshua shrugged. "He's a madman. We can't expect his reasoning to be logical and decipherable."

But Tony was sensitive to the implications of her question. He slid forward on the couch, frowning. "I think I know what you're going to say," he told her. "My God, it gives me goose pimples."

Joshua looked from one to the other and said, "I must be getting slow-witted in my declining years. Will someone explain things to this old codger?"

"Maybe I'm not the first woman he's thought was his mother," Hilary said. "Maybe he killed the others before he came after me."

Joshua gaped at her. "Impossible!"

"Why?"

"We'd have known if he'd been running around killing women for the past five years. He'd have been caught at it!"

"Not necessarily," Tony said. "Homicidal maniacs are often very careful, very clever people. Some of them make meticulous plans—and yet have an uncanny ability to take the right risks when something unexpected throws the plans off the rails. They aren't always easy to catch."

Joshua pushed one hand through his mane of snow-white hair. "But if Bruno killed other women—where are their bodies?"

"Not in St. Helena," Hilary said. "He may have been schizophrenic, but the respectable, Dr. Jekyll–half of his personality was firmly in control when he was around people who knew him. He almost certainly would have gone out of town to kill. Out of the valley."

"San Francisco," Tony said. "He apparently went there regularly."

"Any town in the northern part of the state," Hilary said. "Any place far enough away from the Napa Valley for him to be anonymous."

"Now wait," Joshua said. "Wait a minute. Even if he went somewhere else and found women who bore a vague resemblance to Katherine, even if he killed them in other towns—he'd still have to leave bodies behind. There would have been similarities in the way he murdered them, links that the authorities would have noticed. They'd be looking for a modern-day Jack the Ripper. We'd have heard all about it on the news."

"If the murders were spread over five years and over a lot of towns in several counties, the police probably wouldn't make any connections between them," Tony said. "This is a large state. Hundreds of thousands of square miles. There are hundreds upon hundreds of police organizations, and there's seldom as much information-sharing among them as there ought to be. In fact, there's only one sure-fire way for them to recognize connections between several random killings—and that's if at least two, and preferably three, of the murders take place in a relatively short span of time, within a single police jurisdiction, one county or one city."

Hilary walked away from the desk, returned to the couch. "So it's possible," she said, feeling as cold as the October wind sounded. "It's possible that he's been slaughtering women—two, six, ten, fifteen, maybe more—during the past five years, and I'm the first one who ever gave him any trouble."

"It's not only possible, but probable," Tony said. "I'd say we can count on it." The Xerox of the letter that had been found in the safe-deposit box was on the coffee table in front of him; he picked it up and read the first sentence aloud. " 'My mother, Katherine Anne Frye, died five years ago, but she keeps coming back to life in new bodies.' "

"Bodies," Hilary said.

"That's the key word," Tony said. "Not body, singular. Bodies, plural. From that, I think we can infer that he killed her several times and that he thought she came back from the grave more than once."

Joshua's face was ash-gray. "But if you're right . . . I've been . . . all of us in St. Helena have been living beside the most evil, vicious sort of monster. And we weren't even aware of it!"

Tony looked grim. " 'The Beast of Hell walks among us in the clothes of a common man.' "

"What's that from?" Joshua asked.

"I've got a dustbin mind," Tony said. "Very little gets thrown away, whether I want to hold on to it or not. I remember the quotation from my Catholic catechism classes a long time ago. It's from the writings of one of the saints, but I don't recall which one. 'The Beast of Hell walks among us in the clothes of a common man. If the demon should reveal its true face to you at a time when you have turned away from Christ, then you will be without protection, and it will gleefully devour your heart and rend you limb from limb and carry your immortal soul into the yawning pit.' "

"You sound like Latham Hawthorne," Joshua said.

Outside, the wind shrieked.

•

Frye put the knife on the nightstand, well out of Sally's reach. Then he grabbed the lapels of her uniform dress and tore the garment open. Buttons popped.

She was paralyzed by terror. She did not resist him; she could not.

He grinned at her and said, "Now. Now, Mother. Now, I get even."

He ripped the dress all the way down the front and flung it open. She was revealed in bra and panties and pantyhose, a slim, pretty body. He clutched the cups of her bra and jerked them down. The straps bit into her skin and then broke. Fabric tore. Elastic snapped.

Her breasts were large for her size and bone structure, round and full, with very dark, pebbly nipples. He squeezed them roughly.

"Yes, yes, yes, yes, yes!" In his deep, gravelly voice, that one word acquired the eerie quality of a sinister chant, a Satanic litany.

He wrenched off her shoes, first the right, then the left, and threw them aside. One of them struck the mirror above the dresser and shattered it.

The sound of falling glass roused the woman from her shock-induced catatonic trance, and she tried to pull away from him, but fear sapped her strength; she writhed and fluttered ineffectually against him.

He held her without difficulty, slapped her twice with such force that her mouth sagged open and her eyes swam. A fine thread of blood unraveled from the corner of her mouth, ran down her chin.

"You rotten bitch!" he said, furious. "No sex, huh? I can't have any sex, you said. No sex ever, you said. Can't risk some woman finding out what I am, you said. Well, you already know what I am, Mother. You already know my secret, I don't have to hide anything from you, Mother. You know I'm different from other men. You know my prick isn't like theirs. You know who my father was. You know. You know that my prick is like his. I don't have to hide it from you, Mother. I'm going to shove it into you, Mother. All the way up into you. You hear me? Do you?"

The woman was crying, tossing her head from side to side. "No, no, no! Oh, God!" But then she got control of herself, locked eyes with him, gazed intently at him (and he could see Katherine in there, beyond the brown eyes, glaring out at him), and she said, "Listen to me. Please, listen to me! You're sick. You're a very sick man. You're all mixed up. You need help."

"Shut up, shut up, shut up!"

He slapped her again, harder than he had done before, swinging his big hand in a long swift arc, into the side of her face.

Each act of violence excited him. He was aroused by the sharp sound of each blow, by her gasps of pain and her birdlike cries, by the way her tender flesh reddened and swelled. The sight of her pain-contorted face and her scared-rabbit eyes stoked his lust to an unbearable white-hot flame.

He was shaking with need, trembling, quivering, quaking. He was breathing like a bull. His eyes were wide. His mouth was watering so excessively that he had to swallow every couple of seconds to avoid drooling on her.

He mauled her lovely breasts, squeezed and stroked them, roughed them up.

She had retreated from the terror, had slipped back into that semi-trance, motionless and rigid.

On the one hand, Bruno hated her and did not care how badly he hurt her. He *wanted* to cause her pain. He wanted her to suffer for all the things she had done to him—for even bringing him into the world in the first place.

But on the other hand, he was ashamed of touching his mother's breasts and ashamed of wanting to stick his penis into her. Therefore, as he pawed at her, he tried to explain himself and justify his actions: "You told me that if I ever tried to make love to a woman, she'd know right away that I'm not human. You said she'd see the difference, and she'd know. She'd call the police, and they'd take me away, and they'd burn me at the stake because they'd know who my father was. But you already know. It's no surprise to you, Mother. So I can use my prick on you. I can stick it right up in you, Mother, and no one will burn me alive."

He had never thought of putting it into her while she was alive. He'd been hopelessly cowed by her. But by the time she had come back from the dead in her first new body, Bruno had tasted freedom, and he had been full of daring and new ideas. He realized at once that he must kill her to prevent her from taking over his life again—or dragging him back to the grave with her. But he also realized that he could screw her and be safe, since she already knew his secret. She was the one who had told him the truth about himself; she'd told him ten thousand times. She knew that his father was a demon, a foul and hideous *thing*, for she had been raped by that inhuman creature, impregnated by it against her will. During her pregnancy, she had worn overlapping girdles to conceal her condition. When her time drew near, she went away to give birth under the care of a close-mouthed midwife in San Francisco. Later, she told people in St. Helena that Bruno was the illegitimate son of an old college friend who had gotten in trouble, that his real mother died shortly after his birth, and that her last wish was for Katherine to raise the boy. She brought the baby home and pretended he had been legally placed in her care and custody. She lived in constant, numbing fear that someone would discover Bruno was hers, and that his father was not human. One of the things that marked him as the progeny of a demon was his penis. He had the penis of a demon, different from that of a man. He must always hide it, she said, or he would be uncovered and burned at the stake. She had told him all about those things, had been telling him about them since he was too young to know what a penis was for. So, in a peculiar way, she had become both his blessing and his curse. She was a curse because she kept returning from the grave to regain control of him or to kill him. But she was also a blessing because, if she didn't keep coming back again and again and again, he wouldn't have anyone into whom he could empty the great, hot quantities of semen that built up like boiling lava in him. Without her, he was doomed to a life of celibacy. Therefore, while he regarded her resurrections with horror and outrage, a part of him also eagerly looked forward to each new encounter with each new body that she inhabited.

Now, as he knelt on the bed beside her, looking down at her breasts and at the dark pubic bush that was visible through her pale yellow panties, his erection grew so hard that it hurt. He was aware of the demon-half of his personality asserting itself; he felt the beast surging toward the surface of his mind.

He clawed at Sally's (Katherine's) pantyhose, shredding the nylon as he pulled it down her slim legs. He gripped her thighs in his large hands and forced them apart, and he moved around clumsily on the mattress until he was kneeling between her legs.

She snapped out of her trance again. Suddenly bucking, thrashing, kicking, she tried to rise, but he shoved her back with ease. She pummeled him with her fists, but her punches were without force. Seeing that he was unaffected by her blows, she opened her hands, made claws of them, struck at his face, raked his left cheek with her nails, then went for his eyes.

He jerked back, raised one arm to protect himself, winced as she gouged the back of his hand. Then he fell full-length upon her, crushing her with his big, strong body. He got one arm across her throat and pressed down, choking her.

•

Joshua Rhinehart washed the three whiskey glasses in the sink at the wet bar. To Tony and Hilary, he said, "The two of you have more at stake in this thing than I do, so why don't you come with me tomorrow when I fly down to see Rita Yancy in Hollister?"

"I was hoping you'd ask us," Hilary said.

"There's nothing we can do here right now," Tony said.

Joshua dried his hands on a dishtowel. "Good. That's settled. Now have you gotten a hotel room for the night?"

"Not yet," Tony said.

"You're welcome to stay at my place," Joshua said.

Hilary smiled prettily. "That's very kind. But we don't want to impose on you."

"You wouldn't be imposing."

"But you weren't expecting us, and we—"

"Young lady," Joshua said impatiently, "do you know how long it's been since I've had house guests? More than three years. And do you know why I haven't had any house guests in three years? Because I didn't invite anyone to stay with me, that's why. I am not a particularly gregarious man. I don't issue invitations lightly. If I felt that you and Tony would be a burden—or, worst of all, boring—I wouldn't have invited you, either. Now let's not waste a lot of time being overly polite. You need a room. I have a room. Are you going to stay at my place or not?"

Tony laughed, and Hilary grinned at Joshua. She said, "Thank you for asking us. We'd be delighted."

"Good," Joshua said.

"I like your style," she told him.

"Most people think I'm a grump."

"But a nice grump."

Joshua found a smile of his own. "Thank you. I think I'll have that engraved on my tombstone. 'Here lies Joshua Rhinehart, a nice grump.'"

As they were leaving the office, the telephone rang, and Joshua went back to his desk. Dr. Nicholas Rudge was calling from San Francisco.

•

Bruno Frye was still on top of the woman, pinning her to the mattress, one muscular arm across her throat.

She gagged and fought for breath. Her face was red, dark, twisted in agony.

She excited him.

"Don't fight me, Mother. Don't fight me like this. You know it's useless. You know I'll win in the end."

She writhed under his superior weight and strength. She tried to arch her back and roll to one side, and when she failed to throw him off, she was shaken by violent involuntary muscle spasms as her body reacted to the growing interruption in her air supply and in the supply of blood to her brain. At last, she seemed to realize she would never be able to get free of him, that she had absolutely no hope of escape, and so she went limp in defeat.

Convinced that the woman had surrendered spiritually as well as physically, Frye lifted his arm from her bruised throat. He raised up on his knees, taking his weight off her.

She put her hands to her neck. She gagged and coughed uncontrollably.

In a frenzy now, his heart pounding, blood roaring in his ears, aching with need, Frye got up, stood beside the bed, stripped off his clothes, threw them on top of the dresser, out of the way.

He looked down at his erection. The sight of it thrilled him. The steeliness of it. The size of it. The angry color.

He climbed onto the bed again.

She was docile now. Her eyes had a vacant look.

He ripped off her pale yellow panties and positioned himself between her slim legs. Saliva drooled out of his mouth. Dripped on her breasts.

He thrust into her. He thrust his demon staff all the way into her. Growling like an animal. Stabbed her with his demonic penis. He stabbed and stabbed her, until his semen flowered within her.

He pictured the milky fluid. Pictured it flowering from him, deep inside of her.

He thought of blood blossoming from a wound. Red petals spreading from a deep knife wound.

Both thoughts wildly excited him: semen and blood.

He didn't go soft.

Sweating, grunting, slobbering, he made thrust after thrust after thrust. Into her. Into. In.

Later, he would use the knife.

•

Joshua Rhinehart flipped a switch on his desk phone, putting the call from Dr. Nicholas Rudge on the conference speaker, so that Tony and Hilary could hear the conversation.

"I tried your home number first," Rudge said. "I didn't expect you to be at the office at this hour."

"I'm a workaholic, doctor."

"You should try to do something about it," Rudge said with what sounded like genuine concern. "That's no way to live. I've treated more than a few overly-ambitious men for whom work had become the only interest in their lives. An obsessive attitude toward work can destroy you."

"Dr. Rudge, what is your medical specialty?"

"Psychiatry."

"I suspected as much."

"You're the executor?"

"That's right. I presume you heard all about his death."

"Just what the newspaper had to say."

"While handling some estate matters, I discovered that Mr. Frye had been seeing you regularly during the year and a half prior to his death."

"He came in once a month," Rudge said.

"Were you aware that he was homicidal?"

"Of course not," Rudge said.

"You treated him all that time and weren't aware that he was capable of violence?"

"I knew he was deeply disturbed," Rudge said. "But I didn't think he was a danger to anyone. However, you must understand that he didn't really give me a chance to spot the violent side of him. I mean, as I said, he only came in once a month. I wanted to see him at least once every week, and preferably twice, but he refused. On the one hand, he wanted me to help him. But at the same time, he was afraid of what he might learn about himself. After a while, I decided not to press him too hard about making weekly visits because I was afraid that he might back off altogether and even cancel his monthly appointment. I figured a little therapy was better than none, you see."

"What brought him to you?"

"Are you asking what was wrong with him, what he was complaining of?"

"That's what I'm asking, all right."

"As an attorney, Mr. Rhinehart, you ought to be aware that I can't give out that sort of information indiscriminately. I have a doctor-patient privilege to protect."

"The patient is dead, Dr. Rudge."

"That doesn't make any difference."

"It sure as hell makes a difference to the patient."

"He placed his trust in me."

"When the patient is dead, the concept of doctor-patient privilege has little or no legal validity."

"Perhaps it has no legal validity," Rudge said. "But the moral validity remains. I still have certain responsibilities. I wouldn't do anything to damage the reputation of a patient, regardless of whether he's dead or alive."

"Commendable," Joshua said. "But in this case, nothing you could tell me would damage his reputation one whit more than he damaged it himself."

"That, too, makes no difference."

"Doctor, this is an extraordinary situation. This very day, I have come into possession of information which indicates that Bruno Frye murdered a number of women over the past five years, a large number of women, and got away with it."

"You're joking."

"I don't know what sort of thing strikes you as funny, Dr. Rudge. But *I* don't make jokes about mass murder."

Rudge was silent.

Joshua said, "Furthermore, I have reason to believe that Frye didn't act alone. He may have had a partner in homicide. And that partner may still be walking around, alive and free."

"This is extraordinary."

"That's what I said."

"Have you given this information of yours to the police?"

"No," Joshua said. "For one thing, it's probably not enough to get their attention. What I've discovered convinces *me*—and two other people who are involved in this. But the police will probably say it's only circumstantial evidence. And for another thing—I'm not sure which police agency has primary jurisdiction in the case. The murders might have been committed in several counties, in a number of cities. Now it seems to me that Frye might have told you something that doesn't appear all that important by itself, but which fits in with the facts that I've uncovered. If, during those eighteen months of therapy, you acquired a bit of knowledge that complements my information, then perhaps I'll have enough to decide which police agency to approach—and enough to convince them of the seriousness of the situation."

"Well . . ."

"Dr. Rudge, if you persist in protecting this particular patient, yet more murders may occur. Other women. Do you want their deaths on your conscience?"

"All right," Rudge said. "But this can't be done on the telephone."

"I'll come to San Francisco tomorrow, at your earliest convenience."

"My morning is free," Rudge said.

"Shall my associates and I meet you at your offices at ten o'clock?"

"That'll be fine," Rudge said. "But I warn you—before I discuss Mr. Frye's therapy, I'll want to hear this evidence of yours in more detail."

"Naturally."

"And if I'm not convinced that there's a clear and present danger, I'll keep his file sealed."

"Oh, I have no doubt that we can convince you," Joshua said. "I'm quite sure we can make the hair stand up on the back of your neck. We'll see you in the morning, doctor."

Joshua hung up. He looked at Tony and Hilary. "Tomorrow's going to be a busy day. First San Francisco and Dr. Rudge, then Hollister and the mysterious Rita Yancy."

Hilary got up from the couch where she had sat through the call. "I don't care if we have to fly halfway around the world. At least things seem to be breaking. For the first time, I feel that we're actually going to find out what's behind all of this."

"I feel the same way," Tony said. He smiled at Joshua. "You know . . . the way you handled Rudge . . . you've got a real talent for interrogation. You'd make a good detective."

"I'll add that to my tombstone," Joshua said. " 'Here lies Joshua Rhinehart, a nice grump who would have made a good detective.' " He stood up. "I'm starved. At home I've got steaks in the freezer and a lot of bottles of Robert Mondavi's Cabernet Sauvignon. What are we waiting for?"

•

Frye turned away from the blood-drenched bed and from the blood-splashed wall behind the bed.

He put the bloody knife on the dresser and walked out of the room.

The house was filled with an unearthly quiet.

His demonic energy was gone. He was heavy-lidded, heavy-limbed, lethargic, sated.

In the bathroom, he adjusted the water in the shower until it was as hot as he could stand it. He stepped into the stall and soaped himself, washed the blood out of his hair, washed it off his face and body. He rinsed, then lathered up again, rinsed a second time.

His mind was a blank. He thought of nothing except the details of cleaning up. The sight of the blood swirling down the drain did not make him think of the dead woman in the next room; it was only dirt being sluiced away.

All he wanted to do was make himself presentable and then go sleep in the van for several hours. He was exhausted. His arms felt as if they were made of lead; his legs were rubber.

He got out of the shower and dried himself on a big towel. The cloth smelled like the woman, but it had neither pleasant nor unpleasant associations for him.

He spent a lot of time at the sink, working on his hands with a brush that he found beside the soap dish, getting every trace of blood out of his knuckle creases, taking special care with his caked fingernails.

On his way out of the bathroom, intending to fetch his clothes from the bedroom, he noticed a full-length mirror on the door, which he hadn't seen on his way to the shower. He stopped to examine himself, looking for smears of blood that he might have missed. He was as spotless and fresh and pink as a well-scrubbed baby.

He stared at the reflection of his flaccid penis and the drooping testicles beneath it, and he tried very hard to see the mark of the demon. He knew that he was not like other men; he had no doubt whatsoever about that. His mother had been terrified that someone would find out about him and that the world would learn that he was half-demon, the child of an ordinary woman and a scaly, fanged, sulphurous beast. Her fear of exposure was transmitted to Bruno at an early age, and he still dreaded being found out and subsequently burned alive. He had never been naked in front of another person. In school, he had not gone out for sports, and he had been excused from gymnasium for supposed religious objections to taking showers in the nude with other boys. He had never even completely stripped for a physician. His mother had been positive that anyone who saw his sex organs would know at once that his manhood was the genetic legacy of a demon father; and he had been impressed and deeply affected by her fearful, unwavering certainty.

But as he looked at himself in the mirror, he couldn't see anything that made his sex organs different from those of other men. Shortly after his mother's fatal heart attack, he had gone to a pornographic movie in San Francisco, eager to learn how a normal man's penis looked. He'd been surprised and baffled to discover that the men in the film were all very much like him. He'd gone to other pictures of the same sort, but he hadn't seen even one man who was strikingly different from him. Some of them had bigger penises than his; some of them had smaller organs; some were thicker, some thinner; some were curved slightly; some of them were circumcised, and some were not. But those were all just minor variations, not the awful, shocking, fundamental differences which he had expected.

Puzzled, worried, he had gone back to St. Helena to sit with himself and discuss his discovery. His first thought was that his mother had lied to him. But that was very nearly inconceivable. She had recounted the story of his conception several times every week, for years and years, and each time that she had described the hateful demon and the violent rape, she had shuddered and wailed and wept. The experience had been real for her, not some imaginary tale that she had created to mislead him. And yet. . . . Sitting with himself that afternoon five years ago, discussing it with himself, he had been unable to think of any explanation other than that his mother was a liar; and himself agreed with him.

The following day, he had returned to San Francisco, wildly excited, fevered, having decided to risk sex with a woman for the first time in his thirty-five years. He had gone to a massage parlor, a thinly disguised brothel, where he had chosen a slim, attractive blonde as his masseuse. She called herself Tammy, and except for slightly protruding upper teeth and a neck that was just a bit too long, she was as beautiful as any woman he had ever seen; or at least that's how she seemed to him as he struggled to keep from ejaculating in his trousers. In one of the cubicles that smelled of pine disinfectant and stale semen, he agreed to Tammy's price, paid her, and watched as she took off her sweater and slacks. Her body was smooth and sleek and so desirable that he stood like a post, unable to move, awe-stricken as he considered all of the things he could do with her. She sat on the edge of the narrow bed and smiled at him and suggested he undress. He stripped down to his underpants, but when the time came for him to show her his rigid penis, he was unable to take the risk, for he could see himself in a pillar of flame, put to death because of his demonic blood. He froze. He stared at Tammy's slender legs and at her wiry pubic hair and at her round breasts, wanting her, needing her, but afraid to take her. Sensing his reluctance to reveal himself, she reached out and put one hand on his crotch, felt his penis through his shorts. She slowly rubbed him through the thin cloth and said, "Oh, I want that. It's so big. I've never had one like this before. Show me. I want to see it. *I've never had anything like it.*" And as he spoke those words he knew that somehow he *was* different, in spite of the fact that he could not see the difference. Tammy tried to pull off his shorts, and he slapped her face, knocked her backwards, flat on the bed; she bumped her head against the wall, threw her hands up to ward him off, screamed and screamed. Bruno wondered if he should kill her. Even though she had not seen his demonic prick, she might have recognized the inhuman quality of it merely by feeling it through his underwear. Before he could make up his mind what to do, the door of the cubicle flew open in answer to the girl's screams, and a man with a blackjack stepped in from the corridor. The bouncer was as big as Bruno, and the weapon gave him a substantial advantage. Bruno was certain that they were going to overpower him, revile him, curse and spit upon him, torture him, and then burn him at the stake; but to his utter amazement, they only made him put on his clothes and get out. Tammy didn't say another word about Bruno's unusual penis. Apparently, while she knew it was different, she was not aware of exactly *how* different it was; she didn't know that it was a sign of the demon that had fathered him, proof of his hellish origins. Relieved, he had dressed hurriedly and had scurried out of the massage parlor, blushing, embarrassed, but thankful that his secret had not been uncovered. He had gone back to St. Helena and had told himself about the close call he'd had, and both he and himself had agreed that Katherine had been right, and that he would have to furnish his own sex, without benefit of a woman.

Then, of course, Katherine had started coming back from the grave, and Bruno had been able to satisfy himself with her, expending copious quantities of sperm in the many lovely bodies that she had inhabited. He still had most of his sex alone, with himself, with his other self, his other half—but it was wildly exciting to thrust into the warm, tight, moist center of a woman every once in a while.

Now he stood in front of the mirror that was fixed to the door of Sally's bathroom, and he stared with fascination at the reflection of his penis, wondering what difference Tammy had sensed when she'd felt his pulsating erection in that massage parlor cubicle, five years ago.

After a while, he let his gaze travel upward from his sex organs to his flat, hard, muscular belly, then up to his huge chest, and farther up until he met the gaze of the other Bruno in the looking glass. When he stared into his own eyes, everything at the periphery of his vision faded away, and the very foundations of reality turned molten and assumed new forms; without drugs or alcohol, he was swept into an hallucinogenic experience. He reached out and touched the mirror, and the fingers of the other Bruno touched his fingers from the far side of the glass. As if in a dream, he drifted closer to the mirror, pressed his nose to the other Bruno's nose. He looked deep into the other's eyes, and those eyes peered

deep into his. For a moment, he forgot that he was only confronting a reflection; the other Bruno was real. He kissed the other, and the kiss was
cold. He pulled back a few inches. So did the other Bruno. He licked his
lips. So did the other Bruno. Then they kissed again. He licked the other
Bruno's open mouth, and gradually the kiss became warm, but it never
grew as soft and pleasant as he had expected. In spite of the three powerful orgasms that Sally-Katherine had drawn from him, his penis stiffened
yet again, and when it was very hard he pressed it against the other
Bruno's penis and slowly rotated his hips, rubbing their erect organs together, still kissing, still gazing rapturously into the eyes that stared out of
the mirror. For a minute or two, he was happier than he had been in days.

But then the hallucination abruptly dissolved, and reality came back
like a hammer striking iron. He became aware that he really was not
holding his other self and that he was trying to have sex with nothing
more than a flat reflection. A strong electric current of emotion seemed to
jump across the synapse between the eyes in the looking glass and his own
eyes, and a tremendous shock blasted through his body; it was an emotional shock, but it also affected him physically, making him twitch and
shake. His lethargy burned away in an instant. Suddenly he was re-
energized; his mind was spinning, sparking.

He remembered that he was dead. Half of him was dead. The bitch had
stabbed him last week, in Los Angeles. Now he was both dead and alive.

A profound sorrow welled up in him.

Tears came to his eyes.

He realized that he couldn't hold himself as he once had done. Not
ever again.

He couldn't fondle himself or be fondled by himself as he once had
done. Not ever again.

He now had only two hands, not four; only one penis, not two; only
one mouth, not two.

He could never kiss himself again, never feel his two tongues caressing
each other. Not ever again.

Half of him was dead. He wept.

He never again would have sex with himself as he'd had it thousands
of times in the past. Now he would have no lover but his hand, the limited
pleasure of masturbation.

He was alone.

Forever.

For a while, he stood in front of the mirror, crying, his broad shoul-

ders bent under the terrible weight of abject despair. But slowly his unbearable grief and self-pity gave way to rising anger. *She* had done this to
him. Katherine. The bitch. She had killed half of him, had left him feeling
incomplete and wretchedly empty, hollow. The selfish, hateful, vicious
bitch! As his fury mounted, he was possessed by an urge to break things.
Naked, he stormed through the bungalow—living room and kitchen and
bathroom—smashing furniture, ripping upholstery, breaking dishes, cursing his mother, cursing his demon father, cursing a world that he sometimes couldn't understand at all.

•

In Joshua Rhinehart's kitchen, Hilary scrubbed three large baking potatoes
and lined them up on the counter, so that they were ready to be popped
into the microwave oven as soon as the thick steaks were approaching perfection on the broiler. The menial labor was relaxing. She watched her
hands as she worked, and she thought about little more than the food that
had to be prepared, and her worries receded to the back of her mind.

Tony was making the salad. He stood at the sink beside her, his shirt
sleeves rolled up, washing and chopping fresh vegetables.

While they prepared dinner, Joshua called the sheriff from the kitchen
phone. He told Laurenski about the withdrawal of funds from Frye's accounts in San Francisco and about the look-alike who was down in Los
Angeles somewhere, searching for Hilary. He also passed along the mass
murder theory that he and Tony and Hilary had arrived at in his office a
short while ago. There was really not much that Laurenski could do, for
(so far as they knew) no crimes had been committed in his jurisdiction.
But Frye was most likely guilty of local crimes of which they were, for the
moment, unaware. And it was even more likely that crimes might yet be
committed in the county before the mystery of the look-alike was solved.
Because of that, and because Laurenski's reputation had been stained
slightly when he had vouched for Frye to the Los Angeles Police Department last Wednesday night, Joshua thought (and Hilary agreed) that the
sheriff was entitled to know everything that they knew. Even though Hilary could hear only one end of the telephone conversation, she could tell
that Peter Laurenski was fascinated, and she knew, from Joshua's responses, that the sheriff twice suggested that they exhume the body in
Frye's grave to determine whether or not it actually was Bruno Frye.
Joshua preferred to wait until Dr. Rudge and Rita Yancy had been heard
from, but he assured Laurenski that an exhumation would take place if

Rudge and Yancy were unable to answer all of the questions he intended to ask.

When he finished talking with the sheriff, Joshua checked on Tony's salad, debated with himself about whether the lettuce was sufficiently crisp, fretted about whether the radishes were too hot or possibly not hot enough, examined the sizzling steaks as if looking for flaws in three diamonds, told Hilary to put the potatoes in the microwave oven, quickly chopped some fresh chives to go with the sour cream, and opened two bottles of California Cabernet Sauvignon, a very dry red wine from the Robert Mondavi winery just down the road. He was rather a fussbudget in the kitchen; his worrying and nitpicking amused Hilary.

She was surprised at how quickly she had developed a liking for the attorney. She seldom felt so comfortable with a person she had known only a couple of hours. But his fatherly appearance, his gruff honesty, his wit, his intelligence, and his curiously off-handed courtliness made her feel welcome and safe in his company.

They ate in the dining room, a cozy, rustic chamber with three white plaster walls, one used-brick wall, a pegged-oak floor, and an open-beam ceiling. Now and then, squalls of big raindrops burst against the charming leaded windows.

As they sat down to the meal, Joshua said, "One rule. No one talks about Bruno Frye until we've put away the last bite of our steak, the last swallow of this excellent wine, the last mouthful of coffee, and the very last sip of brandy."

"Agreed," Hilary said.

"Definitely," Tony said. "I think my mind overloaded on the subject quite some time ago. There *are* other things in the world worth talking about."

"Yes," Joshua said. "But unfortunately, many of them are just as thoroughly depressing as Frye's story. War and terrorism and inflation and the return of the Luddites and know-nothing politicians and—"

"—art and music and movies and the latest developments in medicine and the coming technological revolution that will vastly improve our lives in spite of the new Luddites," Hilary added.

Joshua squinted across the table at her. "Is your name Hilary or Pollyanna?"

"And is yours Joshua or Cassandra?" she asked.

"Cassandra was correct when she made her prophecies of doom and destruction," Joshua said, "but time after time everyone refused to believe her."

"If no one believes you," Hilary said, "then what good is it to be right?"

"Oh, I've given up trying to convince other people that the government is the only enemy and that Big Brother will get us all. I've stopped trying to convince them of a hundred other things that seem to be obvious truths to me but which they don't get at all. Too many of them are fools who'll never understand. But it gives me enormous satisfaction just to know I'm right and to see the ever-increasing proof of it in the daily papers. *I* know. And that's enough."

"Ah," Hilary said. "In other words, you don't care if the world falls apart beneath us, just so you can have the selfish pleasure of saying, 'I told you so.' "

"Ouch," Joshua said.

Tony laughed. "Beware of her, Joshua. Remember, she makes her living being clever with words."

For three-quarters of an hour, they spoke of many things, but then, somehow, in spite of their pledge, they found themselves talking about Bruno Frye once more, long before they were finished with the wine or ready for coffee and brandy.

At one point, Hilary said, "What could Katherine have done to him to make him fear her and hate her as much as he apparently does?"

"That's the same question I asked Latham Hawthorne," Joshua said.

"What'd he say?"

"He had no idea," Joshua said. "I still find it difficult to believe that there could have been such black hatred between them without it being visible even once in all the years I knew them. Katherine always seemed to dote on him. And Bruno seemed to worship her. Of course, everyone in town thought she was something of a saint for having taken in the boy in the first place, but now it looks as if she might have been less saint than devil."

"Wait a minute," Tony said. "She took him in? What do you mean by that?"

"Just what I said. She could have let the child go to an orphanage, but she didn't. She opened her heart and her home to him."

"But," Hilary said, "we thought he was her son."

"Adopted," Joshua said.

"That wasn't in the newspapers," Tony said.

"It was done a long, long time ago," Joshua said. "Bruno had lived all but a few months of his life as a Frye. Sometimes it seemed to me that he was more like a Frye than Katherine's own child might have been if she'd had one. His eyes were the same color as Katherine's. And he certainly had the same cold, introverted, brooding personality that Katherine had—and that people say Leo had, too."

"If he was adopted," Hilary said, "there's a chance he *does* have a brother."

"No," Joshua said. "He didn't."

"How can you be so sure? Maybe he even has a *twin!*" Hilary said, excited by the thought.

Joshua frowned. "You think Katherine adopted one of a pair of twins without being aware of it?"

"That would explain the sudden appearance of a dead ringer," Tony said.

Joshua's frown grew deeper. "But where has this mysterious twin brother been all these years?"

"He was probably raised by another family," Hilary said, eagerly fleshing out her theory. "In another town, another part of the state."

"Or maybe even another part of the country," Tony said.

"Are you trying to tell me that, somehow, Bruno and his long-lost brother eventually found each other?"

"It could happen," Hilary said.

Joshua shook his head. "Perhaps it could, but in this case it didn't. Bruno was an only child."

"You're positive?"

"There's no doubt about it," Joshua said. "The circumstances of his birth aren't secret."

"But twins . . . It's such a lovely theory," Hilary said.

Joshua nodded. "I know. It's an easy answer, and I'd like to find an easy answer so we can wrap this thing up fast. Believe me, I hate to punch holes in your theory."

"Maybe you can't," Hilary said.

"I can."

"Try," Tony said. "Tell us where Bruno came from, who his real mother was. Maybe we'll punch holes in *your* story. Maybe it's not as open and shut as you think it is."

•

Eventually, after he had broken and torn and smashed nearly everything in the bungalow, Bruno got control of himself; his fiery, bestial rage cooled into a less destructive, more human anger. For a while, after his temper fell below the boiling point, he stood in the middle of the rubble he had made, breathing hard, sweat dripping off his brow and gleaming on his naked body. Then he went into the bedroom and put on his clothes.

When he was dressed, he stood at the foot of the bloody bed and stared at the brutally butchered body of the woman he had known only as Sally. Now, too late, he realized that she hadn't been Katherine. She hadn't been another reincarnation of his mother. The old bitch hadn't switched bodies from Hilary Thomas to Sally; she couldn't do that until Hilary was dead. Bruno couldn't imagine why he had ever thought otherwise; he was surprised that he could have been so confused.

However, he felt no remorse for what he had done to Sally. Even if she hadn't been Katherine, she had been one of Katherine's handmaidens, a woman sent from Hell to serve Katherine. Sally had been one of the enemy, a conspirator in the plot to kill him. He was sure of that. Maybe she had even been one of the living dead. Yes. Of course. He was positive of that, too. Yes. Sally had been exactly like Katherine, a dead woman in a new body, one of those monsters who refused to stay in the grave where she belonged. She was one of *them*. He shuddered. He was certain that she had known all along where Hilary-Katherine was hiding. But she kept that secret, and she deserved to die for her unshakable allegiance to his mother.

Besides, he hadn't actually killed her, for she would come back to life in some other body, pushing out the person whose rightful flesh it was.

Now he must forget about Sally and find Hilary-Katherine. She was still out there somewhere, waiting for him.

He must locate her and kill her before she found a way to kill him first.

At least Sally had given him one small lead. A name. This Topelis fellow. Hilary Thomas's agent. Topelis would probably know where she was hiding.

•

They cleared away the dinner dishes, and Joshua poured more wine for everyone before telling the story of Bruno's rise from orphan to sole heir of the Frye estate. He had gotten his facts over the years, a few at a time, from Katherine and from other people who had lived in St. Helena long before he had come to the valley to practice law.

In 1940, the year Bruno was born, Katherine was twenty-six years old and still living with her father, Leo, in the isolated clifftop house, behind and above the winery, where they had resided together since 1918, the year after Katherine's mother died. Katherine had been away from home only for part of one year that she had spent at college in San Francisco; she had dropped out of school because she hadn't wanted to be away from St. Helena just to acquire a lot of stale knowledge that she would never use. She loved the valley and the big old Victorian house on the cliff. Katherine was a handsome, shapely woman who could have had as many suitors as she wished, but she seemed to find romance of no interest whatsoever. Although she was still young, her introverted personality and her cool attitude toward all men convinced most of the people who knew her that she would be an old maid and, furthermore, that she would be perfectly happy in that role.

Then, in January of 1940, Katherine received a call from a friend, Mary Gunther, whom she'd known at college a few years earlier. Mary needed help; a man had gotten her into trouble. He had promised to marry her, had strung her along with excuse after excuse, and then had skipped out when she was six months pregnant. Mary was nearly broke, and she had no family to turn to for help, no friend half so close as Katherine. She asked Katherine to come to San Francisco a few months hence, as soon as the baby arrived; Mary didn't want to be alone at that trying time. She also asked Katherine to care for the baby until she, Mary, could find a job and build up a nest egg and provide a proper home for the child. Katherine agreed to help and began telling people in St. Helena that she would be a temporary surrogate mother. She seemed so happy, so excited by the prospect, that her neighbors said she would be a wonderful mother to her own children if she could just find a man to marry her and father them.

Six weeks after Mary Gunther's telephone call, and six weeks before Katherine was scheduled to go to San Francisco to be with her friend, Leo suffered a massive cerebral hemorrhage and dropped dead among the high stacks of oak barrels in one of the winery's huge aging cellars. Although Katherine was stunned and grief-stricken, and although she had to start learning to run the family business, she did not back out of her promise to Mary Gunther. In April, when Mary sent a message that the baby had arrived, Katherine went off to San Francisco. She was gone more than two weeks, and when she returned, she had a tiny baby, Bruno Gunther, Mary's alarmingly small and fragile child.

Katherine expected to have Bruno for a year, at which time Mary would be firmly on her feet and ready to assume complete responsibility for the tyke. But after six months, word came that Mary had more trouble, much worse this time—a virulent form of cancer. Mary was dying. She had only a few weeks to live, a month at most. Katherine took the baby to San Francisco, so that the mother could spend what little time she had left in the company of her child. During Mary's last days, she made all of the necessary legal arrangements for Katherine to be granted permanent custody of the baby. Mary's own parents were dead; she had no other close relatives with whom Bruno could live. If Katherine had not taken him in, he would have wound up in an orphanage or in the care of foster parents who might or might not have been good to him. Mary died, and Katherine paid for the funeral, then returned to St. Helena with Bruno.

She raised the boy as if he were her own, acting not just like a guardian but like a concerned and loving mother. She could have afforded nursemaids and other household help, but she didn't hire them; she refused to let anyone else tend to the child. Leo had not employed domestic help, and Katherine had her father's spirit of independence. She got along well on her own, and when Bruno was four years old, she returned to San Francisco, to the judge who had awarded her custody at Mary's request, and she formally adopted Bruno, giving him the Frye family name.

Hoping to get a clue from Joshua's story, alert for any inconsistencies or absurdities, Hilary and Tony had been leaning forward, arms on the dining room table, while they listened. Now they leaned back in their chairs and picked up their wine glasses.

Joshua said, "There are still people in St. Helena who remember Katherine Frye primarily as the saintly woman who took in a poor foundling and gave him love and more than a little wealth, too."

"So there wasn't a twin," Tony said.

"Definitely not," Joshua said.

Hilary sighed. "Which means we're back at square one."

"There are a couple of things in that story that bother me," Tony said.

Joshua raised his eyebrows. "Like what?"

"Well, even these days, with our more liberal attitudes, we still make it damned hard for a single woman to adopt a child," Tony said. "And in 1940, it must have been very nearly impossible."

"I think I can explain that," Joshua said. "If memory serves me well, Katherine once told me that she and Mary had anticipated the court's reluctance to sanction the arrangement. So they told the judge what they felt was just a little white lie. They said that Katherine was Mary's cousin and her closest living relative. In those days, if a close relative wanted to take the child in, the court almost automatically approved."

"And the judge just accepted their claim of a blood relationship without checking into it?" Tony asked.

"You have to remember that, in 1940, judges had a lot less interest in involving themselves in family matters than they seem to have now. It was a time when Americans viewed government's role as a relatively minor one. Generally, it was a saner time than ours."

To Tony, Hilary said, "You said there were a couple of things that bothered you. What's the other one?"

Tony wearily wiped his face with one hand. "The other's not something that can easily be put into words. It's just a hunch. But the story sounds . . . too smooth."

"You mean fabricated?" Joshua asked.

"I don't know," Tony said. "I don't really know what I mean. But when you've been a policeman as long as I have, you develop a nose for these things."

"And something smells?" Hilary asked.

"I think so."

"What?" Joshua asked.

"Nothing particular. Like I said, the story just sounds too smooth, too pat." Tony drank the last of his wine and then said, "Could Bruno actually be Katherine's child?"

Joshua stared at him, dumbfounded. When he could speak, he said, "Are you serious?"

"Yes."

"You're asking me if it's possible that she made up the whole thing about Mary Gunther and merely went away to San Francisco to have her own illegitimate baby?"

"That's what I'm asking," Tony said.

"No," Joshua said. "She wasn't pregnant."

"Are you sure?"

"Well," Joshua said, "I didn't personally take her urine sample and perform a rabbit test with it. I wasn't even living in the valley in 1940. I didn't get here until '45, after the war. But I've heard her story repeated, sometimes in part and sometimes in its entirety, by people who *were* here in '40. Now you'll say that they were probably just repeating what she had told them. But if she was pregnant, she couldn't have hidden the fact. Not in a town as small as St. Helena. Everyone would have known."

"There's a small percentage of women who don't swell up a great deal when they're carrying a child," Hilary said. "You could look at them and never know."

"You're forgetting that she had no interest in men," Joshua said. "She didn't date anyone. How could she possibly have gotten pregnant?"

"Perhaps she didn't date any locals," Tony said. "But at harvest time, toward the end of summer, aren't there a lot of migrant workers in the vineyards? And aren't a lot of them young, handsome, virile men?"

"Wait, wait, wait," Joshua said. "You're reaching way out in left field again. You're trying to tell me that Katherine, whose lack of interest in men was widely remarked upon, suddenly fell for a field hand."

"It's been known to happen."

"But then you're also trying to tell me that this unlikely pair of lovers carried out at least a brief affair in a virtual fish bowl without being caught or even causing gossip. And *then* you're trying to tell me that she was a unique woman, one in a thousand, a woman who didn't look pregnant when she was. No." Joshua shook his white-maned head. "It's too much for me. Too many coincidences. You think Katherine's story sounds too neat, too smooth, but next to your wild suppositions, her tale has the gritty sound of reality."

"You're right," Hilary said. "So another promising theory bites the dust." She finished her wine.

Tony scratched his chin and sighed. "Yeah. I guess I'm too damned tired to make a whole lot of sense. But I still don't think Katherine's story makes perfect sense, either. There's something more to it. Something she was hiding. Something strange."

•

In Sally's kitchen, standing on broken dishes, Bruno Frye opened the telephone book and looked up the number of Topelis & Associates. Their offices were in Beverly Hills. He dialed and got an answering service, which was what he had expected.

"I've got an emergency here," he told the answering service operator, "and I thought maybe you could help me."

"Emergency?" she asked.

"Yes. You see, my sister is one of Mr. Topelis's clients. There's been a death in the family, and I've got to get hold of her right away."

"Oh, I'm sorry," she said.

"The thing of it is, my sister's apparently off on a short holiday, and I don't know where she's gone."

"I see."

"It's urgent that I get in touch with her."

"Well, ordinarily, I'd pass your message right on to Mr. Topelis. But he's out tonight, and he didn't leave a number where he could be reached."

"I wouldn't want to bother him anyway," Bruno said. "I thought, with all the calls you take for him, maybe *you* might know where my sister is. I mean, maybe she called in and left word for Mr. Topelis, something that would indicate where she was."

"What's your sister's name?"

"Hilary Thomas."

"Oh, yes! I do know where she is."

"That's wonderful. Where?"

"I didn't take a message from her. But someone called in just a while ago and left a message for Mr. Topelis to pass on to her. Hold the line just a sec. Okay?"

"Sure."

"I've got it written down here somewhere."

Bruno waited patiently while she sorted through her memos.

Then she said, "Here it is. A Mr. Wyant Stevens called. He wanted Mr. Topelis to tell Miss Thomas that he, Mr. Stevens, was eager to handle the paintings. Mr. Stevens said he wanted her to know he wouldn't be able to sleep until she got back from St. Helena and gave him a chance to strike a deal. So she must be in St. Helena."

Bruno was shocked.

He couldn't speak.

"I don't know what hotel or motel," the operator said apologetically. "But there aren't really many places to stay in all of Napa Valley, so you shouldn't have any trouble finding her."

"No trouble," Bruno said shakily.

"Does she know anyone in St. Helena?"

"Huh?"

"I just thought maybe she's staying with friends," the operator suggested.

"Yes," Bruno said. "I think I know just where she is."

"I'm really sorry about the death."

"What?"

"The death in the family."

"Oh," Bruno said. He licked his lips nervously. "Yes. There have been quite a few deaths in the family the past five years. Thank you for your help."

"No trouble."

He hung up.

She was in St. Helena.

The brazen bitch had gone back.

Why? My God, what was she doing? What was she after? What was she up to?

Whatever she had in mind, it would not do him any good. That was for damned sure.

Frantic, afraid that she was planning some trick that would be the death of him, he began to call the airlines at Los Angeles International, trying to get a seat on a flight north. There were no commuter planes until morning, and all of the early flights were already booked solid. He wouldn't be able to get out of L.A. until tomorrow afternoon.

That would be too late.

He knew it. Sensed it.

He had to move fast.

He decided to drive. The night was still young. If he stayed behind the wheel all night and kept the accelerator to the floor, he could reach St. Helena by dawn.

He had a feeling his life depended on it.

He hurried out of the bungalow, stumbling through ruined furniture and other rubble, leaving the front door wide open, not bothering to be careful, not taking time to see if anyone was nearby. He sprinted across the lawn, into the dark and deserted street, toward his van.

•

After they enjoyed coffee with brandy in the den, Joshua showed Tony and Hilary to the guest room and connecting bath at the far end of the house from his own sleeping quarters. The chamber was large and pleasant, with deep window sills and leaded glass windows like those in the dining room. The bed was an enormous fourposter that delighted Hilary.

After they said goodnight to Joshua and closed the bedroom door, and after they drew the drapes over the windows to prevent the eyeless night from gazing blindly in at them, they took a shower together to soothe their aching muscles. They were quite exhausted, and they intended only to try to recapture the sweet, relaxing, childlike, asexual pleasure of the bath that they had shared the previous night at the airport hotel in L.A. Neither of them expected passion to raise its lovely head. However, as he lathered her breasts, the gentle, rhythmic, circular movements of his hands made her skin tingle and sent wonderful shivers through her. He cupped her breasts, filled his large hands with them, and her nipples hardened and rose through the soapy foam that sheathed them. He went to his knees and washed her belly, her long slim legs, her buttocks. For Hilary, the world shrank to a small sphere, to just a few sights and sounds and exquisite sensations: the odor of lilac-scented soap, the hiss and patter of falling water, the swirling patterns in the steam, his lean and supple body glistening as water cascaded over his well-defined muscles, the eager and incredible growth of his manhood as she took her turn lathering him. By the time they finished showering, they had forgotten how tired they were; they had forgotten their aching muscles; only desire remained.

On the fourposter bed, in the soft glow of a single lamp, he held her and kissed her eyes, her nose, her lips. He kissed her chin, her neck, her turgid nipples.

"Please," she said. "Now."

"Yes," he said against the hollow of her throat.

She opened her legs to him, and he entered her.

"Hilary," he said. "My sweet, sweet Hilary."

He drove into her with great strength and yet with tenderness, filled her up.

She rocked in time with him. Her hands moved over his broad back, tracing the outlines of his muscles. She had never felt so alive, so energized. In only a minute, she began to come, and she thought she might never stop, just rise from peak to peak, on and on, forever and ever, without end.

As he moved within her, they became one body and soul in a way she had never been with any other man. And she knew Tony felt it, too, this unique and astonishingly deep bonding. They were physically, emotionally, intellectually, and psychically joined, molded into a single being that was far superior to the sum of its two halves, and in that moment of phenomenal synergism—which neither of them had experienced with other lovers—Hilary knew that what they had was so special, so important, so rare, so powerful, that it would last as long as they lived. As she called his name and lifted up to meet his thrusts and climaxed yet again, and as he began to spurt within the deep darkness of her, she knew, as she had known the first time they'd made love, that she could trust him and rely on him as she'd never been able to trust or rely upon another human being; and, best of all, she knew that she would never be alone again.

Afterwards, as they lay together beneath the covers, he said, "Will you tell me about the scar on your side?"

"Yes. Now I will."

"It looks like a bullet wound."

"It is. I was nineteen, living in Chicago. I'd been out of high school for a year. I was working as a typist, trying to save enough money so I could get a place of my own. I was paying Earl and Emma rent for my room."

"Earl and Emma?"

"My parents."

"You called them by their first names?"

"I never thought of them as my father and mother."

"They must have hurt you a lot," he said sympathetically.

"Every chance they got."

"If you don't want to talk about it now—"

"I do," she said. "Suddenly, for the first time in my life, I *want* to talk about it. It doesn't hurt to talk about it. Because now I've got you, and that makes up for all the bad days."

"My family was poor," Tony said. "But there was love in our house."

"You were lucky."

"I'm sorry for you, Hilary."

"It's over," she said. "They've been dead a long time, and I should have exorcised them years ago."

"Tell me."

"I was paying them a few dollars rent each week, which they used to buy a little more booze, but I was socking away everything else I earned as a typist. Every penny. Not much, but it grew in the bank. I didn't even spend anything for lunch; I went without. I was determined to get an apartment of my own. I didn't even care if it was another shabby place with dark little rooms and bad plumbing and cockroaches—just so Earl and Emma didn't come with it."

Tony kissed her cheek, the corner of her mouth.

She said, "Finally, I saved up enough. I was ready to move out. One more day, one more paycheck, and I was going to be on my way."

She trembled.

Tony held her close.

"I came home from work that day," Hilary said, "and I went into the kitchen—and there was Earl holding Emma against the refrigerator. He had a gun. The barrel was jammed into her teeth."

"My God."

"He was going through a very bad siege of . . . Do you know what delirium tremens are?"

"Sure. They're hallucinations. Spells of mindless fear. It's something that happens to really chronic alcoholics. I've dealt with people who've been having delirium tremens. They can be violent and unpredictable."

"Earl had that gun against her teeth, which she kept clenched, and he started screaming crazy stuff about giant worms that he thought were coming out of the walls. He accused Emma of letting the worms out of the walls, and he wanted her to stop them. I tried to talk to him, but he wasn't listening. And then the worms kept coming out of the walls and started slithering around his feet; he got furious with Emma, and he pulled the trigger."

"Jesus."

"I saw her face blown away."

"Hilary—"

"I need to talk about it."

"All right."

"I've never talked about it before."

"I'm listening."

"I ran out of the kitchen when he shot her," Hilary said. "I knew I couldn't make it out of the apartment and down the hall before he shot me in the back, so I ducked the other way, into my room. I closed and locked the door, but he shot the lock off. By then, he was convinced that I was the one causing the worms to come out of the walls. He shot me. It wasn't anywhere close to being a fatal wound, but it hurt like hell, like a white-hot poker in my side, and it bled a lot."

"Why didn't he shoot you again? What saved you?"

"I stabbed him," she said.

"Stabbed? Where'd you get the knife?"

"I kept one in my room. I'd had it since I was eight. I'd never used it until then. But I'd always thought that if one of their beatings got out of hand and it looked like they were going to finish me, I'd cut them to save myself. So I cut Earl about the same instant he pulled the trigger. I didn't hurt him any worse than he hurt me, but he was shocked, terrified at the sight of his own blood. He ran out of the room, back to the kitchen. He started shouting at Emma again, telling her to make the worms go away before they smelled his blood and came after him. Then he emptied his gun into her because she wouldn't send the worms away. I was hurting something terrible from the wound in my side, and I was scared, but I tried to count the shots. When I thought he'd used up his ammunition, I hobbled out of my room and tried to make it to the front door. But he had several boxes of bullets. He had reloaded. He saw me and shot at me from the kitchen, and I ran back to my room. I barricaded the door with a dresser and hoped help would come before I bled to death. Out in the kitchen, Earl kept screaming about the worms, and then about giant crabs at the windows, and he kept emptying the gun into Emma. He put almost a hundred and fifty rounds into her before it was all over. She was torn to pieces. The kitchen was a charnel house."

Tony cleared his throat. "What happened to him?"

"He killed himself when the SWAT team finally broke in."

"And you?"

"A week in the hospital. A scar to remind me."

They were silent for a while.

Beyond the drapes, beyond the leaded windows, the night wind coughed.

"I don't know what to say," Tony said.

"Tell me you love me."

"I do."

"Tell me."

"I love you."

"I love you, Tony."

He kissed her.

"I love you more than I ever thought I could love anyone," she said. "In just a week, you've changed me forever."

"You're damned strong," he said admiringly.

"You give me strength."

"You had plenty of that before I came along."

"Not enough. You give me more. Usually . . . just thinking about that day he shot me . . . I get upset, scared all over again, as if it just happened yesterday. But I didn't get scared this time. I told you all about it, and I was hardly affected. You know why?"

"Why?"

"Because all the terrible things that happened in Chicago, the shooting and everything that came before it, all of that is ancient history now. None of it matters any more. I have you, and you make up for all the bad times. You balance the scales. In fact, you tip the scales in my favor."

"It works both ways, you know. I need you as much as you need me."

"I know. That's what makes it so perfect."

They were silent again.

Then she said, "There's another reason that those memories of Chicago don't scare me any more. I mean, besides the fact that I've got you now."

"What's that?"

"Well, it has to do with Bruno Frye. Tonight I began to realize that he and I have a lot in common. It looks like he endured the same sort of torture from Katherine that I got from Earl and Emma. But he cracked, and I didn't. That big strong man cracked, but I held on. That means something to me. It means a lot. It tells me that I shouldn't worry so much, that I should not be afraid of opening myself to people, that I can take just about anything the world throws at me."

"That's what I told you. You're strong, tough, hard as nails," Tony said.

"I'm not hard. Feel me. Do I feel hard?"

"Not here," he said.

"What about here?"

"Firm," he said.

"Firm isn't the same as hard."

"You feel nice."

"Nice isn't the same as hard either."

"Nice and firm and warm," he said.

She squeezed him.

"*This* is hard," she said, grinning.

"But it's not hard to make it soft again. Want me to show you?"

"Yes," she said. "Yes. Show me."

They made love again.

As Tony filled her up and explored her with long silken strokes, as waves of pleasure crashed through her, she was sure that everything would be all right. The act of love reassured her, gave her tremendous confidence in the future. Bruno Frye had not come back from the grave. She wasn't being stalked by a walking corpse. There was a logical explanation. Tomorrow they would talk to Dr. Rudge and Rita Yancy, and they would learn what lay behind the mystery of the Frye look-alike. They would uncover enough information and proof to help the police, and the double would be found, arrested. The danger would pass. Then she would always be with Tony, and Tony with her, and then nothing really bad could happen. Nothing could hurt her. Neither Bruno Frye nor anyone else could hurt her. She was happy and safe at last.

Later, as she lay on the edge of sleep, a sharp crash of thunder filled the sky, rolled down the mountains, into the valley, and over the house.

A strange thought flashed through her mind: *The thunder is a warning. It's an omen. It's telling me to be careful and not to be so damned sure of myself.*

But before she could explore that thought further, she fell off the edge of sleep, all the way down into it.

•

Frye drove north from Los Angeles, traveling near the sea at first, then swinging inland with the freeway.

California had just come out of one of its periodic gasoline shortages. Service stations were open. Fuel was available. The freeway was a concrete artery running through the flesh of the state. The twin scalpels of his headlights laid it bare for his examination.

As he drove, he thought about Katherine. The bitch! What was she doing in St. Helena? Had she moved back into the house on the cliff? If she had done that, had she also taken over control of the winery again? And would she try to force him to move in with her? Would he have to live with her and obey her as before? All of those questions were of vital importance to him, even though most of them didn't make any sense whatsoever and could not be sensibly answered.

He was aware that his mind was not clear. He wasn't able to think straight regardless of how hard he tried, and that inability frightened him.

He wondered if he should pull over at the next rest area and get some sleep. When he woke he might have control of himself again.

But then he remembered that Hilary-Katherine was already in St. Helena, and the possibility that she was setting a trap for him in his own house was far more unsettling than his temporary inability to order his thoughts.

He wondered, briefly, whether the house was actually his any longer. After all, he was dead. (Or half dead.) And they had buried him. (Or they thought they had.) Eventually, the estate would be liquidated.

As Bruno considered the extent of his losses, he got very angry with Katherine for taking so much from him and leaving so little. She had killed him, had taken himself from him, leaving him alone, without himself to touch and talk to, and now she had even moved into his house.

He pushed his foot down hard on the accelerator until the speedometer registered ninety miles an hour.

If a cop stopped him for speeding, Bruno intended to kill him. Use the knife. Cut him open. Rip him up. No one was going to stop Bruno from getting to St. Helena before sunrise.

chapter seven

Afraid that he would be seen by men on the night crew at the winery, men who knew him to be dead, Bruno Frye did not drive the van onto the property. Instead, he parked almost a mile away, on the main road, and walked overland, through the vineyards, to the house that he had built five years ago.

Shining indirectly through ragged tears in the cloud cover, the cold white moon cast just enough light for him to make his way between the vines.

The rolling hills were silent. The air smelled vaguely of copper sulphate which had been sprayed during the summer to prevent mildew, and overlaying that was the fresh, ozone odor of the rain that had stirred up the copper sulphate. There was no rain falling now. There couldn't have been much of a storm earlier, just sprinkles, squalls. The land was only soft and damp, not muddy.

The night sky was one shade brighter than it had been half an hour ago. Dawn had not yet arrived from its bed in the east, but it would be rising soon.

When he reached the clearing, Bruno hunkered down beside a line of shrubbery and studied the shadows around the house. The windows were dark and blank. Nothing moved. There was not a sound except the soft, whispery whistle of the wind.

Bruno crouched by the shrubs for a few minutes. He was afraid to move, afraid that she was waiting for him inside. But at last, heart pounding, he forced himself to forsake the cover and relative safety of the shrubbery; he got up and walked to the front door.

His left hand held a flashlight that wasn't switched on, and his right hand held a knife. He was prepared to lunge and thrust at the slightest movement, but there was no movement other than his own.

At the doorstep, he put the flashlight down, fished a key out of his jacket pocket, unlocked the door. He picked up the flash, pushed the door open with one foot, snapped on the light that he carried, and went into the house fast and low, the knife held straight out in front of him.

She wasn't waiting in the foyer.

Bruno went slowly from one gloomy, overfurnished room to another gloomy, overfurnished room. He looked in closets and behind sofas and behind large display cases.

She wasn't in the house.

Perhaps he had gotten back in time to stop whatever plot she was hatching.

He stood in the middle of the living room, the knife and the flashlight still in his hands, both of them directed at the floor. He swayed, exhausted, dizzy, confused.

It was one of those times when he desperately needed to talk to himself, to share his feelings with himself, to work out his confusion with himself and get his mind back on the track. But he would never again be able to consult with himself because himself was dead.

Dead.

Bruno began to shake. He wept.

He was alone and frightened and very mixed-up.

For forty years, he had posed as an ordinary man, and he had passed for normal with considerable success. But he could not do that any more. Half of him was dead. The loss was too great for him to recover. He had no self-confidence. Without himself to turn to, without his other self to give advice and offer suggestions, he did not have the resources to maintain the charade.

But the bitch was in St. Helena. Somewhere. He couldn't sort out his thoughts, couldn't get a grip on himself, but he knew one thing: He had to find her and kill her. He had to get rid of her once and for all.

•

The small travel alarm was set to go off at seven o'clock Thursday morning.

Tony woke an hour before it was time to get up. He woke with a start, began to sit up in bed, realized where he was, and eased back down to the pillow. He lay on his back, in the dark, staring at the shadowy ceiling, listening to Hilary's rhythmic breathing.

He had bolted from sleep to escape a nightmare. It was a brutal, grisly dream filled with mortuaries and tombs and graves and coffins, a dream that was somber and heavy and dark with death. Knives. Bullets. Blood. Worms coming out of the walls and wriggling from the staring eyes of corpses. Walking dead men who spoke of crocodiles. In the dream, Tony's life had been threatened half a dozen times, but on each occasion, Hilary had stepped between him and the killer, and every time she had died for him.

It was a damned disturbing dream.

He was afraid of losing her. He loved her. He loved her more than he could ever tell her. He was an articulate man, and he was not the least bit reluctant to express his emotions, but he simply did not have the words to properly describe the depth and quality of his feeling for her. He didn't think such words existed; all of the ones he knew were crude, leaden, hopelessly inadequate. If she were taken from him, life would go on, of course—but not easily, not happily, not without a great deal of pain and grief.

He stared at the dark ceiling and told himself that the dream had not been anything to worry about. It had not been an omen. It had not been a prophecy. It was only a dream. Just a bad dream. Nothing more than a dream.

In the distance, a train whistle blew two long blasts. It was a cold, lonely, mournful sound that made him pull the covers up to his chin.

•

Bruno decided that Katherine might be waiting for him in the house that Leo had built.

He left his own house and crossed the vineyards. He took the knife and flashlight with him.

In the first pale light of dawn, while most of the sky was still blue-black, while the valley lay in the fading penumbra of the night, he went to the clifftop house. He did not go up by way of the cable car because, in order to board it, he would have to go into the winery and climb to the second floor, where the lower tramway station occupied a corner of the building. He dared not be seen in there, for he figured the place was now crawling with Katherine's spies. He wanted to sneak up on the house, and the only route by which he could do that was the stairs on the face of the cliff.

He started climbing rapidly, two steps at a time, but before he went very far, he discovered that caution was essential. The staircase was crumbling. It had not been kept in good repair, as the tramway had been. Decades of rain and wind and summer heat had leeched away much of the mortar that bound the old structure together. Small stones, pieces of virtually every one of the three hundred and twenty steps, broke off under his feet and clattered to the base of the cliff. Several times, he almost lost his balance, almost fell backwards, or almost pitched sideways into space. The safety railing was decayed, dilapidated, missing whole sections; it would not save him if he stumbled against it. But slowly, cautiously, he followed the switchback path of the staircase, and in time he reached the top of the cliff.

He crossed the lawn, which had gone to weeds. Dozens of rose bushes, once carefully tended and manicured, had sent thorny tentacles in all directions and now sprawled in tangled, flowerless heaps.

Bruno let himself into the rambling Victorian mansion and searched the musty, dust-filmed, spider-webbed rooms which stank of mildew that thrived on the drapes and carpets. The house was crammed full of antique furniture and art glass and statuary and many other things, but it did not hold anything sinister. The woman was not here, either.

He didn't know whether that was good or bad. On the one hand, she hadn't moved in, hadn't taken over in his absence. That was good. He was relieved about that. But on the other hand—where the hell was she?

His confusion was rapidly getting worse. His powers of reasoning began to fail him hours ago, but now he couldn't trust his five senses, either. Sometimes he thought he heard voices, and he pursued them through the house, only to realize it was his own mumbling that he heard. Sometimes the mildew didn't smell like mildew at all, but like his mother's favorite perfume; but then a moment later it smelled like mildew again. And when he looked at familiar paintings that had hung on these walls since his childhood, he was unable to perceive what they were depicting; the shapes and colors would not resolve themselves, and his eyes were baffled by even the most simple pictures. He stood before one painting that he knew to be a landscape with trees and wildflowers, but he was not able to *see* those objects in it; he could only remember that they were there; all he saw now were smears, disjointed lines, blobs, meaningless forms.

He tried not to panic. He told himself that his bizarre confusion and disorientation were merely the results of his not having slept all night. He'd driven a long way in a short time, and he was understandably weary. His eyes were heavy, gritty, red and burning. He ached all over. His neck was stiff. All he needed was sleep. When he woke, he would be clear-headed. That was what he told himself. That was what he had to believe.

Because he had searched the house from bottom to top, he was now in the finished attic, the big room with the sloped ceiling, where he had spent so much of his life. In the chalky glow of his flashlight, he could see the bed in which he had slept during the years he'd lived in the mansion.

Himself was already on the bed. Himself was lying down, eyes closed, as if sleeping. Of course, the eyes were sewn shut. And the white nightgown was not a nightgown; it was a burial gown that Avril Tannerton had put on him. Because himself was dead. The bitch had stabbed and killed him. Himself had been stone-cold dead since last week.

Bruno was too enervated to vent his grief and rage. He went to the king-size bed and stretched out on his half of it, beside himself.

Himself stank. It was a pungent, chemical smell.

The bedclothes around himself were stained and damp with dark fluids that were slowly leaking out of the body.

Bruno didn't care about the mess. His side of the bed was dry. And although himself was dead and would never speak again or laugh again, Bruno felt good just being near himself.

Bruno reached out and touched himself. He touched the cold, hard, rigid hand and held it.

Some of the painful loneliness abated.

Bruno did not feel whole, of course. He would never feel whole again, for half of him was dead. But lying there beside his corpse, he did not feel all alone either.

Leaving the flashlight on to dispel the darkness in the shuttered attic bedroom, Bruno fell asleep.

•

Dr. Nicholas Rudge's office was on the twentieth floor of a skyscraper in the heart of San Francisco. Apparently, Hilary thought, the architect either had never heard of the unpleasant term "earthquake country," or he had made a very good deal with the devil. One wall of Rudge's office was glass from floor to ceiling, divided into three enormous panels by only two narrow, vertical, steel struts; beyond the window lay the terraced city, the bay, the magnificent Golden Gate Bridge, and the lingering tendrils of last night's fog. A quickening Pacific wind was tearing the gray clouds to tatters, and blue sky was becoming more dominant by the minute. The view was spectacular.

At the far end of the big room from the window-wall, six comfortable chairs were arranged around a circular teak coffee table. Obviously, group therapy sessions were held in that corner. Hilary, Tony, Joshua, and the doctor sat down there.

Rudge was an affable man with the ability to make you feel as if you were the most interesting and charming individual he had encountered in ages. He was as bald as all the clichés (a billiard ball, a baby's bottom, an eagle), but he had a neatly trimmed beard and mustache. He wore a three-piece suit with a tie and display handkerchief that matched, but there was nothing of the banker or of the dandy in his appearance. He looked distinguished, reliable, yet as relaxed as if he'd been wearing tennis whites.

Joshua summed up the evidence that the doctor had said he would need to hear, and he delivered a short lecture (which seemed to entertain Rudge) about a psychiatrist's obligation to protect society from a patient who appeared to have homicidal tendencies. In a quarter of an hour, Rudge heard enough to be convinced that a claim of doctor-patient privilege was neither wise nor justified in this case. He was willing to open the Frye file to them.

"Although I must admit," Rudge said, "if only one of you had come in here with this incredible story, I'd have put very little credence in it. I'd have thought you were in need of my professional services."

"We've considered the possibility that all three of us are out of our minds," Joshua said.

"And rejected it," Tony said.

"Well, if you *are* unbalanced," Rudge said, "then you'd better make it 'the *four* of us' because you've made a believer out of me, too."

During the past eighteen months (Rudge explained), he had seen Frye eighteen times in private, fifty-minute sessions. After the first appointment, when he realized the patient was deeply disturbed about something, he encouraged Frye to come in at least once every week, for he believed that the problem was too serious to respond to once-a-month sessions. But Frye had resisted the idea of more frequent treatments.

"As I told you on the phone," Rudge said, "Mr. Frye was torn between two desires. He wanted my help. He wanted to get to the root of his problem. But at the same time, he was afraid of revealing things to me—and afraid of what he might learn about himself."

"What was his problem?" Tony asked.

"Well, of course, the problem itself—the psychological knot that was causing his anxiety and tension and stress—was hidden in his subconscious mind. That's why he needed me. Eventually, we'd have been able to uncover that knot, and we might even have untied it, if the therapy had been successful. But we never got that far. So I can't tell you what was wrong with him because I don't really know. But I think what you're actually asking me is—what brought Frye to me in the first place? What made him realize that he needed help?"

"Yes," Hilary said. "At least that's a place to start. What were his symptoms?"

"The most disturbing thing, at least from Mr. Frye's point of view, was a recurring nightmare that terrified him."

A tape recorder stood on the circular coffee table, and two piles of cassettes lay beside it, fourteen in one pile, four in the other. Rudge leaned forward in his chair and picked up one of the four.

"All of my consultations are recorded and stored in a safe," the doctor said. "These are tapes of Mr. Frye's sessions. Last night, after I spoke with Mr. Rhinehart on the phone, I listened to portions of these recordings to see if I could find a few representative selections. I had a hunch you might convince me to open the file, and I thought it might be better if you could hear Bruno Frye's complaints in his own voice."

"Excellent," Joshua said.

"This first one is from the very first session," Dr. Rudge said. "For the first forty minutes, Frye would say almost nothing at all. It was very strange. He seemed outwardly calm and self-possessed, but I saw that he was frightened and trying to conceal his true feelings. He was afraid to talk to me. He almost got up and left. But I kept working at him gently, very gently. In the last ten minutes, he told me what he'd come to see me about, but even then it was like pulling teeth to get it out of him. Here's part of it."

Rudge pushed the cassette into the recorder and snapped on the machine.

When Hilary heard the familiar, deep, gravelly voice, she felt a chill race down her spine.

Frye spoke first:

> *"I have this trouble."*
> *"What sort of trouble?"*
> *"At night."*
> *"Yes?"*
> *"Every night."*
> *"You mean you have trouble sleeping?"*
> *"That's part of it."*
> *"Can you be more specific?"*
> *"I have this dream."*

"What sort of dream?"

"A nightmare."

"The same one every night?"

"Yes."

"How long has this been going on?"

"As long as I can remember."

"A year? Two years?"

"No, no. Much longer than that."

"Five years? Ten?"

"At least thirty. Maybe longer."

"You've been having the same bad dream every night for at least thirty years?"

"That's right."

"Surely not every night."

"Yes. There's never a reprieve."

"What's this dream about?"

"I don't know."

"Don't hold back."

"I'm not."

"You want to tell me."

"Yes."

"That's why you're here. So tell me."

"I want to. But I just don't know what the dream is."

"How can you have had it every night for thirty years or more and not know what it's about?"

"I wake up screaming. I always know a dream woke me. But I'm never able to remember it."

"Then how do you know it's always the same dream?"

"I just know."

"That's not good enough."

"Good enough for what?"

"Good enough to convince me that it's always the same dream. If you're so sure it's just one recurring nightmare, then you must have better reasons than that for thinking so."

"If I tell you . . ."

"Yes?"

"You'll think I'm crazy."

"I never use the word 'crazy.' "

"You don't?"

"No."

"Well . . . every time the dream wakes me, I feel as if there's something crawling on me."

"What is it?"

"I don't know. I can never remember. But I feel as if something's trying to crawl in my nose and in my mouth. Something disgusting. It's trying to get into me. It pushes at the corners of my eyes, trying to make me open my eyes. I feel it moving under my clothes. It's in my hair. It's everywhere. Crawling, creeping . . ."

In Nicholas Rudge's office, everyone was watching the tape recorder. Frye's voice was still gravelly, but there was raw terror in it now.

Hilary almost could see the big man's fear-twisted face—the shock-wide eyes, the pale skin, the cold sweat along his hairline.

The tape continued:

"Is it just one thing crawling on you?"

"I don't know."

"Or is it many things?"

"I don't know."

"What does it feel like?"

"Just . . . awful . . . sickening."

"Why does this thing want to get inside you?"

"I don't know."

"And you say you always feel like this after a dream."

"Yeah. For a minute or two."

"Is there anything else that you feel in addition to this crawling sensation?"

"Yeah. But it's not a feeling. It's a sound."

"What sort of sound?"

"Whispers."

"You mean that you wake up and imagine that you hear people whispering?"

"That's right. Whispering, whispering, whispering. All around me."

"Who are these people?"

"I don't know."

"*What are they whispering?*"

"*I don't know.*"

"*Do you have the feeling they're trying to tell you something?*"

"*Yes. But I can't make it out.*"

"*Do you have a theory, a hunch? Can you make a guess?*"

"*I can't hear the words exactly, but I know they're saying bad things.*"

"*Bad things? In what way?*"

"*They're threatening me. They hate me.*"

"*Threatening whispers.*"

"*Yes.*"

"*How long do they last?*"

"*About as long as the . . . creeping . . . crawling.*"

"*A minute or so?*"

"*Yes. Do I sound crazy?*"

"*Not at all.*"

"*Come on. I sound a little crazy.*"

"*Believe me, Mr. Frye, I've heard stories much stranger than yours.*"

"*I keep thinking that if I knew what the whispers were saying, and if I knew what was crawling on me, I'd be able to figure out what the dream is. And once I know what it is, maybe I won't have it any more.*"

"*That's almost exactly how we're going to approach the problem.*"

"*Can you help me?*"

"*Well, to a great extent that depends on how much you want to help yourself.*"

"*Oh, I want to beat this thing. I sure do.*"

"*Then you probably will.*"

"*I've been living with it so long . . . but I never get used to it. I dread going to sleep. Every night, I just dread it.*"

"*Have you undergone therapy before?*"

"*No.*"

"*Why not?*"

"*I was afraid.*"

"*Of what?*"

"Of what . . . you might find out."
"Why should you be afraid?"
"It might be something . . . embarrassing."
"You can't embarrass me."
"I might embarrass myself."
"Don't worry about that. I'm your doctor. I'm here to lis-
ten and help. If you—"

Dr. Rudge popped the cassette out of the tape recorder and said, "A re-curring nightmare. That's not particularly unusual. But a nightmare fol-lowed by tactile and audial hallucinations—that's not a common complaint."

"And in spite of that," Joshua said, "he didn't strike you as danger-ous?"

"Oh, heavens, no," Rudge said. "He was just frightened of a dream, and understandably so. And the fact that some dream sensations lingered even after he was awake meant that the nightmare probably represented some especially horrible, repressed experience buried way down in his subconscious. But nightmares are generally a healthy way to let off psy-chological steam. He exhibited no signs of psychosis. He didn't seem to confuse components of his dream with reality. He drew a clear line when he talked about it. In his mind, there appeared to be a sharp distinction between the nightmare and the real world."

Tony slid forward on his chair. "Could he have been less sure of real-ity than he let you know?"

"You mean . . . could he have fooled me?"

"Could he?"

Rudge nodded. "Psychology isn't an exact science. And by compari-son, psychiatry is even less exact. Yes, he could have fooled me, especially since I only saw him once a month and didn't have a chance to observe the mood swings and personality changes that would have been more ev-ident if we'd had weekly contact."

"In light of what Joshua told you a while ago," Hilary said, "do you feel you *were* fooled?"

Rudge smiled ruefully. "It looks as if I was, doesn't it?"

He picked up a second cassette that had been wound to a pre-selected point in another conversation between him and Frye, and he slipped it into the recorder.

"You've never mentioned your mother."

"What about her?"

"That's what I'm asking you."

"You're full of questions, aren't you?"

"With some patients, I hardly ever have to ask anything. They just open up and start talking."

"Yeah? What do they talk about?"

"Quite often they talk about their mothers."

"Must get boring for you."

"Very seldom. Tell me about your mother."

"Her name was Katherine."

"And?"

"I don't have anything to say about her."

"Everyone has something to say about his mother—and his father."

For almost a minute, there was silence. The tape wound from spool to spool, producing only a hissing sound.

"I'm just waiting him out," Rudge said, interpreting the silence for them. "He'll speak in a moment."

"Doctor Rudge?"

"Yes?"

"Do you think . . . ?"

"What is it?"

"Do you think the dead stay dead?"

"Are you asking if I'm religious?"

"No. I mean . . . do you think that a person can die . . . and then come back from the grave?"

"Like a ghost?"

"Yes. Do you believe in ghosts?"

"Do you?"

"I asked you first."

"No. I don't believe in them, Bruno. Do you?"

"I haven't made up my mind."

"Have you ever seen a ghost?"

"I'm not sure."

"What does this have to do with your mother?"

"She told me that she would . . . come back from the grave."

"When did she tell you this?"

"Oh, thousands of times. She was always saying it. She said she knew how it was done. She said that she would watch over me after she died. She said that if she saw I was misbehaving and not living like she wanted me to, then she'd come back and make me sorry."

"Did you believe her?"

". . ."

"Did you believe her?"

". . ."

"Bruno?"

"Let's talk about something else."

"Jesus!" Tony said. "That's where he got the notion that Katherine had come back. The woman planted the idea in him before she died!"

To Rudge, Joshua said, "What in the name of God was the woman trying to do? What sort of relationship did those two have?"

"That was the root of his problem," Rudge said. "But we never got around to exposing it. I kept hoping I could get him to come in every week, but he kept resisting—and then he was dead."

"Did you pursue the subject of ghosts with him in later sessions?" Hilary asked.

"Yes," the doctor said. "The very next time he came in, he started off on it again. He said that the dead stayed dead and that only children and fools believed differently. He said there weren't such things as ghosts and zombies. He wanted me to know that he had never believed Katherine when she'd told him that she would come back."

"But he was lying," Hilary said. "he did believe her."

"Apparently, he did," Rudge said. He put the third tape in the machine.

"Doctor, what religion are you?"

"I was raised a Catholic."

"Do you still believe?"

"Yes."

"Do you go to church?"

"Yes. Do you?"

"No. Do you go to mass every week?"

"Nearly every week."

"Do you believe in heaven?"

"Yes. Do you?"

"Yeah. What about hell?"

"What do you think about it, Bruno?"

"Well, if there's a heaven, there must be a hell."

"Some people would argue that earth is hell."

"No. There's another place with fire and everything. And if there are angels . . ."

"Yes?"

"There must be demons. The Bible says there are."

"You can be a good Christian without taking all of the Bible literally."

"Do you know how to spot the various marks of the demons?"

"Marks?"

"Yeah. Like when a man or a woman makes a deal with the devil, he puts a mark on them. Or if he owns them for some other reason, he marks them, sort of like we brand cattle."

"Do you believe you can really make a deal with the devil?"

"Huh? Oh, no. No, that's just bunk. It's crap. But some people do believe in it. A lot of people do. And I find them interesting. Their psychology fascinates me. I read a lot about the occult, just trying to figure out the kind of people who put a lot of faith in it. I want to understand the way their minds work. You know?"

"You were talking about the marks that demons leave on people."

"Yeah. It's just something I read recently. Nothing important."

"Tell me about it."

"Well, see, there are supposed to be hundreds and hundreds of demons in hell. Maybe thousands. And each one of them is supposed to have his own mark that he puts on people whose souls he claims. Like, for instance, in the middle ages, they believed that a strawberry birthmark on the face was the mark of a demon. And another one was crossed eyes. A third *breast. Some people are born with a third breast. It's really not so rare. And there are those who say it's a mark of a demon. The number 666. That's the mark of the chief of all demons, Satan. His people have the number 666 burned into their skin, under their hair, where it can't be seen. I mean, that's what the True Believers think. And twins. . . . That's another sign of a demon at work."*

"Twins are the handiwork of demons?"

"You understand, I'm not saying I believe any of this. I don't. It's junk. I'm just telling you what some nuts out there believe."

"I understand."

"If I'm boring you—"

"No. I find it as fascinating as you do."

Rudge switched off the recorder. "One comment before I let him go on. I encouraged him to talk about the occult because I thought it was just an intellectual exercise for him, a way for him to strengthen his mind to deal with his own problem. I am sorry to say that I believed him when he said he didn't take it seriously."

"But he did," Hilary said. "He took it very seriously."

"So it seems. But at the time I thought he was exercising his mind, preparing to solve his own problem. If he could find a way to explain the apparently irrational thought processes of far-out people like die-hard occultists, then he would feel ready to find an explanation for the tiny piece of irrational behavior in his own personality. If he could explain occultists, it would be an easier matter to explain the dream that he could not remember. That's what I *thought* he was doing. But I was wrong. Damn! If only he'd been coming in more frequently."

Rudge started the tape recorder again.

"You said twins are the handiwork of demons."

"Yeah. Not all twins, of course. Just certain special kinds of twins."

"Such as?"

"Siamese twins. Some people think that's the mark of a demon."

"Yes. I can see how that superstition might develop."

"And sometimes identical twins are born with both heads

covered by cauls. That's rare. Maybe one. But not two. It's very rare for both twins to be born with cauls. When that happens, you can be pretty sure those twins were marked by a demon. At least, that's what some people think."

Rudge took the tape out of the player. "I'm not sure how that one fits in with what's been happening to the three of you. But since there seems to be a dead ringer for Bruno Frye, the subject of twins seemed like something you'd want to hear about."

Joshua looked at Tony, then at Hilary. "But if Mary Gunther did have two children, why did Katherine bring home only one? Why would she lie and say there was just one baby? It doesn't make any sense."

"I don't know," Tony said doubtfully. "I told you that story sounded too smooth."

Hilary said, "Have you found a birth certificate for Bruno?"

"Not yet," Joshua said. "There wasn't one in any of his safe-deposit boxes."

Rudge picked up the fourth of the four cassettes that had been separated from the main pile of tapes. "This was the last session I had with Frye. Just three weeks ago. He finally agreed to let me try hypnosis to help him recall the dream. But he was wary. He made me promise to limit the range of questions. I wasn't permitted to ask him about anything except the dream. The excerpt I've chosen for you begins after he was in a trance. I regressed him in time, not far, just to the previous night. I put him back into his dream again.

> *"What do you see, Bruno?"*
> *"My mother. And me."*
> *"Go on."*
> *"She's pulling me along."*
> *"Where are you?"*
> *"I don't know. But I'm just little."*
> *"Little?"*
> *"A little boy."*
> *"And your mother is forcing you to go somewhere?"*
> *"Yeah. She's dragging me by the hand."*
> *"Where does she drag you?"*
> *"To . . . the . . . the door. The door. Don't let her open it. Don't. Don't!"*

"*Easy. Easy now. Tell me about this door. Where does it go?*"

"*To hell.*"

"*How do you know that?*"

"*It's in the ground.*"

"*The door is in the ground?*"

"*For God's sake, don't let her open it! Don't let her put me down there again. No! No! I won't go down there again!*"

"*Relax. Be calm. There's no reason to be afraid. Just relax, Bruno. Relax. Are you relaxed?*"

"*Y-Yes.*"

"*All right. Now slowly and calmly and without any emotion, tell me what happens next. You and your mother are standing in front of a door in the ground. What happens now?*"

"*She . . . she . . . opens the door.*"

"*Go on.*"

"*She pushes me.*"

"*Go on.*"

"*Pushes me . . . through the door.*"

"*Go on, Bruno.*"

"*She slams it . . . locks it.*"

"*She locks you inside?*"

"*Yeah.*"

"*What's it like in there?*"

"*Dark.*"

"*What else?*"

"*Just dark. Black.*"

"*You must be able to see something.*"

"*No. Nothing.*"

"*What happens next?*"

"*I try to get out.*"

"*And?*"

"*The door's too heavy, too strong.*"

"*Bruno, is this really just a dream?*"

"*. . .*"

"*Is it really just a dream, Bruno?*"

"*It's what I dream.*"

"*But is it also a memory?*"

"*. . .*"

"*Did your mother actually lock you in a dark room when you were a child?*"

"*Y-Yes.*"

"*In the cellar?*"

"*In the ground. In that room in the ground.*"

"*How often did she do that?*"

"*All the time.*"

"*Once a week?*"

"*More often.*"

"*Was it a punishment?*"

"*Yeah.*"

"*For what?*"

"*For . . . for not acting . . . and thinking . . . like one.*"

"*What do you mean?*"

"*It was punishment for not being one.*"

"*One what?*"

"*One. One. Just one. That's all. Just one.*"

"*All right. We'll come back to that later. Now we're going to go on and find out what happens next. You're locked in that room. You can't get out the door. What happens next, Bruno?*"

"*I'm s-s-scared.*"

"*No. You're not scared. You feel very calm, relaxed, not scared at all. Isn't that right? Don't you feel calm?*"

"*I . . . guess so.*"

"*Okay. What happens after you try to open the door?*"

"*I can't get it open. So I just stand on the top step and look down into the dark.*"

"*There are steps?*"

"*Yes.*"

"*Where do they lead?*"

"*Hell.*"

"*Do you go down?*"

"*No! I just . . . stand there. And . . . listen.*"

"*What do you hear?*"

"*Voices.*"

"*What are they saying?*"

"*They're just . . . whispers. I can't make them out. But they're . . . coming . . . getting louder. They're coming closer. They're coming up the steps. They're so loud now!*"

"What are they saying?"

"Whispers. All around me."

"What are they saying?"

"Nothing. It means nothing."

"Listen closely."

"They don't speak in words."

"Who are they? Who's whispering?"

"Oh, Jesus. Listen. Jesus."

"Who are they?"

"Not people. No. No! Not people!"

"It isn't people whispering?"

"Get them off! Get them off me!"

"Why are you brushing at yourself?"

"They're all over me!"

"There's nothing on you."

"All over me!"

"Don't get up, Bruno. Wait—"

"Oh, my God!"

"Bruno, lie down on the couch."

"Jesus, Jesus, Jesus, Jesus."

"I'm ordering you to lie down on the couch."

"Jesus, help me! Help me!"

"Listen to me, Bruno. You—"

"Gotta get 'em off, gotta get 'em off!"

"Bruno, it's all right. Relax. They're going away."

"No! There's even more of them! Ah! Ah! No!"

"They're going away. The whispers are getting softer, fainter. They're—"

"Louder! Getting louder! A roar of whispers!"

"Be calm. Lie down and be—"

"They're getting in my nose! Oh, Jesus! My mouth!"

"Bruno!"

On the tape, there was a strange, strangled sound. It went on and on. Hilary hugged herself. The room suddenly seemed frigid.

Rudge said, "He jumped up from the couch and ran into the corner, over there. He crouched down in the corner and put his hands over his face."

The eerie, wheezing, gagging sound continued to come from the tape.

"But you snapped him out of the trance," Tony said.

Rudge was pale, remembering. "At first, I thought he was going to stay there, in the dream. Nothing like that had ever happened to me before. I'm very good at hypnotic therapy. Very good. But I thought I'd lost him. It took a while, but finally he began to respond to me."

On the tape: rasping, gagging, wheezing.

"What you hear," Rudge said, "is Frye screaming. He's so frightened that his throat has seized up on him, so terrified that he's lost his voice. He's trying to scream, but he can't get much sound out."

Joshua stood up, bent over, switched off the recorder. His hand was shaking. "You think his mother really locked him in a dark room."

"Yes," Rudge said.

"And there was something else in there with him."

"Yes."

Joshua pushed one hand through his thick white hair. "But for God's sake, what could it have been? What was in that room?"

"I don't know," Rudge said. "I expected to find out in a later session. But that was the last time I saw him."

•

In Joshua's Cessna Skylane, as they flew south and slightly east toward Hollister, Tony said, "My view of this thing is going through changes."

"How?" Joshua asked.

"Well, at first, I looked at it in simple black and white. Hilary was the victim. Frye was the bad guy. But now . . . in a way . . . maybe Frye's a victim, too."

"I know what you mean," Hilary said. "Listening to those tapes . . . I felt so sorry for him."

"It's all right to feel sorry for him," Joshua said, "so long as you don't forget that he's damned dangerous."

"Isn't he dead?"

"Is he?"

•

Hilary had written a screenplay that contained two scenes set in Hollister, so she knew something about the place.

On the surface, Hollister resembled a hundred other small towns in California. There were some pretty streets and some ugly streets. New houses and old houses. Palm trees and oaks. Oleander bushes. Because this was one of the drier parts of the state, there was more dust than elsewhere, but that was not particularly noticeable until the wind blew really hard.

The thing that made Hollister different from other towns was what lay under it. Fault lines. Most communities in California were built on or near geological faults that now and then slipped, causing earthquakes. But Hollister was not built on just one fault; it rested on a rare confluence of faults, a dozen or more, both major and minor, including the San Andreas Fault.

Hollister was a town on the move; at least one earthquake struck it every day of the year. Most of those shocks were in the middle or lower range of the Richter Scale, of course. The town had never been leveled. But the sidewalks were cracked and canted. A walk could be level on Monday, a bit hoved up on Tuesday, and almost level again on Wednesday. Some days there were chains of tremors that rattled the town gently, with only brief pauses, for an hour or two at a time; but people who lived there were seldom aware of these very minor tremors, just as those who lived in the High Sierra ski country paid scant attention to any storm that put down only an inch of snow. Over the decades, the courses of some streets in Hollister were altered by the ever-moving earth; avenues that had once been straight were now a bit curved or occasionally doglegged. The grocery stores had shelves that were slanted toward the back or covered with wire screens to prevent bottles and cans from crashing to the floor every time the ground shook. Some people lived in houses that were gradually slipping down into unstable land, but the sinkage was so slow that there was no alarm, no urgency about finding another place to live; they just repaired the cracks in the walls and planed the bottoms off doors and made adjustments as they could. Once in a while, a man in Hollister would add a room to his house without realizing that the addition was on one side of a fault line and the house on the other side; and as a result, over a period of years, the new room would move with stately, turtlelike determination—north or south or east or west, depending on the fault—while the rest of the house stood still or inched in the opposite direction, a subtle but powerful process that eventually tore the addition from the main structure. The basements of a few buildings contained sinkholes, bottomless pits; these pits were spreading unstoppably under the buildings and would one day swallow them, but in the meantime, the citizens of Hollister lived and worked above. A lot of people would be terrified to live in a town where (as some residents put it) you could "go to sleep at night listening to the earth whisper to itself." But for generations the good people of Hollister had gone about their business with a positive attitude that was wondrous to behold.

Here was the ultimate California optimism.

Rita Yancy lived in a corner house on a quiet street. It was a small home with a big front porch. There were autumn-blooming white and yellow flowers in a border along the walkway.

Joshua rang the bell. Hilary and Tony stood behind him.

An elderly woman came to the door. Her gray hair was done up in a bun. Her face was wrinkled, and her blue eyes were quick, bright. She had a friendly smile. She was wearing a blue housedress and a white apron and sensible old-lady shoes. Wiping her hands on a dish towel, she said, "Yes?"

"Mrs. Yancy?" Joshua asked.

"That's me."

"My name's Joshua Rhinehart."

She nodded. "I figured you'd show up."

"I'm determined to talk to you," he said.

"You strike me as a man who either doesn't give up easily or never gives up at all."

"I'll camp out right here on your porch until I get what I've come for."

She sighed. "That won't be necessary. I've given the situation a great deal of thought since you called yesterday. What I decided was—you can't do anything to me. Not a thing. I'm seventy-five years old, and they don't just throw women my age into jail. So I might as well tell you what it was all about, because, if I don't, you'll just keep pestering me."

She stepped back, opened the door wide, and they went inside.

•

In the attic of the clifftop house, in the king-size bed, Bruno woke, screaming.

The room was dark. The flashlight batteries had gone dead while he'd slept.

Whispers.

All around him.

Soft, sibilant, evil whispers.

Slapping at his face and neck and chest and arms, trying to brush away the hideous things that crawled on him, Bruno fell off the bed. There seemed to be even a greater number of bustling, skittering *things* on the floor than there had been on the bed, thousands of them, all whispering, whispering. He wailed and gibbered, then clamped a hand over his nose and mouth to prevent the things from slithering inside of him.

Light.

Threads of light.

Thin lines of light like loose, luminescent threads hanging from the otherwise tenebrous fabric of the room. Not many threads, not much light, but some. It was a whole lot better than nothing.

He scrambled as fast as he could toward those faint filaments of light, flinging the *things* from him, and what he found was a window. The far side of it was covered by shutters. Light was seeping through the narrow chinks in the shutters.

Bruno stood, swaying, fumbling in the dark for the window latch. When he found the lock, it would not turn; it was badly corroded.

Screaming, brushing frantically at himself, he stumbled back toward the bed, found it in the seamless blackness, got hold of the lamp that stood on the nightstand, carried the lamp back to the window, used it as a club, and glass shattered. He threw the lamp aside, felt for the bolt on the inside of the shutters, put his hand on it, jerked on it, skinned a knuckle as he forced the bolt out of its catch, threw open the shutters, and wept with relief as light flooded into the attic.

The whispers faded.

•

Rita Yancy's parlor—that was what she called it, a parlor, rather than using a more modern and less colorful word—almost was a parody of the stereotypical parlor in which sweet little old ladies like her were supposed to spend their twilight years. Chintz drapes. Handmade, embroidered wall hangings—most of them inspirational sayings framed by penny-sized flowers and cute birds—were everywhere, a relentless display of good will and good humor and bad taste. Tasseled upholstery. Wingback chairs. Copies of *Reader's Digest* on a dainty occasional table. A basket filled with balls of yarn and knitting needles. A flowered carpet that was protected by matching flowered runners. Handmade afghans were draped across the seat and the back of the sofa. A mantel clock ticked hollowly.

Hilary and Tony sat on the sofa, on the edge of it, as if afraid to lean back and risk rumpling the covering. Hilary noticed that each of the many knickknacks and curios was dust-free and highly polished. She had the feeling that Rita Yancy would jump up and run for a dust cloth the instant anyone tried to touch and admire those prized possessions.

Joshua sat in an armchair. The back of his head and his arms rested on antimacassars.

Mrs. Yancy settled into what was obviously her favorite chair; she seemed to have acquired part of her character from it, and it from her. It was possible, Hilary thought, to picture Mrs. Yancy and the chair growing together into a single organic-inorganic creature with six legs and brushed velvet skin.

The old woman picked up a blue and green afghan that was folded on her footstool. She opened the blanket and covered her lap with it.

There was a moment of absolute silence, where even the mantel clock seemed to pause, as if time had stopped, as if they had been quick-frozen and magically transported, along with the room, to a distant planet to be put on exhibition in an extraterrestrial museum's Department of Earth Anthropology.

Then Rita Yancy spoke, and what she said totally shattered Hilary's homey image of her. "Well, there's sure as hell no point in beating around the bush. I don't want to waste my whole day on this damn silly thing. Let's get straight to it. You want to know why Bruno Frye was paying me five hundred bucks a month. It was hush money. He was paying me to keep my mouth shut. His mother paid me the same amount every month for almost thirty-five years, and when she died, Bruno started sending checks. I must admit that surprised the hell out of me. These days it's an unusual son who would pay that kind of money to protect his mother's reputation—and especially after she's already kicked the bucket. But he paid."

"Are you saying you were blackmailing Mr. Frye and his mother before him?" Tony asked, astonished.

"Call it whatever you want. Hush money or blackmail or anything you want."

"From what you've told us so far," Tony said, "I believe the law would call it blackmail and nothing else."

Rita Yancy smiled at him. "Do you think the word bothers me? Do you think I'm afraid of it? All quivery inside? Sonny, let me tell you, I've been accused of worse than that in my time. Is blackmail the word you want to use? Well, it's all right by me. Blackmail. That's what it is. We won't put a prettier face on it. But of course, if you're stupid enough to drag an old lady into court, I won't use the same word then. I'll just say that I did a great favor for Katherine Frye a long time ago, and that she insisted on repaying me with a monthly check. You don't really have any proof otherwise, do you? That's one reason I set it up on a monthly basis in the first place. I mean, blackmailers are supposed to strike and run, take it in one big bite, which is easy for the prosecutor to trace. But who's going to believe that a blackmailer would agree to a modest monthly payment on account?"

"We don't have any intention of bringing criminal charges against you," Joshua assured her. "And we haven't the slightest interest in attempting to recover the money that was paid to you. We realize that would be futile."

"Good," Mrs. Yancy said. "Because I'd make a bloody battle of it if you tried."

She straightened her afghan.

I've got to remember this one, everything about her, Hilary thought. She'd make a great little character role in a movie some day: Grandma with spice and acid and a touch of rot.

"All we want is some information," Joshua said. "There's a problem with the estate, and it's holding up the disbursement of funds. I need to get answers to some questions in order to expedite the final settlement. You say you don't want to waste your whole day on this 'damn silly thing.' Well, I don't want to waste months on the Frye estate either. My only motivation in coming here is to get the information I need to wrap up this damn silly thing of *mine*."

Mrs. Yancy stared hard at him, then at Hilary and Tony. Her eyes were shrewd, appraising. Finally, she nodded with evident satisfaction, as if she had read their minds and had approved of what she'd seen in them. "I think I believe you. All right. Ask your questions."

"Obviously," Joshua said, "the first thing we want to know is what you had on Katherine Frye that made her and her son pay you nearly a quarter of a million dollars over the past forty years."

"To understand about that," Mrs. Yancy said, "you'll need a bit of background on me. You see, when I was a young woman, at the height of the Great Depression, I looked around at all the kinds of work I could do to make ends meet, and I decided that none of them offered more than mere survival and a life of drudgery. All but one. I realized that the only profession that offered me a chance at real money was the oldest profession of them all. When I was eighteen, I became a working girl. In those days, in mixed company like this, a woman like me was referred to as a 'lady of easy virtue.' Today, you don't have to tiptoe around it. You can use any damn word you want these days." A strand of gray hair had slipped out of her bun. She pushed it away from her face, tucked it behind her ear. "When it comes to sex—the old slap-and-tickle, as it was sometimes called in my day—I'm amazed at how times have changed."

"You mean you were a . . . prostitute?" Tony asked, expressing the surprise that Hilary felt.

"I was an exceptionally good-looking girl," Mrs. Yancy said proudly. "I never worked the streets or bars or hotels or anything like that. I was on the staff of one of the finest, most elegant houses in San Francisco. We catered exclusively to the carriage trade. Only the very best sort of men. There were never fewer than ten girls and often as many as fifteen, but every one of us was striking and refined. I made good money, as I had expected I would. But by the time I was twenty-four, I realized that there was a great deal more money to be made operating my own house than there was in working in someone else's establishment. So I found a house with a lot of charm and spent nearly all of my savings redecorating it. Then I lined up a stable of lovely and polished young ladies. For the next thirty-six years, I worked as a madam, and I ran a damned classy place. I retired fifteen years ago, when I was sixty, because I wanted to come here to Hollister where my daughter and her husband lived; I wanted to be close to my grandchildren, you know. Grandchildren make old age a lot more rewarding than I'd ever thought it would be."

Hilary leaned back on the couch, no longer worried about rumpling the afghans that were draped across it.

Joshua said, "This is all quite fascinating, but what does it have to do with Katherine Frye?"

"Her father regularly visited my place in San Francisco," Rita Yancy said.

"Leo Frye?"

"Yes. A very strange man. I was never with him myself. I never serviced him. After I became a madam, I did very little bedwork; I was busy with the management details. But I heard all the stories that my girls told about him. He sounded like a first-class bastard. He liked his women docile, subservient. He liked to insult them and call them dirty names while he was using them. He was a strong disciplinarian, if you know what I mean. He had some nasty things he liked to do, and he paid a high price for the right to do them with my girls. Anyway, in April of 1940, Leo's daughter, Katherine, showed up on my doorstep. I'd never met her. I didn't even know he had a child. But he'd told her about me. He'd sent her to me so that she could have her baby in total secrecy."

Joshua blinked. "Her baby?"

"She was pregnant."

"Bruno was her baby?"

"What about Mary Gunther?" Hilary asked.

"There never was such a person as Mary Gunther," the old woman said. "That was just a cover story that Katherine and Leo made up."

"I knew it!" Tony said. "Too smooth. It was just too damn smooth."

"Nobody in St. Helena knew she was pregnant," Rita Yancy said. "She was wearing several girdles. You wouldn't believe how that poor girl had bound herself up. It was horrible. From the time she missed her first period, long before she ever began to swell up, she started wearing tighter and tighter and tighter girdles, then one girdle on top of another. And she starved herself, trying to keep off all the weight she could. It's a miracle she didn't either have a miscarriage or kill herself."

"And you took her in?" Tony asked.

"I'm not going to claim I did it out of the goodness of my heart," Mrs. Yancy said. "I can't stand old women when they're smug and self-righteous, like a lot of the ones I see when I go to the bridge games at the church. Katherine didn't touch my heart or anything like that. And I didn't take her in because I felt I had an obligation to her father. I didn't owe him a thing. Because of what I'd heard about him from my girls, I didn't even like him. And he'd been dead six weeks when Katherine showed up. I took her in for one reason, and I'm not going to pretend otherwise. She had three thousand bucks with her to cover room and board and the doctor's fee. That was a good deal more money then than it is today."

Joshua shook his head. "I can't understand it. She had a reputation as a cold fish. She didn't care for men. She didn't have a lover that anyone knew about. Who was the father?"

"Leo," Mrs. Yancy said.

"Oh, my God," Hilary said softly.

"Are you sure?" Joshua asked Rita Yancy.

"Positive," the old woman said. "He'd been fooling around with his own daughter since she was four years old. He forced her to perform oral sex when she was a small child. Later, as she grew up, he did everything to her. Everything."

•

Bruno had hoped that a good night's sleep would clear his befuddled mind, wash away the confusion and the disorientation that had plagued him last night and early this morning. But now, as he stood in front of the broken attic window, basking in the gray October light, he was no more in command of himself than he had been six hours ago. His mind was writhing with chaotic thoughts and doubts and questions and fears; pleasant and ugly memories tangled like worms; mental images shifted and changed like puddles of quicksilver.

He knew what was wrong with him. He was alone. All alone. He was only half a man. Torn in half. That's what was wrong with him. Ever since the other half of him had been killed, he'd been increasingly nervous, increasingly unsure of himself. He no longer had the resources that he'd had when both halves of him had been alive. And now, trying to stumble along as only half a person, he was unable to cope; even the smallest problems were beginning to seem insoluble.

He turned away from the window and staggered heavily to the bed. He knelt on the floor beside the bed and put his head on the corpse, on its chest.

"Say something. Say something to me. Help me figure out what to do. Please. Please, help me."

But the dead Bruno had nothing to say to the one who was still alive.

•

Mrs. Yancy's parlor.

The ticking clock.

A white cat strolled in from the dining room and jumped up on the old woman's lap.

"How do you know that Leo molested Katherine?" Joshua asked. "Surely he didn't tell you about it."

"He didn't," Mrs. Yancy said. "But Katherine did. She was in a terrible state. Half out of her mind. She'd expected her father to bring her to me when her time drew near, but then he died. She was alone and terrified. Because of what she'd done to herself—the girdles and the dieting—her labor was damned difficult. I called in the doctor who gave my girls their weekly health examinations because I knew he would be discreet and willing to handle the case. He was sure the baby would be born dead. He thought there was a pretty good chance Katherine would die, too. She was in hard, agonizing labor for fourteen hours. I've never seen anyone endure the kind of pain that she went through. She was delirious a lot of the time, and when she had her wits about her, she was desperate to tell me what her father had done to her. I think she was trying to patch up her soul. She seemed to be afraid to die with the secret, and so she sort of treated me as if I was a priest listening to her confession. Her father forced her to provide oral sex shortly after her mother died. When they moved into the cliff house, which I gather is fairly isolated, he virtually set about training her to be a sex slave to him. When she was old enough for intercourse, he took precautions, but eventually, after years and years of it, they made a mistake; she got pregnant."

Hilary had the urge to lift the afghan that was draped on the couch and curl up in it to ward off the chills that swept over her. In spite of the frequent beatings, the emotional intimidation, the physical and mental torture that she suffered while living with Earl and Emma, she knew she was lucky to have escaped sexual abuse. She believed Earl had been impotent; only his inability to perform had saved her from that ultimate degradation. At least she had been spared that nightmare. But Katherine Frye had been plunged into it, and Hilary unexpectedly felt a kinship with the woman.

Tony seemed to sense what was going through her mind. He took her hand, squeezed it gently, reassuringly.

Mrs. Yancy stroked the white cat, and it made a low, rough, purring sound.

"There's something I don't understand," Joshua said. "Why didn't Leo send Katherine to you as soon as he knew she was going to have a baby? Why didn't he ask you to set up an abortion for her? Surely you had the contacts for that."

"Oh, yes," Mrs. Yancy said. "In my line of work, you had to know doctors who would handle that sort of thing. Leo could have arranged it through me. I don't know for sure why he didn't. But I suspect it was because he hoped Katherine would have a pretty baby girl."

"I'm not sure I follow," Joshua said.

"Isn't it obvious?" Mrs. Yancy asked, scratching the white cat under its fat chin. "If he had a granddaughter, then in a few years, he'd be able to start breaking her in, just like he did Katherine. Then he'd have two of them. A little harem of his own."

•

Unable to get a response out of his other self, Bruno got up and walked aimlessly around the huge room, stirring the dust on the floor; hundreds of whirling motes spun in the milky shaft of light from the window.

Eventually, he noticed a pair of dumbbells, each weighing about fifty pounds. They were part of the elaborate set of weights he had used six days a week, every week, between the ages of twelve and thirty-five. Most of his equipment—the barbells, heavier weights, the press bench—was down in the basement. But he had always kept a spare set of dumbbells in his room for use in those idle moments when a few extra sets of bicep curls or wrist flexes was just the thing to drive away boredom.

Now he picked up the weights and started working out with them. His enormous shoulders and powerful arms quickly got into the familiar rhythm, and he began to work up a sweat.

Twenty-eight years ago, when he'd first expressed a desire to lift weights and become a body builder, his mother had thought it was an excellent idea. Long, brutal workouts with weights helped burn up the sexual energy that he was just then beginning to generate, caught as he was in the throes of puberty. Because he didn't dare expose his demonic penis to a girl, vigorous weight training preoccupied him, seized his imagination and his emotions as sex might otherwise have done. Katherine had approved.

Later, as he packed on muscle tissue and became a formidable specimen, she had second thoughts about the wisdom of letting him grow so strong. Afraid that he might develop his body only so he could successfully turn on her, she had tried to take his weights away from him. But when he broke into tears and begged her to reconsider, she realized that she would never have anything to fear from him.

How could she ever have thought differently? Bruno wondered as he curled the dumbbells to his shoulders and then slowly let them down again. Hadn't she realized that she would always be stronger than he was? After all, she had the key to the door in the ground. She had the power to unlock that door and make him go into that dark hole. No matter how big his biceps and triceps became, as long as she possessed that key, she would always be stronger than he was.

It was around that time, when his body began to develop, that she first told him that she knew how to come back from the dead. She'd wanted him to know that, after she died, she'd watch over him from the other side; and she'd sworn that she would come back to punish him if she saw him misbehaving or if he started getting careless about hiding his demonic heritage from other people. She had warned him a thousand times or more that, if he was bad and forced her to come back from the grave, she would throw him into the hole in the ground, lock the door, and leave him there forever.

But now, as he worked out in the dusty attic, Bruno suddenly wondered if Katherine's threat had been empty. Had she really possessed supernatural powers? Could she really come back from the dead? Or was she lying to him? Was she lying because she was afraid of him? Was she afraid he would get big and strong—and then break her neck? Was her story about coming back from the grave nothing more than feeble insurance against his getting the idea that he could kill her and then be free of her forever?

Those questions came to him, but he was not capable of holding on to them long enough to explore each one and answer it. Disconnected thoughts surged like bursts of electric current through his short-circuiting brain. Each doubt was forgotten an instant after it occurred to him.

Contrarily, each fear that rose up did *not* fade away but remained, sparking and sputtering, in the dark corners of his mind. He thought of Hilary-Katherine, the latest resurrection, and he remembered that he had to find her.

Before she found him.

He began to shake.

He dropped one dumbbell with a crash. Then the other one. The floorboards rattled.

"The bitch," he said fearfully, angrily.

•

The white cat licked Mrs. Yancy's hand as she said, "Leo and Katherine worked up a complex story to explain the baby. They didn't want to admit it was hers. If they did that, they had to point a finger at the man responsible, at some young suitor. But she didn't have any suitors. The old man didn't want anyone else touching her. Just him. Gives me the creeps. What kind of man would force himself on his own little girl? And the bastard started on her when she was only *four!* She wasn't even old enough to understand what was happening." Mrs. Yancy shook her gray head in shock and sorrow. "How could a grown man be aroused by a baby like that? If I made the laws, any man who did that sort of thing would be castrated—or worse. Worse, I think. I tell you, it disgusts me."

Joshua said, "Why didn't they just claim Katherine was raped by a migrant farm worker or some stranger passing through? She wouldn't have had to send an innocent man to jail to support a story like that. She could have given the police a totally phony description. And even if, by some wild chance, they'd found a guy who fit that description, some poor son of a bitch who didn't have an alibi . . . well, then she could have said he wasn't the right man. She wouldn't have been forced to rail-road anyone."

"That's right," Tony said. "Most rape cases of that sort are never solved. The police would probably have been surprised if Katherine *had* made a positive identification of anybody they rounded up."

"I can understand why she wouldn't have been eager to cry rape," Hilary said. "She would have had to endure endless humiliation and embarrassment. A lot of people think every woman who's raped was just asking for it."

"I'm aware of that," Joshua said. "I'm the one who keeps saying that most of my fellow human beings are idiots, asses, and buffoons. Remember? But St. Helena has always been a relatively openminded town. The people there wouldn't have blamed Katherine for being raped. At least most of them wouldn't have. She would have had to deal with a few crude characters and a measure of embarrassment, naturally, but in the long run she would have had everyone's sympathy. And it seems to me that it would have been a lot easier taking that route than trying to make everyone believe an elaborate lie about Mary Gunther—and then having to worry about maintaining that lie for the rest of her life."

The cat turned over on Mrs. Yancy's lap. She rubbed its belly.

"Leo didn't want to blame the pregnancy on a rapist because that would have brought in the cops," Mrs. Yancy said. "Leo had great respect for the cops. He was an authoritarian type. He believed the cops were better at their jobs than they really were, and he was afraid they would smell something fishy about any rape story that he and Katherine could concoct. He didn't want to draw attention to himself, not attention like that. He was scared to death the cops would sniff out the truth. He wasn't about to risk going to jail for child molestation and incest."

"Katherine told you that?" Hilary asked.

"That's right. As I said before, she'd been living with the shame of Leo's abuse all her life, and when she thought maybe she was going to die in childbirth, she wanted to tell someone, anyone, what she'd been through. Anyway, Leo was sure he'd be safe if Katherine could conceal her pregnancy, hide it completely, and fool everyone in St. Helena. Then it would be possible to pass the child off as the illegitimate baby of an unfortunate friend from Katherine's college days."

"So her father forced her to wear the girdles," Hilary said, feeling sorrier for Katherine Frye than she would have thought possible when she first walked into Mrs. Yancy's parlor. "He put her through that agony to protect himself. It was his idea."

"Yes," Mrs. Yancy said. "She'd never been able to stand up to him.

She'd always done what he'd told her to do. It wasn't any different this time. She did this thing with the girdles and the dieting, even though it caused her a hell of a lot of pain. She did it because she was afraid to disobey him. Which isn't surprising when you consider that he'd spent twenty-some years breaking her spirit."

"She went away to college," Tony said. "Wasn't that an attempt to gain independence?"

"No," Mrs. Yancy said. "College was Leo's idea. In 1937, he went to Europe for seven or eight months to sell off the last of his holdings in the old country. He saw World War Two coming, and he didn't want to have any assets frozen over there. He didn't want to take Katherine on the trip with him. I suspect he intended to combine business with pleasure. He was a highly-sexed man. And I hear tell some of those European brothels offer all kinds of kinky thrills, just the sort of things to appeal to him. The dirty old goat. Katherine would have been in his way. He decided she should go to college while he was out of the country, and he arranged for her to stay with a family he knew in San Francisco. They owned a company that distributed wine, beer, and liquor in the Bay Area, and one of the things they handled was Shade Tree products."

Joshua said, "He was taking quite a chance, letting her out from under his thumb for so long."

"Apparently, he didn't think so," Mrs. Yancy said. "And he was proved right. In all those months without him around, she never began to come out of his thrall. She never told anyone about the things he'd been doing to her. She never even considered telling anyone. She was a broken spirit, I tell you. Enslaved. That's really the word for it. She was enslaved, not like a plantation worker or anything like that. Mentally and emotionally enslaved. And when he came back from Europe, he made her drop out of college. He took her back to St. Helena with him, and she didn't resist. She couldn't resist. She didn't know how."

The mantel clock chimed the hour. Two measured tones. The notes echoed softly from the parlor ceiling.

Joshua had been sitting on the edge of his chair. Now he slid back until his head touched the antimacassar again. He was pale, and dark rings circled his eyes. His white hair was no longer fluffy; it was lank, lifeless. In the short time that Hilary had known him, he appeared to her to have aged. He looked wrung-out.

She knew how he felt. The Frye family history was an unrelievedly grim tale of man's inhumanity to man. The more they poked around in that mess, the more depressed they became. The heart could not help but respond, and the spirit sagged as one awful discovery followed another.

As if talking to himself, getting it straight in his own mind, Joshua said, "So they went back to St. Helena, and they picked up their sick relationship where they'd left off, and eventually they made a mistake, and she got pregnant—and no one up there in St. Helena ever suspected a thing."

Tony said, "Incredible. Usually a simple lie is the best because it's the only kind that won't trip you up. The story about Mary Gunther was so damned involved! It was a juggling act. They had to keep a dozen balls in the air at once. Yet they brought it off without a hitch."

"Oh, hardly without a hitch," Mrs. Yancy said. "There was certainly a hitch or two."

"Such as?"

"Such as—the day she left St. Helena to come to my place to have her baby, she told people up there that this imaginary Mary Gunther had sent word that the baby had arrived. Now that was stupid. It really was. Katherine said she was going to San Francisco to pick up the child. She told them Mary's message mentioned a lovely baby, but neglected to say whether it was a boy or a girl. That was Katherine's pathetic way of covering for herself, since she couldn't know what her baby's sex was until it was born. Dumb. She should have known better. That was her only mistake—saying that the child was born before she left St. Helena. Ah, I know she was a complete nervous wreck. I know she wasn't thinking straight. She couldn't have been a very well-balanced woman after all that Leo had done to her over the years. And being pregnant, having to hide it under all those girdles, then Leo's death coming at a time when she needed him most—that was bound to drive her even further over the edge. She was out of her head, and she didn't think it out well enough."

"I don't understand," Joshua said. "Why was it a mistake for her to say Mary's baby had already been born? Where's the hitch?"

Stroking the cat, Mrs. Yancy said, "What she should have told the people in St. Helena was that the Gunther baby was about to arrive, that it hadn't been born yet, but that she was going to San Francisco to be with Mary. That way she wouldn't have been committed to the story that there was *one* baby. But she didn't think of that. She didn't realize what might happen. She told everyone that it was just *one* baby, already in hand. Then she came to my place and gave birth to twins."

Hilary said, "Twins?"

"Damn," Tony said.

The surprise brought Joshua to his feet.

The white cat sensed the tension. It lifted its head out of Rita Yancy's lap and peered curiously at each person in the parlor, one after the other. Its yellow eyes appeared to shine with inner light.

•

The attic bedroom was large, but not nearly large enough to keep Bruno from feeling that it was gradually closing in on him. He looked for things to do because idleness made his claustrophobia worse.

He got bored with the dumbbells even before his massive arms began to ache from the exercise.

He took a book from one of the shelves and tried to read, but he wasn't able to concentrate.

His mind still hadn't settled down; it flitted from one thought to another, like a quietly desperate jeweler looking for a misplaced bag of diamonds.

He talked to his dead self.

He searched the dusty corners for spiders and squashed them.

He sang to himself.

He laughed at times without really knowing what had struck him funny.

He wept, too.

He cursed Katherine.

He made plans.

He paced, paced, paced.

He was eager to leave the house and begin searching for Hilary-Katherine, but he knew he would be a fool if he went out in daylight. He was certain that Katherine's conspirators were everywhere in St. Helena. Her friends from the grave. Other walking dead, men and women from the Other Side, hiding in new bodies. All of them would be on the lookout for him. Yes. Yes. Maybe dozens of them. He would be too conspicuous during the day. He would have to wait until sunset before he went looking for the bitch. Although night was the favorite time of the day for the undead, the time when they prowled in especially large numbers, and although he would be in terrible danger while he stalked Hilary-Katherine in the night, he would also benefit from the darkness. A night-shadow would hide him from the walking dead every bit as well as it would conceal them from him. With the scales thus balanced, the success of the hunt would depend only on who was smarter—he or Katherine—and if that was the only criterion, he might have a better than even chance of winning; for Katherine was clever and infinitely wicked and cunning, but she was not as smart as he was.

He believed that he would be safe if he stayed in the house during the day, and that was ironic, really, because he hadn't felt safe for one minute during the thirty-five years he'd lived there with Katherine. Now the house was a reliable haven because it was the last place Katherine or her conspirators would look for him. She wanted to catch him and bring him to this very place. He knew that. He knew it! She had come back from the grave for only one reason: to bring him to the top of the cliff, around the house, to the doors in the ground at the end of the rear lawn. She wanted to put him in that hole in the ground, lock him in there forever. That's what she had told him she would do if she ever had to come back to punish him. He had not forgotten. And now she would expect him to avoid the top of the cliff and the old house at all costs. She would never think to look for him in his long-abandoned attic bedroom, not in a million years.

He was so pleased with his excellent strategy that he laughed aloud.

But then he had a horrible thought. If she *did* think to look for him here, and if she came with a few of her friends, others of the living dead, enough of them to overpower him, then they wouldn't have far to drag him. The doors in the ground were right behind the house. If Katherine and her hellish friends caught him here, they would be able to carry him to those doors and throw him into that dark room, into the whispers, in little more than a minute.

Frightened, he ran back to the bed and sat down beside himself and tried to get himself to reassure him that everything would be all right.

•

Joshua couldn't sit still. He walked back and forth on one of the flowered runners in Mrs. Yancy's parlor.

The old woman said, "When Katherine gave birth to twins, she realized that the elaborate lie about Mary Gunther would no longer hold up. The people in St. Helena had been prepared for *one* child. No matter how she explained the second baby, she'd plant suspicion. The idea that everyone she knew would find out what she'd been doing with her own father. . . . Well, I guess it was too much for her on top of everything else that had happened in her life. She just snapped. For three days, she carried on like someone in a fever delirium, gabbling like a madwoman. The doctor gave her sedatives, but they didn't always work. She ranted and raved and babbled. I thought I'd have to call the cops and let them put her away in a little padded room. But I didn't want to do that. I sure as hell didn't."

"But she needed psychiatric help," Hilary said. "Just letting her scream and carry on for three days—that wasn't good. That wasn't good at all."

"Maybe not," Mrs. Yancy said. "But I couldn't do anything else. I mean, when you're running a fancy bordello, you don't want to see the cops except when you pass out their payoff money. They usually don't bother a classy operation like the one I had going. After all, some of my clients were influential politicians and wealthy businessmen, and the cops didn't want to embarrass any big shots in a raid. But if I sent Katherine off to a hospital, I knew damned well the newspapers would pick up on the story, and then the cops would *have* to shut me down. They couldn't just let me go on doing business after I'd gotten all that publicity. No way. Absolutely impossible. I'd have lost everything. And my doctor was worried that his career would be ruined if his regular patients found out he was secretly treating prostitutes. These days it wouldn't damage a doctor's practice even if everyone knew he gave vasectomies to alligators with the same instruments he used in his office. But in 1940, people were more . . . squeamish. So you see, I had to think about myself, and I had to protect my doctor, my girls . . ."

Joshua walked up to the old woman's chair. He looked down at her, taking in the plain dress and the apron and the dark brown support stockings and the stodgy black shoes and the silky white cat, trying to see through the grandmotherly image to the real woman underneath. "When you accepted Katherine's three thousand dollars, didn't you also take on certain responsibilities for her?"

"I didn't *ask* her to come to my place to have her baby," Mrs. Yancy said. "My business was worth a whole lot more than three thousand dollars. I wasn't going to throw it all away just for principle. Is that what you think I should have done?" She shook her gray head in disbelief. "If that's what you really think I should have done, then you're living in a dream world, my dear sir."

Joshua stared down at the woman, unable to speak for fear he would scream at her. He didn't want to be thrown out of her house until he was certain she had told him absolutely everything she knew about Katherine Anne Frye's pregnancy and about the twins. *Twins!*

Tony said, "Look, Mrs. Yancy, shortly after you took Katherine in, when you discovered that she had wrapped herself up in girdles, you knew she was likely to lose the baby. You admit the doctor told you that might happen."

"Yes."

"He told you Katherine might die, too."

"So?"

"A child's death or the death of a pregnant woman in labor—something like that would have closed up your place every bit as fast as having to call in the cops to deal with a woman who was suffering a nervous breakdown. Yet you didn't turn Katherine away when there was still time to do that. Even after you knew it was a risky proposition, you kept her three thousand dollars, and you allowed her to stay. Now surely you realized that if someone died, you'd have to report it to the police and risk getting shut down."

"No problem," Mrs. Yancy said. "If the babies had died, we'd have taken them away in a suitcase. We'd have buried them quietly in the hills up in Marin County. Or maybe we'd have weighted the suitcase and dropped it off the Golden Gate Bridge."

Joshua had an almost irresistible urge to grab the old woman by her bun of gray hair and yank her out of her chair, jerk her out of her smug complacency. Instead, he turned away and took a deep breath and began to pace along the flower-patterned runner once more, glowering at the floor.

"And what about Katherine?" Hilary asked Rita Yancy. "What would you have done if *she* had died?"

"The same as I'd done if the twins had been born dead," Mrs. Yancy said blithely. "Except, of course, we wouldn't have been able to fit Katherine into a suitcase."

Joshua stopped at the far end of the runner and looked back at the woman, aghast. She wasn't trying to be funny. She was utterly unaware of the gruesome humor in that gross remark; she was merely stating a fact.

"If anything had gone wrong, we'd have dumped the body," Mrs. Yancy said, still answering Hilary's question. "And we'd have handled it so that no one would have known that Katherine had ever come to my place. Now don't you look so shocked and disapproving, young lady. I'm no killer. We're talking about what I'd have done—what any sensible person in my position would have done—if she or the baby had died a natural death. *Natural* death. For heaven's sake, if I were a killer, I'd have done away with poor Katherine when she was out of her head, when I didn't know if she'd ever recover. She was a threat to me then. I didn't know whether or not she was going to cost me my house, my business, everything. But I didn't strangle her, you know. My goodness, such a thought never crossed my mind! I nursed the poor girl through her fits. I nursed her out of her hysteria, and then everything was all right."

Tony said, "You told us Katherine ranted and raved and babbled. That sounds as if—"

"Only for three days," Mrs. Yancy said. "We even had to tie her down to the bed to keep her from hurting herself. But she was only sick for three days. So maybe it wasn't a nervous breakdown. Just a sort of temporary collapse. Because after three days she was as good as new."

"The twins," Joshua said. "Let's get back to the twins. That's what we really want to know about."

"I think I've told you just about everything," Mrs. Yancy said.

"Were they identical twins?" Joshua asked.

"How can you tell when they're just born? They're all wrinkled and red. There's no way to tell that early if they're fraternal or identical."

"Couldn't the doctor have run a test—"

"We were in a first-class bordello, Mr. Rhinehart, not a hospital." She chucked the white cat under the chin, and it playfully waved a paw at her. "The doctor didn't have the time or the facilities for what you're suggesting. Besides, why should we have cared whether the boys were identical or not?"

Hilary said, "Katherine named one of them Bruno."

"Yes," Mrs. Yancy said. "I found that out when he started sending me checks after Katherine's death."

"What did she call the other boy?"

"I haven't the foggiest. By the time she left my place, she hadn't given names to either of them yet."

"But weren't their names on their birth certificates?" Tony asked.

"There weren't any certificates," Mrs. Yancy said.

"How could that be?"

"The births weren't recorded."

"But the law—"

"Katherine insisted that the births not be recorded. She was paying good money for what she wanted, and we made sure she got it."

"And the doctor went along with this?" Tony asked.

"He got a thousand bucks for delivering the twins and for keeping his mouth shut," the old woman said. "A thousand was worth several times more in those days than it is now. He was well paid for bending a few rules."

"Were both of the babies healthy?" Joshua asked.

"They were thin," Mrs. Yancy said. "Scrawny as hell. Two pathetic little things. Probably because Katherine had been on a diet for months.

And because of the girdles. But they could cry just as good and loud as any other babies. And there wasn't a thing wrong with their appetites. They seemed healthy enough, just small."

"How long did Katherine stay at your place?" Hilary asked.

"Almost two weeks. She needed that long to get her strength back after such a hard delivery. And the babies needed time to put a little flesh on their bones."

"When she left, did she take both children with her?"

"Of course. I wasn't running a nursery. I was glad to see her leave."

"Did you know that she was going to take only one of the twins to St. Helena?" Hilary asked.

"I understood that to be her intention, yes."

"Did she say what she was going to do with the other boy?" Joshua asked, taking over the questioning from Hilary.

"I believe she intended to put it up for adoption," Mrs. Yancy said.

"You *believe?*" Joshua asked exasperatedly. "Weren't you even the least bit concerned about what might happen to those two helpless babies in the hands of a woman who was obviously mentally unbalanced?"

"She had recovered."

"Baloney."

"I tell you, if you'd met her on the street, you wouldn't have thought she had any problems."

"But for God's sake, underneath that facade—"

"She was their mother," Mrs. Yancy said primly. "She wouldn't have done them any harm."

"You couldn't have been sure of that," Joshua said.

"I certainly *was* sure of it," Mrs. Yancy declared. "I've always had the highest respect for motherhood and a mother's love. A mother's love can work wonders."

Again, Joshua had to restrain himself from reaching for the bun of hair on top of her head.

Tony said, "Katherine couldn't have put the baby up for adoption. Not without a birth certificate to prove that it was hers."

"Which leaves us with a number of unpleasant possibilities to consider," Joshua said.

"Honestly, you people amaze me," Mrs. Yancy said, shaking her head and scratching her cat. "You always want to believe the worst. I've never seen three bigger pessimists. Did you ever stop to think she might have left the little boy on a doorstep? She probably abandoned him at an orphanage or maybe a church, some place where he would be found right away and given proper care. I imagine he was adopted by an upstanding young couple, raised in an excellent home, given lots of love, a good education, all sorts of advantages."

•

In the attic, waiting for nightfall, bored, nervous, lonely, apprehensive, sometimes stuporous, more often frenetic, Bruno Frye spent much of Thursday afternoon talking to his dead self. He hoped to soothe his roiling mind and regain a sense of purpose, but he made little or no progress along those lines. He decided that he would be calmer, happier, and less lonely if he could at least look into his other self's eyes, like in the old days, when they had often sat and stared longingly into each other for an hour or more at a time, communicating so much without benefit of words, sharing, being one, just one together. He recalled that moment in Sally's bathroom, only yesterday, when he had stopped in front of a mirror and had mistaken his reflection for his other self. Looking into eyes that he had thought were the eyes of his other self, he had felt wonderful, blissful, at peace. Now he desperately wanted to recapture that state of mind. And how much better to look into the *real* eyes of his other self, even if they were flat and sightless now. But himself lay on the bed, eyes firmly closed. Bruno touched the eyes of the other Bruno, the dead one, and they were cold orbs; the lids would not lift under his gently prodding fingertips. He explored the curves of those shuttered eyes, and he felt hidden sutures at the corners, tiny knots of thread holding the lids down. Excited by the prospect of seeing the other's eyes again, Bruno got up and hurried downstairs, looking for razor blades and delicate cuticle scissors and needles and a crocheting hook and other makeshift surgical instruments that might be of use in the reopening of the other Bruno's eyes.

•

If Rita Yancy had any more information about the Frye twins, neither Hilary nor Joshua would get it out of her. Tony could see that much even if Hilary and Joshua could not. Any second now, one of them was going to say something so sharp, so angry, so biting and bitter, that the old woman would take offense and order all of them out of the house.

Tony was aware that Hilary was deeply shaken by the similarities between her own childhood ordeal and Katherine's agony. She was bristling at all three of Rita Yancy's attitudes—the bursts of phony moralizing, the brief moments of equally unfelt and syrupy sentimentality, and the far more genuine and constant and stunning callousness.

Joshua was suffering from a loss of self-esteem because he had worked for Katherine for twenty-five years without spotting the quiet madness that surely must have been bubbling just below her carefully-controlled surface placidity. He was disgusted with himself; therefore, he was even more irritable than usual. And because Mrs. Yancy was, even in ordinary circumstances, the kind of person Joshua despised, the attorney's patience with her could fit into a thimble with room left over for one of Charo's stage costumes plus the collected wisdom of the last four U.S. Presidents.

Tony got up from the sofa and went to the footstool that was in front of Rita Yancy's chair. He sat down, explaining his move by pretending that he just wanted to pet the cat; but in switching seats, he was placing himself between the old woman and Hilary, and he was effectively blocking Joshua, who looked as if he might seize Mrs. Yancy and shake her. The footstool was a good position from which to continue the interrogation in a casual fashion. As Tony stroked the white cat, he kept up a constant stream of chatter with the woman, ingratiating himself with her, charming her, using the old Clemenza soft-sell which always had done well for him in his police work.

Eventually, he asked her if there had been anything unusual about the birth of the twins.

"Unusual?" Mrs. Yancy asked, perplexed. "Don't you think the whole damned thing was unusual?"

"You're right," he said. "I didn't put my question very well. What I meant to ask was whether there was anything peculiar about the birth itself, anything odd about her labor pains or her contractions, anything remarkable about the initial state of the babies when they came out of her, any abnormality, any strangeness."

He saw the surprise enter her eyes as his question tripped a switch in her memory.

"In fact," she said, "there *was* something unusual."

"Let me guess," he said. "Both of the babies were born with cauls."

"That's right! How did you know?"

"Just a lucky guess."

"The hell it was." She wagged a finger at him. "You're smarter than you pretend to be."

He forced himself to smile at her. He had to force it, for there was nothing about Rita Yancy that could elicit a genuine smile from him.

"Both of them were born with cauls," she said. "Their little heads were almost entirely covered. The doctor had seen and dealt with that sort of thing before, of course. But he thought the chances of both twins having cauls was something like a million to one."

"Was Katherine aware of this?"

"Aware of the cauls? Not at the time. She was delirious with pain. And then for three days she was completely out of her mind."

"But later?"

"I'm sure she was told about it," Mrs. Yancy said. "It's not the sort of thing you forget to tell a mother. In fact . . . I remember telling her myself. Yes. Yes, I do. I recall it very clearly now. She was fascinated. You know, some people think that a child born with a caul has the gift of second sight."

"Is that what Katherine believed?"

Rita Yancy frowned. "No. She said it was a bad sign, not a good one. Leo had been interested in the supernatural, and Katherine had read a few books in his occult collection. In one of those books, it said that when twins were born with cauls, that was . . . I can't recall exactly what she said it meant, but it wasn't good. An evil omen or something."

"The mark of the demon?" Tony asked.

"Yes! That's it!"

"So she believed that her babies were marked by a demon, their souls already damned?"

"I'd almost forgotten about that," Mrs. Yancy said.

She stared beyond Tony, not seeing anything in the parlor, looking into the past, striving to remember. . . .

Hilary and Joshua stayed back, out of the way, silent; and Tony was relieved that they recognized his authority.

Eventually, Mrs. Yancy said, "After Katherine told me about it being the mark of a demon, she just clammed up. She didn't want to talk any more. For a couple of days, she was as quiet as a mouse. She stayed in bed, staring at the ceiling, hardly moving at all. She looked like she was thinking real hard about something. Then suddenly, she started acting so damned weird that I had to start wondering if I still might have to send her away to the booby hatch."

"Was she ranting and raving and violent like before?" Tony asked.

"No, no. It was all talk this time. Very wild, intense, crazy talk. She told me that the twins were the children of a demon. She said she'd been raped by a thing from hell, a green and scaly thing with huge eyes and a forked tongue and long claws. She said it had come from hell to force her to carry its children. Crazy, huh? She swore up and down that it was true. She even described this demon. A damned good description, too. Full of detail, very well done. And when she told me about how it raped her, she managed to give me the chills, even though I knew it was all a bunch of crap. The story was colorful, very imaginative. At first, I thought it was a joke, something she was doing just for laughs, except she wasn't laughing, and I couldn't see anything funny in it. I reminded her that she'd told me all about Leo, and she screamed at me. Did she scream! I thought the windows would break. She denied ever having said such things. She pretended to be insulted. She was so angry with me for suggesting incest, so self-righteous, a regular little prig, so de-termined to make me apologize—well, I couldn't help laughing at her. And that made her even angrier. She kept saying it hadn't been Leo, though we both knew damned well it had. She did everything she could to make me believe it was a demon that had fathered the twins. And I tell you, her act was *good!* I didn't believe it for a minute, of course. All that silly stuff about a creature from hell sticking his thing in her. What a bunch of hogwash. But I started to wonder if maybe she had con-vinced herself. She sure looked convinced. She was so fanatical about it. She said she was afraid that she and her babies would be burned alive if any religious people found out that she'd consorted with a demon. She begged me to help her keep the secret. She didn't want me to tell any-one about the two cauls. Then she said she knew that both twins car-ried the mark of the demon between their legs. She pleaded with me to keep that a secret, too."

"Between their legs?" Tony asked.

"Oh, she was carrying on like a full-fledged looney," Rita Yancy said. "She insisted that both of her babies had their father's sex organs. She said they weren't human between the legs, and she said she knew I'd noticed that, and she begged me not to tell anyone about it. Well, that was purely ridiculous. Both those little boys had perfectly ordinary pee-pees. But Katherine jabbered on and on about demons for almost two days. Some-times she seemed truly hysterical. She wanted to know how much money I'd take to keep the secret about the demon. I told her I wouldn't take a penny for that, but I said I'd settle for five hundred a month to keep mum about Leo and all the rest of it, the rest of the *real* story. That calmed her down a little, but she still had this demon thing stuck in her head. I was just about decided that she really believed what she was saying, and I was going to call my doctor and have him examine her—and then she shut up about it. She seemed to regain her senses. Or she got tired of her joke, I guess. Anyway, she didn't say one more word about demons. She behaved herself from then on until she took her babies and left a week or so later."

Tony thought about what Mrs. Yancy had told him.

Like a witch cuddling a feline familiar, the old woman petted the white cat.

"What if," Tony said. "What if, what if, what if?"

"What if what?" Hilary asked.

"I don't know," he said. "Pieces seem to be falling into place . . . but it looks . . . so wild. Maybe I'm putting the puzzle together all wrong. I've got to think about it. I'm just not sure yet."

"Well, do you have any more questions for me?" Mrs. Yancy asked.

"No," Tony said, getting up from the footstool. "I can't think of anything else."

"I believe we've gotten what we came for," Joshua agreed.

"More than we bargained for," Hilary said.

Mrs. Yancy lifted the cat off her lap, put it on the floor, and rose from her chair. "I've wasted too much time on this silly damned thing. I should be in the kitchen. I've got work to do. I made four pie shells this morning. Now I've got to mix up the fillings and get everything in the oven. I've got grandchildren coming for dinner, and each one of them has a different kind of favorite pie. Sometimes the little dears can be a tribulation. But on the other hand, I'd sure be lost without them."

The cat leapt abruptly over the footstool, darted along the flowered runner, past Joshua, and under a corner table.

Precisely when the animal stopped moving, the house shook. Two miniature glass swans toppled off a shelf, bounced without breaking on the thick carpet. Two embroidered wall hangings fell down. Windows rattled.

"Quake," Mrs. Yancy said.

The floor rolled like the deck of a ship in mild seas.

"Nothing to worry about," Mrs. Yancy said.

The movement decreased.

The rumbling, discontented earth grew quiet.

The house was still again.

"See?" Mrs. Yancy said. "It's over now."

But Tony sensed other oncoming shockwaves—although none of them had anything to do with earthquakes.

•

Bruno finally opened the dead eyes of his other self, and at first he was upset by what he found. They weren't the clear, electrifying, blue-gray eyes that he had known and loved. These were the eyes of a monster. They appeared to be swollen, rotten-soft and protuberant. The whites were stained brown-red by half-dried, scummy blood from burst vessels. The irises were cloudy, muddy, less blue than they had been in life, now more the color of an ugly bruise, dark and wounded.

However, the longer Bruno stared into them the less hideous those damaged eyes became. They were, after all, still the eyes of his other self, still part of himself, still eyes that he knew better than any other eyes, still eyes that he loved and trusted, eyes that loved and trusted him. He tried not to look *at* them but *into* them, deep down beyond the surface ruin, way down in, where (many times in the past) he had made the blazing, thrilling connection with the other half of his soul. He felt none of the old magic now, for the other Bruno's eyes were not looking back at him. Nevertheless, the very act of peering deeply into the other's dead eyes somehow revitalized his memories of what total unity with his other self had been like; he remembered the pure, sweet pleasure and fulfillment of being with himself, just he and himself against the world, with no fear of being alone.

He clung to that memory, for memory was now all that he had left.

He sat on the bed for a long time, staring down into the eyes of the corpse.

•

Joshua Rhinehart's Cessna Turbo Skylane RG roared north, slicing across the eastward-flowing air front, heading for Napa.

Hilary looked down at the scattered clouds below and at the sere autumn hills that lay a few thousand feet below the clouds. Overhead, there was nothing but crystal-blue sky and the distant, stratospheric vapor trail of a military jet.

Far off in the west, a dense bank of blue-gray-black clouds stretched out of sight to the north and the south. The massive thunderheads were rolling in like giant ships from the sea. By nightfall, Napa Valley—in fact, the entire northern third of the state from the Monterey Peninsula to the Oregon border—would lay under threatening skies again.

During the first ten minutes after takeoff, Hilary and Tony and Joshua were silent. Each was preoccupied with his own bleak thoughts—and fears.

Then Joshua said, "The twin has to be the dead ringer we're looking for."

"Obviously," Tony said.

"So Katherine didn't try to solve her problem by killing off the extra baby," Joshua said.

"Evidently not," Tony said.

"But which one did *I* kill?" Hilary asked. "Bruno or his brother?"

"We'll have the body exhumed and see what we can learn from it," Joshua said.

The plane hit an air pocket. It dropped more than two hundred feet in a roller coaster swoop, then soared up to its proper altitude.

When her stomach crawled back into its familiar niche, Hilary said, "All right, let's talk this thing out and see if we can come up with any answers. We're all sitting here chewing on the same question anyway. If Katherine didn't kill Bruno's twin brother in order to keep the Mary Gunther lie afloat, then what *did* she do with him? Where the devil has he been all these years?"

"Well, there's always Mrs. Rita Yancy's pet theory," Joshua said, managing to pronounce her name in such a way as to make it clear that even the need to refer to her in passing distressed him and left a bad taste in his mouth. "Perhaps Katherine did leave one of the twins bundled up on the doorstep of a church or an orphanage."

"I don't know. . . ." Hilary said doubtfully. "I don't like it, but I don't exactly know why. It's just too . . . clichéd . . . too trite . . . too romantic. Damn. None of those is the word I want. I can't think how to say it. I just sense that Katherine would not have handled it like that. It's too . . ."

"Too smooth," Tony said. "Just like the story about Mary Gunther was too smooth to please me. Abandoning one of the twins like that would have been the quickest, easiest, simplest, safest—although not the most moral—way for her to solve her problem. But people almost never do anything the quickest, easiest, simplest, and safest way. Especially not when they're under the kind of stress that Katherine was under when she left Rita Yancy's whorehouse."

"Still," Joshua said, "we can't rule it out altogether."

"I think we can," Tony said. "Because if you accept that the brother was abandoned and then adopted by strangers, you've got to explain how he and Bruno got back together again. Since the brother was an unregistered birth, there'd be no way he could trace his blood parentage. The only way he could hook up with Bruno would be by coincidence. Even if you're willing to accept that coincidence, you've still got to explain how the brother could have been raised in another home, in an altogether different environment from Bruno's, without ever knowing Katherine—and yet have such a fierce hatred for the woman, such an overwhelming fear of her."

"That's not easy," Joshua admitted.

"You've got to explain why and how the brother developed a psychopathic personality and paranoid delusions that perfectly match Bruno's in every detail," Tony said.

The Cessna droned northward.

Wind buffeted the small craft.

For a minute, the three of them sat in silence, within the expensive, single-engine, overhead-wing, two-hundred-mile-per-hour, sixteen-mile-per-gallon, white and red and mustard-yellow, airborne cocoon.

Then Joshua said, "You win. I can't explain it. I can't see how the brother could have been raised entirely apart from Bruno yet wind up with the same psychosis. Genetics don't explain it, that's for sure."

"So what are you saying?" Hilary asked Tony. "That Bruno and his brother weren't separated after all?"

"She took them both home to St. Helena," Tony said.

"But where was the other twin all those years?" Joshua asked. "Locked away in a closet or something?"

"No," Tony said. "You probably met him many times."

"What? Me? No. Never. Just Bruno."

"What if. . . . What if both of them were living as Bruno? What if they . . . took turns?"

Joshua looked away from the open sky ahead, stared at Tony, blinked. "Are you trying to tell me they played some sort of childish game for forty years?" he asked skeptically.

"Not a game," Tony said. "At least it wouldn't have been a game to them. They would have thought of it as a desperate, dangerous necessity."

"You've lost me," Joshua said.

To Tony, Hilary said, "I knew you were working on an idea when you started asking Mrs. Yancy about the babies having cauls and about how Katherine reacted to that."

"Yes," Tony said. "Katherine carrying on about a demon—that bit of news gave me a big piece of the puzzle."

"For God's sake," Joshua said impatiently, gruffly, "stop being so damned mysterious. Put it together for Hilary and me in a way we can understand."

"Sorry. I was more or less still thinking aloud." Tony shifted in his seat. "Okay, look. This will take a while. I'll have to go back to the beginning. . . . To understand what I'm going to say about Bruno, you have to understand Katherine, or at least understand the way I see her. What I'm theorizing is . . . a family in which madness has been . . . sort of handed down like a legacy for at least three generations. The insanity steadily grows bigger and bigger, like a trust fund earning interest." Tony shifted in his seat again. "Let's start with Leo. An extreme authoritarian type. To be happy he needed to totally control other people. That was one of the reasons he did so well in business, but it was also the reason he didn't have many friends. He knew how to get his way every time, and he never gave an inch. A lot of aggressive men like Leo have a different approach to sex from the one they have toward everything else; they like to be relieved of all responsibility when they're in bed; they like to be ordered around and dominated for a change—but only in bed. Not Leo. Not even in bed. He insisted on being the dominant one even in his sex life. He enjoyed hurting and humiliating women, calling them names, forcing them to do unpleasant things, being a little rough, a little sadistic. We know that from Mrs. Yancy."

"It's a hell of a big step from paying prostitutes so they'll satisfy some perverse desire—to molesting your own child," Joshua said.

"But we know he did molest Katherine repeatedly, over many years," Tony said. "So it mustn't have been a big step in Leo's eyes. He probably would have said that his abuse of Mrs. Yancy's girls was all right because he was paying them and therefore owned them, at least for a while. He would have been a man with a strong sense of property rights—and with an extremely liberal definition of the word 'property.' He'd have used that argument, that same point of view, to justify what he did to Katherine. A man like that thinks of a child as just another of his possessions—'*my* child' instead of 'my *child*.' To him, Katherine was a thing, an object, wasted if not used."

"I'm glad I never met the son of a bitch," Joshua said. "If I'd ever shaken hands with him, I think I'd still feel dirty."

"My point," Tony said, "is that Katherine, as a child, was trapped in a house, in a brutalizing relationship, with a man who was capable of *anything*, and there was virtually no chance that she could maintain a firm grip on her sanity under those awful conditions. Leo was a very cold fish, a loner's loner, more than a little bit selfish, with a very strong and very twisted sex drive. It's possible, even likely, that he wasn't just emotionally disturbed. He might have been all the way gone, over the edge, psychotic, detached from reality but able to conceal his detachment. There's a kind of psychopath who has iron control over his delusions, the ability to channel a lot of his lunatic energy into socially-acceptable pursuits, the ability to pass for normal. That kind of psycho vents his madness in one narrow, generally private, area. In Leo's case, he let off a little steam with prostitutes—and a lot of it with Katherine. We've got to figure that he didn't merely abuse her physically. His desire went beyond sex. He lusted after *absolute* control. Once he'd broken her physically, he wouldn't have been satisfied until he'd broken her emotionally, spiritually, and then mentally. By the time Katherine arrived at Mrs. Yancy's place to have her father's baby, she was every bit as mad as Leo had been. But she apparently also had acquired his control, his ability to pass among normal people. She lost that control for three days when the twins arrived, but then she pulled herself together again."

"She lost control a second time," Hilary said as the plane bobbled through a patch of turbulent air.

"Yeah," Joshua said. "When she told Mrs. Yancy that she'd been raped by a demon."

"If my theory's correct," Tony said, "Katherine was going through incredible changes after the birth of the twins. She was moving from one severe psychotic state to an even *more* severe psychotic state. A new set of delusions was pushing out the old set. She had been able to maintain a surface calm in spite of her father's sexual abuse, in spite of the emotional and physical torture he put her through, in spite of becoming pregnant with his child, and even in spite of the agony of being girdled in day and night during all those months when nature was insisting that she grow. Somehow she maintained an air of normalcy through all of that. But when the twins were born, when she realized her story about Mary Gunther's baby had come crashing down around her, that was too much to bear. She flipped out—until she conceived the notion that she'd been raped by a demon. We know from Mrs. Yancy that Leo was interested in the occult. Katherine had read some of Leo's books. Somewhere she had picked up the fact that some people believe twins born with cauls are marked by a demon. Because her twins were born with cauls . . . well, she began to fantasize. And the idea that she had been the innocent victim of a demonic creature that had forced itself on her—well, that was very appealing. It exonerated her of the shame and guilt of bearing her own father's babies. It was still something she had to hide from the world, but it wasn't something she had to hide from herself. It wasn't something shameful for which she had to make constant excuses to herself. No one could expect an ordinary woman to resist a demon that had supernatural strength. If she could make herself believe that she'd really been raped by a monster, then she could start thinking of herself as nothing worse than an unfortunate, innocent victim."

"But that's what she was anyway," Hilary said. "She was her father's victim. He forced himself on her, not the other way around."

"True," Tony said. "But he had probably spent a lot of time and energy brainwashing her, trying to make her think she was the one at fault, the one responsible for their twisted relationship. Transferring the guilt to the daughter—that's a fairly common way for a sick man to escape his own sense of guilt. And that sort of behavior would fit Leo's authoritarian personality."

"All right," Joshua said as they fled northward into the yielding sky. "I'll go along with what you've said so far. It may not be right, but it makes sense, and that's a welcome change in the situation. So Katherine gave birth to twins, lost herself for three days, and then got control again by resorting to a new fantasy, a new delusion. By believing that a demon had raped her, she was able to forget that her father was the one who had actually done it. She was able to forget about the incest and regain some of her self-respect. In fact, she probably hadn't ever felt better about herself in her whole life."

"Exactly," Tony said.

Hilary said, "Mrs. Yancy was the only person she'd ever told about the incest, so when she settled into the new fantasy about a demon, she was eager to let Mrs. Yancy know the 'truth.' She was worried that Mrs. Yancy thought of her as a terrible person, a wicked sinner, and she wanted Mrs. Yancy to know that she was only the victim of some irresistible supernatural *thing*. That's why she babbled on about it for so long."

"But when Mrs. Yancy didn't believe her," Tony said, "she decided to keep it to herself. She figured no one else would believe her, either. But that didn't matter to her because she was positive, in her own mind, that she knew the truth, and that truth was the demon. That was a much easier secret to keep than the other one, the one about Leo."

"And Leo had died a few weeks earlier," Hilary said, "so he wasn't around to remind her of what she had forgotten."

Joshua took his hands off the airplane controls for a moment, wiped them on his shirt. "I thought I was too damned old and too cynical to respond to a horror story any more. But this one makes my palms sweat. There's a terrible correlation to what Hilary just said. Leo wasn't around to remind her—but she needed to keep both of the twins around to reinforce the new delusion. They were the living proof of it, and she couldn't put either of them up for adoption."

"That's right," Tony said. "Having them with her helped her maintain the fantasy. When she looked at those two perfectly healthy, unquestionably human babies, she really *did* see something different about their sex organs, like she told Mrs. Yancy. She saw it in her mind, imagined it, saw something that was proof, to her, that they were the children of a demon. The twins were part of her comfortable new delusion—and I say 'comfortable' only in comparison to the nightmares with which she had lived before."

Hilary's mind was racing faster than the airplane engine. She grew excited as she saw where Tony's speculations were leading. She said, "So Katherine took the twins home, to that clifftop house, but she still had to keep the Mary Gunther lie in the air, didn't she? Sure. For one thing, she wanted to protect her reputation. But there was another reason, much more important than just her good name. A psychosis is rooted in the subconscious mind, but, as I understand it, the fantasies a psychotic uses to cope with his inner turmoil are more the product of the conscious mind. So . . . while Katherine believed in the demon on a conscious level . . . at the same time, deep down, subconsciously, she knew that if she went back to St. Helena with twins and let the Mary Gunther story collapse, her neighbors would eventually realize that Leo was the father. If she had to deal with that disgrace, she wouldn't have been able to support the demon fantasy that her conscious mind had fabricated. Her new, more comfortable delusions would be replaced by the old, hard, sharp-edged ones. So to maintain the demon fantasy in her own mind, she had to present only one child to the public. So she gave the two boys just one name. She allowed only one of them to go out in public at any one time. She forced them to live one life."

"And eventually," Tony said, "the two boys actually came to think of themselves as one and the same person."

"Hold it, hold it," Joshua said. "Maybe they were able to double for each other and live under only one name, one identity, in public. Even that's asking me to believe a lot, but I'll try. But for sure, in private they still would have been two distinct individuals."

"Maybe not," Tony said. "We've come across proof that they thought of themselves as . . . sort of one person in two bodies."

"Proof? What proof?" Joshua demanded.

"The letter you found in the safe-deposit box in that San Francisco bank. In it, Bruno wrote that *he* had been killed in Los Angeles. He didn't say his brother had been killed. He said he, himself, was dead."

"You can't prove anything by that letter," Joshua said. "It was all mumbo-jumbo. It didn't make any sense."

"In a way it *does* make sense," Tony said. "It makes sense from Bruno's point of view—*if* he didn't think of his brother as another human being. If he thought of his twin as part of himself, as just an extension of himself, and not as a separate person at all, then the letter makes a lot of sense."

Joshua shook his head. "But I still don't see how two people could possibly ever be made to believe they were only one person."

"You're accustomed to hearing about split personalities," Tony said. "Dr. Jekyll and Mr. Hyde. The woman whose true story was told in *The Three Faces of Eve*. And there was a book about another woman like that. It was a best-seller several years ago. *Sybil*. Sybil had sixteen distinct, separate personalities. Well, if I'm right about what became of the Frye twins, then they developed a psychosis that's just the reverse of split personality. These two people didn't split into four or six or eight or eighty; instead, under tremendous pressure from their mother, they . . . melted together psychologically, melted into one. Two individuals with one personality, one self-awareness, one self-image, all shared. It's probably never happened before and might never happen again, but that doesn't mean it can't have happened here."

"The two would have found it virtually essential to develop identical personalities in order to take turns living in the world beyond their mother's house," Hilary said. "Even small differences between them would ruin the charade."

"But *how?*" Joshua demanded. "What did Katherine do to them? How did she make it happen to them?"

"We'll probably never know for certain," Hilary said. "But I've got a few ideas about what she might have done."

"So do I," Tony said. "But you go first."

•

By mid-afternoon, the amount of light coming through the east-facing attic windows grew steadily less. The quality of the light began to decrease as well; it no longer radiated out from the shaft form that the shape of the window imparted to it. Darkness slowly claimed the corners of the room.

As shadows crept across the floor, Bruno began to worry about being caught in the dark. He couldn't simply snap on a lamp because the lamps weren't in working order. There hadn't been any electric service to the house for five years, since his mother's first death. His flashlight was useless; the batteries were drained.

For a while, as he watched the room sink into purple-gray gloom, Bruno fought panic. He didn't mind being outdoors in the dark, for there was almost always some light spilling from houses, streetlamps, light from passing cars, the stars, the moon. But in a totally lightless room, the whispers and the crawling things returned, and that was a double plague he must prevent somehow.

Candles.

His mother had always kept a couple of boxes of tall candles in the pantry, off the kitchen. They were for use in the event of a power failure. He was pretty sure there would also be matches in the pantry, a hundred or more of them in a round tin with a tight-fitting lid. He hadn't touched any of those things when he had moved out; he had taken nothing but a few personal possessions and some of the collections of artwork that he had acquired himself.

He leaned over to peer into the face of the other Bruno, and he said, "I'm going downstairs for a minute."

The cloudy, blood-muddied eyes stared up at him.

"I won't be gone long," Bruno said.

Himself said nothing.

"I'm going to get some candles so I won't be caught in the dark," Bruno said. "Will I be all right alone here for a few minutes while I'm gone?"

His other self was silent.

Bruno went to the set of steps in one corner of the room. They led down into a second-floor bedroom. The stairwell was not totally dark, for some light from the attic window fell into it. But when Bruno pushed open the door at the bottom, he was shocked to find that the bedroom below was black.

The shutters.

He had opened the shutters in the attic when he'd awakened in the dark this morning, but the windows were still sealed elsewhere in the house. He hadn't dared open them. It wasn't likely that Hilary-Katherine's spies would look up and notice just one pair of opened attic shutters; but if he were to let light into the entire house, they would certainly spot the change and come running. Now the place was like a sepulcher, shrouded in eternal night.

He stood in the stairwell and peered into the lightless bedroom, afraid to advance, listening for whispers.

Not a sound.

No movement either.

He thought of going back to the attic. But that was no solution to his problem. In a few hours, night would have come, and he would be without a protective light. He *must* forge on to the pantry and find those candles.

Reluctantly, he moved into the second-floor bedroom, holding open the stairwell door to take advantage of the meager, smoky light that lay behind and above him. Two steps. Then he stopped.

Waited.

Listened.

No whispers.

He let go of the door and hurriedly crossed the bedroom, feeling his way between pieces of furniture.

No whispers.

He reached another door and then stepped into the second-floor hallway.

No whispers.

For a moment, enveloped in seamless velvety blackness, he could not remember whether to turn left or right to reach the stairs that led to the ground floor. Then he regained his bearings, and he went to the right, arms extended in front of him and hands opened with fingers spread in blindman fashion.

No whispers.

He almost fell down the stairs when he came to them. The floor suddenly opened under him, and he saved himself by reeling to the left and clutching the unseen bannister.

Whispers.

Clinging to the bannister, unable to see anything at all, he held his breath, cocked his head.

Whispers.

Coming after him.

He cried out and lumbered drunkenly down the steps, lost touch with the railing, then with his balance, windmilled his arms, tripped, sprawled on the landing, face down in the musty carpet, pain shooting through his left leg, just a flash of pain and then the dull echo of it in his flesh, and he lifted his head, and he heard the whispers getting closer, closer, and he got up, whimpering in fear, limped rapidly down the next flight, stumbled when he abruptly reached the ground floor, and looked back, stared up into darkness, heard the whispers rushing toward him, building to a roaring hiss, and he shouted—"No! No!"—and started toward the rear of the house, along the first-floor corridor, toward the kitchen, and then the whispers were all around him, rolling over him, coming from above and below and every side, and the things were there, too, the horrible crawling things—or *thing;* one or many; he didn't know which—and as he careened toward the kitchen, bouncing from wall to wall in his terror, he brushed and slapped at himself, desperately trying to keep the crawling things off him, and then he crashed into the kitchen door, which was a swinging door, which swung open to admit him, and he felt along the perimeter of the room, felt over the stove and the refrigerator and the cupboards and the sink until he came to the pantry door, and the things slithered over him all this time, and the whispers continued, and he screamed and screamed at the top of his raspy voice, and he pulled open the pantry door, was assaulted by a nauseating stench, stepped into the pantry in spite of the overpowering odor that wafted from it, then realized he couldn't see and wouldn't be able to find the candles or the matches by touch among all the other jars and cans, whirled around, into the kitchen again, screaming, flailing at himself, wiping the wriggling *things* off his face as they tried to scurry into his mouth and nose, found the outside door that connected the kitchen to the back porch, fumbled with the stiff latches, finally freed them, and threw the door open.

Light.

Gray afternoon light, slanting down the Mayacamas Mountains from the west, rained through the open door and illuminated the kitchen.

Light.

For a while, he stood in the doorway, letting the wonderful light wash over him. He was sheathed in perspiration. His breath came hard and ragged.

When he finally calmed down, he returned to the pantry. The sickening stench came from old cans and jars of food that had swelled and exploded, spraying spoiled goods and giving rise to green-black-yellow molds and fungi. Trying to avoid the mess as best he could, he located the candles and the can of matches.

The matches were still dry and useful. He struck one to be sure. The spurting flame was a sight that lifted his heart.

•

To the west of the northward-streaking Cessna, a couple of thousand feet below the aircraft, at the seven- or eight-thousand-foot level, storm clouds steadily approached from the Pacific.

"How?" Joshua asked again. "How did Katherine make the twins think and act and *be* one person?"

"As I said," Hilary told him, "we'll probably never know for certain. But for one thing, it seems to me that she must have shared her delusions with the twins almost from the day she brought them home, long before they were old enough even to understand what she was saying. Hundreds and hundreds of times, perhaps thousands upon thousands of times over the years, she told them that they were the sons of a demon. She told them they'd been born with cauls, and she explained what that meant. She told them their sex organs weren't like those of other boys. She probably told them that they would be killed if other people found out what they were. By the time they were old enough to question all those things, they would have been so thoroughly brainwashed that they wouldn't have been *able* to doubt her. They'd have shared her psychosis and her delusions. They'd have been two extremely tense little boys, afraid of being found out, afraid of being killed. Fear is stress. And a lot of stress would make their psyches highly malleable. It seems to me that tremendous, unrelenting, extraordinary stress over a long period of time would provide exactly the right atmosphere for the melting together of personalities in the way that Tony has suggested. Massive, prolonged stress wouldn't, by itself, *cause* that melting together, but it would sort of set the stage for it."

Tony said, "From the tapes we heard in Dr. Rudge's office this morning, we know Bruno was aware that he and his brother were born with cauls. We know that he was familiar with the superstition connected with that rare phenomenon. From the way he sounded on the tape, I think we can safely assume he believed, as his mother did, that he was marked by a demon. And there's other evidence that points to the same conclusion. The letter in the safe-deposit box, for instance. Bruno wrote that he couldn't ask for police protection against his mother because the police would discover what he was and what he'd been hiding all these years. In the letter, he said that if people found out what he was, they would stone him to death. He thought he was the son of a demon. I'm sure of it. He had absorbed Katherine's psychotic delusions."

"All right," Joshua said. "Maybe both twins believed the demon bunk because they'd never had a chance *not* to believe it. But that still doesn't explain how or why Katherine shaped the two of them into one person, how she got them to . . . melt together psychologically, as you put it."

"The *why* part of your question is the easiest to answer," Hilary said. "As long as the twins thought of themselves as individuals, there would be differences between them, even if only very minor differences. And the more differences, the more likely it was that one of them would unintentionally blow the entire masquerade someday. The more she could force them to act and think and talk and move and respond alike, the safer she was."

"As for the *how* of it," Tony said, "you shouldn't forget that Katherine knew the ways and means to break and shape a mind. After all, she had been broken and shaped by a master. Leo. He had used every trick in the book to make her what he wanted her to be, and she couldn't have helped but learn something from all of that. Techniques of physical and psychological torture. She could probably have written a textbook on the subject."

"And to make the twins think like one person," Hilary said, "she'd have to treat them like one person. She'd have to set the tone, in other words. She'd have to offer them the exact same degrees of love, if any. She'd have to punish both for the actions of one, reward both for the actions of one, treat the two bodies as if they were in possession of the same mind. She had to talk to them as if they were only one person, not two."

"And every time she caught a glimpse of individuality, she'd either have to make them both do it, or she'd have to eradicate the mannerism in the one who displayed it. And pronoun usage would be very important," Tony said.

"Pronoun usage?" Joshua asked, perplexed.

"Yes," Tony said. "This is going to sound pretty damned far-out. Maybe even meaningless. But more than anything else, our understanding and use of language shapes us. Language is the way we express every idea, every thought. Sloppy thinking leads to a sloppy use of language. But the opposite is also true: Imprecise language causes imprecise thinking. That's a basic tenet of semantics. So it seems logical to theorize that the selectively-twisted usage of pronouns would aid in the establishment of the kind of selectively-twisted self-image that Katherine wanted to see the twins adopt. For example, when the twins spoke to each other, they could never be allowed to use the pronoun 'you.' Because 'you' embodies the concept of another person other than one's self. If the twins were forced to think of themselves as *one* creature, then the pronoun 'you' would have no place between them. One Bruno could never say to the other, 'Why don't you and I play a game of Monopoly?' He'd have to say, instead, something like this: 'Why don't me and I play a game of Monopoly?' He couldn't use the pronouns 'we' and 'us' when talking about himself and his brother, for those pronouns indicate at least *two* people. Instead, he'd have to say 'me and myself' when he meant 'we.' Furthermore, when one of the twins was talking to Katherine about his brother, he couldn't be permitted to use the pronouns 'he' and 'him.' Again, they embody the concept of another individual in addition to the speaker. Complicated?"

"Insane," Joshua said.

"That's the point," Tony said.

"But it's too much. It's too crazy."

"Of course, it's crazy," Tony said. "It was Katherine's scheme, and Katherine was out of her mind."

"But how could she possibly enforce all of those bizarre rules about habits and mannerisms and attitudes and pronouns and whatever the hell else?"

"The same way you'd enforce an ordinary set of rules with ordinary children," Hilary said. "If they do the right thing, you reward them. If they do the wrong thing, however, you punish them."

"But to make children behave as unnaturally as Katherine wanted the twins to behave, to make them totally surrender their individuality, the punishment would have to be something truly monstrous," Joshua said.

"And we know it *was* something monstrous," Tony said. "We all heard Dr. Rudge's tape of that last session with Bruno, when hypnosis was used. If you remember, Bruno said that she put him into some dark hole in the ground as punishment—and I quote—'for not thinking and acting like one.' I believe he meant she put both him and his brother in that dark place when they refused to think and act like a single person.

She locked them in a dark place for long periods of time, and there was something alive in there, something that crawled all over them. Whatever happened to them in that room or hole . . . it was so terrible that they had bad dreams about it every night for decades. If it could leave that strong an impression so many years afterwards, I'd say it was enough of a punishment to be a good brainwashing tool. I'd say Katherine did exactly what she set out to do with the twins: melted them into one."

Joshua stared at the sky ahead.

At last, he said, "When she came back from Mrs. Yancy's whorehouse, her problem was to pass off the twins as the one child she'd talked about, thereby salvaging the Mary Gunther lie. But she could have accomplished that by locking up one of the brothers, making him a house son, while the other twin was the only one allowed to go out of the house. That would have been quicker, easier, simpler, safer."

"But we all know Clemenza's Law," Hilary said.

"Right," Joshua said. "Clemenza's Law: Damned few people ever do anything the quickest, easiest, simplest, and safest way."

"Besides," Hilary said, "Maybe Katherine just didn't have the heart to keep one of the boys locked up forever while the other one was permitted to lead at least a little bit of a normal life. After all the suffering she'd been through, maybe there was a limit to the amount of suffering she could force her children to endure."

"It seems to me she made them endure a whole hell of a lot!" Joshua said. "She drove them mad!"

"Inadvertently, yes," Hilary said. "She didn't intend to drive them mad. She thought she was doing what was best for them, but her own state of mind didn't make it possible for her to *know* what was best."

Joshua sighed wearily. "It's a wild theory you've got."

"Not so wild," Tony said. "It fits the known facts."

Joshua nodded. "And I guess I believe it, too. At least most of it. I just wish all of the villains in this piece were thoroughly vile and despicable. It seems wrong, somehow, to feel so much sympathy for them."

•

After they landed in Napa, under rapidly graying skies, they went straight to the county sheriff's office and told Peter Laurenski everything. At first, he gaped at them as if they had lost their minds, but gradually his disbelief turned into reluctant, astonished acceptance. That was a pattern of reactions, a transformation of emotions that Hilary expected they would all witness a few hundred times in the days ahead.

Laurenski telephoned the Los Angeles Police Department. He discovered that the FBI already had contacted the LAPD in regard to the San Francisco bank fraud case involving a look-alike for Bruno Frye, now believed at large in the LAPD's jurisdiction. Laurenski's news, of course, was that the suspect was not merely a look-alike, but the genuine article—even though another genuine article was dead and buried in the Napa County Memorial Park. He informed the LAPD that he had reason to believe the two Brunos had taken turns killing women and had been involved in a series of murders in the northern half of the state over the past five years, although he could not yet provide hard evidence or name specific homicides. The evidence was thus far circumstantial: a grisly but logical interpretation of the safe-deposit box letter in light of recent discoveries about Leo and Katherine and the twins; the fact that both of the twins had made attempts on Hilary's life; the fact that one of the twins had covered for the other last week when Hilary had first been attacked, which indicated complicity in at least attempted murder; and finally the conviction, shared by Hilary and Tony and Joshua, that Bruno's hatred for his mother was so powerful and maniacal that he would not hesitate to slaughter any woman who he imagined was his mother come back to life in a new body.

While Hilary and Joshua shared the railback bench that served as an office couch, and while they drank coffee provided by Laurenski's secretary, Tony took the phone at Laurenski's request and spoke with two of his own superiors in L.A. His support for Laurenski and the corroboration of facts that he provided were apparently effective, for the call concluded with a promise that L.A. authorities would take immediate action at their end. Operating under the assumption that the psychopath would be keeping a watch on Hilary's home, the LAPD agreed to establish around-the-clock surveillance on the Westwood house.

With the cooperation of the Los Angeles police assured, the sheriff quickly composed a bulletin, outlining the basic facts of the case, for distribution to all law enforcement agencies in Northern California. The bulletin doubled as an official request for information on any unsolved murders of young, attractive, brown-eyed brunettes, in jurisdictions beyond Laurenski's, during the past five years—and especially any murders involving decapitation, mutilation, or evidence of blood fetishism.

As Hilary watched the sheriff issuing orders to clerks and deputies, and as she thought about the events of the past twenty-four hours, she had the feeling that everything was moving too fast, like a whirlwind, and that this wind—filled with surprises and ugly secrets, just as a tornado is filled with swirling clods of uprooted earth and chunks of debris—was carrying her toward a precipice that she could not yet see, but over which she might be flung. She wished she could reach out with both hands and seize control of time itself, hold it back, slow it down, take a few days out to rest and to consider what she had learned, so that she would be able to follow the final few twists and turns of the Frye mystery with a clear head. She felt sure that continued haste was foolish, even deadly. But the wheels of the law, now engaged and rolling, could not be blocked. And time could not be reined in as if it were a runaway stallion.

She hoped there was no precipice ahead.

At 5:30, after Laurenski had gotten the law enforcement machinery moving, he and Joshua used the telephone to track down a judge. They found one, Judge Julian Harwey, who was fascinated by the Frye story. Harwey understood the necessity of retrieving the corpse and putting it through an extensive battery of tests for identification purposes. If the second Bruno Frye was apprehended, and if he somehow managed to pass a psychiatric examination, which was highly unlikely but not altogether impossible, then the prosecutor would need physical proof that there had been identical twins. Harwey was willing to sign an exhumation order, and by 6:30, the sheriff had that paper in hand.

"The workmen at the cemetery won't be able to open the grave in the dark," Laurenski said. "But I'll have them out there digging at the crack of dawn." He made a few more phone calls, one to the director of the Napa County Memorial Park where Frye was buried, another to the county coroner who could conduct the exhumation of the body as soon as it was delivered to him, and one to Avril Tannerton, the mortician, to arrange for him to transport the corpse to and from the coroner's pathology lab.

When Laurenski finally got off the telephone, Joshua said, "I imagine you'll want to search the Frye house."

"Absolutely," Laurenski said. "We want to find proof that more than one man was living there, if we can. And if Frye really had murdered other women, maybe we'll turn up some evidence. I think it would be a good idea to go through the house on the cliff, too."

"We can search the new house as soon as you like," Joshua said. "But there's no electricity in the old place. That one will have to wait until daylight."

"Okay," Laurenski said. "But I'd like to have a look at the vineyard house tonight."

"Now?" Joshua asked, getting up from the railback bench.

"None of us has had dinner," Laurenski said. Earlier, before they had told him even half of what they'd learned from Dr. Rudge and Rita Yancy, the sheriff had called his wife to tell her he wouldn't be home until very late. "Let's get a bite to eat at the coffee shop around the corner. Then we can head on out to Frye's place."

Before they left for the restaurant, Laurenski told the night reception-ist where he would be and asked her to let him know immediately if word came in that the Los Angeles police had arrested the second Bruno Frye.

"It's not going to be that easy," Hilary said.

"I suspect she's right," Tony said. "Bruno has concealed an incredible secret for forty years. He may be crazy, but he's also clever. The LAPD isn't going to lay hands on him that fast. They'll have to play a lot of cat-and-mouse before they finally nail him."

•

When night had begun to fall, Bruno had closed the attic shutters again.

Now there were candles on each nightstand. There were two candles on the dresser. The flickering yellow flames made shadows dance on the walls and ceiling.

Bruno knew that he should already be out looking for Hilary-Katherine, but he could not find the energy to get up and go. He kept put-ting it off.

He was hungry. He suddenly realized that he hadn't eaten since yes-terday. His stomach was growling.

For a while, he sat on the bed, beside the staring corpse, and he tried to decide where he should go to get some food. A few of the cans in the pantry hadn't swelled up, hadn't burst, but he was sure that everything on those shelves was spoiled and poisonous. For almost an hour, he struggled with the problem, trying to think of where he could go to get something to eat and still be safe from Katherine's spies. They were everywhere. The bitch and her spies. Everywhere. His state of mind was still best described as confused, and even though he was hungry, he had difficulty keeping his thoughts focused on food. But at last, he remembered there was food in the vineyard house. The milk would have spoiled during the past week, and the bread would have gotten hard. But his own pantry was full of canned goods, and the refrigerator was stocked with cheese and fruit, and there was ice cream in the freezer. The thought of ice cream made him smile like a small boy.

Driven by the vision of ice cream, hoping that a good supper would give him the energy he needed to begin looking for Hilary-Katherine, he left the attic and made his way down through the house with the aid of a candle. Outside, he snuffed out the flame and tucked the candle into a jacket pocket. He descended the crumbling switchback stairs on the face of the cliff and strode off through the dark vineyards.

Ten minutes later, in his own house, he struck a match and relit the candle because he was afraid that he would attract unwanted attention if he switched on the lights. He got a spoon from a drawer by the kitchen sink, took a one-gallon, cardboard tub of chocolate ripple from the freezer, and sat at the table for more than a quarter of an hour, smiling, eating big spoonfuls of ice cream right out of the carton, until at last he was too full to swallow even one more bite.

He dropped the spoon in the half-emptied carton, put the ice cream back in the freezer, and realized that he ought to pack up canned goods to take back to the clifftop house. He might not be able to find and kill Hilary-Katherine for days, and during that time he didn't want to have to sneak back here for every meal. Sooner or later, the bitch would think to have some of her spies put a watch on this place, and then he would be caught. But she'd never look for him in the cliff house, not in a million years, so that was where he ought to have his food supply.

He went into the master bedroom and got a large suitcase from the closet, took that into the kitchen, and filled it with cans of peaches, pears, mandarin orange slices, jars of peanut butter and jars of olives, and two kinds of jelly—each jar wrapped in paper towels to cushion it and keep it from breaking—and tins of little Vienna sausages. When he finished packing, the big suitcase was extremely heavy, but he had the muscles to handle it.

He had not showered since last night, at Sally's house in Culver City, and he felt grimy. He hated being dirty, for being dirty somehow always made him think of the whispers and the awful crawling things and the dark place in the ground. He decided he could risk taking a quick shower before he carried the food back to the clifftop house, even if that meant being naked and defenseless for a few minutes. But as he walked through the living room on his way to the bedroom and master bath, he heard cars approaching along the vineyard road. The engines sounded unnaturally loud in the perfect stillness of the fields.

Bruno ran to a front window and parted the drapes just an inch and looked out.

Two cars. Four headlights. Coming up the slope toward the clearing.

Katherine.

The bitch!

The bitch and her friends. Her dead friends.

Terrified, he ran to the kitchen, grabbed the suitcase, put out the candle that he was carrying, and pocketed it. He let himself out by the back door and dashed across the rear lawn, into the sheltering vineyards, as the cars stopped out front.

Crouching, lugging the suitcase, anxiously aware of every small sound he made, Bruno moved through the vines. He circled the house until he could see the cars. He put down the suitcase and sprawled beside it, hugging the moist earth and the darkest of the night shadows. He watched the people getting out of the cars, and his heart hammered faster each time that he recognized a face.

Sheriff Laurenski and a deputy. So the police were among the living dead! He had never suspected them.

Joshua Rhinehart. The old attorney was a conspirator, too! He was one of Katherine's hellish friends.

And there *she* was! The bitch. The bitch in her sleek new body. And that man from Los Angeles.

They all went into the house.

Lights came on in one room after another.

Bruno tried to remember if he'd left any signs of his visit. Maybe some drippings from the candle. But the droplets of wax would be cold and hard already. They would have no way of knowing if the drippings were fresh or weeks old. He'd left the spoon in the ice cream carton, but that might have been done a long time ago, too. Thank God, he hadn't taken a shower! The water on the floor of the stall and the damp towel would have given him away; finding a recently used towel, they would have known instantly that he was back in St. Helena, and they would have intensified their search for him.

He got to his feet, hefted the suitcase, and hurried as fast as he could through the vineyards. He went north toward the winery, then west toward the cliff.

They would never come to the cliff house looking for him. Not in a million years. He would be safe in the cliff house because they would think he was too afraid to go there.

If he hid in the attic, he would have time to think and plan and organize. He didn't dare rush into this. He hadn't been thinking too clearly lately, not since the other half of him had died, and he didn't dare move against the bitch until he had planned for every possible contingency.

He knew how to find her now. Through Joshua Rhinehart.

He could get his hands on her whenever he wanted.

But first he needed time to formulate a foolproof plan. He could hardly wait to get back to the attic to talk it over with himself.

•

Laurenski, Deputy Tim Larsson, Joshua, Tony, and Hilary spread out through the house. They searched drawers and closets and cupboards and cabinets.

At first, they couldn't find anything that proved two men had been living in the house instead of one. There seemed to be quite a few more clothes than one man would need. And the house was stocked with more food than one man usually kept on hand. But that wasn't proof of anything.

Then, as Hilary was going through desk drawers in the study, she came across a stack of recently received bills that hadn't been paid yet. Two of them were from dentists—one in nearby Napa, the other in San Francisco.

"Of course!" Tony said as everyone gathered around to have a look at the bills. "The twins would have had to go to different doctors and, especially, different dentists. Bruno Number Two couldn't walk into a dentist's office to have a tooth filled when that same dentist had filled the same tooth in Bruno Number One just the week before."

"This helps," Laurenski said. "Even identical twins don't get the same cavities in the same places on the same teeth. Two sets of dental records will prove there were two Bruno Fryes."

A while later, while searching a bedroom closet, Deputy Larsson made an unsettling discovery. One of the shoe boxes did not have shoes in it. Instead, the box contained a dozen wallet-size snapshots of a dozen young women, driver's licenses for six of them, and another eleven licenses belonging to eleven other women. In each snapshot and in each license photo, the woman looking out at the camera had things in common with all the other women in the collection: a pretty face, dark eyes, dark hair, and an indefinable something in the lines and angles of the facial structure.

"Twenty-three women who vaguely resemble Katherine," Joshua said. "My God. Twenty-three."

"A gallery of death," Hilary said, shivering.

"At least they're not all unidentified snapshots," Tony said. "With the licenses, we've got names and addresses."

"We'll get them out on the wire right away," Laurenski said, sending Larsson out to the car to radio the information to HQ. "But I think we all know what we'll find."

"Twenty-three unsolved murders spread over the past five years," Tony said.

"Or twenty-three disappearances," the sheriff said.

They spent two more hours in the house, but they didn't find anything else as important as the photographs and driver's licenses. Hilary's nerves were frayed, and her imagination was stimulated by the disturbing realization that her own driver's license had nearly wound up in that shoe box. Each time she opened a drawer or a cupboard door, she expected to find a shriveled heart with a stake through it or a dead woman's rotting head. She was relieved when the search was finally completed.

Outside, in the chilly night air, Laurenski said, "Will the three of you be coming to the coroner's office in the morning?"

"Count me out," Hilary said.

"No thanks," Tony said.

Joshua said, "There's really nothing we can do there."

"What time should we meet at the cliff house?" Laurenski asked.

Joshua said, "Hilary and Tony and I will go up first thing in the morning and open all the shutters and windows. The place has been closed up for five years. It'll need to be aired out before any of us will want to spend hours poking through it. Why don't you just come on up and join us whenever you're finished at the coroner's?"

"All right," Laurenski said. "See you tomorrow. Maybe the Los Angeles police will get the bastard during the night."

"Maybe," Hilary said hopefully.

Up in the Mayacamas Mountains, soft thunder roared.

•

Bruno Frye spent half the night talking to himself, carefully planning Hilary-Katherine's death.

The other half, he slept while the candles flickered. Thin streams of smoke rose from the burning wicks. The dancing flames cast jiggling, macabre shadows on the walls, and they were reflected in the staring eyes of the corpse.

•

Joshua Rhinehart had trouble sleeping. He tossed and turned, getting increasingly tangled in the sheets. At three o'clock in the morning, he went out to the bar and poured himself a double shot of bourbon, drank it fast. Even that didn't settle him down a whole lot.

He had never missed Cora so much as he did that night.

Hilary woke repeatedly from bad dreams, but the night did not go by slowly. It swept past at rocket speeds. She still had the feeling that she was hurtling toward a precipice, and she could do nothing to stop her forward rush.

•

Near dawn, as Tony lay awake, Hilary turned to him, came against him, and said, "Make love to me."

For half an hour, they lost themselves in each other, and although it was not better than before, it was not one degree worse either. A sweet, silken, hushed togetherness.

Afterwards, she said, "I love you."

"I love you, too."

"No matter what happens," she said, "we've had these few days together."

"Now don't get fatalistic on me."

"Well . . . you never know."

"We've got years ahead of us. Years and years and years together. Nobody's going to take them away from us."

"You're so positive, so optimistic. I wish I'd found you a long time ago."

"We're through the worst of this thing," he said. "We know the truth now."

"They haven't caught Frye yet."

"They will," Tony said reassuringly. "He thinks you're Katherine, so he's not going to stray too far from Westwood. He'll keep checking back at your house to see if you've shown up, and sooner or later the surveillance team will spot him, and it'll all be over."

"Hold me," she said.

"Sure."

"Mmmm. That's nice."

"Yeah."

"Just being held."

"Yeah."

"I feel better already."

"Everything's going to be fine."

"As long as I have you," she said.

"Forever, then."

•

The sky was dark and low and ominous. The peaks of the Mayacamas were shrouded in mist.

Peter Laurenski stood in the graveyard, hands in his pants pockets, shoulders hunched against the chill morning air.

Using a backhoe for most of the way, then tossing out the last eight or ten inches of dirt with shovels, workmen at Napa County Memorial Park gouged into the soft earth, tearing open Bruno Frye's grave. As they labored, they complained to the sheriff that they were not being paid extra for getting up at dawn and missing breakfast and coming in early, but they got very little sympathy from him; he just urged them to work faster.

At 7:45, Avril Tannerton and Gary Olmstead arrived in the Forever View hearse. As they walked across the green hillside toward Laurenski, Olmstead looked properly somber, but Tannerton was smiling, taking in great lungfuls of the nippy air, as if he were merely out for his morning constitutional.

"Morning, Peter."

"Morning, Avril. Gary."

"How long till they have it open?" Tannerton asked.

"They say fifteen minutes."

At 8:05, one of the workmen climbed up from the hole and said, "Ready to yank him out?"

"Let's get on with it," Laurenski said.

Chains were attached to the casket, and it was brought out of the ground by the same device that had lowered it in just last Sunday. The bronze coffin was caked with earth around the handles and in the frill work, but overall it was still shiny.

By 8:40, Tannerton and Olmstead had loaded the big box into the hearse.

"I'll follow you to the coroner's office," the sheriff said.

Tannerton grinned at him. "I assure you, Peter, we aren't going to run off with Mr. Frye's remains."

•

At 8:20, in Joshua Rhinehart's kitchen, while the casket was being exhumed at the cemetery a few miles away, Tony and Hilary stacked the breakfast dishes in the sink.

"I'll wash them later," Joshua said. "Let's get up to the cliff and open that house. It must smell like hell in there after all these years. I just hope the mildew and mold haven't done too much damage to Katherine's collections. I warned Bruno about that a thousand times, but he didn't seem to care if—" Joshua stopped, blinked. "Will you listen to me babble on? Of *course* he didn't care if the whole lot of it rotted away. Those were Katherine's collections, and he wouldn't have cared a damn about anything she treasured."

They went to Shade Tree Vineyards in Joshua's car. The day was dreary; the light was dirty gray. Joshua parked in the employees' lot.

Gilbert Ulman hadn't come to work yet. He was the mechanic who maintained the aerial tramway in addition to caring for all of Shade Tree Vineyards' trucks and farm equipment.

The key that operated the tramway was hanging on a pegboard in the garage, and the winery's night manager, a portly man named Iannucci, was happy to get it for Joshua.

Key in hand, Joshua led Hilary and Tony up to the second floor of the huge main winery, through an area of administrative offices, through a viniculture lab, and then onto a broad catwalk. Half the building was open from the first floor to the ceiling, and in that huge chamber there were enormous three-story fermentation tanks. Cold, cold air flowed off the tanks, and there was a yeasty odor in the place. At the end of the long catwalk, at the southwest corner of the building, they went through a heavy pine door with black iron hinges, into a small room that was open at the end opposite from where they entered. An overhanging roof extended twelve feet out from the missing wall, to keep rain from slanting into the open chamber. The four-seat cable car—a fire-engine-red number with lots of glass—was nestled under the overhang, at the brink of the room.

•

The pathology laboratory had a vague, unpleasant chemical odor. So did the coroner, Dr. Amos Garnet, who sucked vigorously on a breath mint.

There were five people in the room. Laurenski, Larsson, Garnet, Tannerton, and Olmstead. No one, with the possible exception of the perennially good-natured Tannerton, seemed happy to be there.

"Open it," Laurenski said. "I've got an appointment to keep with Joshua Rhinehart."

Tannerton and Olmstead threw back the latches on the bronze casket. A few remaining chunks of dirt fell to the floor, onto the plastic dropcloth that Garnet had put down. They pushed the lid up and back.

The body was gone.

The velvet- and silk-lined box held nothing but the three fifty-pound bags of dry mortar mix that had been stolen from Avril Tannerton's basement last weekend.

●

Hilary and Tony sat on one side of the cable car, and Joshua sat on the other. The attorney's knees brushed Tony's.

Hilary held Tony's hand as the red gondola moved slowly, slowly up the line toward the top of the cliff. She wasn't afraid of heights, but the tramway seemed so fragile that she could not help gritting her teeth.

Joshua saw the tension on her face and smiled. "Don't worry. The car seems small, but it's sturdy. And Gilbert does a fine job with maintenance."

As it ground gradually upward, the car swung slightly in the stiff morning wind.

The view of the valley became increasingly spectacular. Hilary tried to concentrate on that and not on the creaking and clattering of the machinery.

The gondola finally reached the top of the cable. It locked in place, and Joshua opened the door.

When they walked out of the upper station of the tramway system, a fiercely-white arc of lightning and a violent peal of thunder broke open the lowering sky. Rain began to fall. It was a thin, cold, slanting rain.

Joshua, Hilary, and Tony ran for shelter. They stomped up the front steps and across the porch to the door.

"And you say there's no heat up here?" Hilary asked.

"The furnace has been shut down for five years," Joshua said. "That's why I told both of you to wear sweaters under your coats. It's not a cold day, really. But once you've been up here awhile in this damp, the air will cut through to your bones."

Joshua unlocked the door, and they went inside, switching on the three flashlights they'd brought with them.

"It stinks in here," Hilary said.

"Mildew," Joshua said. "That's what I was afraid of."

They walked from the foyer into the hall, then into the big drawing room. The beams of their flashlights fell on what looked to be a warehouse full of antique furniture.

"My God," Tony said, "it's worse than Bruno's house. There's hardly room to walk."

"She was obsessed with collecting beautiful things," Joshua said. "Not for investment. Not just because she liked to look at them, either. A lot of things are crammed into closets, hidden away. Paintings stacked on paintings. And as you can see, even in the main rooms, there's just too damned much stuff; it's jammed too close together to please the eye."

"If every room has antiques of this quality," Hilary said, "then there's a fortune here."

"Yeah," Joshua said. "If it hasn't been eaten up by worms and termites and whatnot." He let his flashlight beam travel from one end of the room to the other. "This mania for collecting was something I never understood about her. Until this minute. Now I wonder if. . . . As I look at all of this, and as I think about what we learned from Mrs. Yancy. . . ."

Hilary said, "You think collecting beautiful things was a reaction to all the ugliness in her life before her father died?"

"Yeah," Joshua said. "Leo broke her. Shattered her soul, smashed her spirit flat and left her with a rotten self-image. She must have hated herself for all the years she let him use her—even though she'd had no choice but to let him. So maybe . . . feeling low and worthless, she thought she could make her soul beautiful by living among lots of beautiful things."

They stood in silence for a moment, looking at the overfurnished drawing room.

"It's so sad," Tony said.

Joshua shook himself from his reverie. "Let's get these shutters open and let in some light."

"I can't stand this smell," Hilary said, cupping one hand over her nose. "But if we raise the windows, the rain will get in and ruin things."

"Not much if we raise them only five or six inches," Joshua said. "And a few drops of water aren't going to hurt anything in this mold colony."

"It's a wonder there aren't mushrooms growing out of the carpet," Tony said.

They moved through the downstairs, raising windows, unbolting the inward-facing latches on the shutters, letting in the gray storm light and the fresh rain-scented air.

When most of the downstairs rooms had been opened, Joshua said, "Hilary, all that's left down here is the dining room and the kitchen. Why don't you take care of those windows while Tony and I tend to the upstairs."

"Okay," she said. "I'll be up in a minute to help out."

She followed her flashlight beam into the pitch-black dining room as the men went down the hall toward the stairs.

•

When he and Joshua came into the upstairs hallway, Tony said, *"Phew!* It stinks even worse up here."

A blast of thunder shook the old house. Windows rattled icily. Doors stuttered in their frames.

"You take the rooms on the right," Joshua said. "I'll take the ones on the left."

Tony went through the first door on his side and found a sewing room. An ancient treadle-powered sewing machine stood in one corner, and a more modern electric model rested on a table in another corner; both were bearded with cobwebs. There was a work table and two dress-maker's forms and one window.

He went to the window, put his flashlight on the floor, and tried to twist open the lock lever. It was rusted shut. He struggled with it as rain drummed noisily on the shutters beyond the glass.

•

Joshua shone his flashlight into the first room on the left and saw a bed, a dresser, a highboy. There were two windows in the far wall.

He crossed the threshold, took two more steps, sensed movement behind him, and he started to turn, felt a sudden cold thrill go through his back, and then it became a very hot thrill, a burning lance, a line of pain drawn through his flesh, and he knew he had been stabbed. He felt the knife being jerked out of him. He turned. His flashlight revealed Bruno Frye. The madman's face was wild, demoniacal. The knife came up, came down, and the cold thrill shivered through Joshua again, and this time the blade tore his right shoulder, from front to back, all the way through, and Bruno had to twist and jerk the weapon savagely, several times, to get it out. Joshua raised his left arm to protect himself. The blade punctured his forearm. His legs buckled. He went down. He fell against the bed, slid to the floor, slick with his own blood, and Bruno turned away from him and went out to the second-floor hall, out of the flashlight's glow, into the darkness. Joshua realized he hadn't even screamed, had not warned Tony, and he tried to shout, really tried, but the first wound seemed to be very serious, for when he attempted to make any sound at all, pain blossomed in his chest, and he could do no better than hiss like a goddamned goose.

•

Grunting, Tony put all of his strength against the stubborn window latch, and abruptly the rusted metal gave—*sweeek*—and popped open. He raised the windows, and the sound of the rain swelled. A fine spray of water misted through a few narrow chinks in the shutters and dampened his face.

The inward-facing bolt on the shutters also was corroded, but Tony finally freed it, pushed the shutters open, leaned out in the rain, and fixed them in their braces so they wouldn't bang about in the wind.

He was wet and cold. He was anxious to get on with the search of the house, hoping the activity would warm him.

As another volley of thunder cannonaded down from the Mayacamas, into the valley, over the house, Tony walked out of the sewing room and into Bruno Frye's knife.

•

In the kitchen, Hilary opened the shutters on the window that looked onto the back porch. She fixed them in place and paused for a moment to stare out at the rain-swept grass and the wind-whipped trees. At the end of the lawn, twenty yards away, there were doors in the ground.

She was so surprised to see those doors that, for a moment, she thought she was imagining them. She squinted through the sheeting rain, but the doors didn't dissolve miragelike, as she half expected.

At the end of the lawn, the land rose up in one of its last steps to the vertical ramparts of the mountains. The doors were set into that hillside. They were framed with timbers and mortared stones.

Hilary turned away from the window and hurried across the filthy kitchen, anxious to tell Joshua and Tony about her discovery.

•

Tony knew how to protect himself against a man with a knife. He was trained in self-defense, and he'd been in situations like this one on two other occasions. But this time he was caught off guard by the suddenness and total unexpectedness of the attack.

Glaring, his broad countenance split by a hideous rictus grin, Frye swung the knife at Tony's face. Tony managed to turn partly out of the blow, but the blade still tore along the side of his head, ripping scalp, drawing blood.

The pain was like an acid burn.

Tony dropped his flashlight; it rolled away, causing the shadows to leap and sway.

Frye was fast, damned fast. He struck again as Tony was just going into a defensive posture. This time the knife scored solidly if peculiarly, coming down point-first on the top of his left shoulder, driving through jacket and sweater, through muscle and gristle, between bones, instantly taking all the strength out of that arm and forcing Tony to his knees.

Somehow Tony found the energy to swing his right fist up from the floor, into Frye's testicles. The big man gasped and staggered backwards, pulling the knife out of Tony as he went.

Unaware of what was happening above her, Hilary called up from the foot of the stairs. "Tony! Joshua! Come down here and see what I've found."

Frye whirled at the sound of Hilary's voice. He headed for the steps, apparently forgetting that he was leaving a wounded but living man behind him.

Tony got up, but a napalm explosion of pain set fire to his arm, and he swayed dizzily. His stomach flopped over. He had to lean against the wall.

All he could do was warn her. "Hilary, run! Run! Frye's coming!"

•

Hilary was about to call up to them again when she heard Tony shouting to her. For an instant, she couldn't believe what he was saying, but then she heard heavy footsteps on the first flight, thumping down. He was still out of sight above the landing, but she knew he couldn't be anyone but Bruno Frye.

Then Frye's gravelly voice boomed: *"Bitch, bitch, bitch, bitch!"*

Stunned, but not frozen with shock, Hilary backed away from the foot of the stairs, and then she ran as she saw Frye reach the landing. Too late, she realized she should have gone toward the front of the house, outside, to the cable car; but she was streaking toward the kitchen instead, and there was no turning back now.

She pushed through the swinging door, into the kitchen, as Frye jumped down the last few steps and into the hallway behind her.

She thought of searching the kitchen drawers for a knife.

Couldn't. No time.

She ran to the outside door, unlocked it, and bolted from the kitchen as Frye entered it through the swinging door.

The only weapon she had was the flashlight she had been carrying, and that was no weapon at all.

She crossed the porch, went down the steps. Rain and wind battered her.

He was not far behind. He was still chanting, *"Bitch, bitch, bitch!"*

She would never be able to run around the house and all the way to the cable car before he caught her. He was much too close and gaining.

The wet grass was slick.

She was afraid of falling.

Of dying.

Tony?

She ran toward the only place that might offer protection: the doors in the ground.

Lightning flickered, and thunder followed it.

Frye wasn't screaming behind her any more. She heard a deep, animal growl of pleasure.

Very close.

Now *she* was screaming.

She reached the doors in the hillside and saw that they were latched together at both the top and bottom. She reached and threw back the top bolt, then stooped and disengaged the one on the bottom, expecting a blade to be slammed down between her shoulders. The blow never came. She pulled open the doors, and there was inky blackness beyond.

She turned.

Rain stung her face.

Frye had stopped. He was standing just six feet away.

She waited in the open doors with darkness at her back, and she wondered what was behind her other than a flight of steps.

"Bitch," Frye said.

But now there was more fear than fury in his face.

"Put the knife down," she said, not knowing if he would obey, doubting it, but having nothing to lose. "Obey your mother, Bruno. Put the knife down."

He took a step toward her.

Hilary stood her ground. Her heart was exploding.

Frye moved closer.

Shaking, she backed down the first step that lay beyond the doors.

•

Just as Tony reached the head of the stairs, supporting himself with one hand against the wall, he heard a noise behind him. He looked back.

Joshua had crawled out of the bedroom. He was splashed with blood, and his face was nearly as white as his hair. His eyes seemed out of focus.

"How bad?" Tony asked.

Joshua licked his pale lips. "I'll live," he said in a strange, hissing, croaking voice. "Hilary. For God's sake . . . Hilary!"

Tony pushed away from the wall and careened down the stairs. He weaved back down the hall toward the kitchen, for he could hear Frye shouting out on the rear lawn.

In the kitchen, Tony pulled open one drawer, then another, looking for a weapon.

"Come on, dammit! *Shit!*"

The third drawer held knives. He chose the largest one. It was spotted with rust but still wickedly sharp.

His left arm was killing him. He wanted to cradle it in his right arm, but he needed that hand to fight Frye.

Gritting his teeth, steeling himself against the pain of his wounds, lurching like a drunkard, he went out to the porch. He saw Frye at once. The man was standing in front of two open doors. Two doors in the ground.

Hilary was nowhere in sight.

•

Hilary backed off the sixth step. That was the last one.

Bruno Frye stood at the head of the stairs, looking down, afraid to come any farther. He was alternately calling her a bitch and whimpering as if he were a child. He was clearly torn between two needs: the need to kill her, and the need to get away from that hated place.

Whispers.

Suddenly she heard the whispers, and her flesh seemed to turn to ice in that instant. It was a wordless hissing, a soft sound, but growing louder by the second.

And then she felt something crawling up her leg.

She cried out and moved up one step, closer to Frye. She reached down, brushed at her leg, and knocked something away.

Shuddering, she switched on the flashlight, turned, and shone the beam into the subterranean room behind her.

Roaches. Hundreds upon hundreds of huge roaches were swarming in the room—on the floor, on the walls, on the low ceiling. They were not just ordinary roaches, but enormous things, over two inches long, an inch wide, with busy legs and especially long feelers that quivered anxiously. Their shiny green-brown carapaces appeared to be sticky and wet, like blobs of dark mucus.

The whispering was the sound of their ceaseless movement, long legs and trembling antennae brushing other long legs and antennae, constantly crawling and creeping and scurrying this way and that.

Hilary screamed. She wanted to climb the steps and get out of there, but Frye was above, waiting.

The roaches shied away from her flashlight. They were evidently sub-terranean insects that survived only in the dark, and she prayed that her flashlight batteries would not go dead.

The whispering grew louder.

More roaches were pouring into the room. They were coming out of a crack in the floor. Coming out by tens. By scores. By hundreds. There were a couple of thousand of the disgusting things in the room already, and the chamber was no more than twenty feet on a side. They piled up two and three deep in the other half of the room, avoiding the light, but getting bolder by the moment.

She knew that an entomologist would probably not call them roaches. They were beetles, subterranean beetles that lived in the bowels of the earth. A scientist would have a crisp, clean, Latin name for them. But to her they were roaches.

Hilary looked up at Bruno.

"Bitch," he said.

Leo Frye had built a cold storage cellar, a common enough conve-nience in 1918. But he had mistakenly built it on a flaw in the earth. She could see that he had tried many times to patch the floor, but it kept open-ing each time that the earth trembled. In quake country, the earth trem-bled often.

And the roaches came up from hell.

They were still gushing from the hole, a wriggling, kicking, squirm-ing mass.

They mounted up on one another, five- and six- and seven-deep, covering the walls and the ceiling, moving, endlessly moving, swarming restlessly. The cold whisper of their movement was now a soft roar.

For punishment, Katherine had put Bruno in this place. In the dark. For hours at a time.

Suddenly, the roaches moved toward Hilary. The pressure of them building up in layers finally caused them to spill at her like a breaking wave, in a roiling green-brown mass. In spite of the flashlight, they surged forward, hissing.

She screamed and started up the steps, preferring Bruno's knife to the hideous insect horde behind her.

Grinning, Frye said, "See how you like it, bitch." And he slammed the door.

•

The rear lawn was no more than twenty yards long, but to Tony it appeared to be at least a mile from the porch to the place where Frye was standing. He slipped and fell in the wet grass, taking some of the fall on his wounded shoulder. A brilliant light played behind his eyes for a moment, and then an iridescent darkness, but he resisted the urge to just lay there. He got up.

He saw Frye close the doors and lock them. Hilary had to be on the other side, shut in.

Tony covered the last ten feet of the lawn with the awful certainty that Frye would turn and see him. But the big man continued to face the doors. He was listening to Hilary, and she was screaming. Tony slipped up on him and put the knife between his shoulder blades.

Frye cried out in pain and turned.

Tony stumbled backwards, praying that he had inflicted a mortal wound. He knew he could not win in hand-to-hand combat with Frye—especially not when he had the use of only one arm.

Frye reached frantically behind, trying to grab the knife that Tony had rammed into him. He wanted to pull it out of himself, but he could not reach it.

A thread of blood trickled from the corner of his mouth.

Tony backed up another step. Then another.

Frye staggered toward him.

•

Hilary stood on the top step, pounding on the locked doors. She screamed for help.

Behind her, the whispering in the dark cellar grew louder with each shattering thump of her heart.

She risked a glance backward, shining the light down the steps. Just the sight of the humming mass of insects made her gag with revulsion. The room below appeared to be waist-deep in roaches. A huge pool of them shifted and swayed and hissed in such a way that it seemed almost as if there was only one organism down there, one monstrous creature with countless legs and antennae and hungry mouths.

She realized that she was still screaming. Over and over again. Her voice was getting hoarse. She couldn't stop.

Some of the insects were venturing up the steps in spite of her light. Two of them reached her feet, and she stamped on them. Others followed.

She turned to the doors again, screaming. She pounded on the timbers with all her strength.

Then the flashlight went out. She had thoughtlessly hammered it against the door in her hysterical effort to get help. The glass cracked. The light died.

For a moment, the whispering seemed to subside—but then it rose rapidly to a greater volume than ever before.

Hilary put her back to the door.

She thought of the tape recording she had heard in Dr. Nicholas Rudge's office yesterday morning. She thought of the twins, as children, locked in here, hands clamped over their noses and mouths, trying to keep the roaches from crawling into them. All of that screaming had given both of them coarse, gravelly voices; hours and hours, days and days of screaming.

Horrified, she stared down into the darkness, waiting for the ocean of beetles to close over her.

She felt a few on her ankles, and she quickly bent down, brushed them away.

One of them ran up her left arm. She clapped a hand on it, squashed it.

The terrifying susurration of the moving insects was almost deafening now.

She put her hands to her ears.

A roach dropped from the ceiling, onto her head. Screaming, she plucked it out of her hair, threw it away.

Suddenly, the doors opened behind her, and light burst into the cellar.

She saw a surging tide of roaches only one step below her, and then the wave fell back from the sun, and Tony pulled her out into the rain and the beautiful dirty gray light.

A few roaches clung to her clothes, and Tony knocked them from her.

"My God," he said. "My God, my God."

Hilary leaned against him.

There were no more roaches on her, but she imagined she could still feel them. Crawling. Creeping.

She shook violently, uncontrollably, and Tony put his good arm around her. He talked to her softly, calmly, bringing her down.

At last she was able to stop screaming.

"You're hurt," she said.

"I'll live. And paint."

She saw Frye. He was sprawled on the grass, face down, obviously dead. A knife protruded from his back, and his shirt was soaked with blood.

"I had no choice," Tony said. "I really didn't want to kill him. I felt sorry for him . . . knowing what Katherine put him through. But I had no choice."

They walked away from the corpse, across the lawn.

Hilary's legs were weak.

"She put the twins in that place when she wanted to punish them," Hilary said. "How many times? A hundred? Two hundred? A thousand times?"

"Don't think about it," Tony said. "Just think about being alive, being together. Think about whether you'd like being married to a slightly battered ex-cop who's struggling to make a living as a painter."

"I think I'd like that very much."

Forty feet away, Sheriff Peter Laurenski rushed out of the kitchen, onto the back porch. "What's happened?" he called to them. "Are you all right?"

Tony didn't bother to answer him. "We've got years and years together," he told Hilary. "And from here on, it's all going to be good. For the first time in our lives, we both know who we are, what we want, and where we're going. We've overcome the past. The future will be easy."

As they walked toward Laurenski, the autumn rain hammered softly on them and whispered in the grass.

AFTERWORD BY
DEAN KOONTZ

afterword

In 1979, when I wrote *Whispers*, I was less well known than the young Harrison Ford before he appeared in *American Graffiti*—and a *lot* less handsome. I was slightly better looking than J. Fred Muggs, a performing chimpanzee on TV at that time, but also less well known than he was. Although I had been a full-time writer for several years, and though I had a file drawer full of good reviews, I had never enjoyed a bestseller and, in fact, had never known enough financial security to guarantee that I would always be able to earn a living at my chosen art and craft. Writing novels was the only work for which I'd ever had a passion. Although I put in sixty- and seventy-hour weeks at the typewriter, I worried that I might eventually have to find new work. Because I had no other talent, skill, or ability, I would no doubt have turned to a life of crime. Robbing banks, hijacking airliners to hold the passengers for ransom, and knocking over armored cars is undeniably more exciting than sitting at a typewriter all day; however, with associates named Slash and Scarface and Icepick, the office Christmas party each year tends to be deadly.

Whispers was the last book I wrote in total obscurity and the last book I wrote on a typewriter. In those days, personal computers were not universally in use, though a few writers had them. (To help you understand this ancient era: Most of the dinosaurs had died off by that time; we had indoor plumbing, electricity, and the internal-combustion engine; abductions by extraterrestrials were not yet an everyday occurrence back then; but most people were naive enough to believe that Elvis Presley was dead—when, as we now know, he had moved to a fabulous mansion on a moon of Jupiter.) My wife, Gerda, had been urging me to trade my typewriter for a computer. When I finished *Whispers*, she informed me that she had tracked our office supplies, and that for every page in the final manuscript, I had used thirty-two pages of typing paper, which meant that I had done thirty-one discarded drafts of every page, typing eight hundred pages of text again and again to polish it. Although I was aware of my obsessive-compulsive rewriting, I hadn't realized quite how many revisions I usually undertook. With a computer, revision didn't require re-typing an entire page to make half a dozen changes. I bought an IBM Dis-playwriter (now as extinct as the T-Rex) and never looked back.

During the last few months that I sat at the typewriter, working on this novel, I lost twenty pounds. I was not overweight when I started the project, and I didn't diet while writing. When I finished the script—which took nearly a year of long hours—I was not only thinner but both physi-cally and emotionally exhausted. For years, I didn't realize why this proj-ect drained me. A decade later, I could look back on the book and understand that I was writing out of painful personal experience, which I couldn't acknowledge at the time. Virtually all the characters in *Whispers* suffer terrible, violent childhoods. Some overcome those traumas, and some do not; indeed, one of them becomes a serial killer. I, too, had lived through a childhood marked by physical and psychological violence. Al-though my experience was not like that of Hilary in *Whispers*, and cer-tainly not like that of Bruno, I was nevertheless drawing upon my own life for the *emotional* content of the novel, while only half realizing what I was doing, which is why the writing of it left me so depleted.

When the book was delivered to the publisher, I was asked to slash the manuscript in half. I was told that the story was too long and that I was "a mid-list suspense writer" who had overreached. The publisher was smart, successful, and perceptive, but I felt that this particular judgment was wrong. Although I desperately needed to be paid for the acceptance of the manuscript, I found only five pages to cut out of eight hundred pages of manuscript, less than one percent, and I declined to delete any more.

For the next four months, as the debate continued and my career seemed doomed, I studied the help-wanted ads with growing panic. I had taught high-school English for a year and a half before becoming a full-time writer; perhaps I could return to the classroom. Perusing the employ-ment opportunities, I saw that exotic dancers earned more than teachers, but to achieve the highest earnings as a stripper, I would need to have a sex-change operation as well as a great deal of body contouring.

At last, the publisher reluctantly accepted the book and issued it with-out enthusiasm in a small printing of seven thousand hardcovers, which wasn't enough to put even one copy in every bookstore. Fortunately, I was kept afloat by a motion-picture rights sale, a bookclub sale, and the enthusiasm of a paperback publisher who believed *Whispers* could be a major success. Eventually, when issued in paperback, it rose into the top five of the *New York Times*'s paperback bestsellers list. As I write this afterword, *Whispers* has been published in thirty-three languages and has been continuously in print for nearly two decades.

The lesson for me was one I had already learned well as a child under the thumb of an alcoholic father: In the face of adversity, it's important to persevere, to be optimistic, and to be true to your personal vision. This insight is, in fact, expressed by the actions of the lead characters—Hilary and Tony—in *Whispers*, and is one of the themes of the novel.

Primarily, however, *Whispers* explores the forces that affect our lives but that we often do not—or refuse to—contemplate. Geography and climate (in this novel, California) deeply influence us in more ways than we generally recognize on a conscious level. The subculture in which we choose to involve ourselves can either inspire us to be great or diminish us. And family history, for better or worse, shapes us more profoundly than anything else.

I still like this novel and feel that it was a milestone for me. I regret only the rigid Freudian nature of the psychology underlying the history. In the years since, I've come to believe that Freudianism is pure bunkum and to deplore the culture of victimization that it has generated. John D. MacDonald—the brilliant novelist whose work most influenced mine when I was young—might say, "Kid, don't worry about it. Freud or no Freud, the yarn is still good." That is, of course, the right attitude, and I hope that the yarn in *Whispers* is, indeed, still good.

Anyway, this is the book that saved me from a life of crime. No banks robbed. No airliners hijacked. No armored cars hit. I've had a couple speeding tickets over the past two decades, but in neither case did the authorities consider the offense serious enough to throw me in the slammer. Furthermore, I've gained back the twenty pounds—plus a few.